William Riddle

Nicholas Comenius

Ye Pennsylvania schoolmaster of ye olden time. Second Edition

William Riddle

Nicholas Comenius
Ye Pennsylvania schoolmaster of ye olden time. Second Edition

ISBN/EAN: 9783337402488

Printed in Europe, USA, Canada, Australia, Japan

Cover: Foto ©Andreas Hilbeck / pixelio.de

More available books at **www.hansebooks.com**

Nicholas Comenius.

NICHOLAS COMENIUS:

OR

YE PENNSYLVANIA SCHOOLMASTER

OF

YE OLDEN TIME.

BY

WILLIAM RIDDLE.

SECOND EDITION.

LANCASTER:
T. B. & H. B. COCHRAN, PRINTERS.
1898.

TO THE FEW

Old Schoolmasters

WHO YET LINGER AMONG MEN

IN THE SILVERY HALO OF

A RIPE OLD AGE,

THIS WORK

IS AFFECTIONATELY DEDICATED BY

The Author,

PREFACE.

In the reminiscences of Nicholas Comenius, the aim has been to present a faithful picture of conditions in school life, which during the past forty years have come within the observation and experience of the writer but which now exist only in memory.

The book has been written, not to glorify the old nor to reflect unjustly on the new, but rather with the hope that it may deepen a love and inspire a more lasting veneration for the old schoolmasters of other days, around whose memory still linger, in the hearts of the older generation, so many endearing recollections of their boyhood days.

Believing that there was enough of good in the older dispensation to make it worthy of the younger—the young men and women who have so recently entered the teacher's calling—some of its salient features have been thrown into contrast with the new order of things. If the comparison is not always to the advantage of the present, it is to be hoped that this fact may indicate the value of a closer study of the past.

If, upon the whole, the work shall be found to lean too strongly toward the old, at the expense of the new, fifty years of service in various relations to the school work, as pupil under one of the old masters, teacher,

(vii)

director, and for a quarter of a century a member of that class of public benefactors whose services are not at all times recognized and appreciated, may plead the writer's excuse. But in view of the extravagant claims and concessions of the new order of development, perhaps such a slight leaning toward one's own generation may only serve to restore a just balance.

The few whose memory goes back with the writer's to personal relations with the old masters, will unite in blessing their memory; and we hope the younger, matter-of-fact reader, while he may smile at the grotesque side, will not overlook the other characteristics we have sought to portray.

The writer is little disposed to apply to the newer order the caustic criticism of a new book, that "what was good was not new and what was new was not good." Nor can such a spirit be justly attributed to this book, which aims to favor the liberal yet judicious doctrine: "Prove all things, hold fast that which is *good*."

Wherein our pages deal with history we have tried to catch the spirit of the times, and need not apologize for our word of tribute to the great men whose self-sacrificing devotion to the cause of popular education should inspire their descendants to a more lasting appreciation of their deeds and services.

If the book shall help the reader to *appreciate the old* without *depreciating the new*, to receive from those who went before the truth they held, and apply it in sifting wheat from chaff, the labors of the author will not have been in vain. W. R.

Lancaster, Pa.

CONTENTS.

(ix)

Contents.

ILLUSTRATIONS.

Contents.

(xiv)　　　　GOV. ANDREW G. CURTIN.

INTRODUCTION.

SOMETIMES one wishes there was less truth in the old saying "of the making of books there is no end" (Eccl. xii. 12), so many books are made of nothing and for nothing and get nowhere. The book here presented is not of that class. In my judgment it is a valuable contribution to our educational literature, because the incidents and the pictures which it gives of bygone days, show wherein true progress has been made. Every chapter bears evidence of the author's desire to preserve in the form of anecdote and story the things connected with our educational history which are rapidly passing into oblivion. In a pleasant way he seeks to teach the lesson that the new is not to be accepted without question because it is new, nor is the old to be rejected because it is old. True progress is made by pointing out and eliminating the defects of the present and by preserving and perpetuating at the same time the essence of what the past and the present have achieved and are achieving for the benefit of future generations.

The author is fond of the old, and seeks to do justice to the men of former days. He exposes their follies, prejudices and superstitions, and yet credits them with good sense in accepting the new after they saw its real merit and superiority. If here and there he seems to lean too strongly toward the older period, it is an amiable weakness in contrast with the current methods of heralding what are claimed as discoveries and reforms.

The sketches strung upon the thread of Nicholas Comenius' narrative are true to life, as many of the older readers will recognize; to the younger generation they will be ancient history in a form that they too will enjoy, and from which they can scarcely fail to draw the lesson which the author means to teach.

Here and there the characters may be somewhat exaggerated, especially where the humorous side of the author came uppermost, but even this adds to the originality and piquancy of the whole.

The story of Robert and Hannah is suited to the taste of a class of readers—we are glad to believe a growing one—who do not read for excitement so much as for quiet enjoyment; and in this we find good judgment.

If the criticisms on some forms of our educational system seem severe, we may remember that the author knows whereof he speaks, and that in this as in other fields, "all is not gold that glitters."

The strictures upon the method of conducting the county institute deserve the attention of those entrusted with the management of these annual gatherings. Pennsylvania has the best system of institutes that can be found anywhere in the United States; but it would be folly to claim that no improvement is possible in the method of conducting them, or in the quality of the instruction that is given by the lecturers.

The anecdote in which the book agent wins the School Board by the judicious present of a book, is inimitable. It is indeed difficult to determine where legitimate influence stops and bribery begins. The present of a drink or of a cigar, of a hospitable meal or of a free car ride, may be in essence of the same nature as the bribe which secures pernicious legislation or large appropriations. That this sin should have crept into our School Boards and thus poisoned the very fountains of our system of public instruction, may well cause the friends of popular government to sit like Marius and meditate upon the future of the republic.

Tricks at examinations belong to the lower type of school morality. A higher stage in the growth of the will is reached when the idea of right inspires the teacher and his pupils and enables them to say: "I would sooner fail than cheat." The school must cause those connected with our system of public instruction to value right above success; otherwise we cannot hope for the revival of an order of statesmen who "would sooner be right than President"

Ignorance is the mother of superstition. Although the early settlers of Pennsylvania never burned witches at the stake, they cherished many superstitions of which sad traces still remain in the life of the people. The closing chapters of the book show how a good teacher may revolutionize the thinking of a community; how sound knowledge gradually dissipates prejudice and superstition, and silently begets higher forms of piety and religious life.

The chief merit of the book lies in the fact that it

pours a flood of light upon the two most critical periods in the educational history of Pennsylvania. One of these culminated in a victory that was achieved not by the sword, but by the greatest speech Thaddeus Stevens ever made. The other came with the creation of the County Superintendency and the establishment of our system of State Normal schools. While the Act of 1854 was pending, Henry Barnard examined its provisions and assured its friends that if it should become a law, Pennsylvania would have the best common school system of any state in the Union. Ex-State Supt. H. C. Hickock calls this period "one of the most disturbed and difficult and critical periods ever known in our school history. Its like can never be seen again." Effort after effort was made to abolish the office of County Superintendent.

The fact that Gov. Bigler had signed the Act of 1854 helped to defeat him at the next election, and his successor, Gov. Pollock, in speaking of the pressure upon him, remarked that it was about as much as a man's life was worth to stand by the County Superintendency at that period. It was also during Gov. Pollock's administration that the fight for Normal schools was made. The character of this fight is not as well understood as it should be, and a few details will help the reader to appreciate the situation. The Act creating State Normal schools was drawn in an emergency on a Sunday by Dr. Burrowes, and was put through the House by Andrew G. Curtin, then ex-officio Superintendent of Common Schools, and by his deputy, H. C. Hickok, under the most adverse circumstances. It had passed the Senate without a dissenting vote. "It so happened," says Mr. Hickok, "that the bill could not be called up for consideration until the last day of the session on which bills could be considered, and there were a number of important bills in which leading members were interested that were before it. Mr. Curtin in consultation with the Speaker and Committee on Education, and other friends of the cause in the House, arranged to have the Normal school bill taken up on motion out of its order, and had as he believed secured votes enough to sustain the motion. . . . The leader of the House, Mr. Foster, a liberally educated gentleman of great influence, and a good common school man in a general way, had an important bill of his own on the calendar, and was not likely to yield precedence to the Normal school bill without a struggle, in which case the odds would be heavily against us. Although politically opposed, Mr. Curtin and Mr. Foster were warm personal friends, and Curtin took it upon himself to hold Mr. Foster in check if possible until the required forms of legislation could be gone through with. When the time came for action, Mr. Curtin and Mr. Foster were standing in the aisle near Mr. Foster's desk, engaged in earnest conversation. The motion to take up the Normal school bill was instantly challenged by a call for the yeas and nays, but being carried, the Clerk, Captain Jacob Ziegler, who was in the secret, proceeded to the second reading of the bill, which being a long one, took some time, although rapidly done. Mr. Foster became very restive before it was completed, and turned to the Speaker twice to move its indefinite postponement; but Mr. Curtin, with court-

cous insistence, persuaded him to let the reading go
on, as the bill would be through in a very few minutes.
The House was very still during the reading, and
many curious eyes were turned toward those two distinguished gentlemen conversing so earnestly, but
very few knew what that colloquy meant. They had
before them the remarkable spectacle of the premier
of an administration standing on the floor of an opposition House, holding the opposition leader under
moral duress against his will while passing a bill over
his head—a piece of diplomatic audacity, skill and success without a parallel in parliamentary history that I
ever heard of. . . . If the bill had not passed at that
session, it would not have been passed to this day; because by the next session combinations would have
been made amongst the higher institutions of learning
and some potential friends of education to compass its
defeat or make sweeping changes in its character and
provisions, whether for the better or not cannot here
be discussed."

Two Governors, Wolf and Bigler, failed to be re-
elected largely on account of the stand which they had
taken in the interest of common schools. In each instance, their successors, Ritner and Pollock respect-
ively, although of opposite political faith, took up the
work in spite of popular clamor and the most bitter
opposition, and carried it forward to the lasting benefit
of posterity. Thaddeus Stevens, although elected on
an anti-school ticket, saved the system by his eloquence and his logic, and proved that although a poor
plank in a platform may be helpful in stepping into
office, it is not a good thing to stand on after the ship

of state is moving forward. At a later day, Andrew
G. Curtin, by work more effective than oratory, saved
the County Superintendency and paved the way for
the establishment of our splendid system of State
Normal schools. If a politician differs from a states-
man in that the former looks forward to the next
election, while the latter looks toward the next generation, then surely Wolf and Ritner and Stevens and
Curtin deserve to rank as statesmen.

Through the epoch-making period in which these men
were the moulding factors of our educational history,
the author of this book asks the reader to follow the narrative of Nicholas Comenius, who was an interested eye-
witness of the first examination in which the County
Superintendent took the place of the Squire and the
Committeemen of former days. That other states are
now following the Pennsylvania plan of prescribing literary and professional qualifications for those who hold
the office of County Superintendent, argues well for the
wisdom of the men who framed the Act of 1854, and
lends additional interest to the portions of the book
which bear upon this epoch in our educational history.

The author of Nicholas Comenius deserves the special
gratitude of those who feel an interest in rescuing
from oblivion the factors that gave us our beneficent
system of Common Schools.

NATHAN C. SCHAEFFER.

Department of Public Instruction,
  Harrisburg, Pa., July 13, 1897.

THE NEW AND THE OLD.

NICHOLAS COMENIUS.

CHAPTER I.

FROM THE OLD TO THE NEW.

It was the year that marked the sixtieth anniversary of the adoption of the Common School System in Pennsylvania. Around the old Court House in the metropolis of Blackwell county had congregated, on a bright, crisp November morning, a throng of young men and women, exchanging greetings and congratulating themselves upon the prospect of a week of professional work and entertainment. They were teachers gathered from all parts of a great county, in attendance at the Annual Teachers' Institute.

Beyond the mirth in store for them and the fond dreams of pleasant associations to be found, their thoughts did not seem to wander. They had severed the ties of the school-room, at least for a season, and come forth with joyous hearts to enter a new field of intellectual activity.

The cosy, well-equipped rural school far away on some lone hillside, and the numerous little temples

of learning dotted here and there over the broad
acres of Blackwell county, stood deserted and forsaken during this bounteous Thanksgiving week.
The merry voices and the gay shouts of laughter
of the little ones were no longer to be heard on the
playground. Their books were resting high up on
the shelf in the sitting-room of the unpretentious
homestead, out of reach; while the boys and girls,
forgetful of their daily tasks, were playing hide-
and-seek around the shocks of golden fodder.

Only an occasional constituent, on his way to
partake of a neighbor's Thanksgiving hospitality,
would stop in front of some deserted school-house
and wonder how the teacher's stock of new-fangled
notions was to compensate for the increased tax-rate
and a week's time frittered away at the teachers'
meeting. But the young educators of Blackwell
county, buoyed up with the last month's salary and
the pleasures that only a week's professional enjoyment can give, gave little heed to their far-off
routine of duty.

The antiquated Court House, in which many a
hotly-contested legal battle had been fought, around
which tradition still lingers, was the center of at-
traction. Within its time-stained walls had congregated a fair percentage of the teaching force of
a great Commonwealth. Its interior was tastefully
decorated with choice flowers and evergreens, while
directly over the judicial altar was suspended the
American flag—emblem of our cherished liberties.

But aside from these decorations, the old flag, and a few patriotic remarks, was there anything of such special importance as to give to this reunion precedence over that of the year previous? At all events, it was such a gathering of enthusiastic teachers, as in the judgment of the young superintendent was best adapted to the county in which it was held. The programme was of the pre-arranged stereotyped order, and when set in motion by the presiding officer, moved with the regularity of well-adjusted mechanism. The list of professional instructors was in many respects the best the Literary Bureau could command or the institute afford; while the only conditions imposed upon the members were first, the annual membership fee, and second, prompt daily attendance.

Some years previous, a change had taken place in the management of the schools of the county. Nicholas Comenius, who had held the position of Superintendent, with the exception of a short interval, for nearly a quarter of a century from the date of the act creating the office, having failed to keep in touch with the advanced public sentiment the spirit of the times seemed to demand, had been ruthlessly thrust aside, and a young Normal School graduate elected in his place. At many consecutive elections in that long series of years, Nicholas Comenius had been his own worthy successor; but after his defeat the tenure of each superintendent was limited to a single term. This triennial rota-

tion, in a most responsible office, was due in part
to the large number of political aspirants, with
whom qualification is always of secondary importance, but in the main to that peculiar tendency in
the human mind to oscillate from one extreme to
the other; to that untiring zeal after the unattain-
able, that causes men to transcend the bounds of
experience and prudence. One class proposed to
root out the very last remnant of old-fogyism,
whether relating to teacher or director, to make
room for the new; to remove the landmarks set by
the wisdom of the past, and erect them on new
lines of advanced thought. Another, and the more
numerous class, argued that no system of education
was useful except the practical kind—that which
had for its ultimate object and aim, pecuniary gain.
A few, however, believed that education based
merely on the accumulation of wealth was in direct
conflict with the spirit, if not the letter, of the act
creating the common school system. Between
these conflicting opinions the constituents of Blackwell county found themselves at the close of the
official career of Nicholas Comenius.

Whatever may have been the shortcomings of
Nicholas, he was in the broadest sense of the word
one of the pioneers of the system. There was
neither system, classification, nor unity of action
on the part of the directorship, nor a progressive
public school sentiment on the part of the masses.
There were times, indeed, when Nicholas was wont

to say, "Truly the lights are dim, the foundations insecure, and nothing seems certain save the uncertainty that everywhere prevails." To harmonize conflicting opinions, to go forth like the early missionary, preaching the light of the new doctrine on highway and byway, among the rich and the poor, the ignorant and the learned, was the mission of Nicholas Comenius. The wrath which the various acts of the Legislature passed from time to time had engendered among the masses, found vent at times and fell with crushing force on the head of this public benefactor. He, however, never took a backward step, but like a faithful pioneer, kept straight on in the line of his professional duties as he understood them.

Nicholas Comenius, who claimed to be the lineal descendant of the distinguished John Amos Comenius, had received more than an average education. Being a favorite with old Jimmy, the master of the school at Emden, he continued to plod along within its dusky walls until he had passed well into his teens. It was then that fortune favored young Nicholas, despite the general protest of the rural population. After leaving the village school, Nicholas Comenius fell heir to the proud distinction of being the only country lad of Emden who had ever been permitted to attend a distant academic institution. This special privilege accorded him was due more to the noble name he bore than to any special desire on the part of his parents to

favor such a course of instruction. Indeed, the
tendency of the times was directly the opposite;
for the thrifty settlers at that early day were content to live within themselves and for themselves,
having their own peculiar customs, traditions and
local history, and caring little for the bustling
world without. A common bond of good fellowship, a generous hospitality, a deep affection for all
old-time customs and a marked respect for old age,
were virtues of which these people could rightfully
boast. It was this reverence for the traditions of
other days, and especially for that staid old philosopher of the sixteenth century, that gave to young
Comenius a standing in the community that he
could have attained in no other way. It was but
natural, then, that Nicholas as he grew in years
should appreciate the distinction accorded him, for
the name of Comenius was a household word,
revered by these sturdy tillers of the soil.

It is not, however, to the early period immediately preceding the adoption of the new school
system, nor to that somewhat later period when
Nicholas Comenius was monarch of all he surveyed, that I would now direct the attention of the
reader, but rather to a time when the new conditions were pressing hard upon the old, and when
self-preservation with him became indeed the first
law of nature.

Opposition had now begun to manifest itself
from a source wholly unexpected. If there was

one thing in the work of Comenius on which he
prided himself more than any other, it was his
manner of conducting the County Institute. Economy with Nicholas was neither a penny-wise nor a
pound-foolish theory. He was an ardent, firm believer in the principle that on all important questions pertaining to the practice and theory of
teaching, careful, thoughtful conference of one
teacher with another always produced the best results; and in this view he was at all times sustained
by the great majority, at least of the older teachers.
Nicholas, in justification of his course, was at all
times prepared to back up his arguments by excellent authorities, among whom none stood higher
than his ancestor, John Amos Comenius, whose life
and example he had ever held as the *ne plus ultra*
of all that was truly noble and enduring. But
Nicholas failed to realize that among the new conditions that were forging their way to the front, the
teachings of that staid old philosopher had few
advocates. And so, when the Literary Bureau
directed his attention from time to time to the
growing wants of the system and the beneficial
effects resulting from the employment of a corps of
highly eminent instructors from abroad, Nicholas
only smiled, shook his head, and continued in the
line of his professional work. It was strongly intimated in many of these gratuitous communications
that the old man was steering dangerously close to
the dead line, and that to prevent a fatal collapse

or early disintegration of the entire educational
fabric, a living, vital force was necessary. It was
also pointed out, in unmistakable language, that
too great a percentage of old fossils was to be found
in the ranks of the profession, in a county esteemed
for its general intelligence in other directions. It
was even intimated that a radical change in the
personnel of the institute was most desirable; and
that the pruning-knife should be brought into service, and much of the dead timber that for years
had proven a hindrance to a vigorous, healthy
growth of the system, should be lopped off. In
fact, the day came when the institute of Nicholas
Comenius was spoken of at all modernly equipped
teachers' meetings, as "a thing of the past," notwithstanding the fact that the practical results
attained, as shown in the various schools of the
county, were of the highest order. While Nicholas
Comenius, now well up in years, had a profound
respect for the young Normal School graduate,
there lingered in the bosom of this faithful public
servant a mine of pure love for the little army of
old schoolmasters who had grown gray in the
service. Nicholas was in no sense of the word "a
back number." He fully appreciated the growing
wants of the system, but he was, at the same time,
loath to break in on a class of old teachers in any
single locality, when he felt assured that honest
service was being rendered alike to rich and poor.

Nicholas Comenius, in the goodness of his

rugged nature, may have discriminated at times in
favor of some old veteran, with a big heart and a
growing family; but he always satisfied his conscience with the thought that the young could
afford to wait, at least until they had reached the
years of discretion. But above all these minor
considerations, to Nicholas important in themselves, there were other binding ties—associations
of a personal nature—that he could not overlook.
For had Comenius not lived through that exciting
period that gave birth to the Common School system? Was he not the same Nicholas who was a
living witness of the first public examination ever
held in the little red sandstone school house at
Emden, in 1854, by one who held the position of
superintendent but one short year, and who, in the
discharge of the duties of his office, had laid down
his young life for the cause he so much loved?
Had he not seen the eight old masters thrust into
the cold world by one sweep of the pen, to make
room for an equal number of New England professors? Could these early impressions ever be
entirely eliminated from his memory?

Dear reader, have you ever taught a district
school in some remote place, far away from kind
friends and among strangers, where a familiar face
is seldom if ever seen? If so, can you recall the
first visitation by the county superintendent—more
especially if he were one of those big-hearted men
whose very presence is an inspiration to all that is

good and noble? Then you can appreciate the emotions of many another lone schoolmaster when brought into communion with the object of many longing desires. Have you ever known a Nicholas Comenius, as kind and loving in his rugged nature as a child, and yet as broad, as brilliant and as comprehensive as it seems possible for man to become? Has such a broad and loving nature ever come in upon your little school on a cold bleak February day? Can you, if teacher you be or have been, picture a scene in life's battle around which cluster more endearing reminiscences of by-gone days? Did you forget to offer him the old arm-chair as you stirred up the half-dead coals in the stove beside which you asked him to sit? Did you feel his magnetic influence as it permeated and electrified the whole school? The parental in-fluence of home life may be sacred and lasting, but that of the school-room, under such hallowed sur-roundings, has no parallel in the broad field of child nature. The tender and generous impulses unconsciously displayed in early manhood or womanhood may for the time be forgotten; but as years roll on they will as surely return as the sun after a passing cloud. The world may never know and perhaps little cares to learn the true relation-ship which existed between Nicholas Comenius and many an old-time schoolmaster, when he directed, as superintendent, the school affairs of Blackwell county.

But as has been said, the time came at last when Nicholas Comenius was to transfer the mantle of his authority to one younger in years and more closely in touch with the advanced public school sentiment the times seemed to demand. Was there sympathy for Nicholas when the vote was counted and the result announced? It was not sympathy for himself that Nicholas wanted. He had simply done his duty as he understood it, and accepted the result when it came with that perfect inner contentment that duty well performed always brings. Were tears shed when Nicholas passed through the doorway and down the great stone steps? Yes, tears of rejoicing and tears of sorrow—rejoicing by the younger teachers, who felt that a new era had at last dawned on the profession; sorrow by the old masters for their head and chief. The defeat of Nicholas Comenius, they felt, carried with it a meaning that could not be mistaken. It was the handwriting on the wall, the passing away of the Old, the incoming of the New. When Comenius passed out of the active professional work of the superintendency, he had also passed beyond his three-score, the allotted time of most men, especially in the field of active life as educators. And so within a few brief years thereafter, the last old master disappeared from the rural school, leaving Nicholas to be remembered only by the few who yet lingered among men. How few of the hundreds of young teachers in

attendance at the institute could recall even the name of Nicholas Comenius! And who can wonder at this, when we see how great had been the change in the educational world which left him the representative of the Old, while these young people aspired to be considered typical of the New?

For a new era had truly dawned upon the Pennsylvania teacher. The old educational ship, in the opinion of many, had become waterlogged and loaded down with antiquated ideas and discarded methods. Having undergone extensive alterations and repairs, the anchor was now to be raised and the double rigged, modernly equipped vessel launched forth on an experimental sea of uncertainty. The few remaining trusty old seamen were either superseded at the very outstart, or thrust overboard at the first opportune moment.

This new educational ship, in its onward course, was no longer to be guided by the teachings and experiences of such old mariners as Pestalozzi, Froebel and Krusi, those master minds of nearly two centuries before, who had given to the world the very highest conceptions of child nature and child culture. A younger generation of teachers had now taken possession of the helm, and in their superior wisdom were to be guided in the future by a theoretical compass and the modern text-book. Whatever inspiration Pestalozzi's little school at Stanz may have thrown around the old schoolmasters of earlier years, was now to be swept aside.

These were the conditions, dear reader, that prevailed in the closing years of the official career of the venerable Nicholas Comenius. But, far off in the distant horizon, under the guiding star of a trusty captain, we now may see the dim outlines of the old educational ship returning to the harbor of its earlier days. Let us hope that the life, the light and the inspiration which hovered around the school of Pestalozzi may yet serve to guide the old ship in the direction of a more permanent and lasting future.

But in this stirring age of future possibilities, how many of my younger readers, following the example of the antiquarian, who delves among buried cities in search of some lost art or hidden treasure, stand ready to buckle on the armor of investigation and follow Comenius down this enchanted highway to the birth of the new system? And how many, having resolved to make the journey, will have the fortitude to continue to the end? A few, no doubt, will make the attempt; here and there one genial spirit may be found willing to complete a chapter or two, and then turn aside, leaving the task to be completed by some old-time pedagogue. "Life is too short," says one, "to waste in rummaging through the cobwebs of antiquity." Another shakes his head, turns his back to the past, and rushes forward to join the multitude in its onward march for what the future may have in store.

But, dear reader, before entering on our journey,
let us take a retrospective view of the educational
pathway. As we stand upon our lofty eminence
and survey this extended avenue, what a panorama
is spread before the patient and observant reader!
Midway in the distance we behold the half-way
mile-stone, the dividing line between the Old and
the New. Beyond that line the great majority of
our teachers are as strangers in a strange land.
Along that section of the highway of time, to their
young minds all is a wilderness. Here and there,
it is true, may yet be seen the remnants of some
long-since-abandoned academic institution, and by
the wayside the ruins of some lone school-house,
but the last old schoolmaster has passed away forever.

Ah, but let us reverse the search-light of investigation and throw it forward upon this, the
close of the nineteenth century, and how vastly
different are the conditions to be met on every
hand. Along this modern highway, an army of
young, enthusiastic teachers from the thousands of
cosy, well-equipped rural schools, step forward to
bid us welcome. In the distance loom up before
us the Normal schools, so bountifully endowed by
a generous people, and from whose spacious halls
have gone forth this army of young educators to
bless the land. But even from this luminous highway, guarded by its long line of illustrious sentinels, branch off many by-ways and cross-roads that

modern engineering has constructed. Where the sun shines brightest are many blind leaders of the blind, wearing the garb of the professional teacher. Follow the footsteps of Nicholas Comenius, dear reader, and he will lead you in safety down through the sixty years of that exciting period that gave birth to the common school system.

2

CHAPTER II.

THE recollections and experiences of Nicholas
Comenius, as they are related in the following
chapters, may not be altogether new to many of the
older teachers who have passed through an era
contemporaneous with that of our aged historian.

Here and there in the Commonwealth of Pennsylvania, a few old residents may yet be found who
can point, with more or less pride, if not to
Nicholas Comenius in person, at least to his counterpart; for the Act of Assembly that forty odd
years ago created the Superintendency, applied to
all the counties of the State. It is safe to say that
in three-fourths of the districts, a large majority of
the rural population was arrayed in open opposition, not only to the law but to the individual in
office as well. There was no one single official,
with the possible exception of the tax collector,
that was more intensely hated. Few Superintendents were fortunate enough to escape this unreason-
able crusade, that at times enlisted the sympathies

18

of even the better class of the community. An outward expression of sympathy in favor of either the law or the man in office, rendered the unfortunate individual who uttered it, whether of high or low degree, an object of ostracism. Men of business, of known literary taste and of social position, if once suspected of sympathizing with the new system of education, were made to suffer the hate and vengeance of the anti-school men. More than one public examination was broken up and the Superintendent driven from the school-house by a squad of the unruly element, equipped with drum, fife and horn, in defence of what they had been led to believe were their sacred rights and franchises. Only a few years ago what a volume might have been written by many of these faithful pioneers. But, alas! most of them have passed over the river of time, leaving Comenius and his few remaining colleagues as the last frail span connecting the past with the present, the Old with the New.

Ah! how many times have we heard him relate his personal experiences as we sat beside the open fire in his low dingy office, on his return from one of his lonely pilgrimages. I remember one evening, after glancing over his note-book, he said:

"Made up my mind a year ago that I'd have to shelve the old gentleman at my next visitation. You see, he's been a little careless in his discipline, and don't appear to be holding up his end of the line with the other boys. I visited his school the

other day, but couldn't see any marked change. It was an awful day, my friend—snowing and blowing, with roads blocked and night coming on, and no public stopping-place within three miles. There we stood facing each other, Cornelius on one side of the wood stove, I on the other, while Nelly, the mare, stood without, buried to her hips in a snow-drift. What to do or where to go?—that was what bothered Nicholas," continued he, as he raked the half-dead coals into a blaze. "Yes, there we stood, peering out into the storm, and before us, huddled together on the long bench, sat a half dozen ill-clad lads, stormstaid also. 'Fear not, my little fellows,' said the master, as he saw the tears trickling down the faces of the lads. 'The cabin of Cornelius isn't very large, my boys, but the old master will always be taking good care of his little flock. We'll give you all a good warm supper, my lads, and then we'll pack you all together in the old buffalo robe, and when morning comes round you'll all feel like a piece of toast fresh from the oven.'

"Then there came a rap at the door and a pleasant voice from without: 'Cornelius! I say Cornelius! Give the Superintendent an invite to step over and partake of the hospitality of one who will never see a lone traveler and his poor brute perish in such a storm.'

"Then Cornelius, looking me squarely in the eye, said in a half-mistrustful tone: 'Will you, Mr. Superintendent, condescend to accept lodgment in the humble cabin of an old schoolmaster, such as you may find it?'

"'Accept it?' said I; 'why bless you, my old friend, the comforts of your little home, Cornelius, unpretentious though it be, are to me a thousand times more acceptable than the most lavish hand could provide in a palace where love is a stranger. But Nelly, the mare, Cornelius?'

"'Never mind Nell, Nicholas, but follow the lads and the old lady, who's been making a path for our convenience. Brindle will be only too glad to share her bed with the young critter on such a night,' was the reply of the tender-hearted schoolmaster, as he began to cover a few live coals for an early morning fire. Ah," added Nicholas, as he wiped away a tear, "and such a repast! And what a bed of downy feathers, thought I, as I laid myself down to offer a prayer of thanksgiving that Nicholas Comenius still lived to protect the old schoolmaster and his willing helpmate."

"Then you did not cancel his certificate?" we asked.

"Cancel it!" he replied; "Cancel it, did you say?—and could you have done it?"

Then, after raking up the dying embers, and watching the curling smoke as it circled upward through the old chimney-place, Nicholas turned from the pathetic to the humorous, and with a twinkle in his eye, remarked: "Ever hear of old Zaccheus and his telescope? Beats all how slow

some people are to catch on to the improvements
of the age! Zaccheus, you see, was president of
the boys' academy over at the forge. 'Twas along

ZACCHEUS AND THE TELESCOPE.

about harvest that Zaccheus employed an astrono-
mer to give the lads a peep through that wonderful
instrument; for the astronomers had been predict-
ing a total eclipse of the moon for months previous.
Well, there stood the telescope in front of the

Academy, pointing squarely at the old gentleman in the heavenly orb at an angle of fifteen degrees, when old farmer Nathan came riding along, all out of breath.

"'Zaccheus!' exclaimed he, at the top of his voice, 'if it's that infernal cannon you're after firing, it might be well to shift the nozzle a little to windward, as the old farm buildings are in direct line, and without a dollar of insurance either.'

"'Why Nat, my honest old friend,' retorted Zaccheus, 'it isn't a cannon at all; only a telescope, that the scientists have invented for making observations of the moon.'

"'A telescope! What's a telescope, Zaccheus? Thought sure it was one of the old Revolutionary field-pieces that had been resurrected from over beyond the Forge,' was the reply of Nathan, with a sigh of relief. 'But, Zaccheus,' came the inquiry, as the old farmer began to grow impatient, 'what's in the moon, anyway, that's causing you to be wasting your precious time over such a new-fangled machine? Seems you arn't being paid by the constituents for such silly nonsense! Better keep directing the minds of the lads to earthly affairs, instead of soaring around among the heavenly planets in search of the spiritual, that the parsons are employed to gather out of the Scriptures. Time enough, Zaccheus—time enough, old man, to be soaring around when you hear old Gabriel's trumpet summoning you to make the ascension.

Mighty uncertain kind of notions, Zaccheus, for one of your years to be instilling into the minds of growing lads!'

"Just then Zaccheus, by a neat adjustment of the instrument, caught a beautiful view, unusual even in the moon, and waving his hand and beckoning to the boys, said: 'Come here, boys, and see what a fine view lies over there. It is simply grand, and another proof that the unaided eye of man is blind to the greater glories of God's creation.'

"The boys, one after another, gazed through the telescope and expressed their delight and astonishment at so wonderful a revelation. One of the lads, who was more of a wag than a scientist, said he fancied he saw some familiar faces staring at him in the moon, and continued to gaze through the instrument, talking as he gazed: 'By Jove, I believe they are having a harvest picnic over yonder! There is a large hamper filled, no doubt, with summer sausage; the best of cheese, bread and butter, and a few jugs of well-brewed home mead, such as old Blackwell county is famous for. Save me, boys! if one of the stoppers hasn't popped out, and I see the foaming liquid running down the sides of the jug! It makes my lips water! What a sight of a lifetime, boys! But I feel very sorry for the good stuff that is going to waste over there.'

"Old Nat couldn't stand the pressure any longer —indeed he couldn't," chuckled Nicholas; "so leaping from his mare, he rushed up to catch a view of this wonderful picture, portrayed by the waggish young student. Nat gazed intently, but failed to discover any familiar faces, or any signs of the harvest picnickers; but he did own that the sight was most astonishing, and that there might be a good chance over in the moon for some enterprising fellow to plant a colony of farmers and give a new impetus to the Homestead Law. Then turning from the instrument and mounting his old nag, he turned and said: 'All very well Zaccheus: It may be very good farming up there in the moon for some, but old farmer Nathan would sooner have a half acre right here beside the old Academy than a whole plantation up there.' "

And so for hours Nicholas would sit and recount his reminiscences of by-gone days, while actively engaged in his official labors as Superintendent of Blackwell county. Casting his eye toward the dingy wall, upon which was suspended a time-worn map of the United States, with the Great American Desert conspicuously portrayed in its outlines, he'd smile and say: "Common enough, these wall maps, in every district in Blackwell county nowadays; not so, however, in the early times. I remember well when the first set was placed on exhibition in Bear Creek school. Why bless me, the whole neighborhood turned out, bent on burning the maps and smoking out the master. 'Twas along about Thanksgiving that word reached the office

that the school was to be closed and the maps con-
fiscated. There wasn't any time to be lost, my
friend, I can assure you, to make the ten miles
drive and be on hand before the commotion began.
I found the door of the old house surrounded by a
cordon of angry tax-payers, demanding entrance,
and swearing vengance on the head of the agent
who had placed the maps in the school, and who
was now inside explaining them to four of the
trustees. First one of the constituents would step
up and take a peep through the window; then
another would follow; then they'd beckon to the
others and exclaim: 'Come men, take a peep, and
see what new-fangled nonsense they're introducing
into the schools of Bear Creek district, anyway.'

"'What are they for, Mr. Superintender?' said
the President of the Board, 'except to ornament
the walls?'

"'I'll tell you what they're for, men,' replied
old Jeremiah, the charcoal burner over beyond the
Ridge, with a flourish of his long arms; 'it's an
advertisement by some Western land speculator, to
entice the young men to desert the plantations of
Blackwell county, and get scalped in the end by
the Indians, or lost in the Great American Desert,
of which I've been reading quite considerable of
late. Yes, men, that's what they're for, if I am a
judge of such tomfoolery.'

"'My sentiments, gentlemen,' 'and mine,' 'and
mine,' came a dozen voices; 'and it's out of the

THE MAP AGENT.

(28)

school the maps and that agent must go, Mr.
Superintender, or we'll smoke the master out in
short order. Mount the roof, boys!' came the
word of command, 'and close up the chimney!'"

"Did they smoke him out?" I asked, as Nicholas
fell into a reverie.

"Why bless you, no, my young friend," retorted
he, with his eyes still fixed upon the old map:
"they didn't do anything of the kind. It was a
trying time, though, such as I have had to meet
many times before and since, whenever a new
branch was added to the course of study or a patent
blackboard placed in any one of the schools.
'Come, men,' said I, as I looked them squarely in
the face, 'follow me, and we'll go into the school
and find out what the queer-looking things are
made for; and if they are pernicious to good morals,
or conflict in any way with the Scriptures, or with
the teachings of John Amos Comenius, we'll yank
them into the old wood-stove in short order."

"And did they follow you?"

"Follow *me?* No! It wasn't Nicholas Comenius that was the touchstone, but a certain charm
that the name of John Amos Comenius always possessed for this honest, but at times misguided yeomanry. What name in history was more inspiring
to these hardy tillers of the soil than the name of
this sterling educator of more than two centuries
ago? Was it not with this same John Amos
Comenius that thousands of their early ancestors

were compelled to flee and take refuge, some among the mountain defiles and others in a foreign land, to escape the intolerance of a religious crusade? Ah, my friend, to this day the name of Comenius is dear to the hearts of these people.

"Well, into the old house they marched, one after the other, where they all stood at the doorway with eyes on the maps and the four trustees, ready to desert the premises at the first signal of command. Took mighty careful handling," said Nicholas, as he stepped over and examined the date on the old map, that had become blackened with smoke and age almost beyond recognition. "Quite an old stager, published away back in the forties; but it's the only one of the set remaining that caused all that excitement in Bear Creek district. See, there's nothing beyond the Missouri but wild lands and the great unexplored desert."

"Part with the old map for a consideration?" I made bold to ask.

"No, not for a fortune," came the quick response. "It's a picture that conveys a lesson full of meaning to young and old," added Nicholas with a sigh. "From a barren waste, as I recall the western country, it's been turned into an empire more powerful than the world has ever known. Of course, as a guide for the present the old map isn't very valuable; but as a reminder of the past, it's like the old text-book, full of prophecy for what the future is to be.

"Yes, yes," he continued, regaining the thread of his story; "this same old map was hanging against the wall, with the constituents eying it from the rear of the room. It wasn't long until the school was called to order, and the lads drawn up in line, like young soldiers on dress parade. Beginning with the far-off state of Maine, the agent kept pointing and naming, and the young-sters repeating, so that before the old men could recover their senses, the class had gone clear through the country from Canada to the Gulf and from the Atlantic to the Missouri, without a mishap. But the climax was reached when Gideon, the master, who had been taking private drills on the maps the evening previous, stepped forward, and endeavored to play upon the credulity of old Jeremiah. 'Jerry,' as was known to Gideon, had been a drover, and had traveled some in his time; and so, when the master started to point out many of the towns the old man had visited in the line of his business operations, the old drover turned, shook his head and said: 'True enough, men, the Yankee who invented that map, as they call it, managed to place the towns where they belong, for I've been there myself many a time; but it's as true as preaching that it costs plenty of solid cash to get there, with no free ride on the packet line or stage-coach either, as I have reason to know from experience.'

"'Yes, men,' chimed in the little Dutch squire,

'and it's the solid cash these map agents are after, and no mistaking it.'

"It stirred up a pretty stiff breeze," said Nicholas, as he rolled up the map, "but it's all blown over long ago, and now there's a full set of the latest improved maps in every school in Bear Creek district."

CHAPTER III.

LADAMUS AND MARINDA.

It was late in the evening when I arose to leave the veteran educator, and, as we stood within the open doorway of his low, dusky office, watching the moon as it came into view, a single horseman rode up and dismounted.

"Oh, it is only Ladamus, one of the six men of Brimstone district school board; comes regularly once a month for legal advice covering some knotty point in the school law," said Comenius, as the backwoodsman stepped into the post-office opposite. "Come inside, if not too much in a hurry, and I'll relate a little episode that the old gentleman will illustrate before an hour goes by."

"You expect to meet him then, on official business?" I remarked, as I stepped within and closed the door.

"O yes; and there isn't a section of the school law that I haven't gone over time and again for the benefit of Brimstone School Board."

"Rather a difficult undertaking, to find authority for the multiplicity of legal questions submitted annually for your decision," I suggested.

3

"Oh no, not by any means, my friend," he replied. "You see, the common school law was framed to meet every phase of the public school question, and is susceptible, pro and con, of almost any construction desirable. As a whole, it is both contractive and expansive, and affords those high in authority an easy avenue of escape from what otherwise might involve school boards in endless litigation."

"Then you seem to anticipate the purpose of the old gentleman's mission?"

"Fully, my friend; and if you are not averse to a little innocent amusement, I will illustrate to your satisfaction the versatility of the law, and how it can be twisted to meet the whims and caprices of the average school trustee. But in order that you may appreciate more fully the object of his visit, it may be necessary to acquaint you with the preliminary facts before the arrival of President Ladamus."

Nicholas then hastily sketched the history of the case. For many years Brimstone School, over in the charcoal region, had been under the control of a crusty, old, one-legged schoolmaster, whose only boast was that he had thrashed as many lads daily as there were months in the year. The school board, unhappily, was composed of this same kind of knotty timber; honest, well-meaning, but rough, rugged, and at times superstitious—firm believers in the teaching of Solomon, that to spare the rod is to spoil the child. Once in possession of the school interests of Brimstone district, these six wise men of the charcoal-pits were destined to continue in office to their souls' content. If any of the lads returned home showing marks that had been inflicted by the strong arm of "Old Obstinate," as he was familiarly known among the dusky constituents of the ridge, a repetition of even greater severity was sure to follow. If the lads outwardly respected him, it was only for the ability he displayed in swinging the shillalah. To the true character of Old Obstinate, Comenius was not blinded. He had visited his school, denounced with severity his mode of treatment, spoken plainly to the trustees, but all without avail. In the estimation of the Board, Old Obstinate's systematic mode of flogging had endeared him to the hearts of the populace, the most important of whom was the President.

Ladamus, in addition to being a school trustee, was the fortunate possessor of the old forge and the finest six-mule team that ever drew a load of charcoal over the ridge. He had in his employ at the same time a young teamster, Sandoe by name, whose chief recommendation was his ability to outdo Old Obstinate in the use of the raw-hide, which often fell with unerring accuracy on the bare backs of the poor dumb brutes. The crack of his whip as it circled through the air and fell first on one, then on the other, of his spanking

team, was music to the ears of the President of
Brimstone School Board.

Ladamus had but one child in the world, an
intelligent, bright-eyed lad of twelve. Many indeed were the times that Sim returning from
school, and feeling the welts of Old Obstinate's
birch rod beneath his flimsy jacket, would stop and
listen to the whacks of Sandoe's raw-hide. He
could bear the itching pain left by the blows on his
own back, but he rebelled inwardly against the
severity of the castigation administered to the poor
animals. As time ran on, a bond of the closest
sympathy sprang up between Sim and the "black
beauties," as he was proud to call them. Between
school hours, he would slip into their respective
stalls, pat them gently on the mane, and tell them
of his own trials and difficulties. Through these
repeated visits a friendship sprang up between Sim
and the poor abused creatures, that appealed with
much force to his young nature, even though it
failed to produce an outward expression of recipro-
city on the part of the "black beauties."

But all things are destined to change sooner or
later, and Brimstone school was to be no exception
to this inexorable law of nature. Nicholas Comenius had waited long and patiently for some avenue
through which another teacher might be, with
safety installed there. At last, Old Obstinate fell
into the meshes of the law, and his schoolmastership, after forty years of uninterrupted sway, came

to an untimely end. To supply the vacancy fell in part to the lot of Comenius, who was not unmindful of the conditions to be met. As it happened, a middle-aged Yankee schoolmistress made application for a position at this opportune moment; and as Nicholas was not slow in discovering the inherent qualities of the "little midget," as he termed her—characteristics the very opposite of those possessed by Old Obstinate—the necessary machinery was put in operation to place her in the school. This being accomplished, Nicholas, after visiting the school on two occasions, composed himself to await developments. Two long months had since passed by, and Comenius had almost forgotten the occurrence, until our attention was attracted to the President of Brimstone School Board as he dismounted and entered the post-office.

Nicholas had scarcely concluded this preliminary history when there came a rap at the door.

"Ah, my worthy friend, rather a late hour to be skylarking around through the metropolis of Blackwell county, with only the man in the moon to guide your footsteps," said Nicholas, in his affable manner, as he shook the dusky charcoal-burner by the hand and invited him to a seat.

"Oh yes, Mr. Superintender, rather a late hour to be 'skylarking' around," was the curt rejoinder; "but business means business, Mr. Superintender, and when duty calls it isn't the President of Brimstone School Board that's to be found wanting."

With this drawling rejoinder, he thrust one hand into his trousers pocket, and grasping the back of the chair with the other, stood staring at Nicholas for a moment, and then added: "There's a mountain of trouble brewing over among the constituents of Brimstone school, that I've had the honor to oversee for more than thirty years, Mr. Superintender; and if it isn't squelched before election day comes around, there will be one trustee less to guide the affairs of Brimstone school district."

"Ah, more trouble in the old school?" smiled Nicholas, as he turned and caught my eye. "Strange, passing strange, that Marinda should be getting into trouble with the charcoal-burners before the term is more than half up."

"Oh yes, there's trouble, and plenty of it, in the old gal's school, Mr. Superintender; and I thought I'd slip over under cover of darkness to get an opinion favorable to the trustees, before the Yankee schoolmistress could put in her appearance."

"Ah, I see! I comprehend! Nothing like taking time by the forelock, Mr. President! Charges of a serious nature and well substantiated?—or only exaggerated rumors based largely on gossip?"

"Well, Mr. Superintender, there's where the trouble comes in; some say one thing, some another; and betwixt and between lies the pint I'd have you decide."

"Oh, we are now beginning to reach an understanding, Mr. President." (Nicholas turned, reached for quill and paper and pretended to write, as he humorously continued the dialogue.) "And can it be possible, Mr. President, that Marinda, the Yankee schoolmistress whom I so highly recommended to the trustees on account of her literary ability and high standing as a disciplinarian, has gone off and married the pious old parson, who it is true has grown pretty lonely of late, as he's grown older? A mighty serious condition for the trustees to meet, Mr. President." He reached down a volume of school laws, adjusted his spectacles and continued: "Ah, here is a provision that covers your case in a nutshell. No cause for action, I regret to say; comes within the law of supply and demand, and bears out the inference to be drawn that what's Marinda's gain is the school's loss. You see, here is where the law of supply and demand comes in; eliminate this wholesome provision, and you blight the future prospects of more than nine-tenths of all the school-ma'ams in the land."

"Good Heavens, Mr. Superintender! There isn't any wedding ceremonies connected with the fracas."

"Oh, now I comprehend the situation! Died of a broken heart—been jilted by the hypocritical old parson, and you've come to secure a memorial tribute. Mighty considerate in the President of Brimstone School Board, and shows a tender regard for the memory of the little schoolmistress. Leave any bequests, my friend? And were her last moments peaceful and happy?"

"For the Lord's sake, Mr. Superintender, Marinda didn't—"

"One moment more, my venerable friend; calm yourself while I refer to the moral status of her school" (turning over the leaves of his note-book, while Ladamus stroked his long gray beard, strutting to and fro and gesticulating with both arms): "Ah, here's her record without a blemish:— 'Discipline, perfection; rod abandoned and moral suasion substituted—the first instance of the kind on record; methods of teaching far above the average; general deportment of pupils of the highest standing'—a splendid record, my worthy old friend, to which I shall only be too happy to testify."

"Holy St. Peter! Marinda didn't marry the parson, and she isn't dead either, Mr. Superintender! The plain truth is, the old lady's as lively as a cricket, practicing moral suasion, as they call it, over in Brimstone school, at a rate that calls for prompt action. Think of it, Mr. Superintender! Think of the old gal departing from the law as laid down by old Solomon in the Scriptures," (swaying his long slender form backward and forward and from side to side, and gesticulating,) "and it's for practicing such infernal nonsense, that's never been heard of before around the old forge, that I've come, Mr. Superintender, to ask for the old lady's dismissal!"

"Oh beg your pardon, Mr. President! Now I fully realize the importance of your visit" (stepping over and shaking Ladamus by the hand). "Quiet your emotions, my old friend. These little misunderstandings are always liable to occur among those holding responsible official positions under the common school system." (Ladamus gives a nod of grateful acknowledgment.) "And so you have come over to ask for Marinda's discharge, for substituting moral suasion in place of the ferule, or the shillalah, as you term it?"

"Well, that's about the size of it, Mr. Superintender."

"Ah! now, Mr. President, have you any well-defined ideas as to the way in which Marinda has violated the provisions of the law? If so, please state them in as few words as possible, and I shall then be prepared to render an opinion."

Ladamus stood erect, balancing himself first on one foot then on the other; transferring his quid of tobacco from right to left, then vice versa, and proceeded with his statement: "You know Sim, Mr. Superintender, that uncommon spry chap of mine; up early and late, assisting the old man over at the charcoal beds during the summer months, and attending school over at the old Brimstone house during the three winter months."

"Oh yes, Mr. President, I well remember Sim, and a most precocious lad he is," was the reply of Comenius, with a look of approval.

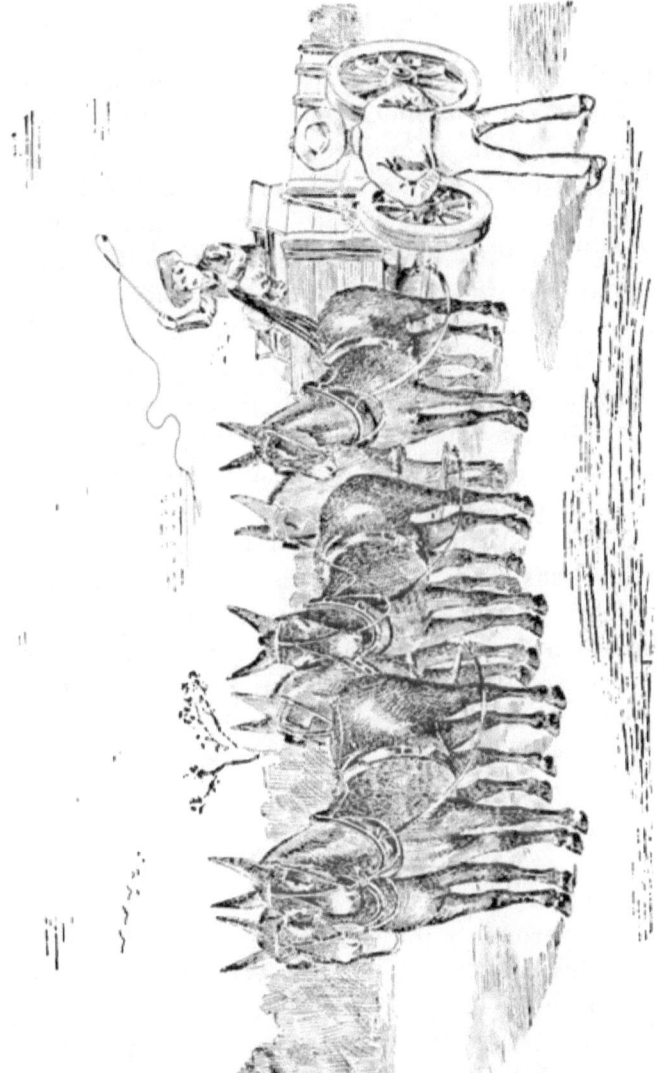

THE BLACK BEAUTIES.

(42)

"Glad to hear your good opinion of the lad; he is a chip o' the old block, and the very image of his father. Well, as I started out to say, Sim, you recollect, attended school under the old school-master a year ago, in readin', writin', and 'rith-metic, with a little chemistry beaten into his head by way of assistin' the old man in diagonosing the kind o' metal around the ore banks. This of course, Mr. Superintender, gave the lad a fine standing among the gentry of Brimstone school district. There was some fault-finding on account of the chemistry, which was only natural: for many believed that readin', writin' and 'rithmetic, with a little spellin' thrown in to round up his edication, was more than enough for any youngster who wasn't born to be hankering after any of the hifalutin callings. But Mr. Superintender, the trouble with Marinda wasn't on account of the chemistry nor the spellin'; and if hadn't been for the moral suasion racket, there'd have been clear sailing for the old edicational ship o' state around through the charcoal region.

"It was long about sun-up this morning, Mr. Superintender, that Sandoe started out to hook up that obstreperous six-mule team, that's got a record for pure, downright cussedness. Well, things were moving along with Sandoe and the sly critters as smooth as old Dan Rice's circus on dress parade; and if it hadn't been for Sim and that dastardly off-side mule, that began kicking and backing be-

fore Sandoe had given the others more than a half-
dozen whacks with his long raw-hide, everything
might have gone 'long without a mishap. But
while Sandoe was whacking away at that off-side
critter, Sim, that edicated lad o' mine, came flying
up as fast as his legs could carry him, calling out
at the top of his voice : 'Sandoe, I say Sandoe, use
a little of Marinda's school-room tactics on the
black beauties.' '.And what kind o' medicine is
that, Sim, you'd be after giving the ondacent
beasts?' cried Sandoe, between the lashes of his
raw-hide. 'Oh, it's only a new kind of discipline
the mistress has been practicing over in Brimstone school, but it beats lickin' all hollow ! You
see, Sandoe,' said Sim, in a soft persuasive tone, a
way he had of handling the young teamster, 'it's
been a pretty good kind o' medicine for old Tom
Brown's son Ned, who only yesterday declared to
the mistress that it was the first school he had
attended in his lifetime that he didn't get at least
five wallopings a day, from crusty old one-legged
Obstinate.' Then Sandoe dropped the long raw-
hide and stepped over to Sim and said : 'Sim, my
boy, I ain't much in favor of lickin' anyway ; so
tell me how in the deuce the mistress managed to
break the spirit of young Ned Brown without the
use of the shillalah ;' and so after whispering some
nonsense in his ear and saying he'd tell him all
about it some time on the sly, Sim started right
over to the six-mule team, patted each of the

critters on the neck, and after whispering some
hocus-pocus nonsense into their ears, took the
reins in his own hands and started the unruly
critters off at a rate faster than they'd ever been
driven under the lash of Sandoe. Then Sim
halted the six-mule team at the top of the hill and
handed the lines to Sandoe; and true as you're a
living man, Mr. Superintender, Sandoe started
them off without a crack of the whip, and they've
been going along under the influence of Marinda's
moral-suasion racket ever since.

"But, Mr. Superintender, while Sim was practicing this hocus-pocus nonsense on Sandoe and
the six-mule team I wasn't to be caught napping,
for I was prying through the bars over at the old
wagon-shed, and I riz right up and followed that
edicated chap of mine down by the foot of the long
slope. Says I, 'Sim,' says I, 'what kind of hocus-
pocus nonsense have you been instilling into the
brain of Sandoe about the dumb creatures?' Then
Sim looked straight up in my eyes and told me all
about how the Yankee schoolmistress had been
practicing moral suasion among the wild lads of the
school. 'Dad,' said he, 'there isn't any hocus-
pocus about Marinda's teaching. It is only a way
she has of appealing to a boy's honor. There's old
Tom Brown's son Ned, the worst chap in the
school! You see, Dad, Ned had made up his mind
on the first day of school to carry the little schoolmistress out of the school and then take possession

himself. All the larger boys were in the secret, and a jolly good time they were going to have at Marinda's expense! Ned said he didn't see any use, anyway, for the Yankee school-marm to be taking the place of Old Obstinate, whose teaching suited him, even if the lickings didn't. Well, Dad, some how or other the mistress got wind of Ned's intentions, and so, after the reading of the Scriptures, she called about a dozen of the larger boys up in a row, and said: "Boys, I want to form a 'Law and Order Society,' and I want the largest boy in the school to be chairman." Then we all turned and looked at Ned, who was standing at the end of the row, looking down through the opening in the floor with a tired sort of look on his face. "Will Master Ned consent to accept the honor of the chairmanship? I see," said she, "that he's the tallest boy in the school, and looks like an intelligent, manly lad, who would give honor and dignity to the society." Then Ned looked up, and with tears running down his face, said: "Teacher, I never in all my life heard such kind words before; they make me feel half ashamed of what I had been thinking about doing." "Will you, Master Ned, accept the Chairmanship?" said the mistress, as she took him by the hand, not noticing his attempt at confession. And so Ned told the mistress that he'd be willing, provided the other boys were; and so we took a vote and elected Ned by what the mistress called a unanimous vote. Since

then, Dad, we've been holding weekly meetings
over in the old school-house, and the mistress is the
secretary and keeps a record of what's going on in
the society. Oh, it's a splendid time we're having,
Dad, and the mistress is so kind and loving, and
uses such kind words that there isn't a boy in the
school who would say an unkind word to hurt her
feelings. And it's the same with the girls, Dad, for
she started a little sewing circle, with Widow Mar-
shall's daughter Fannie as chairman, and they
meet every rainy day at noon-time in one corner
of the room, while the boys are holding society
meetings in the other. It would soften your heart,
Dad, for the "black beauties," I know it would, if
you would drop into the school some rainy day
when there isn't any hauling to be done over at the
charcoal-pits. Oh, Dad, the little mistress said only
yesterday that she hadn't seen the face of a trustee
inside the school-room for the three months that
she had been in charge; but she told me she would
be only too happy to have the President of the
Board visit the school; said she knew he was a
generous, kind-hearted man who meant to do his
duty.' 'Sim,' said I, 'you kind of touch a tender
spot in the old man's heart, my lad'; for I began to
feel, Mr. Superintender, that I hadn't been doing
my duty to the school, and that Sandoe hadn't been
treating the black critters more than half right.

"Yes, Mr. Superintender, such a heavy feeling
came over me when Sim finished telling all about

the little mistress, that I made up my mind then
and there to join Sim and take a peep inside the
school; for I felt at the moment that there might
be something more good than bad in the moral
suasion racket, and that the little mistress was
after all making the right kind of a man out of
Sim. But just as I was getting ready to join Sim,
the other trustees came riding up to the gate, boiling all over with rage and inquiring about the
moral-suasion racket. One said the mistress wasn't
engaged to do the sewing for the children; another
said he was dead against the 'Law and Order
Society,' and that the best thing to be done was to
move on the school in a body and bounce the little
mistress instanter. I tried to argue the case, Mr.
Superintender, as Sim had with me; but I couldn't
make the words fit as Sim did, and what I said in
my rough way only riled them and made their
blood boil all the worse. So as a sort of compromise I told them I'd start to the county-seat to see
the Superintender. But since I've been standing
here, Mr. Superintender, reflecting over the words
of Sim, they all come back to me with such deep
meaning that I feel like going back to Brimstone
school district, taking off my coat, and making the
fight of my life for that little school-mistress.''

"Ah, my sturdy old mountaineer," said Nicholas,
as he saw a big tear rolling down the face of the
sturdy backwoodsman: "you're the right man in
the right place. Go back to the school; **stand** by

the mistress, stand by Sim, and stand by the black
beauties, and I pledge you my word that when the
critical moment comes you shall have the earnest
and unfaltering support of Nicholas Comenius."

"Thank you, thank you, Mr. Superintender, and
may God bless you for the light that has dawned
upon the mind and soul of Ladamus."

Then with a fervent shake of the hand, and the
soft words of Sim pressing hard in upon his rugged
nature, he stepped without, closed the door, and
with a look of resolve upon his face, mounted one
of his black beauties and rode westward toward his
mountain home.

One, two, three years had gone by, and the little
episode was all but forgotten, when meeting Comenius one day he said with a pleasant smile: "Ah,
my friend, have you forgotten Ladamus, President
of Brimstone School Board, and the little Yankee
schoolmistress?"

"Oh bless you, no," I replied, " but how did it all
turn out?"

"Turn out," he responded: "Why, would you
believe it, Ladamus turned out to be one of the
most progressive school directors in Blackwell
county; and the little Yankee schoolmistress, following the law of supply and demand, only a week
ago became the wife of the pious old parson."

CHAPTER IV.

ARCHEY McFADDEN AND TIPPECANOE.

"THERE is at all times a peculiar flavor associated with a good story of certain irrepressible old schoolmasters," resumed Comenius, as he drew me aside and closed the door of his official sanctum. "Here, for instance," continued he, as he turned down a leaf of his old note-book, "is a short sketch of Archey McFadden, who was known throughout Blackwell county as 'The Long Man of the Emerald Isle.' Born and educated among the blackthorn hedges of the North of Ireland, Archey started out when a young man, gravitated to America, finally rounding up among the charcoal pits of Blackwell county under the euphonious title of Professor. This broad and comprehensive evidence of distinction at once made him a formidable rival of the many old schoolmasters of Blackwell county. Commanding in appearance, and blessed as he was with two well-formed pedal extremities, Archey was never known to walk to a teachers' meeting if it were possible for him to secure the services of any old quadruped within a dozen miles of his school.

50

To start out for a ten miles' walk, before the break of day, to borrow an old nag to cover an equal distance only in an opposite direction from his log school, was no unusual undertaking for Archey McFadden. Whether the old schoolmaster, during his latter days, was actuated more by a desire to quench an inherent thirst, at any one or all of the many 'tippling stations' that lay in his way, or to pose before his many rivals at each teachers' meeting astride of some old roadster, as the exponent of a high and dignified calling, has never been definitely determined.

"It was, however, on the day preceding an important spelling contest, as the story runs," continued Comenius, "in which Gad Day, the 'walking dictionary' of Sassafras Ridge, and the shortest-set schoolmaster that ever swung a ferule, was arrayed on one side, with Archey on the other, that the latter began to scour the country round for some stray 'critter,' but without avail.

"As the old schoolmaster's eccentricities were well known to many of his pupils, it was determined to humor his whims in a way he least expected. After a protracted search, their labors were at last rewarded by the discovery of the remnants of a once celebrated roadster, that had already passed his thirtieth mile-stone, and as a reward for past services had been turned loose to spend his last days in an adjoining pasturage. Little time was lost in communicating to their respected tutor the many sterling qualities of Tippecanoe. It was clearly set forth by the spokesman that the owner of old Tip, who resided some ten miles distant in one of the 'Distillery districts,' for which the Ridge was noted, was not averse to entrusting this famous record-breaker to the respected master of Sassafras Ridge, whom he knew to be a man of steady habits and stern qualities as a disciplinarian.

"To the mind of Archey McFadden, whose eyesight through age had become somewhat impaired, there were good and bad qualities in every horse, as in every boy. As to appearances—well, they were the most deceptive things in the world, as he had discovered on more than one occasion. If a horse had a record, he stood, in the estimation of Archey McFadden, the equal of any old schoolmaster with a university diploma. To appear at the metropolis, among his many rivals, as the 'champion speller,' astride of Tippecanoe—the very thought threw Archey into ecstasies of delight!

"Long, pinched and grim, with ruffled shirt front, high standing collar, plaited stock with silver buckle, coat with long skirts, high-topped beaver with broad brim perched at an angle of ten degrees on his well-shaped cranium, was Atchey McFadden, the respected schoolmaster, as he started out afoot before the break of day to secure the services of Tippecanoe, once the most famous trotter in Blackwell county.

"After paying his respects to the numerous

tippling stations, to partake of an occasional 'eye opener,' Archey reached the end of his journey, as he supposed, long before the owner of Tippecanoe had awakened from his peaceful slumbers. Having thrown aside his austere deportment of the school-room, and being at this moment in a happy frame of mind, he stepped cautiously around the rickety farm buildings, where, to his delight, he beheld Tip, the object of his longing desires, munching away beside a pile of hay, oblivious of the old schoolmaster's presence.

"'And indade, and here ye air, me darlint, grazing away, and none the worse for a night's outing, save the night air and the fear of being kidnaped by some jedge of valuable horse-flesh. And a splendid specimen ye are, me spirited pet, for a truth,' soliloquized Archey, as he stood in the early morning twilight surveying Tip from head to foot. 'A little weak about the groins and a wee bit sprung at the joints, ye are; but its a lean nag for a long race, as I've often discivered in me own case. But its all owing to the precious care they've been taking of ye and the low diet you've been receiving for the hard work that's before ye, me darlint beauty.'

"Then stepping up and placing his brawny hand upon old Tip's shaggy mane, he continued: 'Och, me darlint, and it's a handsome figure you'll be cutting, with a saddle and a bridle, and Archey McFadden astride o' you, entering the metropolis of Blackwell county! Now, if ye'll be only after acting a little dacent by a stranger, me pet, I'll be after mounting yer hide for a trial of yer speed before yer master can catch a sight of yer actions.'

"As the old schoolmaster with one bound landed squarely over the back of old Tip, he was startled by the sound of 'Stop thief!'

"'Och and it's a mighty onpleasant predicament for a respected schoolmaster to be occupying; it is for a truth,' soliloquized Archey, as he caught sight of the owner leaping over a five-rail fence.

"'Oh, ho! a pretty time of day, stranger, to be caught prowling around the old plantation, astride the finest roadster in Blackwell county! You may be a judge of blooded stock, old man, but to get away with anything more than your own hide this fine morning will require a little more nerve than you can muster up, when you're caught in the act of spiriting away my famous 'Tippecanoe,' exclaimed the now seemingly exasperated owner, as he caught the old schoolmaster by his plaited stock, landing him squarely on the broad of his back. 'And who would have believed it? None other than old Archey McFadden, the respected schoolmaster of Sassafras Ridge! Pretty late in life for an old man of threescore years to be deserting the school-room for a calling that'll land him in the penitentiary for the balance of his days.'

"'True enough,' replied Archey, almost choking for breath, as he set to readjusting his neck-stock and the folds of his coat-tails; 'it's a blasted reputation and a broken character, it is for a truth. But may the holy angels bear me witness, it's only for the loan of the handsome critter that I'm bothering ye at this time o' day.'

"'Ah, ha! it's to the county-seat to attend the spelling contest, then, that brings you here,' exclaimed farmer Stern, as he assisted Archey to his feet and grasped him by the hand.

"'It is, and may the holy St. Patrick witness me words,' came the cringing reply.

"'Oh, then take him, my old friend, but on one condition—promise me that under no circumstances will you allow his speed to exceed the three-minute limit, unless hard pressed by some gallant knight of the turf.'

"It took but a few moments to place old Tip under saddle, and as Archey mounted and rode away exultantly toward the metropolis, he was followed by the voice of farmer Stern: 'Remember, a safe return of Tippecanoe, at a risk of a hundred dollars upon the head of your schoolmastership!'

"The sun had risen high over the broad acres of Blackwell county, as Archey made his way through the little hamlet, near by which stood his own temple of learning. To the right and to the left he cast furtive glances, but no human form was to be seen. From remote nooks and corners, however, were eyes peering out at the ungainly object of their cruel imposition. The snorting and

wheezing of old Tip could be distinctly heard;
while soaring around and above, a stray vulture
was awaiting a favorable opportunity to pounce
down on its helpless prey. The old schoolmaster,
conscious of the rich blood that was flowing
through the veins of Tippecanoe, and the reception
which awaited himself at the county seat, was in a
state of most perfect contentment. He neither
heard the snorts and wheezes, nor felt the pressure
of his own weight on the dry bones of his gallant
steed, for his mind was dwelling on more momentous issues.

"Up hill and down hill, Archey continued to
plod along, in all the dignity becoming the tallest
schoolmaster in Blackwell county. Failing at a
critical moment, however, to keep a stiff rein on
the blooded roadster in descending a hill, by a
sudden mishap Archey went sprawling headlong
to the earth beneath. Gathering himself together
as best he could, his first effort was to assist old
Tip to his feet; when to his astonishment he beheld the loss of one eye and the partial eclipse of
the other. By one of those sudden gasps, so peculiar to confirmed cribbers, he made another important discovery—that the celebrated trotter was
not only deficient in eyesight, but was, at the same
time, as toothless as himself. A further inspection
satisfied him that while he was resting firmly on
his 'all fours,' the shoes had disappeared, but how
or where was not so clear to his now befuddled

comprehension. To provide for the loss of the shoes was to the mind of Archey an easy matter; but to equip the old nag with a pair of new eyes and a full set of teeth, required a knowledge of veterinary surgery which he did not possess.

"A crisis had now arisen in the life of Archey McFadden. His first purpose was to retrace his steps in search of the missing property; but the thought of Gad Day, the shortest-set school master in Blackwell county, carrying off first honor at the spelling contest, was more than human nature could endure. Reaching a level stretch of road in the suburbs of the metropolis, with the sun at its highest meridian, Archey made one desperate effort to revive the latent energies of his trusty steed. Arranging his hat on the side of his head at an angle of ten degrees to windward, to catch the breeze, and spreading the flaps of his coat-tails on either side of Tip, he pressed first one heel and then the other into the ribs of the snorting nag. To and fro, up and down, the tall, slender form of Archey McFadden swayed from side to side, singing aloud his favorite song of 'Tippecanoe and Tyler too,' as he entered the main thoroughfare of the county seat.

"'Clear the track, men, for there he comes, like one of the knights of the seventeenth century,' cried one, as he waved his hat to the crowd. 'Out with your old time-pieces, men, and give him the benefit of the record! he's making,' cried another!

'Give him the spur, old man, and keep a stiff rein on him,' came the voice of Gad Day, as the hat of the rider went sailing off in a gust of wind over the heads of the by-standers. 'You're a horseman worthy of the name of Archey McFadden!' came the voice of Farmer Stern, with a wave of his hand.

"But with these words there was a momentary pause. Men and women came flocking into the street, uttering shrieks and throwing up their hands in despair; for the famous roadster had made another and a fatal misstep—had collapsed and fallen into a heap before their very eyes, where, after a few spasmodic gasps, came the end of all that was mortal of old Tippecanoe.

"But what had become of Archey, the old schoolmaster, who a moment before was shooting through the town, like a meteor—but now nowhere to be seen? Old men rubbed their eyes and shook their heads, declaring that the sudden disappearance of old Archey McFadden baffled their comprehension. 'Summon a jury, men,' said one; and 'Let the evidence be taken to be handed down to posterity,' cried another.

"The first witness was the little Dutch Burgess, who, after crossing his breast three times in succession, declared that he had actually seen the old schoolmaster caught in the talons of one of those unearthly scavengers that had been hovering over the carcass of the old horse at the very moment that Archey had ascended high up into the air.

"'Call for old Mother Gramm!' exclaimed the Burgess. 'Open the way, men;' and a moment later there stood the little shriveled body, the great expounder of the doctrine of 'Faith Cure,' holding in her hand a copy of the 'Long Lost Friend,' a book of divination, at that early day exceedingly popular among the superstitious. After repeating certain disarranged letters of the alphabet, and casting her eyes first in one direction, then in another, she proceeded to account for the sudden and miraculous disappearance of Archey McFadden, the respected schoolmaster, in the following graphic manner: She confirmed the statement of the Dutch Burgess in one particular; declared that after Archey had ascended to a great height the weight of his sins had suddenly turned his course in a downward direction; that after striking the earth, his Satanic majesty had carried him down into perdition, through the soft stratum of mud for which the streets of the metropolis had for generations been noted.

"This explanation, conforming in every particular to an old traditionary legend that had been handed down from generation to generation, was accepted by the knowing ones as in all respects the most plausible and convincing; for there at the very spot at which Archey had gone down as a punishment for his many sins of omission and commission, lay his high-crowned beaver. At this important juncture and by way of additional testimony, the 'oldest inhabitant' stepped up and declared that some years before, a young book-agent on his way to attend a school board meeting had actually disappeared from view, going down at that identical spot.

"As old Granny Gramm was in the act of placing her 'Long-Lost Friend,' within the folds of her dress, preparatory to her departure, a loud shrill voice came from the off side of a big board fence directly opposite. 'And remember it's a hundred dollars that will be placed as embargo on the head of Archey McFadden for the loss of the baste.' Old men and young men stretched their long necks forward in the direction whence the sound came. 'There he is, and may the Lord preserve his soul in peace!' cried Gad Day, who had mounted the carcass of old Tip by way of adding to his own stature. With one bound the tall slender form of Archey McFadden cleared the high fence and stood with tears in his eyes weeping over the remains of old Tippecanoe, none the worse for the exciting escapade which had landed him unharmed on the remnants of an adjacent straw-pile.

"Words of congratulation now began to pour in upon Archey for his miraculous escape. But old Granny Gramm with her 'Long-Lost Friend' had quietly escaped in the excitement of the moment. A reconciliation was now effected, and Farmer Stern relieved the old schoolmaster from the hundred-dollar embargo on his schoolmastership. Then,

with Archey in the lead, they all betook themselves to the old school-house, where the luckless
rider of Tippecanoe succeeded in carrying off the
first honor.

"For years thereafter Archey McFadden, the
old schoolmaster of Sassafras ridge, continued to
keep school in the old log house," concluded
Comenius, "but he was never seen thereafter
astride of any old nag, preferring, as he declared,
to depend on his own shanks to carry him in safety
to and from teachers' meeting."

CHAPTER V.

DWELLING IN THE SHADOW.

It was on the morning succeeding my visit to the office of Comenius, that I found him in earnest conversation with a number of teachers. They had come for consolation and friendly advice, touching important issues involved in their daily routine of labor. Among the number were two or three, bent and haggard, resting under the educational burdens of many winters; while of the others, a few were young women, upon whose pallid features was distinctly traceable the imprint of the burdens they too had been carrying to and from the school-room in their daily walks.

"You seem to be in a more than usually happy frame of mind," I suggested to Nicholas, as one after the other had departed.

"Yes," he replied, "it requires a happy disposition to be an educator, for there is no other profession in the world where a kind and loving nature is more necessary than in the teacher's calling; and yet in the school-room, where all should be love and sunshine, may often be found teachers old and young, of both sexes, living in the

62

very darkness of their own shadow. Indeed, my friend," he continued, as we walked along arm in arm, " I have often thought that old John Bunyan must have been inspired by some faithful, conscientious teacher, when he wrote his famous Pilgrim's Progress. If Christian, the pilgrim, had his share of trials and difficulties of a spiritual nature, the overworked teacher is not without his share of burdens, although of a somewhat different character. Of those whom I met only a few moments ago," he added after a moment's hesitation, "each had his tale of woe—all heavily mortgaged with a weight of cares and responsibilities resting upon their shoulders, some real, others imaginary. These burdens once assumed, oftentimes continue to follow the young teacher even into the social walks of life, endangering health and strength of body and mind.

"Ah, my friend," said he, after another pause, "if teachers would only cultivate the habit of looking on the sunny side of life, how much sooner would they forget its shadows! How often have I looked in upon a school only to find the master sullen and dejected. No pleasant smile caught my eye as I stepped forward and shook him by the hand. And as I cast my eyes over the school, looking for a ray of sunshine which failed to greet me, how often would I say, 'Old man, you are dwelling in the shadow, instead of on the sunny side of life.'

"Only a short time ago, in one of my official visits to a district school, it was my good fortune to meet a young lady teacher—young did I say?—oh, no, my friend," said Nicholas, "for during her short experience she had changed from a rosy-faced girl of eighteen into a little, nervous, old woman. One glance at her pinched features and sallow complexion satisfied me that she had been living in the shadow; but where to locate the cause that had produced the gloom, whether in the school or in her own home life, I did not know.

"The school-room was large, and the ventilation, while not what it should have been, was above the average. I examined the roll-book, and in punctuality and prompt attendance there was little cause for complaint. A score or more of young faces would now and then bob up and catch my eye, and as suddenly disappear behind their books or slates. Yes, there too I saw the same shadow that was hanging like a pall over the young teacher. It hung over the recitations in grammar, in arithmetic, in geography; it rested over the pages of the reading-book, blighting every poetic inspiration; it would follow the little ones to the playground, thence, by the rippling brook and smiling meadow, to their homes, there perchance to find lodgment in the heart of some fond mother. For an hour or more I sat watching for a ray of sunshine, for I felt that deep down in those tender hearts was hidden a spark which needed but a kind word from the teacher to dispel the surrounding gloom.

"At last, the exercises being over, with much solicitude and a heavy heart the teacher stepped to my side and said: 'Oh, Mr. Superintendent, I am *so* happy to meet you! I want to open my heart to you and tell you of my many trials and difficulties. Indeed, Sir, I know that you will sympathize with one whose troubles are almost too weighty to bear.'

" 'Oh, have you met with the loss of some dear friend?' I soothingly replied.

" 'No,' she answered as she shrugged her shoulders in a nervous manner, 'all my troubles are to be found right here in the school-room ; and if something isn't soon done to bring John into subjection, I fear I shall be compelled to resign my position.'

" 'Is John the only lad who has clouded all the sunshine of your life?' I asked.

" 'Oh, no,' came her hesitating reply ; 'if it isn't John it is sure to be one of the other boys.'

" 'Come, now, my young friend,' I suggested in the same subdued tone, 'point out this shadow that has driven all the sunshine out of your little school.'

" 'Over there in the corner, by the water pail, he stands, Sir, as a punishment for his misdeeds,' came the reply, as she pointed to a half-grown lad who stood alone, with trousers tucked into his raw-hide boots.

5

"'Is he maliciously inclined?' I asked, 'and have you resorted to every effort to bring his refractory nature under control?'

"'Oh, no, not particularly maliciously inclined, not by any means; but he is given to so many annoying pranks as to almost exhaust one's patience.'

"'Ah, I see; but have you spoken kindly to him, reasoned with him as you would with this curly-haired girl by your side—in other words, have you endeavored to reach the sunny side of his life?'"

"'The sunny side of his life, Mr. Superintendent! Why, what is the use of looking for what he doesn't possess?'

"'Well, suppose you, in a kindly way, step over and tell him the Superintendent wishes to speak to him.'

"'It will afford me pleasure to do so, Mr. Superintendent—only too willing to perform an act of duty.' Then turning and stamping her foot on the hard floor, she called out in a shrill commanding tone: 'John, come forward this very moment; do you hear, or must I repeat the summons?'

"For a moment or two John, the young culprit, stood almost paralyzed; then, with the hot blood rushing to his face and the eyes of the school resting upon him, he came straggling forward to meet his doom.

"'Here he is, Mr. Superintendent, and the worst boy in the whole school,' came the shrill voice of the teacher, as if the more completely to envelop him in shadow.

"Believing in the efficacy of kind words, I said: 'Come, come, my lad, give me your hand; do not hesitate, for I too was a boy once upon a time.' Then placing my hand upon his head, I caught a momentary glimpse of his large blue eyes and continued, 'Do you ever smile, my boy?''

"'I—I—never—smile—in—the—school-room, Mr., for the mistress never smiles at me.'

"As these words came in half-suppressed sobs, his eyes fell and tears covered his face.

"Ah, my friend, the veil might here be drawn, for the victory had been won, in so far, at least, as John was concerned," added Comenius, as he continued to draw a series of hieroglyphics with the point of his cane in the hard dry sand. "As I looked around over the school I noticed here and there a little coat-sleeve as it was drawn over eyes from which flowed tears of sympathy for John, their comrade and playmate. But there stood Mary, the young mistress! It was necessary to go a step further, for she still stood in the shadow.

"'Now, tell me, my lad,' I continued, as I drew him closer to my side, 'have you a pleasant home, and are your father and mother, sisters and brothers kind and loving?'

"'Haven't got any, Mr.'

"'No home? no father or mother, sisters or brothers?'

" ' No, I've never had any sisters or brothers, and father and mother died before I could remember.'

" ' And where do you live, my lad?'

" ' Am doing days' work, Mr., for farmer Nash, who lives four miles beyond the school.'

" ' Well, has he any boys or girls, my lad?'

" ' Never saw any, Mr., that I can remember.'

" ' Can you sing, John?' I asked, as I watched the effect on the teacher's expression.

" ' No, it's not allowed around the farm, Mr., and the mistress won't permit it in the school-room.'

" ' Come, come,' I said, as I arose and looked, first at the conscientious but misguided teacher, and then at the long rows of anxious faces: ' what this school needs, what the boys and girls need, and what the teacher needs too, is plenty of warm sunshine. Throw open the windows of your young hearts, and let the light dispel the shadows. Mary,' I said, as I took her by the hand, ' cultivate the habit of looking on the sunny side of life, and you will soon forget the time when you dwelt in the shadow. John, my rough diamond, give your hand to the teacher, and promise her before the whole school that on each morning you will meet her with a pleasant smile on your face.'

" As the sunny side of John's better nature caught a glimpse of the sunlight that had broken through the shadow of the young teacher's soul, Mary turned to me and said : ' Oh, Mr. Superintendent, I am so glad you came.'

"Then I drew forth the following beautiful lines, and leading off we sang:

" 'Let us gather up the sunbeams, lying all around our path;
Let us keep the wheat and roses, casting out the thorns and chaff;
Let us find our sweetest comforts in the blessings of to-day,
With a patient hand removing all the briers from the way.'

"There wasn't much music in the boys and girls, nor in the little mistress, but there was plenty of love and warm sunshine.

"Yes, my friend," added Nicholas, as I turned to leave him; "in that short hour's visit, I saw the shadow lifted from that little school. As the mistress bade me good-bye, she turned and said, with a smile that for months had been hidden under the shadow: 'Oh, Mr. Superintendent, John isn't at all the boy that I imagined him to be. I now see that his little heart is full of sunshine.' 'Ah? I replied, as I withdrew, 'cultivate the habit of looking on the sunny side of life, and you will soon forget you were dwelling in its shadow.'

"And so, my friend, when I see an old school-master crochety and out of touch with the school and its environment, I am inclined to say: 'Get out of the shadow and into the sunshine.' When I meet, as I often do, the young beginner who is forever complaining of the salary, the length of school term and the school officials, I am prone to remark: 'Young man, keep on the sunny side of life and avoid the shadow.' Above all others, let

the Superintendent, in his official visits, not forget
that over and around the young teacher he may
cast a shadow that will darken each little heart,
and cling to the teacher forever after.

"Ah," concluded Nicholas, as I took my departure, "life consists not so much in length of
years as in a sunny disposition! Cultivate the
habit of looking on the sunny side of life, and the
battle is won from the very beginning."

CHAPTER VI.

"MOTHER, HOME AND HEAVEN."

As the reader has already noted, with Nicholas Comenius a good story, like a faithful old schoolmaster, always had the right of way. His sense of humor was not dulled by advancing years. I remember once in his later days, when we were together looking back on the past, he smiled and said:

"Ah, my friend, a good school yarn is always in order. They are apt to come to the surface at each directors' meeting, or teachers' examination, when least expected. Some, it is true, are remembered for a day and then forgotten; while others, like hard cider, increase in flavor the older they get. There, for instance, is the 'Mother, Home and Heaven' yarn, which isn't as old as Zaccheus and his telescope, nor has it the age of the time-worn map hanging over on the office wall; but it well illustrates the methods of the modern school-book peddler on one hand, and the susceptibility of the average school trustee to fall from grace on the other.

"'Twas along about six months ago, as the story

71

runs, that the little episode occurred," said Nicholas,
as he arose, only to recognize, on the opposite side
of the street, the veritable Deacon Green.   "It was
at a season of the year, too, when school boards are
always sure to have a fair crop of book agents, even
though they should fall short of a plentiful supply
of the necessaries of life, that Ned Pendegrist, the
authorized agent of a Chicago book concern, accidentally happened to learn of a contemplated
change in the reading books of Stormtown District. Jumping into his conveyance one fine July
morning, Ned started out, bent on converting the
deacon, the President of the Board, to a favorable
consideration of his own particular series of Readers, before the secular affairs of the week could in
any way affect the religious impressions made upon
his mind the day previous.   But to work the
deacon was a mighty ticklish operation, for the
reason that he had been elected a school trustee on
account of his high standing in the village church,
and the forcible way he had of saying *No* at the
opportune moment. In fact, on more than one
occasion at a school board meeting he had been
known to spring to his feet and exclaim, 'No!
emphatically *No!*' to the consternation of the
other members, even before he had fully stated the
motion, on which a vote was to follow.   Prior to
his own election, as a member of Stormtown school
board, when hearing of any purchases in the way
of globes, maps or charts, he'd exclaim in his most

emphatic manner : 'What I regard, gentlemen, as
the greatest weakness in our whole educational
system, is the cowardice of our local directorship—
their lack of moral courage to say *No* at the proper
time.'

"Ned Pendegrist, you see, was not without his
misgivings as to his ability to meet and overcome
the whims and caprices of the deacon's strong individuality. It is true he had in a theoretical way
studied the old man's peculiarities ; had prepared
no less than half a dozen well-digested plans for
attacking the weaker part of his nature ; had
studied his physiognomy as he walked the streets
of the metropolis on special occasions ; but withal,
when the time came to put his theories into practice, there was doubt and uncertainty depicted on
the young agent's countenance. However, when
he reached the farm, there stood the pious deacon
by the roadside, engaged in superintending the adjustment of a newly-purchased reaping machine.
This was more than the young man had antici-
pated, for while he was prepared to take a hand in
a general discussion involving even the Scriptures,
in the quiet retreat of the deacon's home life, he
was hardly prepared to encounter him on the public
thoroughfare. Drawing his team squarely up to
the fence, and motioning the deacon to the side of
his conveyance, he began in his most gracious
manner :

"'I believe I have the honor of addressing

Farmer Green, the President of Stormtown School Board, and at the same time a deacon in the village parish?'

"'You have, young man,' came the curt rejoinder of Deacon Green; 'but as I've little time to waste on strangers, your name and business would greatly facilitate matters at the very outstart. So your name and the purpose of your visit, young man, for I am a man of few words.'

"'My — my name is Pendegrist, Ned Pendegrist; in other words, Sir, I am a traveling book'—

"'Never mind sir, your business I fully comprehend. You're not the first book peddler that's been strolling round through the district, worrying the very life out of the other members of the Board, who haven't the moral courage to say *No*. Only yesterday, one of your clan followed the deacon into the very sanctuary of the village church, knelt in the same pew, and more than outdid him in his profession of faith. But it wouldn't work, young man. The deacon, you see, is a little too well up to the tricks of the trade to be caught napping in meeting by a pious young book peddler, whose professions of faith bore the ear-marks of his daily occupation.'

"'But—as I have been credibly informed,' ejaculated Ned in a half-hearted way, 'that Stormtown School Board propose to make a change in their reading books at the coming meeting, I concluded to pay my respects to your honor, with the

purpose of presenting you with a set of the Automatic, Self-adjusting Readers for comparison and
examination.' Having succeeded in breaking the
ice, his next move was to unstrap his grip-sack,
which stood before him within easy reach.

"'Hold on, young man,' came the voice of the
deacon ; 'too late, too late!'

"Straightening himself up, Ned replied: 'Why,
has action already been taken by the school
Board?'

"'No; the meeting is still some days off; but
only a week ago I received a set of Readers, post-
paid, and if the deacon's judgment can be relied
on, and he thinks it can, they are the best that
have entered Stormtown district since the creation
of the new system.'

"'Ah, then you haven't seen the very latest
Automatic Series, handsomely bound, beautifully
illustrated, and warranted to teach the whole subject of reading by the simple device of touching a
button within the cover of the book. Science, you
see,' continued Ned, now that he had struck upon
a train of thought purely original with himself, 'has
been accomplishing wonders of late in the material
world, and is liable at any moment to enter the
broad domain of education, with most astonishing
results to follow in the near future. Why bless
me, Deacon ! everything connected with the school-
room is liable at any moment to partake of automatic propulsion. Both teachers and directors,

many of whom are nothing more nor less than automata, are destined sooner or later to step down and out for the automatic dispenser of knowledge of the most improved pattern. Better get yourself into line, Deacon, by taking hold of the Automatic Series! Many of the school-rooms, you see, are already being heated by electricity, and I am credibly informed that all charts, globes, and in fact, all other school-room paraphernalia, are so artistically adjusted as to convey to the mind of the pupil all important information by an automatic arrangement that will insure to the rising generation a most thorough education at the lowest possible cost. So you see, my worthy friend,' continued Ned, in his persuasive manner, 'the average school-book agent should have a loftier and holier purpose in view than the low, mercenary one, that has for its object purely selfish gain. I claim, Mr. President, to be somewhat of a—Can I not induce you, Deacon Green, to accept a set of the Automatic Readers, for the reasons given?'

"'No, young man! The reading books I received may not contain the improvements you mention, but they nevertheless fill the bill, and when the Board meets they'll go in sure as the deacon's a living man. I want to say in conclusion, young man, that when the deacon was a lad, attending school over in the log house, he didn't know very much about geography, history, arithmetic and grammar, but he was always the best reader in

the school. And so when the Board starts out
nowadays on a visiting crusade, one of the members manages to swing the geography class clear
around the world in short order; another steps forward, plants himself in the centre of the room, and
with history in hand, rushes the class like an
electric motor clear through the whole line of
Presidents from the time of the immortal George
Washington down to the present day, without a
mishap. But, young man;' and here the deacon
assumed his favorite attitude when in the school-
room, 'when it comes to conducting the reading
exercises, the Secretary says, " Deacon Green, step
forward and show the young teacher how to conduct a reading class with life and animation ! Read
them a paragraph or two, Deacon, from one of old
Dan Webster's masterpieces, that used to sway the
masses away back in the thirties!" It takes, of
course, considerable persuasion to get the deacon
started; but once under the inspiration of the old
Senator, there are lively times around that old
school-house, I can assure you, young man. But
when I've concluded the rendering of that historical speech, there sit the teacher and the whole
school in tears, while over on the long bench sit
the trustees weeping more like children than full-
grown men. Then the Secretary, looking up and
wiping away the big tears, will say: " Now, Deacon
Green, give the young lads a taste of something
that'll thrill their young natures with joy, and

make them feel that they're all soaring off among
the heavenly planets; read them, Deacon, your
favorite poetical selection, written by one of your
distant relatives; read them Darius Green and his
flying machine." Inside of a minute, young man,
I'll have the whole school in a commotion; some
holding on to the desks, while others keep dancing
around, feeling that they are sitting right beside
the deacon on Darius Green's flying machine, soaring around among the planets. Talk about your
electric motor, young man—why, the deacon's got
more pent-up electricity in his system than would
run a reaping machine, if it could be properly gen-
erated.'

"'Deacon Green, you are just the kind of an
electrician I am in search of,' was Ned's rejoinder.
'With a set of the Automatic Readers in your
hands it is difficult to say where the school
might not eventually land. You see, the books
furnish the motor, while you supply the electric
current—connect the two, and the whole problem
of electrical propulsion is solved, and Deacon
Green becomes a millionaire! Think of it Deacon,
ponder and meditate over what possibilities are in
store for Deacon Green's family.—Allow me, Deacon, to insist upon your accepting a set of the
Automatic Readers.'

"'Impossible, young man; for when the deacon's
mind's made up there isn't any power under
heaven that's going to change it.'

"Ned Pendegrist, reins in hand, was in the act of starting hopelessly disgusted towards the metropolis of Blackwell county, when the deacon hailed him again: 'I say, my young friend, does your firm publish "Mother, Home and Heaven?" See, there was a smart sort of a chap around about the farm only a week ago, trying to sell a copy to Grandmother Green, who's already passed her eighty-ninth milestone; but as the young peddler was selling on the subscription plan, and not inclined to favor the deacon with a free copy, I concluded I'd wait for a more favorable opportunity. Since then, the pious old lady's been worrying herself into spasms over the loss of that book, and if anything of a serious nature should overtake the tender-hearted old soul, there'd be a frightful responsibility resting upon the deacon's conscience.'

"'Mother, Home and Heaven! Why bless you, my pious friend,' retorted Ned—now that a bright ray of hope had illumined the gloom—'the truth is, deacon, while I've never heard of "Mother Home and Heaven," there isn't a book of any kind published *under* heaven that Ned Pendegrist can't secure, if he has to scour the world to find it.'

"'By the way, young man,' continued the deacon, growing more familiar and patronizing, 'what will that work cost?'

"'Oh, never mind the cost, deacon; leave the cost to Ned Pendegrist, who'll charge it up to profit and loss.'

"'Ah! mighty kind and considerate of the old lady's feelings you are, young man. Now, let me take a peep through that First Reader of the Automatic Series, for your arguments have been kind of working on the deacon's feelings.' (Adjusts his glasses, reaches for and examines it with the eye of a trained critic, and then inquires:) 'How soon will that book reach the old lady?'

"'Oh, I'll write for it this very evening, and by Friday it'il be in the hands of Grandmother Green,' replied Ned as he drew himself together.

"'Now, young man, let me take a peep through the Fifth Reader, for a good series is always judged by the higher work.' (Fumbles over page after page, nods his head approvingly, readjusts his spectacles, rubs a leaf between his fingers, holds it up between his eyes and the sun and soliliquizes:) 'Seems to have the staying qualities for wear and tear, and the magnetic touch calculated to thrill a boy's very nature! And the illustrations and the typography! No second rate workmanship on these! Why bless me, if here isn't a speech from old Dan Webster, another from the immortal George Washington, and a third from Abe Lincoln. None of these to be found in the other series. And best of all, my favorite poem (worth the price of the whole set) Darius Green and his Flying Machine! Are you sure, dead sure, that book'll come through the mail in a few days, young man?' exclaimed the now converted deacon. 'Well now,

Pendegrist, if Deacon Green, the President of Stormtown district, is a judge of good reading, and he thinks he is, the Automatic Series has the inside track by a large majority. Take the advice of the deacon, young man, and strike for the metropolis of Blackwell county. No use wasting any of your valuable time on the other trustees! Be sure to call around at the little log school-house, two p. m. Saturday, and you'll find the contract signed, sealed and ready for delivery.'

"'Oh, ever so considerate, deacon! Much obliged for the timely examination you have given the Automatic Series,' was Ned's parting salute as he drew the reins on his trusty mare.

"'Don't mention it, young man ; its all for the good of the cause,' responded the deacon, as he set to readjusting certain parts of the newly invented reaper—musingly humming 'Mother, Home and Heaven,' to which he had unconsciously applied an old familiar air.

"As Ned Pendegrist drove up to the little log school-house at the appointed hour, his heart was full of doubt and uncertainty as he caught a glimpse of the deacon, surrounded by a covey of book agents with whom he seemed to be in earnest conversation.

"'A little late, Ned," observed the president at the first opportune moment.

"'Why?—anything gone wrong?'

"'Oh, no, but the other agents have been prowl-

6

ing around the district since sun-up, and they've
just been comparing notes and showing their
hand. All seem to have the same number of
promises, five in all, which clearly prove the charge
frequently made by the deacon, that the average
director don't know how or when to say No.

"'Mother, Home and Heaven reach you all right
side up with care?' good-naturedly inquired Ned.

"'Better believe it, young man, and it proves
beyond doubt that Ned Pendegrist is a man of his
word.'

"An hour later, as Ned was industriously engaged in repacking his grip, to the discomfiture of
the half-dozen other agents who were standing
round lamenting their fate, the deacon beckoned
him to the rear, handed him the contract duly
signed, and said: 'Went through all right, eh, and
proves that when the President of Stormtown
School Board makes up his mind, there isn't any
power under heaven that's going to change it.
Now, hurry that contract off by the first mail—and
by the way, young man, old Grandmother Green's
been having more peaceful hours over "Mother,
Home and Heaven," than she's had in forty years.
She seems almost to grow young again over its
many beautiful passages. Now there's only one
other work necessary to reconcile the old lady to
the inevitable. Ned Pendegrist' (placing his hand
tenderly upon the shoulder of the young agent),
'there's a counterpart to "Mother, Home and

Heaven," and if the pious old lady could but lay
her failing eyes on " Clinging to the Cross," her
last few remaining hours would certainly be peaceful and happy. Ned Pendegrist, may I presume
upon your generous '—

" ' Deacon Green,' retorted Ned, rising to the
full height of his manhood, as he departed with
grip in hand, ' I am extremely sorry to say, that
" Clinging to the Cross " is out of print.' "

CHAPTER VII.

STEPHEN, THE GATE-KEEPER.

LONG before the morning sun had cast its beams over the hillsides and valleys of beautiful Emden, on this bountiful Thanksgiving morning, an aged father had arisen. Bridled and in waiting in front of the old homestead stood his faithful mare, Nelly, ready to convey him to the county seat, where he had an important mission to perform. A little later, with his top-coat buttoned securely around his slender form, this lonely traveler might have been seen jogging along over the rough Macadam roadway, in communion with his own thoughts.

"Twenty miles is a pretty long stretch of road," soliloquized he, as he caught the first faint outlines in the distance of the long pole that spanned the ancient highway. "But what is distance compared with time, and sixty years at that? True, the system has been making a pretty fair showing since sixty years ago—when Simon, driver of Packet Line No. 10, brought the startling news that the Legislature had passed the free school bill. Don't believe there'll be a soul around the Court House this fine Thanksgiving morning to welcome

84

an old educator. There'll be plenty of young folks
hanging round, true enough, but there'll be no
Cornelius to grasp the hand of the old man—
blessed schoolmaster he was in his day! Yes, yes,
times have been changing, and things are not as
they were when Stephen, the gate-keeper, and I
were attending school together away back in the
twenties. Whoa, Nell! Going to cheat Stephen
out of his honest dues this fine Thanksgiving
morning? Why, we'll both be arrested for violating the statutes," exclaimed the lonely traveler, as
his trusty mare struck the pole squarely in the
center.

"Hallo, Steve, my venerable friend! Hurry
along and give an early riser the right o' way.
Come now, old boy, and open the gate, and finish
your nap at high noon, when the constituents are
feasting on roast goose and hard cider!"

"Hum! hum!" came the low muttering so peculiar to these lonely gate-keepers, as a faint glimmer
from his lantern appeared through the crevice of
the doorway. "A pretty time 'o day anyway for a
stranger to be loafing along the king's highway,
trying to steal his way through without paying his
honest dues."

A moment later the long, slender form of
Stephen Smithers stood with distended eyes,
swinging the lantern over his head and peering out
at an indistinct object that stood before him.

"It's the old mare, 'tis for a fact!" soliloquized

NICHOLAS AWAKENS HONEST STEPHEN.

(86)

Stephen. "Been spirited away from the old homestead, sure as Steve's a living man! Yes, yes, it isn't the first critter that's left his master's stable before he'd eaten his morning oats, and it isn't likely to be the last, in these degenerate days." Then, in a commanding tone: "Guess you'd better dismount, stranger, and make the next twenty miles on foot if you're aiming for the county seat— which I'm pretty certain you aren't, for I've never yet seen one of your kind, and I've seen a good many in my day, who didn't switch off at the first cross-road. You're not the first that I've yanked up before the light o' day, reward or no reward," said Stephen, as he grasped the old nag by the bridle with a vice-like grip.

"Hold on, my venerable friend," came a voice that sent the cold shivers down the spinal column of Stephen Smithers.

"Why bless my eyes if it isn't Nicholas Comenius! Why, the top o' the morning and a thousand apologies to you, my old-time educator," came the good-natured reply, as Stephen grasped the hand of the octogenarian. "Mighty glad to meet you, my venerable friend: the old gate-keeper's as good as ever on a grip, but his eyesight's been failing a good deal since we last met."

Then he muttered to himself, with a shake of the head, as he fumbled over a handful of pennies for the exact change: "There's an important school meeting holding forth somewhere over at the county seat, sure as Steve's a living man. Yes, yes, something more powerful than roast turkey and cranberry sauce has been enticing Nicholas Comenius to be deserting the old homestead at such an hour on this glorious Thanksgiving morning."

"Pretty stiff breeze blowing," said Steve, looking up into the old man's face, that was partly concealed by an old-fashioned three-ply scarf that had protected him for many a long year from the cold winter's blasts. "Any one over along Sassafras Ridge or at Shaky Hollow getting planted or spliced this fine morning?" he continued, as he threw the long pole into a perpendicular position.

"Well, no, Steve, my faithful watchman, there isn't any one getting planted or spliced that I can recall," came the laconic reply. "The plain unvarnished truth is, Stephen my boy, it's just sixty years ago that old Governor Wolf disappointed more than nine-tenths of his Dutch constituents by planting his signature squarely on the Common School law. After thinking the matter over, it occurred to me to take a run over to the county seat and take a peep in at the teachers' institute. You see, the old folks around the village called a meeting, and the chairman said : " Nicholas Comenius, as you're the one man in the whole country round whose name stands first on the list among the pioneers, it will never do to let the exercises of the young educators on this Thanksgiving anni-

versary slip by without your being present to tell
them a fact or two worth knowing about the olden
times.'"

"True as preaching," replied Stephen; "hope
they'll be inviting you to a front seat on the judges'
stand. But I've been reading the papers, Nicholas,
and it strikes me there isn't anything mentioned
in the programme about any Thanksgiving anniversary. You see, it's been a rule of the institute
ever since you were voted out of the office, to have
the programme cut and dried for more than a
month before the time for setting it in motion; and
reminiscences of the olden time aren't likely to cut
much of a figure these days. There's one professor, Nicholas, to lecture on philosophy of teaching; another on physiology—new-fangled subjects,
that have just been added to the curriculum, as
they call it; another on deduction and induction—
things that didn't have a place in the schools when
Nicholas Comenius was running the machine, or
when you and I were attending school as boys
over in the little red sandstone school-house."

"Steve, old boy," replied the aged father, as
memory carried him back to other days, "those
were happy times, when old Jimmy kept the village school, and went boarding around among the
wild lads of the village. Bless me, it starts the
tears flowing when I think of the days when you
and I were boys, Stephen, sitting on the slab seats
by the old wood stove. There's a history about

the little old school-house that's never been written, but as you say, it isn't the kind of history the young professors are looking for nowadays. Come, my pet, hurry along, for the sun's well-nigh risen, and your old bones are shaking from the fresh morning air. Good bye, Stephen, and be sure to keep a sharp lookout for the light-fingered gentry, and make them render a good account of themselves as they go prowling along over the king's highway before the break of day," was the parting salutation of Nicholas Comenius, as he galloped on toward the county seat, twenty miles away, leaving Stephen standing in the open doorway meditating.

"Sixty years ago!" soliloquized Stephen Smithers. "Who would have thought it? And Nicholas Comenius as hale and hearty as on the first day he was elected Superintendent of Blackwell county! In those days no man did greater service, and no man stood higher in his own county, than young Nicholas Comenius. Yes, yes, young Nicholas then, old Nicholas now," was the gate-keeper's revery as he followed the long stretch of road, to make sure that his old friend had passed safely beyond the dangerous hill that lay before him. Passing into his cabin and throwing himself on his low cot, he buried his face in his hands and wept. What thoughts passed through the mind of Stephen Smithers the world may never know, and perhaps as little cares. Let it be here said that the gate-keeper was possessed of more than average intelli-

gence; had held the honorable position of squire as
well as schoolmaster; had served under Zachary
Taylor in the Mexican war, and for thirty years
had earned his bread in his present humble position. But woe to the wild lads who undertook to
play their pranks upon this defender of the king's
highway! On his feet he was as swift as an ante-
lope, as many a wayward lad had discovered to his
sorrow in attempting to evade his honest dues.
Without hat, coat or shoes, Stephen was known to
keep well on the trail of the swiftest horse, and,
when least expected, would pounce down upon his
unsuspecting victim, demanding what in justice be-
longed to the gate known by his name as "Honest
Stephen."

The sun was well up when Stephen awoke from
the sweet slumber into which he had unconsciously
fallen, and, going to the door that led to the loft
above, said: "Ted, my young urchin, it's about
time for you to be stirring yourself this fine
Thanksgiving morning. Get a move on, my spry
young chap, and see that Captain Jack gets a good
square meal, for there's twenty miles twixt the
county-seat and the sly critter, that will have to be
covered before the teachers' meeting ends this very
noon."

A few moments later little Ted, a lad of nine,
stood face to face with his aged grandfather, with
whom he was spending his Thanksgiving vacation.
Patting the little fellow on the head, and looking

down into his large blue eyes, he exclaimed: "Teddy, my boy, it's a fine man you'll be making of yourself one of these days if you keep growing as you've begun." Then raising the young lad and holding him at arm's length on the palm of his large, brawny hand, he said: "Teddy, my young hopeful, there's a teachers' meeting over at the county-seat this very Thanksgiving day."

"Knew that more than a month ago, grandpa; yes, more than two months ago; for if there hadn't been, your little grandson wouldn't be assisting you in collecting toll this fine Thanksgiving day," came the quick response.

"A mighty knowing lad, my precious darling," retorted the old gate-tender as he clasped the lad to his bosom. "Ah, ha, I see, I see! These teachers' meetings have their uses, if they do have their abuses. Ha, ha! no teachers' meetings, no vacation for the young chaps! Bless me, it takes a growing lad, and a city chap at that, to straighten out an old man's ideas," added Stephen, as he set to whistling one of his old familiar airs. Drawing the little fellow beside him on the low cot, he stopped whistling long enough to remark:

"Master Ted, my boy, can I trust you?"

"Trust me, your own little Teddy? Why grandpa, of course you can trust me."

"You see, Teddy my lad, there's a feeling against these city chaps coming out into the country visiting. Too much schooling, they say, isn't helping their manners and their morals, and makes them proud and 'stuck up,' and not as polite and accommodating to strangers as they ought to be. There's been a falling off in good manners, Teddy, among the young folks since I was a lad. See it every day, right here, on the old State Road. It's been my experience, Teddy, that not more than one out of a hundred ever tips his hat or hails the old gate-keeper with, 'It's a bright spring morning,' or 'How is the health of Stephen Smithers to-day?' No, no, it's either 'Hello there, old man!' or a dozen ill-mannered expressions that aren't a credit to the fine school buildings they're having over at the county seat."

"Why, grandpa, you talk like an old school-master. Did you ever teach school?"

"Yes, yes, but 'twas many years ago, when old Nicholas Comenius, whom you've never heard of, my little grandson, was the Superintendent. In those days the young lads didn't know so much, but it was hats off and a "Good morning, master,' when they entered the school. But Teddy, my boy, it's to the county seat old Stephen must go this very hour, and it's to your charge the gate is to be entrusted during this Thanksgiving day, if I can trust to your carefulness. Teddy, my boy, did you ever keep books?"

"Keep books, grandpa? Why no, I've never kept books, but I've read through more than a hundred over at the Boys' Library."

"No, Teddy, I mean did you ever keep accounts in a book or on a slate?"

"Of course I have, grandpa. Why, my slate and scrap book, over in the teacher's desk, are all covered over with figures; some in addition, some in subtraction, others in multiplication and division, with fractions too."

"Come now Ted, what are you giving the old man, anyway?"

"True, grandpa, true every word. And besides, I've been studying reading, spelling, grammar, composition and language, geography, history and physiology. Then I've been taking private lessons in vocal and instrumental music; practising in the gymnasium, on the typewriter, and in the military drills."

"Why, who'd have believed it?" replied Stephen, with a doleful shake of the head. "It don't seem at all natural; for when Stephen Smithers was attending school over at the village it took a whole winter to learn the multiplication table and the alphabet, and when a young man of nineteen struck vulgar fractions he was away up at the head of the graduating class. There's something mighty queer about this new education that's puzzling to an old man's brain! Come here, my young mathematician," continued Stephen, emptying a bag of coin into the lad's hat. "Count this, and if there be no mistake in the reckoning its your old grandfather that'll have use for your services on this Thanksgiving day."

With this, the lad's first practical lesson in numbers, Stephen Smithers took his way to the door, looking first in one direction, then in the other, for he hadn't taken in a stray copper since Nicholas Comenius had disturbed his early slumbers.

"Ho! grandpa," cried little Ted: "the count is completed, with a big lot of the queerest kind of money left over that I ever laid my eyes on. It isn't like anything the city folks have, grandpa. Why, where did it all come from?"

"Ah ha, my lad," chuckled Stephen, as he instinctively kept his eye along the great stretch of road that lay like a panorama before him. "It needs a sharp eye and a clear conscience to be an honest gate-keeper. You see, my young lad, these spurious coins fell into the till in a way you've never dreamed of."

"Weren't given then by honest travelers, were they, grandpa?" asked the little fellow.

"Well, no, not exactly by travelers, but by some of Stephen Smithers' honest neighbors, who wouldn't think of robbing Stephen out of a cent in a business transaction. You see, Teddy, as it may be a lesson for you in morals, I'll give you an example that you may profit by in the future. Along comes honest John Smith, who's been attending market over at the county seat. Now honest John discovers on his way home that he'd been nipped by a city chap with a pewter or Mexican dollar. Says he to his good wife who sits by his side: 'Nancy, it's a shame to stick an honest, hard-working farmer, who's been up early and late, trying to make an honest penny tending market.' So he fumbles that spurious coin over and over, saying to his willing helpmate: 'It's the profit on a barrel of apples, or a basket of butter! Guess we'll stick it on to honest Stephen.' So he nudges the old lady as he says: 'It's a fine morning, Mr. Smithers,' or it's been a long dry or a long wet spell; or 'the times are growing so hard that an honest farmer can't make a living any more,' and slips the spurious coin into the gate-keeper's hand. But when Stephen Smithers makes the discovery, Teddy, as he sometimes does, if not too dark, and turns and says: 'This stuff's no good; only so much base metal that isn't worth more than a nickel a pound,' the old gentleman reaches for it, adjusts his spectacles, looks it over and over, then hands it to Nancy, and she holds it up likewise, turns it round and round, and with a knowing shake of the head says: 'What's the country coming to, any way, Stephen Smithers, when these vile city hypocrites set to robbing an honest farmer out of the profit of a whole day's marketing?''

"But grandpa," asked little Ted, "were all those queer-looking pieces given you by such people?"

"Oh, yes, my inquisitive pupil, they're all my best neighbors, whom I have known for many years," was the old gate-keeper's reply, as he caught sight of Captain Jack standing without, ready to convey him to the county seat. Once more the old gate-keeper drew the lad to his side; this time as he sat astride of Captain Jack, the trusty roadster that had been presented to him when a mere colt, as a token of friendship and esteem, by his Board of Directors—and once more he embraced the lad, printed a kiss upon his forehead and said :

"Teddy, my boy, keep a smile on your face and a kind word on your lips for the stranger, be he the judge of the court or the lowly in station. Be sure, first, to render the exact change to the outside penny ; then pull the long rope, and the lifting of the pole will give to every honest man the right o' way over the king's highway."

With this wholesome advice, Stephen Smithers, the rough diamond, beloved for his simple manners, esteemed for his sterling integrity, took his way westward, but for what purpose he alone knew.

7

CHAPTER VIII.

THE SCHOOL-HOUSE AND THE OAK—THE SMITH SHOP—OLD BLIND TOM.

As Nicholas Comenius passed safely beyond the dangerous cliff, known at an earlier day as the "Round Up," his thoughts naturally wandered back to his boyhood days, and thence to the scenes of his later struggles, when he was the most important factor in the educational councils. Now he was to all intents and purposes as dead to the outer world as though he had never had an existence. What had impelled him, at such an advanced age, and at such an unseemly hour, to wander forth from the old homestead on an errand for which the world little cared? Was he simply dreaming his life over again? Was his mission but an hallucination of the mind, enfeebled by declining old age? These were the thoughts uppermost in the minds of the few who had recognized Nicholas, as he jogged along on his gray mare, that had reached an age relatively as great as his own.

What had induced Stephen to entrust the gate known as "Honest Stephen" to Teddy, a lad of

98

nine, while he went galloping on toward the
county-seat? Was he also impressed with the conviction that perhaps a change in the mental condition of Nicholas Comenius had actually taken
place? Indeed, there was room for well-grounded
belief that Nicholas had simply strayed away from
the old homestead, under the delusion that he was
still in charge of the institute that was in active
operation on this Thanksgiving morning.

But if Nicholas Comenius was dead, so to speak,
to the outer world, in his inner life, around which
clustered the reminiscences of a sweet and fragrant
memory, he was an active, living personality.
There, within the limits of his own pleasant home,
he had retired years before from active life, and
the cares that so often follow in its train. But
Nicholas never grew old, in the ordinary accepta-
tion of the term. His genial disposition, kind and
loving nature, and the love he bore the old town,
with its traditions extending back over two centuries, were a panacea for all the ills and shortcomings consequent to frail human nature. Nicholas
firmly believed in the preservation of at least the
inspiration surrounding many of the traditionary
landmarks that still lingered among the new conditions that time and an enlightened public sentiment had so marvelously wrought. If others,
younger in years, contemplated the destruction of
the little red sandstone school-house, and the
cherished oak under which it had stood for so

many long years, Nicholas would exclaim, with a
shake of the head:

"Yes, yes, the hillsides and valleys, the meadows
and water-courses, may have their charms for
others; but to the heart of Nicholas Comenius this
giant of the forest conveys a lesson full of meaning." Looking upward among its branches he'd
add: "Was it not here, around its huge trunk,
that the boys and girls formed a circle, taking each
other by the hand, as Lafayette, that noble French
patriot, on his triumphal march through the land,
away back in the early thirties, consecrated the
very ground upon which we are now standing to
the cause of religious liberty? Has the old man
forgotten," he would appealingly say, "that stirring event and the parting words of the hero of
many a hard-fought battle, as he gave one and all
a fervent good-bye, and a 'God bless the school,'
ending with: 'Boys, have respect for the master,
love and honor him, and guard the old tree; care
for and protect it in the years to come, as it now
protects the old school-house, the master and his
little flock?' What a beautiful lesson of admonition," Nicholas would conclude, as the young
officials stood by the old tree, with axe and saw in
hand, "and how appropriate to the authorities of
every school-house in the land!"

"And were the words of the patriot heeded in
after years?" comes the suggestive question from a
score or more young teachers. My young friends,

the words so often uttered in defense of some old
landmark have not been without result; for Emden
is known far and wide for its stately and majestic
trees. And beyond the town, on the sites where
the old school-houses once stood, but where the new.
ones now stand, and towering upward as a protection to each, you will find a stately oak; young in
years, it is true, and only a sapling compared with
the parent tree, but in coming years, as other boys
and girls sit beneath its shadow, it too will equal
in size the giants of the forest. Take the lesson
with you, my young friends, to the beautiful
valleys and fertile fields where the blessings of the
new system have been most largely felt, and where
oak and hickory, elm and birch, were once the
pride and glory of man. There, on the sloping
hillside, or in the valley below, stands perchance
your own temple of learning, perfect in architectural design and equipped with all the latest
school-room appliances, but as desolate without as
the sands of the desert. No tree, no shrubbery, as
a protection against the rays of the summer sunshine or the blasts of the fierce gales of winter.
Why should this ever be so? Why should not
each school in the land lay claim to some cherished
oak, and once a year meet with appropriate exercises beneath its overhanging branches? And, before the first signs of decay set in, why should not
some lad, following the example of Nicholas Comenius of sixty years ago, plant an acorn close by

the parent tree, and thenceforth care for and watch
its growth, from early boyhood to manhood, and
thence into declining old age?

Nicholas Comenius may have been a back number in the eyes of many of his illustrious successors,
the modern educators, but he was a firm believer
in the beautiful sentiment that "he who makes
two blades of grass grow where only one grew before is a public benefactor." And as he saved the
old oak from the woodman's axe, Nicholas also
protected the little red sandstone school-house.
"Yes," he'd say, when it was proposed to demol-
ish the old structure, "there isn't much left of the
old house, boys; it's like the old man himself, only
a relic of former days and unfit for use; but it's the
only friend and companion that's left me. It isn't
at all handsome in the eyes of the lad who keeps
school in the new house over there; but it suited
me and the other boys, and Jimmy the master, and
I'll see no harm come to it now."

Is it at all surprising, then, that on the day preceding this lovely Thanksgiving morning, Nicholas
had resolved to re-visit the scenes of his early boyhood days? From this long-deserted structure and
its surroundings had come an inspiration that took
possession of his very nature. For a moment he
stood beneath the now lifeless branches of the venerable oak, where he had stood so many times before; then he passed along the old pathway, once
so familiar to other footsteps but now overgrown

with gray, coarse weeds and brambles, and reached the door of the old house with its rusty, creaking hinges. There, upon an old desk, shattered and time-worn, he beheld the inscription, the work of his own handicraft, "Nicholas Comenius, 1834," and a few paces beyond, the old jack-knife, rusty and broken. Ah, what fond recollections of by-gone days crowded themselves one upon the other, as Nicholas bent over the frail slab desk to make sure that his failing eye-sight had not deceived him. There, true enough, were the letters en-graven deep into the hard, yellow pine slab, and there the one-bladed knife, with its rough bone sides still intact. Then, like the shifting scenes of a panorama, the recollections of a lifetime passed before the mind of Nicholas Comenius.

"Yes, yes," soliloquized Nicholas, as he rode onward, "I recall the occasion as if it were but yesterday. We were all sitting about on the long slab seats, I a lad and Jimmy a young stripling of a master, when old Simon, the driver of Mail Coach No. 10, rapped at the door and in a loud voice ex-claimed, 'Jimmy, my man, have you heard the latest news, that I'm after breaking to you!' 'And what sort of news? good, bad or indifferent, my good man?' was Jimmy's rejoinder. 'Well, Jimmy,' came the doleful reply, 'it may be good news for some, but it's mighty discouraging to the old schoolmasters—'tis for a fact. It's the Legis-lature that's passed the free school bill, and it's the little Dutch Governor that's inscribed his signature to the infernal State System, sure as you're a living master!' was Simon's quick rejoinder, as he landed upon the high seat of the old coach.

"Little thought I at the time," reflected the old father, "of the effect the act thus announced was ultimately to have on hundreds of old school-masters throughout the Commonwealth. But times have changed, and for the better I hope."

For the early morning hours of this charming Thanksgiving brought no despondency to Nicholas. To one of his genial nature, the crisp morning atmosphere was a tonic, giving renewed vigor to his rugged manhood. To this well known thoroughfare Nicholas was no stranger, as many a lone monarch of the forest, still standing in all its primitive glory, stood ready to testify. Here and there, before some familiar landmark, his trusty mare would halt, sniffing the air, before Nicholas could recover from the reverie into which he had fallen. At length, suddenly looking up and catching a glimpse of the object which had last attracted his faithful roadster's attention, he leaned forward, patted her gently on the mane and exclaimed:

"Taking a view of the old school-house and thinking of old Tommy, the master, whom you haven't seen for more than twenty years, eh, my knowing critter? Ah, you've a memory, my worthy steed, that discounts the old man's two to one; and if you were as well gifted in the power of

language as you are in remembering all the old
school-houses in Blackwell county, you could give
the young chaps over at the institute a lesson that
they've never dreamed of.

"Yes, yes, Nell, you've good reason to remember Old Blind Tom, for many an extra meal he
turned into your crib on the sly! But don't you
know, pet, that the old schoolmaster has long
since passed over the river of time, to keep company with Cornelius, and the hundreds of others
who were as prompt in providing for the wants of
Nicholas and the mare as they were in caring for
the young lads of the school? Come, come,
straighten up, stop your whinnying, and hurry
along; no use shedding tears over Old Blind Tom,
who's dead and gone these many years.

"But there's no use trying to forget him,
either," sighed Nicholas, as his eyes took in a
small enclosure by the wayside, surrounded by a
square stone wall and a cluster of cedars. "There
we laid him long years ago, and over there beside
the old smith-shop stands the low thatched cottage
with the great oak towering over it, as young and
green as on the day we laid the old schoolmaster
to rest under the cedar in this little family burying
ground. Yes it seems but yesterday, but 'twas
many years ago that Comenius was summoned to
the bedside of Old Blind Tom, as the wild lads
around the district school named him in later
years. 'Twas a sad scene and well nigh forgotten,

but Nell, the companion of my earlier days, has brought it all back again." As these sad recollections throbbed through the mind of Comenius, he was startled by a voice that came from the rickety smith-shop.

"Lost your way, stranger, or perhaps only a shoe from the old mare? About the loss of your way, I'm not so certain; but that there's a missing shoe from the right front foot of the old nag, I am as sure as that it's Thanksgiving morning, and a mighty fine one at that. You see, my friend, a traveler may occasionally lose his way or his wits, or perchance forget to pay old Stephen Smithers his honest dues; but it will never do for a horse to lose a shoe, with Tommy, the blacksmith, doing business at the old stand."

"Whoa, Nell," cried Nicholas, as he drew the reins on his trusty mare. Then casting his eyes in the direction from which the sound came, he beheld above the door the sign, "Tom, the Smith;" and leaning against a post, a heavy-set individual with a happy smile upon his good-natured countenance.

"Ride the old critter in under the roof of the old shop, my good man, and I will make an examination in short order; for it'll hardly do to openly violate the law, when the Governor's Proclamation calls for a strict observance of Thanksgiving by every loyal son of the Commonwealth."

It took but a moment to remove the fractured

parts of the old shoe, and as the jolly smith forged
away at the new one to the sound of the anvil's
ring, he merrily sang: "The Life of a Smith is
the Life for Me." As Nicholas stood by and observed in astonishment the strength of his large

and sinewy hands and the muscles of his brawny
arms, coupled with a happy smile and a pleasant
disposition, he remarked: "Truly a happy life
you're leading, my good man!"

"Oh, yes," came the good-natured reply, "it's the master who shapes the mind, and the smith who shapes the iron; the only difference being the kind of material at their disposal. You see," he musingly said, as he forged away, giving the shoe a delicate touch here and there, and then holding it first in one direction and then in another before his trained eye, "it was always a question with grandfather, or 'Old Blind Tom,' as the boys around the district school used to call him, whether his little namesake should be a schoolmaster or a blacksmith. It was old Tommy, who kept school in the little stone house when Nicholas Comenius was in command of the school affairs of the county, that settled young Tom's fate; and it all came about in a way that some people call superstitious. It was on the day before his last visit to the school, from which he never returned alive, that he took me on his knee out on the old porch, as was his custom, keeping time with his frail staff to the music of the birds over in the flowery meadow by the running brook. 'Tom,' said he (for he always called me Tom), 'it's the master who shapes the mind, and the smith who shapes the iron. It takes a heavy stroke and a strong arm at times, Tom, to wield the rod as well as the sledge; but there's this difference, Tom, my lad—the strokes that fall from the brawny arm of the smith are lost with the ring of the anvil, but those that fall from the master's arm, necessary at

times to shape aright the young mind, are apt after
long years to come knocking at the silent chamber
of the master's heart. And oh, Tom, my lad, they
carry a weight heavier than the heaviest sledge
ever wielded by the strong arm of the village
smith.'

"But the saddest part of my story is yet to be
told, and there's no better time to tell it than this
bright Thanksgiving morning," continued young
Tom, as he leaned his heavy form against the
patient mare, driving nail after nail with the unerring aim of a trained workman. "It was on the
day following the one that decided the fate of
young Tom, as I well remember. There, surrounded by a half dozen grandchildren and Nicholas Comenius, the beloved apostle of the free school
system, sat old Tommy, blind and tottering, as the
little ones gathered around him not knowing what
to do or say.

"Ah, my old friend, is it the crisp morning air
or the effect of my story that causes the tears to
flow?" said Tom, as he turned and glanced at his
visitor. "It's had the same effect on Tommy the
smith, many, many times as I've thought it over;
but then the sound of the anvil always drove it
away, as it has many other strange thoughts that
came creeping over Tommy in the little smith-shop
during the long winter days.

"It is true I was only a lad at the time, but I
well remember when Old Blind Tom turned to

Nicholas and touchingly said: 'Take me once more, my old friend, to the district school, where old associations yet linger, and thence to the little burying ground, and there let the discarded school-master rest in peace.' In vain did those around him endeavor to dispel the strange fancy that had so suddenly taken possession of his mind, but his only reply was, 'Take me once more to the old school-house.' The saddest moment of all came after every other effort had failed to restore the old father to consciousness. It was then that sister Elsie, his blue-eyed darling, whose golden ringlets he had so often caressed, stepped forward and placing her delicate arms gently around his neck, in a soft child-like voice whispered: 'Why, grandpa, have you forgotten your own little grand-daughter Elsie? Touch my hair, grandpa, and press your cold face to mine. Ah, you know Elsie, do you not, grandpa?' But with a wave of the hand he motioned her aside."

For a moment a death-like stillness prevaded the old smith shop. Then there came a voice in low and measured tones, not unlike the soft voice of Old Blind Tom. It was the voice of the stranger who stood by the side of young Tom, the smith. "And have you, Tommy, forgotten Nicholas Comenius?"

"Nicholas—Nicholas!" And with these words the stalwart frame of the young smith swayed to and fro. "Nicholas Comenius, the bosom friend of Old Blind Tom!" And with these words he turned and fell upon the old man's neck and wept.

"Ah, Tom, many, many times have I recalled this incident in my lonely pilgrimages through Blackwell county," said Nicholas, as they sat side by side on a low trestle—Nicholas, the tall, venerable educator; Tom, the young blacksmith, with muscles and sinews of iron. "Little thought I, Tommy, my boy, as long years ago I sat beside Old Blind Tom on that momentous occasion, that years later I should meet this same lad, now a full grown man. But 'tis only one of the many sad reminiscences that Nelly, my mare, occasionally awakens within me as I go strolling along the king's highway.

"Yes, Tommy, I well remember the day when Old Blind Tom passed away to his rest. It was late in the day, Tommy, one of those perfect October days that always brought sweet consolation to the old master's heart, when tender hands gently raised the dying veteran from his lowly couch, made their way through the narrow open doorway, thence to the district school, where they tenderly placed him in the old arm-chair. Not a sound could be heard, Tom, but the neighing of Nelly, who stood by the road-side, apparently conscious of all that was taking place within. There in the old chair he sat for a moment, oblivious of those who stood tearfully by his side. Then standing erect as in the strength of his earlier

manhood, he turned his head from side to side and
gave the word of command: 'Give the bell rope a
good jerk, Ned, my trusty standby.' And as the
old familiar sound of years gone by broke upon his
ear, he turned, and with a grim smile playing
upon his pallid features, exclaimed: 'Now I know
I am once more the master of the old school, for I
hear the sound of the bell in the belfry above.'

BLIND TOM'S SCHOOL HOUSE.

Oh, Tom, it was I, Nicholas Comenius, that held
you in my arms as Old Blind Tom, the venerated
schoolmaster, fell back in the old arm-chair and
peacefully died, under the firm belief that he was
still the master of the district school. We shall

never hear the bell again, Tommy; I passed the old school to-day, and the belfry is gone, like the old master.''

Then Nicholas whispered a few cheering words to Tommy the smith, jumped astride of Nell, and hurried onward toward the metropolis of Blackwell county.

8

CHAPTER IX.

SIMON, THE DRIVER OF PACKET LINE MAIL COACH NO. 10.

As Comenius, now so full of ardent devotion to
the scenes and recollections of his boyhood days—
a devotion that clings to the soul of the aged
patriarch like the ivy to the massive oak—continued his early morning's journey along the king's
highway, his thoughts instinctively reverted to that
historic day, sixty years before, when Simon, driver
of Packet Line Mail Coach No. 10, drove his gallant steeds six in hand into the very heart of Emden
town. There may seem little of more than passing
interest, dear reader, in this announcement; but
were a messenger direct from the halls of legislation to convey to a modern teachers' convention
the information of the repeal of the common school
law, the tumult could scarcely equal that which
fell with such crushing force on the constituency
of Emden when Simon landed his six-in-hand at
the very door of the little red sandstone school-
house. Swinging his long raw-hide in a graceful
circle through the air, and uttering an unearthly
yell between the trumpet blasts that had already

114

startled the rural population from their peaceful surroundings, in thundering tones came the news that, within a brief period thereafter, was to prove such a disturbing factor to many a household in Blackwell county.

"It is true, I was but a lad," mused Nicholas, as he gave Nell an extra spur, "when Simon drove up to the school-house door, threw the whole school into commotion, and set the master's head to buzzing like an old-fashioned spinning wheel; but I've never forgotten the most trusty driver that ever sent a mail coach flying over the king's highway at the rate of twenty miles an hour. Illiterate as he was from an educational standpoint, Simon was none the less an educator worthy of more than passing notice; and bore the same relation to the public, as a dispenser of general information, that Jimmy bore to the village school. In stature and in courage, he was as far above the average coachman of his day as in trustworthiness and general intelligence. His long, dull-bronze hair, which hung in strands over his broad shoulders, and his small round hazel eyes, which shone at times like miniature stars, gave to his round, red face an expression that once seen was ever to be remembered. Indeed, it was firmly believed by many of the gentry who sat behind this knight of the road on more than one of his lonely pilgrimages, that through his wide receding nostrils he could scent coming danger for miles distant. But if nature favored Simon in this particular above others of his class, he was even more generously blessed with a sonorous, well-rounded voice, and an atmospheric pressure behind it that in times of extreme danger sent a thrill of terror through his trumpet, and then 'one blast upon his bugle horn was worth a thousand men.' Many indeed were the mishaps that had befallen more than one of the many trusty coachmen of the government service in passing over that dangerous stretch of road known as the 'Round Up;' but while Simon had his share of experiences at the hands of numerous bands of highwaymen, he never failed to deliver his precious freight in safety at their point of destination.

"But above all, to the sound of Simon's bugle, on momentous occasions, there was attached a superstitious significance that no convincing proof to the contrary could dispel. When the melodious tones of his horn fell like the strains of an æolian harp on the ears of the good housewives, as he swept onward along the roadway, it was but a gentle reminder that peace and good-will reigned supreme over the inhabitants of Blackwell county. But when a long series of those unearthly blasts, to which the screechings of a locomotive whistle in moments of greatest danger bear no comparison, fell upon the ears of the rural population in the quietude of their home life, it was positive evidence that Simon had come into possession of news that was to affect, in some way, their cherished rights.

"As the intelligent yeomanry of Blackwell county, in this enlightened age, pin their faith largely to the newspaper and the magazine, to the telegraph, the telephone and the weather bureau, so their worthy ancestors of two generations ago reposed even greater confidence in the bugle blasts of Simon, driver of Packet Line Mail Coach No. 10. On this occasion Simon, after leaving the village school, yanked his six in hand up to the very door of the rickety post-office building, followed by Jimmy McCune, the master, and the lads of the school. A moment later the old stage-coach was surrounded by a mass of interested spectators, while at the head of his gallant steeds stood Simon, bugle in hand. That this trusty government official was possessed of information of a most startling nature, none could doubt. Many openly asserted their belief that Simon was ready to proclaim the final dissolution of the world, in the coming of which there was a widespread belief on the part of the old parson's followers; others were simply dumfounded, not knowing how to account for the old coachman's performances.

"It was not, however, until Squire Benton elbowed his way through the crowd and stood face to face with Simon, that the alarming news, conveyed to Jimmy the master a moment before, was fully confirmed. Mounting the platform of the old coach and breaking the seal of an official document from the Secretary of State, he read aloud:

"'Thomas Benton, Esq.,

"'Take notice, and convey the information to the constituents of Emden district, that the Act creating the Common
School System has become the law of this Commonwealth.'

"A change of steeds; the replacing of the old
mail-pouch under the seat; a good-by salute that
'set the wild echoes flying;' and with reins well in
hand, Simon disappeared, leaving the parson and
the squire in earnest communion with Jimmy the
master, on whose features was depicted that deep
distress which eventually was to overtake every old
schoolmaster in the Commonwealth."

This, dear, reader, is but one of the many reminiscences of other days that the thoughts of Old
Blind Tom had suggested to the mind of Nicholas,
in his last half hour's journey toward the county
seat.

"Ah Nell, a few more paces and we shall be feasting on the best that the hospitality of the old town
can afford," was his consoling remark, as his eyes
took in the tall spires for which the metropolis of
Blackwell county has ever been famous. As the
chimes of the distant church bells broke upon his
ear and disturbed the reverie into which he had
fallen, his attention was attracted to a dilapidated
structure that once upon a time was the most pretentious and noted hostelry along this section of the
king's highway. This now antiquated and weather-
beaten inn might easily have been overlooked, but
for the conspicuous sign-post that stood promi-

nently by the road-side, on the large round swinging sign of which was to be seen the faded inscription, "The Trumpet," under a picture of that
instrument.

"Ah, Nelly, you seem to remember this rough-
hewn ,water trough," muttered Comenius, as his
thirsty nag drew up in front of the running pump,
famous in days gone by for its clear, sparkling
draughts that quenched the thirst of man and
beast. As he cast his eyes down into the flowing
stream that ran clear and bright before him.
thoughts of Simon crowded upon his mind. What
had riveted the attention of Nicholas to this placid
pool of water, supplied by the running brook that
gurgled down the hillside? On the old sign-board
had he not beheld only a moment before an exact
counterpart of Simon's trumpet? He understood
its meaning, knew the old inn had adopted this
emblem many long years before in honor of Simon;
but there, reflected from the mirror-like surface,
was the very picture of the old mail coach! What
could it mean? Was it only a reflection from his
own mind? He rubbed his eyes in despair, adjusted his spectacles, but there was the very image
of the old Tally-Ho coach. The felloes had fallen
from the tires; the spokes had become tainted
with rust and showed signs of decay; but here was
still the inscription, reflected in the sun's early
morning rays: "Packet Line Mail Coach No. 10."

"You seem to recognize the old stage, my early

PACKET LINE MAIL, COACH NO. 10.

visitor," came a voice as a stout-set, elderly person
stepped from the rear. "And maybe you've sat
behind the old driver on more than one of his trips,
as he went flying over the king's highway at a rate
that has never been equaled. He was a record-
breaker, was Simon, and up to the last trip he ever
made, held the post of honor in the government
service. You, see, stranger, I was only a lad when
Simon drove his steeds up to the old barn door,
side-tracked the rickety concern, and with tears in
his eyes sang me a song that I've never forgotten.
It wasn't much of a song, my old friend, and it
didn't make much impression on my young mind
then; but since the old inn has gone to ruin for
want of custom, and the pike to seed for want of
traffic, I've found more truth than fiction in the old
song. You see, it was one of Simon's own compo-
sitions, and if you're not too much in a hurry I'll
sing you a verse or two to revive old recollections
as you continue your journey toward the county
seat." And so, forgetful of the condition of mind
into which Comenius had fallen by the reflection
of the old coach in the sparkling water before him,
the good-natured landlord sang aloud:

> "You'll hear no more the clanking hoof,
>   And the stage-coach rattling by;
> For the steam-king rules the traveled world,
>   And the pike is left to die.
>
> "The grass grows over the flinty path,
>   And the bright-eyed daisies steal

Where Simon's stage horse, day by day,
   Lifted his iron heel.

"No more you'll hear the cracking whip,
   Or the blast of the trumpet's sound;
For ah! the water drives us on,
   And an iron horse is found!

"The coach stands rusting in the yard,
   And the horse has sought the plow;
They've spanned the world with an iron rail,
   And the steam-king rules us now."

"There's more of the old song, my friend, but whenever I get to singing it, there's such a heavy feeling comes over me that it sets my head swimming and drives all the poetry out of it," was the doleful comment, as he wiped away a big tear.

"Ah," sighed Nicholas, as he kept his eyes riveted on the fast-receding shadow as it flickered in the sun's bright rays, "it's many long years since Simon paid the debt of nature and was laid away in some lone burying-ground."

"Why bless you, no, not if the reports that every now and then reach the old inn be true, he isn't," came the quick response, as the old innkeeper stepped up and extended his hand to Comenius. "Dead he may be, but if so his spirit and the echo of his bugle-horn are still hovering around among the defiles of Shaky Mountain, where he was last seen only a short time ago. It may be only a superstition, my wise old friend, that's taken possession of the minds of some; but it was only yester-

day that old Eusebius came flying up to this very
watering-trough all flustrated, declaring on his
word of honor 'The world's coming to an end, to-
morrow, Thanksgiving, as sure as gospel preaching.' Said he, 'There were three blasts of Simon's
trumpet in quick succession, and as three blasts
of Simon's horn are equal to one from the trumpet
of old Gabriel, it's time for every old sinner to be
making preparation for the upward journey!' You
see he was only half in earnest until his eyes
caught on to the shadow of the old coach deep
down in the shining pool, when he fell over on his
old nag's mane in a dead faint. Thinking that
possibly he'd gone off for good, I gathered him up
and carried him over beside the bar, where a little
spirits out of Simon's old decanter soon brought
him to his senses."

At the conclusion of this little episode, the burly
innkeeper burst into a hearty laugh. Then looking straight into the face of Comenius, he smilingly
added: "You see, my old friend, that of the hundreds who draw up in front of the running pump,
there's scarcely one who ever thinks of looking up
yonder on the old platform. When they see the
reflection in the pool, and hear the gurgling sound
of the water running through the pipe, it's ten to
one they go away believing that the spirit of Simon
is still hovering around the old stage coach."

But to this plausible narrative, concocted by the
jolly landlord to perpetuate the memory of Simon

and to preserve the reputation of the old hostelry, Nicholas gave little heed. He well understood the philosophy that had produced this optical illusion, yet to satisfy his curiosity as well as his failing eyesight, he dismounted, ascended the frail stairway, and a moment later stood face to face with the old time-saver he had known so many years before. What a strange combination of circumstances had suddenly brought him into communion with this memento of other days! But what to the mind of Nicholas had seemed like an apparition a moment before was now a reality; for there on the side of the time-worn body of the coach was the inscription corresponding with the reflection he had seen deep down in the shining pool: " Packet Line Mail Coach No. 10." And strange as it may seem, there on its side was the small round indendenture made fifty years before by a well directed shot. He inserted his long slender finger, and vividly recalled how one stormy night a bullet had whizzed by his own head, while Simon was driving his spanking team of six in hand along that dangerous tract of woodland known as the " Round Up."

As Nicholas stood thus recalling the many experiences of his long and eventful life, he was startled by the sweet strains of a trumpet. For a moment he stood spellbound, listening to what seemed like the dying echoes of some far-off buglehorn. But the next instant there came a soul-

thrilling blast that almost shook the platform
beneath his feet. Paralyzed by the peculiar quality
of the intonation and by a musical accentuation
which had never been equaled since Simon's day,
Comenius stood tottering on the frail support.
Then, as the notes ceased to vibrate, he hurried
down the narrow steps to behold an object from
which for a moment he instinctively recoiled.
There in the bright sunlight before him were the
now shriveled features, out of which shone the
same round hazel eyes—eyes once seen never to be
forgotten. And there over his now shrunken
shoulders still hung his long strands of dull-bronze
hair. The tall, slender form, that once towered a
head above all his competitors, was now bent and
haggard. But there before his doubting eyes stood
the very image of Simon, with trumpet in hand.
As Nicholas trembling approached this figure that
seemed more like an apparition than a human
being, he raised the trumpet to his lips for a second
time and sent forth such a blast as shook the very
foundation walls of the old inn. And as the strain
fell to a whisper, with a smile of recognition upon
his disturbed features and without uttering a word,
Simon reeled, fell back into the arms of Comenius
and expired. But though the bugle of Simon,
driver of Packet Line Mail Coach No. 10, hangs
still in the old hostelry, the echoes of his last bugle-
blast are said still to be heard reverberating over
the hillsides and valleys of Blackwell county.

CHAPTER X.

WHEN Nicholas reached the main thoroughfare, near by which stood the temple of justice, his attention was attracted by a moving mass of young men and women, all wending their way toward the objective point, the court room, for the time had nearly arrived for the exercises to begin. In the midst of a small circle of teachers stood the young Superintendent, anxiously awaiting the arrival of the principal lecturer of the day.

"Ah, here he comes, with the pockets of his great-coat crammed with manuscripts bearing on every phase of the olden-time dispensation," humorously suggested one of the committee, as he caught sight of an old man jogging along head and shoulders above the average backwoodsman.

"Come, boys, no time for jesting," replied the Superintendent, whose eyes were turned in the direction of the station from which the speaker of the day was momentarily expected.

"He bears a striking resemblance to Nicholas Comenius, the first County Superintendent of Blackwell county," chimed in a rather prepossessing individual of more than the average intelligence.

"Acquainted with the old gentleman?" inquired another bystander.

"Nicholas Comenius?" replied the committee-man addressed, with a look of half-suppressed contempt, "No, not exactly acquainted with the old pedagogue, although I have frequently heard his name mentioned," and the speaker turned on his heel and glanced at the venerable stranger.

"Would it not be in keeping with the early history of the common school system to give these old defenders of the cause a chance to be heard before the institute, and to keep alive the memory of their services in the school libraries of the state?" continued the gentleman who had recognized Comenius, directing his remarks to the Superintendent.

"The truth is," was the curt rejoinder, "there are so many live issues demanding the attention of our young teachers, that any reference to these old-timers must of necessity be brief and to the point. Indeed, an effort has frequently been made by our more experienced educators to commemorate the services of several of these early leaders, but it is a very difficult matter to awaken much enthusiasm. You see," he continued, somewhat annoyed by the necessity of explanation, "there isn't one teacher out of a score of our Normal School graduates, who will remain in the profession longer than is absolutely necessary to fit him for some other professional calling."

"They wouldn't subscribe, then, for a handsomely illustrated volume on Nicholas Comenius, at a reasonable price?" was smilingly suggested.

"No; while the great majority of our teachers are very enthusiastic, and very attentive at the institute, they are not much given to reading of a miscellaneous character. There are so many subjects, you see, in the school curriculum, that few of our teachers can find time to read the daily newspapers or the leading magazines."

"So much in the school curriculum that teachers cannot find time to read newspapers and magazines! What a commentary on the free school system in Blackwell county! How then, Mr. Superintendent," he asked, "do you account for your institute being among the foremost in the State for attendance, and the interest taken by the public?"

"That is easily accounted for," he replied. "In the first place, if the Superintendent of any county is wide awake and enthusiastic, he'll find many important phases of education, new and improved methods, outside of the newspapers and magazines, for the instruction of the young. I am ever on the lookout for what are recognized in certain circles as professional experts; and as soon as one is brought to my notice, through the journals or Literary Bureau, I secure his services if possible;

and the greater his notoriety, the higher his price, the greater the guarantee for the highest literary attainments. You see, we must keep abreast of the age; and in order to do so, we must employ only the best and the newest to be had in the domain of education. The moss-backs and intellectual fossils of years ago would only be a dead weight to the institute work; and for that reason I have seldom recalled an instructor who has once appeared before the institute. The minds of the teachers, especially the older ones, need some friction and polish; and new instructors from a distance are apt to fill the bill better than those who have a personal acquaintance with the needs of the teachers. Many instructors deal out good solid information, but it is often from the old rack, and hence is not the kind of knowledge expected at teachers' institutes. We must have something electrical, bewildering, so as to make a profound impression on the minds of all present—directors as well as teachers. An aurora borealis exhibition, you see, is highly attractive, and has a two-fold use; it raises the instructor to a lofty niche in the estimation of the teacher, and disabuses the minds of the public school teachers as to their own efficiency. It also creates a habit of close attention and takes away the habit of inquiry. By this I mean, the teachers do not feel warranted in asking questions; in fact, they are for the time overwhelmed by the irresistible way in which the

9

modern educator presents his views. There are always some teachers of independent thought and speech, who if they are not overawed by the superior and startling manner of the speaker, are apt to quibble and raise objections, and so bring chaos into the established order of things, and break up the regularity so necessary to a well-conducted teachers' institute. The public of Blackwell county assume that their teachers, while institute is in session, are getting the best intellectual diet to be had; in fact, that the institute is an ideal mental feast, abounding in choice viands, and served with that pedagogic skill characteristic of master minds. This is the secret of a successful institute, and I hope it answers fully the question you put to me."

"Quite to the point—but supposing a teacher does not comprehend a subject as presented?" suggested the stranger.

"It is the teacher's business to comprehend; and besides, no teacher claiming familiarity with the theory and practice of teaching would venture to expose his ignorance. Every teacher knows that the eyes of the institute would be upon him, and that likely he would be made the butt of unlimited jest and ridicule. It is practically understood by teachers that they are to take notes of the subject matter presented, and not interpose any questions, apt or otherwise. In other words, the institute is not intended to furnish brain or brain material, but rather to serve as a grindstone, to point and sharpen the information which the teachers bring with them."

"A most excellent idea," was the reply, after a moment's hesitation, "and no doubt it has the effect desired. Of course the majority of the teachers of your institute are young and bright, and not like elderly folks, slow to catch on. When attending one of the recent sessions I saw but few gray heads, and I wondered what becomes of the teachers when they are advanced in years."

"Teachers nowadays seldom remain in the profession long enough to get gray hairs," was the Superintendent's apt rejoinder. "The young men are aspiring to other and more lucrative callings, and use the school-room only as a stepping-stone to something better. And the girl teachers are ever on the lookout for desirable matrimonial engagements, hence they do not play pedagogue longer than they must. Besides, I do not particularly favor old teachers, because they are apt to get the intellectual dry-rot, and you see there is no remedy for that disease. Give me young, ardent, enthusiastic teachers, full of fire and fervor, and I can organize an army that will prove invincible. The young people are more apt to excel in all the later theories, and are more perceptive and receptive."

"But one more suggestion, Mr. Superintendent— Do you not find that the experienced teacher gives better satisfaction, and produces better results?

And is it not true that public sentiment is averse to having the schools experimented upon by mere novices, who use the school-room simply as a means to an end?"

"You see," was the somewhat impatient reply, with a glance at his time-piece, "both the results and the satisfaction with the teachers' work are largely determined by the Superintendent. But stranger," said he, turning to depart, "as this is a delicate question, I hope you will excuse further reference to it."

"You have certainly enlightened me on the secret of your success, Mr. Superintendent, and I feel indebted to you for the freedom with which you have stated the case." And with a wave of the hand the stranger disappeared among the multitude of young professional teachers.

But, dear reader, be not dismayed at what may seem like a reflection upon the modern teachers' institute, or the earnest, conscientious Superintendent. Far be it from the writer to unduly reflect upon any such faithful officer, or the great body of the teachers directly entrusted to his charge. If abuses have crept into the system; if the teacher's institute has become, in many instances, the modern Superintendent's hobby; if the system itself has failed in that higher order of development essentially necessary to fit the average boy for the responsible duties of every-day business; if, as must be evident to all who are not blinded to the fact, the common schools were not conceived for the ostensible object of educating the masses for one single purpose, and that the teacher's profession ; then it behooves the master minds of the profession to ask themselves the question, "What shall we do to be saved?" Shall we call a halt in the onward rush for additional legislation, that is neither demanded by public sentiment on the one hand nor the absolute wants of the schools on the other?

But this clamoring for additional legislation rests not alone with the body of professional teachers. At the recent organization of a State Directors' convention, this remarkable statement was openly set forth by one high in authority: "The Legislature," said he, "advances and educates public sentiment; the latter is secondary and must follow." And in the discussion that followed, another, prominent in the department of state, gloried in the fact that when he was a member of the lower House he had voted in direct opposition to the prevailing sentiment of his constituency on an important school measure. And still another boldly advanced the doctrine that after he had been elected director, he had felt it to be his bounden duty to ignore public sentiment, and vote in accordance with his own individual judgment on all questions pertaining to the schools of his district. "Give us a system," cries one, "which in order and method is a model of perfection, and as perfectly adjusted in all

its parts as the phonograph;" while another
clamors for the Legislature to assume entire control of the machinery, with the hope that the tax-
payer may eventually rest happy under the delusion that he has been relieved from all local taxation for school purposes. But may not the old
adage, "What is everybody's business is nobody's
business," then be exemplified in the management
of the schools? Directors will, in a manner, be
elected as agents of the State, to apportion the
money to the wants of the schools, rather than as
custodians of the best interest of the district. Who
will particularly care for the schools, when public
sentiment shall have become dead, and the school
system an absolute part of the machinery of the
State, and under direct State control? And what
will become of the tax-payer's interest in the
schools, when he shall have been relieved of all
local taxation?

Has the annual appropriation of over five and
one-half million dollars, actually strengthened the
system? comes the pertinent question—in a whisper
only. Has the percentage of better qualified
teachers been increased? Has the school term,
excepting in a few instances, been lengthened?
Have the salaries been materially increased? Has
it broadened and deepened public sentiment? On
the other hand, has it not engendered a disposition
toward indifference on the part of the School
Boards, as well as on the part of the tax-payer?

Perhaps years hence, when the teacher's calling shall have become a profession—for at the present day it is merely a stepping-stone to some other more remunerative avocation—when the teacher shall receive adequate pay; when the most intelligent and best equipped teachers shall be found in the primary department of city and borough schools; when the graduate of the Normal school shall become a professional teacher, instead of a member of some other profession; when a system of schools for the rural districts shall not have for its sole object and purpose the training of boys and girls for the industrial centres of population—when all these and many other improvements in the right direction shall have been made, then perhaps some reminiscent grandfather may tell the story of the present system from the standpoint of the future, as Nicholas Comenius proposes to judge the present from the standpoint of the past.

CHAPTER XI.

AN INSTRUCTOR'S VIEW OF INSTITUTE.

THE passing of an old man on horseback through one of the principal streets of the metropolis in the early morning, being a frequent occurrence, little heed was given to the mention of the name Nicholas Comenius. There were other more weighty thoughts occupying the minds of the committee of arrangements, whom the Superintendent had dispatched to the station to await the arrival of the fast express, thirty minutes behind schedule time, from aboard of which stepped a most important personage.

"Allow me, Professor, to welcome you back to the metropolis of Blackwell county, and to extend my personal congratulations, as a slight manifestation of my hearty approval of the able manner in which you enlivened the proceedings of the institute during your short stay with us a year ago. Your powers of mimicry and your impersonations of 'Ye old-time Schoolmaster' seemed to keep the audience in a constant state of hilarity and good humor. In fact, Professor, the dullness of the proceedings during the past three days has only tended to sharpen the appetite of the rank and file of our teachers for a grand literary treat at your hands." These complimentary remarks came from the spokesman of the committee, and were addressed to the star lecturer of the occasion, a middle-aged gentleman of culture, grace and refinement.

"Allow me in return to thank you, my young friends, for the compliment paid me," came the felicitous recognition, as he gave each a hearty shake of the hand. "Then you were entertained, and I hope instructed at the same time," continued he, in his affable manner.

"Indeed, Professor, we were more than entertained, we were simply captivated by the power of your eloquence; and I feel at this very moment," smilingly continued the spokesman, "as though I were a thousand miles removed from the drudgery of the school-room. Why, under the influence of your inspiration, the humdrum of school life vanished like a dream ! It makes one feel that there are many phases of our modern school life never dreamed of by the pedantic old-time schoolmasters of a generation ago."

"Yes, yes, my young friends," came the suggestive reply; "but what to teach and how to teach, thoroughly and well, in the common schools of the land, are problems that still await definite solution. We are drifting so rapidly from one extreme to another, or rather skimming over the surface, that the leading educators of the country stand appalled at the outlook. That this feeling is prevalent throughout every State in the Union is made manifest at every county and city superintendents' convention, state and national teachers' association, the country over. There no longer seems to be any common ground upon which any two minds can fully agree. Indeed, the system still seems to be in a state of transition, only to become more and more involved by yearly additions to the school curriculum. On this line, the processes of addition and multiplication seem to dominate in the educational world. The inventive faculty of the modern educator is unexcelled in the scientific world; and to this inventive genius, when displayed upon the platform, the great body of teachers are ever ready to pay homage. To keep alive the spirit of enthusiasm, upon which the very foundation of the system is supposed to rest, the educational pendulum must be kept swinging rapidly backward and forward, all at the expense of the taxpayer. Year by year the arc of movement is increased and the curriculum enlarged. The correlated processes of subtraction or division, whereby this often unwieldly curriculum might be kept within reasonable limits, are seldom suggested, and almost never considered.

"I can in no way better illustrate my meaning, my young friends, than by quoting from a recent speech of a prominent Normal Principal. 'The

great trouble,' said he, 'with the work and theory
of our new education is the crowding of the school
curriculum. The modern theorist takes some
point for a start and then he calmly proceeds to
analyze, synthesize, induce and deduce, until he
gets that point connected with everything else in
the universe that he has seen, heard or thought of.
Basing their plan on the assumption that some
time a child will need certain facts and principles,
these foolish teachers cram the mind and dissipate
the energies of their pupils with an endless series
of observations, inductions and deductions in the
realms of all the "ologies" and "isms." The
little minds are filled with a jumble of monads,
protoplasm, bacteria, late novels, ichthyosaurus,
dinosaurus, and examples of creation generally,
from the primordial protoplasm to the attenuated
theory of a Boston transcendentalist. Each teacher
and specialist in turn pounces on the hapless child,
and each little faculty, as it were, is taken out of
each little head and given a special twist in the
direction of some new fad—for, like Cicero, these
mighty leaders of thought take little stock in the
work begun by other men. Each is a champion
of something that in his opinion will shake the
earth to her center. Such theories and such work
are worthy of nothing but ridicule. Such a system
of education can result in nothing to the average
pupil but a smattering. He is dragged from Dan
to Beersheba, somewhat like a boy holding on to

the tail-board of a wagon drawn by a runaway
team. He doesn't even have time to touch terra
firma or to admire the scenery as he passes. That
which made great men in the past will make them
to-day. With all of them—Franklin, Lincoln,
Garfield and the rest—it was some task that required the putting forth all of their power.'

"Under our new dispensation, we hear far too
little of this educational gospel, which is as true
now as ever. The fact is, there is entirely too
much costly display in nearly every department of
our new education ; and your own institute, I am
compelled to say, is no exception. These entertaining 'talks,' as you aptly designate them, it is
true may for the time being lift the institute into
an atmosphere of enthusiasm ; but they are not the
kind of talks calculated to advance the profession
along the line of advanced thought, nor to place it
where the early promoters of the system intended
it should stand, on a permanent foundation."

As these remarks, so manifestly at variance with
the tenor of the lecturer's own addresses before the
previous institute, fell upon the ears of this little
circle of professional teachers, there was a momentary pause, as if they were conscious of the awkard
dilemma into which their ill-considered remarks
had led them.

"I fail to comprehend, professor, how you, a
prominent institute instructor, can reconcile your
position with that assumed before the institute, if

I correctly interpret your statement," came in a
half apologetic tone from the tallest of the little
circle of teachers.

"It is easily explained, gentlemen, and if you
will bear with me for another moment," said he,
with a wave of the hand and a slight twinkle of
the eye, "I will illustrate my meaning in a way
that cannot be misunderstood. As an example,
take the teachers of your own county, of whom you
no doubt constitute an important factor, if I am to
judge by the interest you have manifested in my
behalf, and for whose benefit I have traveled over
one thousand miles, at an expense to your Superintendent of nearly three hundred dollars, and mark
the result. As most of the teachers of Blackwell
county are young, ardent and enthusiastic, I am
presumed, as a matter of course, to anticipate their
wants and to give them, in my daily discourses,
such information as will best aid them in the practical operations of the school-room. But while the
kind of information they most need is at times dry
and insipid, that which they receive must of necessity be of such a character, I regret to say, as will
appeal in the most direct way to their vanity and
their emotional nature, rather than to their sense
of reason and sound judgment.

"But to go a step further: Institute instructors
who are annually called upon to meet the whims
and caprices of superintendents, teachers and directors, and more especially the public at large, which

of late years has become an important element in these annual educational gatherings, have learned by sad experience how to handle a modern teachers' convention to advantage. On more than one occasion have I been met by a committee of teachers at the station, and after an all-around hand-shake and a few passing remarks about the weather and the crops, the chairman would elbow himself to my side, grasp my satchel, and as we jogged along arm in arm to my hotel quarters, with the other members at a safe distance in the rear, would remark in a confidential way: ' Professor, the institute is anticipating, at your hands, a perfect literary treat; the posters containing your lithograph have already gone into every nook and corner of the county, and the indications are that you will be complimented by one of the largest audiences you have ever had the pleasure of addressing.' Then after a moment he would proceed: ' Now Professor, I hope that, in the time set apart for you, you will manage to steer clear of the dry platitudes of the school-room curriculum; of these we have had an ample sufficiency. What we most need is a series of talks that will appeal directly to our emotional nature, in order that the murky atmosphere of the school-room may be forgotten, at least for the time being.' This is but a sample, my young friend, of the kind of instruction expected at many of these annual teachers' meetings. Dry facts, unless sugar-coated or dealt out

in homeopathic doses, make little or no impression
on the rank and file. Indeed, I can in no way
more fully emphasize my concluding remark than
by reading an extract or two from a letter received
from your own Superintendent engaging my services for this occasion." Opening the letter he
read as follows:

"In my humble efforts to provide for our coming Thanksgiving week's entertainments in such a way as to eclipse those
of my worthy predecessor, I am constrained to suggest that, in
your allotted time, you will intersperse whatever dry facts you
may have to offer with matter calculated to lift our teachers to
a higher sphere of professional standing.

"P. S.—It has been suggested in a casual way by the committee of arrangements, composed of five of our leading
teachers, that a few well-chosen anecdotes apropos to the subject matter in hand might prove a wholesome panacea for the
otherwise dull routine of the daily exercises."

Refolding the letter and casting a glance at the
members of the committee, he beheld a scene even
more sensational than any of his talks had produced among the audience at the institute. A
death-like pallor had spread over their heretofore
cheerful countenances, as each in turn began looking at the others and then for the nearest avenue
of escape.

"Only a few moments more, gentlemen, while
I fully define my position. Acting on the principle
that to be forewarned is to be forearmed, I came to
the institute a year ago at the committee's suggestion, prepared to amuse and entertain, rather

than to instruct. It is true, at the close of my first hour's talk I was somewhat apprehensive as to the effects my humble efforts had produced ; but at the conclusion of the last of my discourses, I felt reasonably confident that I had not only carried the convention by storm (thanks to the generous support which was given by the committee of arrangements), but that I had left my personality indelibly impressed upon the hearts of the teaching force of Blackwell county. I must agree with you, gentlemen, when I say that the outburst of applause which followed my closing remarks was simply bewildering; and when I took my seat beside the Superintendent, he leaned over and whispered : 'Your highly entertaining talks, Professor, have acted like magic, insuring renewed interest in every district in the county.'

"And now, my patient young friends, if not too much trouble, I should be pleased to have you assist me in looking up the committee of arrangements of a year ago, that I may thank them for their untiring exertions in my behalf."

Not being able longer to withstand the mortification depicted on the faces of the committeemen, an older teacher who was within hearing stepped forward and said : "Allow me, Professor, to introduce to you the chairman and other members of the standing committee of arrangements of Blackwell County Teachers' Institute." And just here let us drop the veil.

CHAPTER XII.

IN the delay occasioned by the tardy arrival of the fast express, bearing the distinguished institute instructor, Nicholas had ample time, after entrusting Nelly to the care of the old hotel-keeper, to be on hand before the exercises began. For some moments after reaching the great stone steps he was swayed to and fro, now on one side, then on the other, but apparently making little headway in his efforts to seek admission to the main corridor leading to the various offices set apart for the transaction of all court proceedings. On both sides of this avenue were long rows of stands containing an ample supply of the latest improved text-books, educational magazines, and other school-room appliances; while in close proximity stood the representatives of numerous school-book publishers. As Nicholas stepped within the doorway he was besieged on all sides by a motley crowd of urchins —dispensers of every variety of pamphlets and circulars, advertising the wares of every conceivable traffic, from the peanut vender up to the latest treatise on the philosophy of teaching. Even the

IN THE COURT-HOUSE CORRIDOR.

tiles of the floor were literally carpeted with an assortment of circulars bearing on every subject known even to a modern teachers' institute. As Nicholas cast his eyes around, his first impression was that he had entered a book-store, and in his movements he endeavored if possible to avoid stepping on any of the handsome engravings that lay at his feet. "Ah," thought Nicholas, as the young lads gathered around him, crowding circular after circular into his hands and even forcing them into the capacious pockets of his great top-coat, "truly, Nicholas Comenius is no stranger after all among the young lads of the institute." But when he protested that he was not disposed to purchase any of the costly material thrust upon him, the young lads only chuckled and said: "It's not necessary to pay for these, old man; given away free to everybody who attends the institute."

At last, as Nicholas began to feel himself at home, he was approached by a stylishly-attired representative of one of the leading publishing houses, who, taking him aside, remarked in a very confidential manner: "What School Board in the county, my venerable friend, have you the honor to represent? You see," handing him his card, "while I am a perfect stranger in this locality, the firm I represent has the very best line of text-books in America. What I say to you must be said in a whisper and in the strictest confidence, for the agent directly to my right is an old stager at the business, and claims to carry most of the School Boards of your county in his vest pocket. Think of it, Mr. President, as no doubt you are. Think of these immense, overgrown corporations, fastening their talons like an octopus upon every self-respecting district in the state!''

''I am not''—was Nicholas' attempted reply.

"One moment, one moment more, my friend," continued this silver-tongued representative. "Now if you can guarantee me a hearing with any degree of assurance that our full line of books will receive favorable consideration at your next meeting, it will afford me the greatest pleasure to remember you regularly with a free copy of our latest monthly publication, entitled 'The Director's Friend.' '' ·

"Your attention, for only a moment or two, my worthy friend," came a voice from his left, as a delicate hand was gently laid upon his shoulder. "As you are no doubt," remarked this enthusiastic rival, "a very influential Director, consequent to your age, allow me to caution you against the flattery of those Bostonian agents. They are," said he, in a patronizing tone of voice, "a most unscrupulous set, plying their nefarious traffic in the very face of our own state publications, which you will agree with me should at all times have priority—other things of course being equal. Now here, my friend, is a new work" (holding it up and running through its pages with the

expertness of a trained critic), "on the Philosophy
of our New Education. As a highly meritorious
treatise on this important subject, and partly as a
compliment to the distinguished author, whose
services the Superintendent was enabled to secure
only at great expense to the institute, the Committee on the Course of Study has unanimously
recommended it to the various School Boards as an
invaluable addition to the school libraries of the
county."

Before this enterprising knight of the literary
world had fully stated the conditions for the introduction of this modern aid to the professional
teacher, and before Nicholas could make reply, he
was accosted on his right by an active, prepossessing young individual, who grasping him by the
hand led him aside and in a pleasing tone remarked: "I have a few words of caution I desire
to impress upon you, my venerable friend. You
are evidently a director of the old school, and I
should judge from your appearance the other members are equally conservative and little disposed to
take kindly to any of the new-fangled publications
these book-fiends are ever ready to force upon the
conscientious and unsuspecting director. The very
name of that book, the Philosophy of our New
Education—should be sufficient to condemn it in
the eyes of conservatism. This continual prating
about our new education is all wind—in fact, our
new education is nothing but a rehash of the old

under a flaming new title and cover, to catch the
eye of the young. Now, the publications I represent are late editions of a line of educational works,
published first away back in the early forties—
books that were in common use fifty years ago,
when you were, no doubt, a teacher. Our Arithmetics, for example, are reproductions of the very
best that swayed the mathematical world over two
generations ago, with the double rule of three,
mensuration and vulgar fractions, the three pre-
dominating essentials. Our Spellers strictly ad-
here to the old pronunciation of Scriptural names,
omitting many outlandish words invented by the
successors of old Noah Webster. (Knew him well,
I presume, in your early days, eh?) Then our
Geographies, you will observe on careful examination, conform to what, in these days of high pressure, is sneeringly termed the 'question and answer' method, in contradistinction to what the
enthusiast is pleased to designate 'the search light
of geographical teaching'—the one claiming to
furnish ideas only, the other strictly adhering to
the memory process of fifty years ago. Now, my
old friend, with the educational world rushing
headlong from one extreme to the other, it is certainly reassuring to find, among the older Directors,
at least one with a disposition to move slowly.
Ah, but best of all are our Readers—reproductions
of the series known when you were a lad for their
many most excellent scriptural quotations from the

proverbs of Solomon; and based on the principle laid down two centuries ago by old John Amos Comenius, references to whose writings you may have noticed in the olden times. And who ever heard of Comenius wasting his time on such modernized theories as the Quincy, the Grube, the Phonic or the Word method? Yes, yes, the whole line of our publications possess a two-fold advantage: first, old-time methods and contents; second, modern manufacture. With these two weapons, offensive and defensive, I am invincible, and at all times prepared to meet every shade of public opinion. For instance, in canvassing the young teachers, and especially the younger members of the Boards, I seldom, if ever, refer to the contents. It's the binding that captures the young chap, if it's red, yellow or crimson, with a handsomely colored chromo for the frontispiece. Not so, however, with the conservatives, whose eyes are seldom dazzled by the colors of the rainbow. With them, it's a speech of old Dan Webster or Henry Clay, the statesmen of your day, that brings the answer every time. And now, my venerable friend, as I have enlightened you on a good many important subjects, in a confidential way, I hope"—

"Oh, give the old man a rest, Ned!" broke in a chorus of voices, with a good-natured chuckle. "What are you giving the old gentleman, anyway? He's no school trustee—only some superannuated old-time pedagogue, whom the convention is al-

ways certain to resurrect once a year on these festive occasions.''

"Hold on, my versatile young friends!" came
the reply, as Nicholas Comenius, with his well-
preserved vigor and commanding physique, faced
his besiegers. "You must not let your ardor run
away with your discretion, nor let your flippancy
delude you with a false estimation of your smart-
ness. I am neither a school director nor intellectual fossil, as your duplex opinion would have me.
Your gushing enthusiasm and modernized cuteness
have mistaken the man, but have most unmistakably and satisfactorily delineated your mental
status. What I am, it does not become me at this
moment to dwell upon, nor might you care to
know—yet suffice it to say, fifty years ago it would
not have been safe for such characters as you to run
at large. The tendency of the times is toward lax
discipline, of which you seem to be not unworthy
exponents; and the 'wide and liberal culture'
afforded by our modern teachers' institutes seems
not to have been bestowed upon you in vain.
These text-books may indeed be the best ever
printed, and the celebrated author, who you say is
one of the instructors of the institute, may be
worth the high price paid him by the County Superintendent; but neither the excellency of the books,
nor the ability of the noted author, can atone for
the rude display of freshness and frivolity given by
you so gratuitously in my behalf. If I must take

your conduct and these incidents as an index to the institute, it may be feared that the stern and rugged discipline of the old schoolmasters has given way to misdirected zeal in the interest of the so-called 'New Education.'"

The reproof so forcibly administered had the desired effect of putting to flight the raw and undisciplined book-agents who had imagined they could make capital, for their fun or profit, of the venerable stranger. It was a stinging rebuke, though spoken in tones so low that the attention of the ordinary passer-by would not have been arrested. Too well Comenius knew and appreciated the services of the well-equipped book agent; for it was the text-book in the hands of these thrifty adventurers that preceded the County Superintendent and the best equipped educator in many a backwoods district. Comenius fully realized that while their mission in the broad field of literature had at times added a multiplicity of branches to the school-room curriculum, the good results attained during his incumbency in office more than compensated for any injury done the system. They may at times have overstepped the bounds of propriety and expediency, but wherever their influence had been most largely felt, there a preponderance of healthy public sentiment had ever existed.

As Nicholas was in the act of ascending the long winding stair that led to the platform above, he was startled by the mention of his own name.

"Ah," thought he, "here, after all, is some old-time educator, claiming recognition from his old friend." As he turned, an elderly gentleman, of perhaps sixty, grasped him by the hand.

"Can it be possible," exclaimed this apparent stranger, for such he seemed in the eyes of Nicholas, "that the pleasure has been afforded me of meeting Nicholas Comenius, whom I have not seen for over twenty years?"

"You are a stranger to me: in fact, I have not the slightest recollection of ever meeting you," exclaimed Nicholas, who was not without his misgivings lest a repetition of the little episode that had occurred a moment before might be the result.

"Why! have you forgotten your old friend Reynolds—Frank Reynolds, of the old house of Brazer Bros., Boston?" came the interrogatory, as a bright smile illumined his face. "The same individual, grown a little older and a little grayer, that's all; but still following in the same line of business, since the time we both went coasting around through Blackwell county, thirty-odd years ago; you as Superintendent, and I, with satchel in hand, trying to persuade the trustees to part with old Noah Webster's Spelling-book and Pike's old Arithmetic. How are all the boys flourishing anyway, over at Shaky Hollow and along the Ridge? Still keep the Lyceum alive? and are the young chaps still discussing the Kansas-Nebraska Bill, the Dred Scott decision, and hundreds of kindred subjects that kept the young folks from deserting the old homestead?"

"Oh, glad to see you my old friend," replied Nicholas. "But the young folks, did you say? No, it's not around the homestead you'll find the young men nowadays: and there's a reason for it, that you'll soon discover if you've an observing eye, and are not too much wrapped up in the new conditions to acknowledge the truth when you hear it. Yes, yes, there have been many changes throughout Blackwell county since you were an active factor in the agency field, but there aren't as many young men around the farms nowadays as thirty years ago. Of course, the first break occurred more than a generation ago; but as the system kept growing and the old academic institutions disappearing, the number of runaways kept on increasing, so that at the present day there aren't enough hanging around to keep the crops moving. It's the plain truth, my friend, and I've been preaching it to the young men for a good many years. 'Stick to the old plantation, boys;' I'd tell them; 'it'll carry you through life with less worry of mind and body than the world can give in any other place or at any other calling.' You see, when a young lad nowadays graduates over at the Normal school in all the scientific studies that the new system's invented, it don't generally take more than a week's persuasion to induce the old gentleman to execute a mortgage,

sufficient to start him off to the University. Talk
about poverty among the constituents of Blackwell
county! Why, bless me! during the last thirty
years I've counted no less than threescore of these
educated professors leaving Emden district for the
law, or for some other professional calling. And
for every one that's deserted the farm there's been
a pretty stiff mortgage entered up over there in the
Recorder's office. But, confidentially speaking,
while it's no reflection on the institute, it'll never
do to preach it round in open meetings among the
young educators. Here my friend, is a case in
point that I've no objection to refer to, if you care
to listen before the exercises begin," continued
Nicholas Comenius, as he braced himself against
the heavy railing for support.

"As there's still a half hour before train time, I
shall be only too happy to listen," replied Frank
Reynolds, as he shifted his position to let a stray
absentee pass.

"Now," continued Nicholas, "there was old Ike
Smith's boy Tom, and a right sprightly chap was
he; but the young teacher kept patting him on the
head and sending word to the old man that his boy
Tom was never born to be a farmer, but to be
President some day."

"Oh, I comprehend," was Frank's quick reply.

"Well, this so inflated the old man with new
ideas of Tom's future greatness, that one day he
mortgaged the best farm in the district, and sent

him off to the University. This was about four years ago, and since then what was left of the old homestead took a notion to pull up stakes and follow the lad to keep him company. From that time on, Ike's been living on hope, a mighty uncertain article these days. Day after Thanksgiving last, if my memory serves me right, Ike received a letter from the President of the Faculty, and when the squire read it to him and his neighbors, who had a kindly feeling for the old man, that Thomas Washington Smith had been elected President of the 'College Base Ball Team' and needed a little more ready cash, he never even smiled, but kept looking straight through the window over at the farm, where his other three boys were doing days' work while Tom was making a record at college.''

''True, my good old friend, true every word. Seems to strike pretty close to home, though; for I've wasted a mighty comfortable little property in that direction myself, but what the harvest's to be is pretty difficult to say,'' came the reply, with a shake of the head, as Frank Reynolds, the old school-book agent, gave a sigh of regret. ''But how is old Parson Hoskins, who years ago dwelt in the ivy-covered parsonage; Squire Benton, who dealt out mercy and justice in his rough way to the denizens of Shaky Hollow; and last, though not least, old Oscar Bently, the host of the General Washington, and Ebenezer Lukins, the worthy President of Emden School Board?''

"Sorry to say, my friend," was the reply of Nicholas, "they're all keeping company with Jim and Tim, the old schoolmasters, over in the little burying-ground beside the moss-covered church. And besides, there isn't a single director living who was active in the cause when you were operating in Blackwell county."

"Yes, there's been a tremendous change in the directorship all over the country," was Frank's suggestive response; "younger men are forging their way to the front, who are susceptible to the same influences that control the teacher's profession."

"A little too much extravagance for the practical results obtained, you perceive, but it must be spoken in a whisper—never do to attempt to speak your mind in the convention," replied Nicholas, with a smile. "What in the early days were necessary aids to the young teacher, you will observe during recent years have been thrust by the wholesale on School Boards. It's a fact worth thinking about," he continued, as he kept his eye on the young agents, who were casting sly glances at him. "And from the most favorable standpoint, primary instruction, the great bulk of these self-acting, automatic dispensers of knowledge— the modern charts—presuppose the teacher to be nothing more or less than an automatic machine, capable of pressing the button in order that the light of two centuries may be visibly reflected back

upon the mind of every pupil within the walls of a
rural school.''

''A pretty logical conclusion,'' was the half-
apologetic response: ''and proves beyond question
that you have kept pace with the current events of
the day.''

Then Frank Reynolds, whose firm had but recently published a set of self-adjusting charts,
looked at his watch, shook Nicholas Comenius by
the hand, and directed his way towards the station.

''True, every word,'' soliloquized Frank, as he
hurried down the great stone steps. '' Seems these
old-timers can see further into the new conditions
than those who are entrusted with the education
of the young. But who's to blame? Certainly
not the agent, nor the publisher! It's the short
way to knowledge the public's seeking, and any
school-room appliance that'll get a boy there in the
shortest time is what the people want. If one set
fails to bring the answer, the very next session the
Board'll be casting around for something only a
little more costly. Seems to be a trait of human
nature to revel among the theories and generalities,
accepted to-day and discarded to-morrow,'' he concluded, as he boarded the fast express.

NICHOLAS INVITED TO A SEAT.

CHAPTER XIII.

INSTITUTE IN OPERATION—MODERN ENTERPRISE VERSUS OLD FOGYISM.

As the hand of the court house clock marks the appointed hour, Nicholas stands at the extreme end of the room, already crowded by curious spectators. For a long time after the devotional exercises he stands, listening to the singing of "My Country 'Tis of Thee," and to an ardent speaker, who is talking on the glories of popular education and the rapid strides of intellectual progression. Presently a young lady, noticing the old gentleman, rises, steps over to his side, and offers him her seat. With grateful recognition he accepts, and all through the exercises follows the proceedings with unabated interest. But who, in all this assembly, can estimate the intensity of feeling that throbs within the bosom of Nicholas Comenius, as his eyes take in the surrounding mass of young men and women, with no one to extend the hand of good fellowship save the young miss whose sweet voice had asked: "Are you looking for a seat, my aged friend? Come, and I will give you mine." And yet, had this young teacher, if such she were, done anything more than what common politeness should at all times demand, whether in a convention of teachers or in the humblest walks of life? Of course, for the moment, many eyes were turned from the speaker toward the young lady; but how many understood the purely unselfish motive that prompted the act? Were there not ushers—active, intelligent young men—providing seats, here and there, for the strong and vigorous? and had they simply overlooked the aged father in the excitement of the moment?

"A very gracious, lady-like act," I remarked to an intelligent young teacher beside me.

"Rather officious on her part, if anything," was his indifferent response, as he kept his eye on the speaker. "The fact is," he continued, after a moment's hesitation, by way of gentle rebuke for our implied reflection upon the stronger sex, "these old folks are not interested particularly in the cause, and drop in on the institute more through curiosity than from a desire to give encouragement to the proceedings."

"Are you then, acquainted with that old gentleman?" I ventured to ask.

"Oh, no. He is, no doubt, one of the olden-time educators who were active in the field when Nicholas Comenius had charge of the institute."

"Nicholas Comenius?" I replied; "seems that name is not altogether unfamiliar. Were you acquainted with Nicholas?"

"No, never remember having met the old peda-gogue; but I've heard his name mentioned, at times, in connection with the proceedings. Many amusing incidents are going the rounds of the pro-fession, as to the way he ran the machine. He was set in his ways, and couldn't be induced to inaugurate any new reforms."

"Why, wherein did his methods differ from those of the present Superintendent?"

"Differ? why bless me, there's all the difference in the world! To tell the truth, Comenius didn't run the institute himself; the old masters ran it for him. First one old chap would stand up and give his experience in the school-room; then another would read an essay on the Practice of Teaching, that had taken him all winter to pre-pare; then one after another would rise in his place and discuss its merits. After this, old Nicholas would divide the institute into more than a dozen classes, in charge of the best masters of the county."

"Not an unpractical course of procedure, by any means," I hinted.

"No, perhaps not at that early day," was his equivocal response, as he caught the eye of the Superintendent. Following the line of thought, he continued, a moment later: "It was rather em-barassing, though, to those who were called upon to give expression to their own views."

"Made them thoughtful and self-reliant, and better adapted for practical work," I suggested.

"You are mistaken in your premises, stranger," said he, with eyes riveted on the speaker.

A moment later, and while the audience were singing "Columbia, the Gem of the Ocean," he turned, and in a half-suspicious manner said : "It is useless for the professional teacher to do what the institute pays others to do for him. Our worthy Superintendent has entire charge, employs the very best professional services he can command, and they in turn, who really know better the wants of the average teacher than he does himself, conduct the proceedings."

"A logical, well-digested conclusion, and admirably put," was our unspoken reflection, as we beheld in the rear of the room the stalwart form of Stephen Smithers leaning against the wall.

"Ah, how many times have I looked in upon a similar body of educators in this same old court room, a generation ago," suggested I, to a promising young professional gentleman to my left, who was at the moment engaged in humming a familiar air from an institute note-book, provided gratuitously by one of the school-book publishers.

"Been a teacher, in your day?" was his significent question.

"No, not exactly a teacher, but an observer of current events," I replied. "But alas, what a contrast! In those days there were gray hairs; young and middle-aged men and women—all engaged in a common cause, the education of youth."

"True enough, old man," came a home thrust, that made our own few hairs rise in righteous indignation.

"Old man?" thought I, as I looked around for the nearest avenue of escape; "Old man!" why, bless me! and still on the sunny side of fifty! What in the name of conscience was the world coming to, any way?

"Gray hairs, then," I said aloud, "are in these advanced times no longer commendable in the eyes of the Superintendent and the great body of teachers. What then has become of the old veterans, and what will be the ultimate fate of this great body of educators, when they shall have reached the 'dead line,' so to speak? Are they to be retired on a snug pension, as a reward for past services and a protection against the vicissitudes incident to declining old age?"

"Never reach it, my friend."

"Ah, friend," thought I, "that sounds better, and doesn't grate so harshly on the sensitive nerves."

"Experience," he continued, as he kept time with his finger to the music, "has long since taught the great bulk of the profession the danger of steering too close to the rapids. Occasionally some poor, unfortunate wayfarer, with his whole soul wrapped up in the cause, may continue to hang on to a rural school; but in the end you'll find him twirling round in the whirlpool of despondency, with none to do him reverence."

"And so this, then, accounts for the lack of gray hairs, eh?"

"That's about the size of it," was his parting salute, as he joined in the chorus of the "Hymn of Thanksgiving."

At the conclusion of this national air, a well-dressed gentleman arose, amid tremendous applause. It was his third annual visit to the institute. That he stood at the head of one of the leading institutions of pedagogics may be assumed; for in presenting his name to the Superintendent the Literary Bureau had taken occasion to say: "The distinguished institute instructor whose name we have the honor to present for your consideration, stands foremost among the literary personages of the day. In the science underlying the philosophy of our modern theory and methods of teaching, he stands without a rival. In the exposition of ideal truths, in the diversity and unification of methods, and in the elucidation of the various teaching processes, you will find him without an equal in the broad field of literary pursuits." With this splendid recommendation, known only to the Superintendent, and after the rapturous applause had subsided, he started out by saying:

"Ladies and gentlemen, and teachers of this grand old county, it becomes my pleasant duty to meet with you once again, on this charming Thanksgiving morning—this festive occasion.

Having lectured before nearly every teachers' convention in this broad Commonwealth, I am but giving expression to my inmost convictions when I say that this immense body of young educators is the most intelligent, the most highly cultured, and altogether the most attentive, it has ever been my good fortune to address. And as to your most worthy Superintendent, ladies and gentlemen, permit me to say, preparatory to my opening address, that in all respects he best represents the vital, underlying principles, upon which rests our glorious free school system. And now, fellow teachers," said he, preparing to launch forth into the wide realm of unsettled problems and unproven theories, "as the teacher's profession, like the great scientific world at large, is yearly undergoing many radical changes, it may be necessary for the speaker to reverse himself on certain very essential points, as the Honorable Court would express it were he occupying the bench instead of myself." (Continued applause and clapping of hands.) "And now, if there be any among you, my young friends, who can recall any one of the half-dozen propositions laid down as a basis in my talks of a year ago, I shall be only too happy to have him rise and do so."

At the conclusion of this appeal, and while he stood awaiting a reply that came not, a buzz of excitement pervaded the entire assembly. The young ladies cast wistful glances over at the young gentlemen—all endeavoring to recall some portion of the speaker's remarks, but without avail.

"While I cannot recall any portion," remarked one, in a whisper, "it was, nevertheless, the most delightful talk I have ever listened to."

"Indeed, it fairly sparkled with well-rounded metaphors," said another.

"And how it appealed to the higher attributes of our nature," chimed in a third.

"But while I, at the time, was charmed by the flights of eloquence, I must confess," ventured a timid young lady, "it was quite beyond my comprehension."

And so, while this great body of teachers had for the moment felt the force of an inspiration that seemed to thrill their very natures, there had been little or nothing in the talks that the average teacher could retain for practical use in the school room.

After a few remarks in which the last speaker on the programme paid a glowing tribute to the old flag and thanked an all-wise Providence for the bounteous blessings which this beautiful Thanksgiving had brought to one and all, a messenger forced his way to the front and handed the Superintendent a sealed note. After scrutinizing its contents, he turned and said : "It is to be regretted exceedingly that the request of my legal friend can not be complied with, for the reason that any departure from the pre-arranged programme could only result in the disarranging of the entire week's proceedings."

And so with a tap of the bell ended the first Thanksgiving session of Blackwell County Teachers' Institute. Ended, to the relief of the hundreds of patient, earnest workers, who for three long hours had endured the stifling air of a poorly-ventilated court room.

"Rather tiresome," I suggested to a modest-looking lady, whose pallid cheeks and frail form bore the imprint of earnest, conscientious work in the school-room.

"Yes," was her reply: "it's awfully tiresome to be compelled to sit daily for six long hours in this place and on the hard benches that may answer for witnesses and jurymen, but are scarcely in keeping with the conditions of a teachers' institute."

Was the Superintendent, who was at this moment surrounded by a number of leading citizens of the town, eager to compliment him, altogether responsible for the conditions that prevailed? He was simply the exponent of misdirected public opinion. Having direct charge of a great body of mostly young and inexperienced teachers, he was trying to direct it along the placid stream to the fountain head of knowledge. Was his institute a success? Yes, in the highest degree; for had not the very highest authority, the Department of Public Instruction, publicly pronounced it such? And were there not, at this very moment, a score

or more in waiting to shake him by the hand,
ready to congratulate him on the attention and
splendid order maintained? In fact, had not the
young judge of the court said only a moment before, "Professor, your institute has proven a
wonderful success; growing better every year."
And when the Superintendent blushed and said,
"Judge, do you mean it?" had he not replied,
"Of course I do!—most undoubtedly; and none
but an old fogy would pronounce it otherwise!"

And who in all this vast assembly, in the closing
years of the nineteenth century, would submit to
being called an old fogy? To be termed a schoolmaster or a schoolma'am might be tolerated—but
to be designated an "old fogy," never!

Old fogyism in the teacher's profession of Blackwell county? Why, the term is as obsolete as
Pike's Arithmetic, or the double rule of three. Indeed, there is so little of the old to be found among
the new conditions, that it is almost as difficult to
determine how, when or whence came the system,
as to predict whither we are drifting, or where we
shall ultimately arrive. But who among all the
young educators of Blackwell county particularly
cares whether the common school system ever had
a beginning or whether it shall ever have an end,
so long as the enthusiasm holds out and the tax-
payer stands ready to provide the means? Where
among the rank and file can one be found who has
the moral fortitude to stand before this great body

of teachers and incur the odium of being called an
"old fogy?" He may have his own convictions,
may possibly have lived long enough to see the last
swing of the educational pendulum in the direction
of abstract theories and extravagant tendencies.
He may have studied the significant lesson, felt the
pressure of methods and devices, aids and appliances; but could he afford to run counter to that
so-called larger faith that emanates directly from
the teachers' institute?

Happily for the young executive officer, the day
of old fogyism has passed away with the last old
master from the old log school-house by the wayside. And who mourns either for the old schoolmaster, the old school-ma'am, or the old school-
house? Who longs for the old text-books, the
birch rod, and the old methods? But following
these, the capacious playground, the old games and
pastimes, are fast disappearing from the rural
school, and the narrow basement of the modernly
equipped house is set apart for the physical culture
of the young. Our tender offspring must be nursed
in these hot-houses and nourished on a concoction
of physiology and hygiene, which the state has so
liberally provided as a panacea for all the ills and
shortcomings of their young nature.

On the other hand, the young teacher, a product of the nursery of the Normal school, is oftentimes feeble in both mind and body, and yet
possessing enough stock in trade to command a

fair position and a reasonable salary before he has
passed beyond his teens. By a little judicious tact
and "enterprise," he not infrequently manages to
secure the choice of several positions during a
single year, while he is scarcely able to fill either
with entire satisfaction. Of course these are ex-
ceptional conditions, and have no reference to that
large and respectable body of enthusiastic instructors who now possess the land.

"Well," thought I, as the crowd began to dis-
perse, "this is truly a modern teachers' institute,
with few of the older customs and ideas that pervaded the ranks of the profession when Nicholas
Comenius held the official reins of government."
And as I joined the young and happy throng passing down the winding stairs and into the outer
world, I naturally fell into a reflective frame of
mind. Yes, the boys may cheer the old flag, but
who ever hears them cheer the old sun-burnt veteran who patriotically bears the flag-staff? They
may hurrah for the Fourth of July, celebrating
each incoming anniversary with fire-crackers, but
how many can repeat the Declaration of Independence, or care to study its suggestive meaning?
What a long line of hallowed traditions yearly
cluster around Christmas day; but how many of our
boys and girls are taught to revere its sacred associations? It too, with its old-time child-like simplicity, has grown out of date, and a new Christmas,
with all its accompanying extravagant tendencies,

has taken its place. Thanksgiving, with its bounteous harvest, comes once a year to rich and poor, to young and old; but apart from its festivities and pleasures, how many are taught to remember with gratitude Him from whom every good thing cometh? New Year's day comes with its hopes and anticipations, but the old year cannot be too soon forgotten, and the good resolutions of the day share the same fate. Eastertide, commemorative of the glad tidings of the Resurrection—the harbinger of spring, with its fragrant lilies and its richly-colored eggs—soon follows the Christmas-tide, only to be forgotten before the sun goes down.

The same careless disregard of the past runs all through our modern life. Books of historic value are sold to the junk-dealer, while shelves are piled with trashy literature bound in finest morocco. The old homestead with its many time-scarred imprints disappears, and with it the antiquated furniture, save perhaps the old 'grandfather's clock,' and even this old monitor can scarcely be distinguished from the modern imitations. Old associations of a life-time are severed for newer acquaintances without the slightest compunction. Indeed, so gradually and imperceptibly have old habits and customs, as well as many an old landmark, passed from the world about us, that they are as little missed, possibly, as was the last of the sturdy oaks that clustered around the old farm-house of our boyhood days. And yet can we or should we

forget how during the long years it protected the
old homestead from the wintry blasts, and that
beneath its clustering branches we spent many
joyful hours of early childhood? But that monarch of the forest has fallen before the woodman's
axe, notwithstanding the admonition of the poet,

> " Woodman, spare that tree!
>   Touch not a single bough,
> In youth it sheltered me
> And I'll protect it now."

It is true the old oaken bucket and the old town
pump have been enbalmed by the poet in letters
of gold; but as the well has long since run dry,
who now cares for either? The old wine in the
cellar, perhaps, is guarded with a sparing hand,
while the old grandfather sits alone in the sitting-
room above, perchance, neglected and almost forgotten. With equal force may it not be said, that
the old Bible is being cast aside as too antiquated
to satisfy the craving propensity for our cheap
latter-day literature? And have not many of our
text-books, and notably our modern series of Readers, fallen from grace, so to speak? Do they not
partake of a grade and quality of literature that
could not have gained a foothold in the schools of
the land forty years ago? Or am I simply clamoring for the reinstatement of old fogyism, from the
standpoint of the mistaken judgment of the olden
times?

CHAPTER XIV.

EVERY department of the educational system is included in the crusade against "old fogyism." The sturdy old school director, who is perhaps unable to repeat all the branches of the school-room curriculum in their regular order, and who occasionally shakes his head when a new branch is added, is being rapidly eliminated.

"He has become too old to keep up with the educational procession," jocularly suggested one young lady teacher to another, as they stood commenting on the changes that had taken place in the schools of Blackwell county during the year previous. "Served twenty-seven years, and never missed a meeting of the board."

"Who?" came the quick response.

"Why, old Solomon McMurdy, or 'Uncle Sol,' as he is familiarly known to every boy and girl in the district."

"Progressive?"

"Never had a director that was more so, and as

175

honest and reliable as his old time-piece; but you
see, he didn't take kindly to some of the latest innovations, especially physiology and hygiene and
the military drills. Thought there ought to be
more attention given to reading, spelling, arithmetic, and an occasional lesson in book-keeping,
instead of wasting so much time on theory and
philosophy of teaching. Yes, the old man had to
succumb to the march of events, but it's been a
blessed thing for the whole district."

"Longer term and an increase of salary followed
of course," suggested the other.

"No; salary and term the same. Old Sol, you
see, had arranged for the longest term and the highest salary the year previous."

"Well, in what way then was his loss a gain?"
was the natural question.

"In more ways than one," continued the other,
in a confidential tone. "You see, while the old
man visited the schools regularly once a month,
he couldn't make a speech to save his life; and
when he undertook to express himself, his language was so full of grammatical errors that many
of the larger pupils began to notice them. Then
he often came into the school-room without the
slightest warning to the teacher; was rather un-
couth in his manners, blunt and outspoken in his
expressions. Just think of it, girls! For a broken
window-pane or the slightest injury to one of the
young trees, he'd call the offenders up and lecture

them before the entire school ; and this, of course,
didn't suit the parents. And yet, it must be con-
fessed, Uncle Sol, while a man of few words, was a
consistent member of the board."

"Any improvement in the new director?" asked
one.

"Improvement? well, I should rather conclude
there is, and in the proper direction at that—in
fact, old Sol's successor is a young physician, who
was a teacher for a term or two, is somewhat of a
local politician, and a warm personal friend of the
Superintendent's, whose election was secured
largely through his instrumentality. These influences always count, you know, at the examination."

"Of course they do," suggested another young
miss, whose brother was president of the board.
"I want to bear witness," she added, with a smile,
"to the standing of the doctor. He is so polished
in his manners, and so exquisitely polite when he
enters the school room ; and his well-rounded sentences are perfectly charming! Besides, under his
directorship each school has been furnished with
a fifty-dollar set of Astronomical Charts and a
Manual on Military Tactics—essentials that old
Sol couldn't be induced to purchase."

By this time a number of teachers had joined the
group, and the discussion, if such it may be called,
ranged all along the line of advanced ideas. "But
the tax-payer may eventually object," remarked one
who had up to this time been discreetly silent.

12

"'The tax-payer!" answered a half dozen voices: "'There it is again!—the old fogy cry of 'tax-payer,' that's been heard at every institute for the last thirty years."

And another took up the word : "I tell you, my friends, it's not the tax-payer that supplies the revenue, but the State : and the eleven million dollars voted biennially by the Legislature, the doctor claims, should be applied to whatever the Board may determine, independent of the tax-payer. On this point Doctor Jones is as level-headed as he is on all other questions. These are my sentiments, ladies."

"And mine," "And mine," came several replies, with nodding of heads.

"But where does the Superintendent stand on this question?" inquired one whose actions were at all times in harmony with those of that important functionary.

"Oh, that is rather a close question to be asking in a promiscuous gathering ; and hardly permissible at this time, with the triennial election so near at hand," was the cautious reply. "The Superintendent, you see, must be very judicious and considerate in his expressions—must adapt himself to local conditions. Among the old-fogy directors, he is extremely cautious and politic ; knows what to say and how to say it, and in that way manages to maintain his official standing." And with this the little group broke up, and my attention was

attracted by a pleasant voice at the opposite side
of the corridor.

"Suppose we take a look in at the Directors'
Convention; there are still a few moments before
adjournment," one young lady teacher was saying
to a half dozen others, as they passed in the direction of the lower court room.

"Yes, girls; come this way, and follow your
leader," came the familiar voice of one whom they
recognized as the young physician previously referred to as the successor of old Sol McMurdy, who
with report in hand was passing from a committee
room to the convention, to present the same before
the hour for adjournment arrived. Young in
years but old in experience was the irrepressible
Sam Jones, M. D. With a tremendous responsibility resting upon his individual shoulders; with
the determination to accomplish in one short term
of three years what had taken others half a life-
time; with an enthusiasm that overleapt the
bounds of prudence and discretion, this champion
of the new dispensation smilingly remarked, as he
waved his report over his head:

"If this goes through without a mishap, girls, it
will be the grandest event in the educational history of Blackwell county, since the inauguration
of the common school system itself. Think of a
ten months' term and an average salary of a round
one hundred dollars per month, and no deduction
for lost time either! How does such a report

strike you, girls—with a school library and a full
set of automatic, self-adjusting charts in each
school in Blackwell county?" continued this enthusiastic director, as he waved his paper right
and left to emphasize the important victory he had
just achieved in committee. "Only needs a little
determination and self-assurance to revolutionize
the entire educational system, and place it where
it properly belongs—under the direct control of the
State Legislature, where our forefathers intended
it should rest."

"Oh, doctor! it's awfully considerate in you,"
chimed in a half dozen voices.

"Don't mention it, girls; it's only a duty the
doctor owes to the rising generation. Some one,
you see, must lead off in these very essential reforms; otherwise the entire fabric would soon fall
into 'innocuous desuetude.' Never do to trust
these necessary reforms to the old fogy tax-payers!
In fact, my friends, it's no longer a question of
local taxation, for this report presupposes the State
shall provide the means and foot the bills. There's
an old song my father used to sing years ago, entitled, 'Uncle Sam is rich enough to give us all a
farm.' We'll change the wording of that old song,
girls, and make it read: 'This grand old State is
rich enough to build and run the schools.' There'll
be pretty lively times, girls, when the institutes
throughout the State get to whooping up that
song! It'll spread like wildfire into the very halls

of legislation, for if there's any one thing calculated to stir the members to action, it's a good
song."

"But my dear doctor! is there no possibility of
the report being defeated in convention?" suggested one, more thoughtful than the others.

"Defeated? Oh, no! It may meet with some
opposition, as it did in committee, where the only
vote recorded against it came from the doctor; but
it'll go through all the same, and be referred to
the Legislative Committee, the chairmanship of
which I was compelled to accept, against my earnest protest."

"Why, doctor!—oppose your own report?" came
the startled rejoinder.

"Yes, opposed it in the interest of the cause."
Then, more confidentially, he continued: "Opposition, at times, is a most potent weapon—as was
best illustrated in the purchase of the nineteen sets
of Astronomical charts, a short time ago, when the
only dissenting vote was that of Jones."

"Your own vote? Why doctor, it isn't possible!"

"Yes, yes; all things are possible in these degenerate days," chuckled the young practitioner,
growing more communicative, as was his custom
when in the presence of the gentler sex—"the
truth is, few fully comprehend the *modus operandi*
of running a school board or a directors' convention. Same, you see, as maneuvering a political

meeting, only on a smaller scale; both requiring knowledge of parliamentary tactics, a little political sagacity, and an intuitive knowledge of the weakness of human nature. Hence all that's necessary is to have a half dozen well-defined speeches, pro and con, cut and dried for the occasion. A good speech, abounding in well-rounded adjectives, descriptive of our glorious free school system, and delivered in a commanding tone of voice, is morally sure to overawe and intimidate the weak and unreflecting, and strengthen the side of the speaker."

"But doctor, as you are generally credited by the tax-payers with the responsibility for having expended over a thousand dollars for those charts, which are considered by many of our teachers worthless, some explanation may be necessary on your part to disabuse the average mind," came the friendly suggestion.

"Ah, girls," ironically smiled the young physician; "another proof that it isn't always necessary to advocate a measure to secure success. It all occurred in a way you'd never have dreamed of. See, when the young agent reached the office he was all broken up over his cold reception elsewhere.

"'Been interviewing the other members,' I asked? 'Yes,' he replied, with a doleful shake of the head. 'Well, with what success?' 'Sworn to oppose any measure advocated by young Doc.

Jones,' was the reply. 'Did I ever promise to vote for your charts, young man?' 'No! but'— 'Well, go and tell the other members that Doctor Jones will be on hand at the meeting this very evening, and will have something to say on the chart question—and don't show yourself in the doctor's presence until the meeting's over.' Pretty good advice, eh? So, when I reached the school, there stood the agent explaining the chart, and there sat the five directors, looking at the moon and stars and figuring up the cost. 'It's a little too far advanced and too costly for the rural school,' I suggested as a feeler, 'and furthermore, it isn't practical economy to go into the chart business when so many other more desirable appliances are absolutely necessary. I would therefore move, Mr. Chairman, that the purchase of these charts be indefinitely deferred.' 'Mr. Chairman!—I say Mr. Chairman! What I want the Chair to decide is, whether this young fledgling of a doctor is to run this school board? I would therefore move, Mr. Chairman, to amend the motion of the gentleman—that the President be authorized to purchase one chart for each of the nineteen schools,' said Patrick McGallagher, with a flourish of his long brawny arm. 'And I would second the motion, Mr. Chairman,' came the voice of a colleague. 'One word more, Mr. Chairman,' I interposed; 'if this motion prevails, I shall most certainly appeal to the court for an injunction to restrain the President from drawing his warrant.' 'Let him proceed to restrain, Mr. Chairman: it's the motion that's in order first, and the injunction at another time,' retorted McGallagher."

"And did the measure pass?"

"Why bless me," he exclaimed, in an ecstasy of delight—"pass? Better believe it passed, and by a unanimous vote at that. It wasn't the doctor that was going to get left; so before the result was announced, I rose and said, 'Mr. Chairman, in order that the action of the board may be entirely harmonious, I would move to make the adoption unanimous.'"

At this juncture the door of the Directors' room suddenly opened, and from within came a voice that attracted the attention of the little circle of teachers : "Your report, Mr. Chairman, please : the Convention's ready to receive it."

"Oh! hope you'll excuse me, young ladies: almost lost sight of the convention and the report."

And so, tipping his hat to one and all, he gracefully bowed his way into the crowded assembly of the patient, law-abiding school officials of Blackwell county.

A half hour later, as one after another filed out of the dingy court room, I stepped up and asked a conscientious-looking, middle-aged gentleman : "Adopt the report, eh?"

"Oh, yes: couldn't well do anything else after that great speech of Dr. Jones."

"Ten months' school term and a hundred dollars per month salary! Pretty steep, isn't it, for Blackwell county?"

"Oh, it makes no difference to the tax-payer! See, the doctor had it all figured out how the State Legislature's to supply the money to run the schools," was his reply.

"But where is the State to get the money wherewith to run the schools?"

"Never thought of that," came the hesitating answer, with a doleful shake of the head.

And so this vivacious young director, serving the second year of his first term, had bamboozled the sturdy old farmers into the belief that the State is great enough, rich enough and willing enough to build and furnish all the school-houses in Blackwell county, to the absolute relief of the tax-payers!

CHAPTER XV.

"PARDON me, my friend, but can you give me the name of the gentleman who occupied the seat directly to the right of the Superintendent during the morning's exercises?" I asked of a middle-aged teacher, as we went strolling along one of the leading thoroughfares of the town, immediately after adjournment.

"He," replied the teacher, "is the Superintendent of our city schools, and our first vice-president."

"He seems somewhat disinclined to move along in perfect harmony with the educational procession of the institute," I ventured the further remark.

"That is easily accounted for," was his prompt reply; "you see, the city school system, in the estimation of both the Board of Control and the Superintendent, is far in advance of the rural schools, and we city teachers are supposed to gain very little from these annual conclaves of the country teachers."

"It is a remarkable coincidence," I replied, "that while every city in the Commonwealth is so directly connected with the county in business and

186

commercial relations, there should be such diversity of sentiment with reference to active co-operation in the matter of popular education. Do not these two active forces, the City and the County Superintendent, operate along parallel lines of advanced thought?"

"No," was the reply; "the city schools are supposed to have reached the summit years ago, and until the rural schools shall have struggled up the mountain side, intellectually speaking, and placed themselves on the city level, there is no advantage in our mingling with the rural pedagogues. Understand me, I do not say this is my personal view, but the professional opinion, as derived from my frequent association with the various Superintendents. I have been principal of a grammar school for many years, and at each recurring county teachers' convention I find many valuable aids and suggestions for my work in the classroom; but unless they are in strict conformity with the ideas enunciated by our City Superintendent, there is absolutely no avenue open through which the individuality of the teacher can be brought into active co-operation with that of the pupil. Our system is as perfect and as well-adjusted in its various departments as the phonograph, so that by pressing a button in the office of the Superintendent, each and every section moves with the precision of well-adjusted mechanism."

"Then your schools have reached perfection?"

"No, not by any means. On the contrary, I
know that there are lamentable defects in the city
school system, and if permissible, let me point out
some of the bad features. In the first place, there
is too much of the cramming—too much of the
sieve process; this everlasting pouring in one day
and drawing out the next, which has proven a
severe strain and drain on the grammar school and
primary teachers, as well as on the minds of the
boys and girls."

"But have you not followed the annual reports
of the various City and County Superintendents to
the Department of Public Instruction; and have
you not noticed the wonderful wisdom and enthusiasm displayed in these yearly messages?"

"Followed them? of course I have. These
stereotyped reports reach the Department once
a year, are alphabetically arranged, handsomely
bound and distributed to the various Superintendents for circulation, at great expense; but wherein
does one differ from another, except possibly in the
first year's report of some newly-elected official,
whose standing at the fountain-head is largely dependent upon the earnestness and enthusiasm displayed in covering the whole educational field,
from the time of the adoption of the system to the
pres nt day? He generally starts out by saying:

"'Since my own election to the important office
of Superintendent of schools, so long presided over
by one whom some are pleased to designate as my

old-fogy predecessor, I have visited every portion
of this great and growing city (or county, as the
case may be). The interest manifested in popular
education, the wonderful progress apparent on
every hand, the unparalleled prosperity attending
my first year's experience, have encouraged me
during coming years to press forward along entirely
new and advanced lines, never before dreamed of in
the broad domain of popular education.'

"Abundant space is devoted to the enlargement
of the school-room curriculum, to physical culture,
to the introduction of a text-book, and to numerous
other innovations. Nothing, however, is said about
the forcing process which endangers health, and
causes headaches and sleepless nights in the preparation for the Superintendent's hobby—the periodical examination. No mention is made of the
desperation to which the rank and file of our teachers are driven in their efforts to conform to a course
of study, the prevailing tendency of which is to
subordinate both teacher and pupil to the text of
the book. No intimation is given of the insidious
influences of politics—for the reason, perhaps, that
his own election may have depended largely on the
political 'pull.' Not a word is said in these graphically prepared reports of the modern appliance
known as the educational school-room ladder.
Every Superintendent has one of his own conception, which the teacher is instructed to keep con-
stantly before the school. Some are so high and

the topmost rong so far out of sight as to make it
almost impossible for any but the brightest to hope
to reach it. Have you ever watched the struggle
as it goes on from month to month and year to
year, as each little worker strives manfully in his
vain endeavor to reach the topmost rong, up to-day
and down to-morrow, ever on the strain to gain a
permanent foot-hold at the summit?"

"But a moment, if you please," I interrupted:
"I notice that your Superintendent, in his last
annual report, mentioned a number of very important improvements; among them the erection of a
hundred-thousand-dollar high school, with all the
appurtenances necessary to a well-equipped institution, such as instrumental music, military drill,
etc."

"Ah, the high school! 'the people's college,' in
which ninety-four per cent. of our boys and girls
never set their foot, and out of which only one per
cent. of the school population ever graduate!
Verily, the high school is marching on at the expense of the tax-payer, at a rate that reflects the
utmost credit upon the directorship of the metropolis of Blackwell county!"

"Is the high school, then, not the people's college?" I asked with a look of surprise, as my eyes
took in the most imposing structure in Blackwell
county.

"Yes, it still conveys that meaning to some, and
should in consequence supply the various avenues

of the commercial and business world with those
who are ultimately to fill its positions of trust and
responsibility; but the promise is not borne out by
the facts. You see," he continued, as we leisurely
strolled along the main avenue, "some still entertain the idea that a system of common schools
should be adjusted to benefit the greatest number.
There are, as you will observe by the Superintendent's report —— thousand pupils in the various
departments of our city schools: ninety-four per
cent. of whom, as I have said, never enter the
high school, and this large number must complete
their education, if at all, in the lower grades."

" Then the grammar school—the school of the
people—is, according to your own inference, the
key to the business world, and should possess, only
in a smaller degree, all the advantages to be found
in the high schools?"

" Yes, this should be the object and aim of our
Board of Education, and the public is so led to believe; but the results are not in harmony with the
supposition. The average grammar school is such
only in name, and bears no relation to the defini-
tion of the term given by Webster. For instance,"
he went on to illustrate: " How frequently do we
hear it said by those who have reason to know,
that the pupils of our grammar schools are oftentimes unable to answer the simplest questions from
a business standpoint: have little or no knowledge
of practical book-keeping; are unreliable in the

ordinary mathematical operations, requiring accuracy and dispatch; poor in penmanship, and even more so in spelling and the proper use of words in ordinary conversation.

"Give us a dozen or more well-equipped grammar schools—not simply feeders to the high school, but schools of practical utility, in which a sound business education can be depended on by each boy or girl who enters them—and you at once meet the requirements for which the public school system was originally created. If the term grammar schools be considered too low in the educational scale, call them industrial schools. They will at once attract the hundreds of school children who now fall out of the primary and secondary grades and complete their education in the workshops or in other avocations of life long before their school days should have ended. As statistics prove that only five out of a hundred in all the cities in the land ever enter the high school, more ample provision should be made for the great army of school children within the walls of well-arranged grammar schools, from which all could go forth fairly fitted for life's various duties. Reduce the school-room curriculum to the minimum; eliminate from the mind of the average boy the fatal error of supposing that because his name happens to be George, he is destined to be a second George Washington. Economize time and direct it along the lines to which the child's inclination may eventually turn. How much valuable time is wasted on certain non-essentials in the school-room, is little appreciated by the public at large.

"Take for example the time wasted on the technicalities of the subject of physiology, the school-boy's nightmare, and apply it to something more useful, practical and mind-invigorating, and how much happier, stronger in mind and body, and ready for life's battles, our young people would be. I wish you could see some of the examination papers prepared by the Superintendent, and then look in upon a teacher here and there, or step into the private study-rooms of many of our young pupils, during the long hours of drudgery that should be given to sleep and rest. I know you would smile at many of the questions. Here are a few taken from a list of several hundred prepared for the use of each teacher:

" 1. What is haemogloblin, and how is it affected by the absence of oxygen?

" 2. Name the proteid elements, and state how much nitrogen they contain.

" 3. How does the sympathetic system influence the viscera and the body at large?

" 4. Define peritoneum, parenchyma, perimysium, peduncles, corpora quadrigemina, olecranon and microcephalitis.

" By the way, this last term, I suppose, was invented to describe the condition of the author of the present physiology craze in our schools. These

13

are fair samples of the stuff crammed into our boys
and girls at the expense of sensible facts and ideas
that would prove of substantial benefit."

"And do the rank and file of your teachers rest
content under such pressure?"

"No; but what redress have they, except to resign, and thus give place to the hundreds who
are yearly clamoring for positions."

"From whom then do the teachers draw their
inspiration?"

"From the Superintendent, of course. He is the
mainspring of our whole educational system. He,
it is who lays down the course of study from month
to month and year to year—to-day the same as yesterday, and likely so to remain indefinitely. It was
plodding along through the text-book a decade ago
—everlasting preparation for the final examination;
it is the same to-day. Study accumulates upon
study; the child is rushed from one department to
another with a smattering of abstract ideas, until
there is no relation existing between the result and
the cause which produced it. This course of instruction, I presume, is based on the broad principle that all minds are created alike, and susceptible to the same influences which govern the
material world. The individuality of the average
teacher is subordinated to the perfect system that
springs from the one over-ruling mind—the City
Superintendent. The time may come," said he as
he turned to leave me, "when a legislative com-

mission may be appointed whose direct object will be to rescue the thousands of overworked teachers and school children from a condition more detrimental to health and strength than that which, for years, has existed in the mills and workshops of the land."

" Ah, a little old-fogyism still to be found among city teachers, as well as in the country," was my mental comment, as I took my way toward the leading hotel of the metropolis, in search of the venerable Comenius. "Yes, my young enthusiastic educators, be not dismayed ; a few more years of active service in the ranks of the profession, and the place of our friend in the grammar school will be filled by one younger in years and more closely in touch with the prevailing sentiment of the times. His opinion may be only the expression of a superannuated pedagogue, disgruntled perhaps, and out of harmony with the modern methods, theories, inductions and deductions, that now control the entire educational fabric of the common school system."

Let us not part company, dear reader, but travel together down the path of time to the birth of the New System, and there, perchance, gather consolation from the discomfiture of a Jimmy McCune, or from the triumphant success of a Robert Rayland.

CHAPTER XVI.

NICHOLAS AT THE HOTEL.

In an unpretentious sitting-room, in one of the leading hotels of the town, had gathered, on this auspicious Thanksgiving noon, a goodly number of young educators. Having partaken of a sumptuous repast, such as this day is always sure to provide, they were leisurely lounging before a blazing fire in an old-fashioned fire-place, engaged in discussing the latest improved methods of teaching, when the door opened and in stepped an aged man, whose locks were whitened by the frosts of nearly eighty winters, followed by a number of young teachers. Silently and unobserved he moved toward the only vacant chair in the room, when he turned and greeted them pleasantly with, "Good morning, boys, and a bounteous Thanksgiving may you have, one and all, for your devotion to the great cause of popular education." Drawing his chair closer to the blazing fire, he continued in the same tone: "It's a fine teachers' meeting you're having, my lads, over in the old court house; beats the old-timers of forty years ago, two to one."

These remarks, from such an unexpected source,

197

naturally attracted the attention of the score or more of professors, who now began nudging each other, and casting sly glances over at their strange visitor.

"Who can this 'back number' be—this 'hayseed' of forty years ago, who expects to find the educators of Blackwell county among the lads, or boys as he calls them?" came the supercilious remark, in an undertone, from a young teacher who was in attendance at the institute for the first time by virtue of a provisional certificate granted at a rural examination.

Encouraged by the sly nods of approval, another important individual made bold to ask: "A stranger in these parts, looking for a school?"

"Well, no, my inquisitive young friend; not exactly a stranger looking for a school, nor a professor either." was the reply. "The fact is, boys," added he, "I've been attending these teachers' meetings off and on for nearly forty years, and I still have a good many things to learn."

"Ha, ha, think of it, professors! A pretty specimen of a back number," suggested a third, whose attention had been temporarily diverted from an essay on the relation of the young teacher to the teacher's profession.

"Why bless me, he must be a walking encyclopedia, or a second edition of old Rip Van Winkle," remarked a short-set, pompous-looking individual, in well-fitting clothes which constituted his principal claim to notice. "Let's wake him up from his fifty years' sleep, and find out what he knows about keeping school in the old times, when the masters went boarding round, with Noah Webster's spelling-book under one arm and a birch rod under the other."

The last remark created subdued merriment among the younger teachers, while those who had reached years of discretion simply listened in silence to this rather spicy dialogue, in which the advantage seemed all in favor of the young teachers.

Were these young professional gentlemen maliciously inclined? Were they actuated by a spirit of ridicule or intentional wrong-doing? Not by any means. There was nothing malicious in their nature; they were prompted simply by a desire for a little harmless amusement at the expense (as they supposed) of a defenseless old man. Their politeness and refinement of manners, in the presence of the Superintendent and the gentler sex, were unexceptionable. Was the system then responsible for the outburst of youthful indiscretion on this occasion? To answer this, it may be necessary to recall the playground and the associations surrounding the district school which they had attended as boys. Had they there been taught gentleness and kindness? Was it a cardinal principle with the teacher who taught the school to demand at all times of his pupils, whether in the school-room or on the by-way, politeness and true manliness toward those older than themselves—and especially toward declining old age?

To make the question more general, let me ask, is there, or is there not, a growing disrespect for the common civilities of life among the young lads of our city and district schools? How many teachers place the cultivation of the manners and morals of their pupils above that of the ordinary branches of the school-room curriculum? What can be thought of a teacher who permits his pupils to designate him, on the playground or on the public thoroughfare, with the opprobrious title of "Old Dad"? And yet not many years ago a respected teacher was laid to rest in one of our leading cities, and mourned by the lads as they followed his remains, as "Old Dad Smith;" and when these young lads, now grown into manhood, refer to his memory, as they occasionally do, it is always by that title. How many times have we walked by his side, and listened to the salutation, "Good morning, Old Dad." No particular disrespect was intended. He responded in the same inappropriate manner, applying the nickname of the playground to each and every boy whom he chanced to meet.

While it may be true as claimed, that our common school system is the best the world has ever known, conferring inestimable blessings upon rich and poor alike, let it not be so loudly heralded

from the platform that all the virtues and moral
forces are contemporaneous with the incoming of
this new dispensation. Self-laudation of the new
and denunciation of the old have characterized the
writings and utterances of a large percentage of the
"new lights." Let it not be forgotten that the
development of character, broad and comprehensive
in its simplicity, as exemplified in the personality
of many an aged citizen nurtured under the fostering care of the old academic institutions, was a
cardinal principle held as sacred as that of the
cause itself. Is the tendency of the profession
to-day toward the development of character, of the
moral forces inherent in the nature of the child?
The disposition to magnify the shortcomings of
o'd-time customs, to hold the stern disciplinarian
up to scorn and ridicule, is only equaled by the
intense desire to hurrah for our modern system
and to laud it from the platform as the greatest in
human history. The only wonder would seem to
be how the generation that grew up under the old
conditions had sufficient self-sustaining force of
character to inaugurate a system such as the present has proved to be.

Would that we could instil into the heart of
every young teacher a greater reverence for a type
of old men like Nicholas Comenius, and hundreds
of others whose names might be mentioned. His
methods may have been of the primitive kind,
even at times confined to the three R's and the

Bible, but from the latter were indelibly impressed
on the minds and hearts of the young many wholesome lessons. True, education may have been at
times a pounding or pouring in process, rather
than the drawing-out method in vogue to such an
exaggerated extent at the present day—based apparently on a principle of which the only mathematical description is, that if nothing be taken
from nothing, naught remains. However, much
that was taught under the direction of Nicholas
Comenius took deep root, producing some thirty,
some sixty, and some a hundred fold. Since the
old settlers were a God-fearing people, it is safe to
infer that the great majority of the teachers of
Blackwell county were imbued with the same
spirit. Let the modern teacher then not lose sight
of the all-important fact that the real teacher is by
no means a modern invention, product or discovery. Many an old time-worn structure or academic
institution, so numerous in earlier days, yet stands
to testify to the educational sentiment of the people; and the few of their pupils who yet linger
among us, ladies and gentlemen "of the old school,"
by their manners and character make illustrious
the memory of their early instructors.

But we must return to our little group in the
hotel sitting room. Whence came this aged patriarch, who has been sitting so quietly before the
blazing fire in the midst of the little circle, as they
humorously exchange their pleasantries at his

expense? At last there came a pause, broken only
by the low and measured tic-toc of the old grandfather's clock. In a distant part of the room sat a
middle-aged gentleman known to some of the
teachers as a distinguished lawyer, apparently dozing. Had he been awakened by the ticking of the
faithful monitor that had stood for eighty years a
silent observer in moments of prosperity and rejoicing, as well as during the long hours of adversity?
Silently he arose, made his way toward the object
of so many attempts at wit, and grasping the aged
man by the hand, said:

"Glad to see you, my venerable friend, this
bright Thanksgiving noon. Taking a day off at
the convention, eh? Why bless me, attending
these annual meetings and associating with these
young teachers, seems to keep old Father Time,
with his sharpened scythe, at a pretty safe distance!"

Then turning and facing the little circle of professionals, upon whose countenances were depicted
the very depths of chagrin, he said:

"Gentlemen, representing as you do one of the
noblest of professions, permit me to introduce to
one and all Nicholas Comenius, who for a quarter
of a century was the worthy Superintendent of
Blackwell county. Come, my lads, and gather
round this 'back number,' and extend the hand of
good-fellowship to one who during the early struggles in the cause of popular education, was the
earnest and devoted friend of the old masters, as he

has ever since been the champion of the cause represented by the professional teacher of to-day. He may be a 'walking encyclopedia' or a 'second Rip Van Winkle,' but you will ever find him in the foremost rank, battling for a broader faith."

After a few spasmodic apologies, accompanied by a mortified look and a nervous shake of the hand, the little band of modern educators formed a circle, in the centre of which sat Nicholas Comenius, the hero of the hour.

"Now, my venerable friend," concluded the gentleman, with a half-suppressed chuckle that brought a smile to the face of Nicholas, "since we have all become better acquainted, we shall call upon you to give these boys the story of the little red sandstone school-house."

"Yes, yes, Nicholas Comenius," came a chorus of voices. "Call us boys, or lads, or anything you will, but pardon our youthful indiscretion."

A moment later, Nicholas Comenius was resting in an easy reclining-chair that one of the young teachers had provided, and silence pervaded the room. But, it was different outdoors! The report of the little episode had passed from teacher to teacher, and soon they came crowding into the hotel. All could now remember the old man standing alone in the court-room, and the courtesy of the young lady who said so pleasantly: "Are you looking for a seat, my aged friend? Come, and I will give you mine."

CHAPTER XVII.

NICHOLAS ADDRESSES THE INSTITUTE—HIS GUARD OF HONOR—TEDDY DEFENDS HIS GATE.

THE court-house bell was striking for the exercises to begin when a committee, headed by the young Superintendent, were pressing their way toward the old hotel. There could be no mistaking their mission, for the name of Nicholas Comenius was the only one in all that vast concourse that seemed at that moment to call for recognition. Old men, with silvery locks, pressed their way forward; for did they not remember Nicholas Comenius, when his name was a household word beloved by old and young? As the young Superintendent forced his way through the open door-way, did he wait for a formal introduction? No! But grasping Nicholas by the hand, with moistened eye he atoned for the apparent rudeness displayed in refusing to honor the request that came from his legal friend—the same who had befriended Nicholas in the hour of need, taking in the situation while apparently dozing in a remote corner of the room. Was Nicholas permitted to tell the story of the olden-time dispensation to those who had gathered

205

NICHOLAS TAKEN BY STORM.

round? This was not the place for Nicholas
Comenius to be heard; for strong and willing
hands tenderly lifted the old patriarch from his
easy reclining-chair, passed through the open doorway and thence to the old court-room, where they
placed him in the seat of honor, beneath the old
flag.

What unseen hand on this Thanksgiving day—
this sixtieth anniversary of the adoption of the
school system—was invisibly protecting Nicholas
Comenius like a guardian angel? Who was it that
had prompted the lawyer to send the messenger
with a note to the president of the convention; and
who, failing in this act of homage to his old friend,
had arranged that the same eminent gentleman
should be present in the hotel sitting-room?
Stephen Smithers had not entrusted the gate
known as "Honest Stephen" to the charge of his
little grandson Teddy, the lad of nine, only to enjoy the festivities of the institute. And Stephen
Smithers, of all that crowded assembly, was the
only one who had thus faithfully remembered
Nicholas Comenius. As "one touch of nature
makes the whole world kin," so through this in-
tervention of Stephen the gate-keeper, hundreds
of hearts now beat in unison with that of the aged
father.

As the bell ceased ringing, the audience that
filled the court house—young men and old, matronly women and tender-hearted maidens, awaited

the opportunity of extending the hand of fellowship to Nicholas Comenius, the last frail span that
yet linked the past with the present, the Old with
the New. The effigy of justice, whose scales on
more than one memorable occasion had trembled
in the balance, now looked smilingly down upon
the crowded court-room, as if to whisper, " Nicholas Comenius, for sixty years *thou* hast been
weighed in the balance, and never found wanting."

In the midst of this profound silence the Superintendent arose, and in a speech of deep emotion,
as well as of stirring diction, presented Nicholas to
the institute. Deafening applause greeted the
patriarchal educator as he advanced to the front of
the platform, and with a smile radiant with the
sweetness of a hallowed life, acknowledged the
honor that had come to him so bountifully, yet un-
solicited.

"I am," said Comenius, "in the presence of a
great though unseen power, to which in years gone
by I have done homage, and to which I still remain
loyal, and shall while life endures. It is a long
stretch of time, fellow teachers, a long train of
events, a marvelous procession of deeds and lives
and service, since the day sixty years ago when
old Simon brought us the startling news of the
adoption of the common school law. By all the
memories that cluster round the system, by the
influences which touch and move us, it is meet and
proper at this time to consider what that system

stands for, what it is to me and to you. Its history
is a record of solid and triumphant success, not
only in its specific purpose of education, but in
promoting religion and morality, education, and
all things which go to make a people prosperous,
contented and happy. As the acorn came from the
bud and blossom of the old oak, can we or should
we forget that from a Pestalozzi and Comenius
came the light, the life and the inspiration of the
New? Can we forget that out of the ignorance of
the masses was sifted a trained, organized body of
enthusiastic workers, whose self-sacrificing devotion to the cause of humanity has been felt wherever the rural school has found an abiding-place?
Can we fail to reverence the memory of the men
of our own state who have assured to future generations the untold blessings of the public school?
Can we forget that they are of 'those immortal
dead who live in minds made better by their presence?' The destiny of Blackwell county has been
confided to you in trust, my young teachers; and
it is this responsibility, so vast and weighty, that
you as educators will have to meet and discharge
with fidelity. Owing to want of time, and in
deference to the work already mapped out, I do not
wish to address you at length; but wishing you God
speed in your onward course, and deeply grateful
to you for the opportunity afforded me, I hope at
some future time to carry you back to the birth
and infancy of the common schools, to tell you

14

NICHOLAS ADDRESSES THE INSTITUTE.

the story of the little red sandstone school house, around which still cluster many fond recollections of my early boyhood days."

As Nicholas ended, a profound silence rested upon every hearer for a moment, only to be broken by a wave of enthusiasm which rolled over the audience like the surf on the shore, and ended in a demonstration such as is not often seen in the old court house, and not likely soon to be forgotten. One of the teachers sprang to his feet, and making himself heard, said :

"Mr. Chairman, I move a unanimous vote of thanks to Nicholas Comenius, a worthy and beloved teacher, for his words and his presence, which are alike inspiring to us all." Another teacher added: "And that an escort of honor be appointed to accompany the venerable educator to his home in Emden."

This was heartily agreed to, and Nicholas left the room accompanied by a committee of five teachers and followed by the singing of "Auld Lang Syne," and the prayer that a life so rounded and beautiful might be prolonged indefinitely.

Those who live amid the active scenes of city life may now and then be touched to the very depths of their nature by separation from old friends and associations; but only those who have followed the rippling stream as it gushes from the mountain side, drank of its sparkling waters, climbed the mountain path, and communed with nature in all its varied forms, can measure the love and intensity of feeling that found expression, as Nicholas Comenius bade one and all a fervent farewell to begin his homeward journey.

It was an ideal November noon; the stage-coach stood ready to receive its guests; the steeds were champing their bits, eager for the word to start; all the passengers had taken their seats, with Nicholas Comenius occupying the place of honor. Young Patrick, the driver, took the reins, and amid joyful shouts and gay peals of laughter, the coach spun onward over the king's highway, through fertile fields, by farm-house and village, toward beautiful Emden, the home of Nicholas Comenius. From crowded sidewalks came the clapping of hands and waving of kerchiefs, "God bless the venerable educator," and "Safe journey to one and all."

"Good-bye, Stephen Smithers," shouted his legal friend, as the keeper of "Honest Stephen," astraddle of Captain Jack, followed at a safe distance, leading Nelly the mare.

On all sides, as far as eye could penetrate, the unpretentious farm-house, as well as every old landmark, conveyed a lesson freighted with interest to the young students. What a picture lay before the observing mind of Nicholas Comenius, so full of tradition and historic reminiscences!

But as they reached the dangerous cliff, known in years gone by as the Round Up, with night

coming on, there was one whose mind began to
realize the grave responsibility resting upon his
own conscience, as well as upon Teddy, his loving
grandson. That Nicholas was returning triumphant from the scenes of his early exploits, full of
honors, only added to the intensity of the anxiety
that throbbed in the bosom of Stephen Smithers,
for Teddy, alone in the old gate-house. Had some
mishap befallen the faithful Teddy? Had he
been spirited away in the darkness; or perhaps
stricken down for the little cash the old gate-
keeper was ever suspected of having concealed in
some secluded nook or cranny of the old gate-
house? Sad indeed, were the forebodings of
Stephen Smithers as he rode along within easy
reach of the fast-moving coach, whose occupants
little imagined the state of mind into which he had
fallen. However, as Stephen drew nearer and beheld the flickering light from the old lamp that,
for so many years, had stood within the window of
the lone gate-house, his doubts for the safety of the
lad began to disappear; and he thereupon determined to subject him to a further test, the result
of which would practically demonstrate to his own
mind the effect the teachings of the early morning
were to have on the mind of the youth. Well he
understood the wild and rugged nature of Pat, the
driver, ready at all times to force his way through
every gate on the road. But was not Stephen
Smithers within easy reach of the lad's rescue?

and were not Nicholas Comenius and the young students ready to defend the helpless lad?

"Whoa!" came the burly voice of Pat, as he drove his four-in-hand squarely up to the closed gate. "Up with your pole, old man, or Pat

TEDDY HOLDS THE FORT.

Murphy 'll be after plunging through pole, gate-house and all!"

"Pay your dues to the gate known as 'Honest Stephen,' and the pole will rise to the perpendicular, and give you the right of way," came a voice that startled even this rough native of the Emerald Isle.

"And who are you, my young fledgling, anyway, that would be after dictating to one who always claims the right of way over the road, gate or no gate?" responded Pat, flourishing his long raw-hide over his head.

"Oh, no, Mr. Driver, there's just forty cents due 'Honest Stephen,' and no spurious coin at that," came the quick reply of Teddy, who stood firmly at his post, with his lantern in one hand and the bag of change in the other.

"And where is the old gate-keeper who's been entrusting the king's highway to one of your years?" came the reply of Patrick, who had failed to recognize the presence of Stephen Smithers.

"Never mind; just hurry along with the exact change," retorted Teddy, in a voice that betrayed neither fear nor emotion.

"Better out with the change," suggested Comenius, who had taken the precaution to supply the needed toll-money; and who, at the same time, had received a nod of recognition from Stephen Smithers, who was at that moment enjoying the little dialogue with a good-natured chuckle.

"Well, here, my young scalawag," replied Pat, drawing from his pocket a large shining coin, and placing it in the hand of the youth; "take this, and be sure to render the exact change to a farthing, or I'll be after whaling the life out of ye. Be quick, my young chap, and stop fumbling the precious coin 'twixt your fingers.''

"But its no good, Mr. Driver; only so much base metal, that isn't worth more than a nickel a pound,'' was the lad's rejoinder, as he handed back the spurious coin.

"No good! and surely you're a chip of the old block! No good, eh? By the holy Saint Patrick it's a tender of America's money I've been after making ye, my young sapling, and it's through the gate I'll be after driving my four-in-hand, as sure as Pat's an American citizen," continued the now exasperated coachman, as he gathered the reins in hand, ready for a forward move.

At this moment, and while Teddy grasped at the bridle of the offside horse, came the voice of Stephen Smithers, as he rode up and dismounted: "Hold on, not a step further at the risk of your life!"

The next instant the astonished driver lay at the feet of Stephen Smithers, begging for mercy.

"Now rise, and beg the young lad's pardon," said Stephen, "and hand over the exact change to the penny, or there'll be one coach-driver less in the world to worry Honest Stephen."

Before the others could dismount, Stephen had clasped the lad to his bosom, printed a kiss upon his forehead, and then, relieved from the anxiety that had been resting upon him, exclaimed:

" Teddy, my little hero, this is Nicholas Comenius, whom you have never before seen."

" Yes, my gallant little defender of the king's highway," said Nicholas, as he drew the lad toward him, "the days may come and the days may go, old associations may pass away, but the world will ever grow better and richer with the display of such youthful heroism and self-sacrificing devotion. Who is the lad, and whence came he?" he added, addressing Stephen, wishing to learn the history of one of such tender age, and yet possessing such true manly character. And Stephen proudly answered, " He is my grandson."

For hours Comenius and his little escort sat within the old gate-house, and there for the first time Nicholas learned, from the lips of Stephen Smithers the part the latter had so adroitly played in the old educator's behalf. And it may here be said, that Teddy is now the boon companion of Nicholas Comenius, and that ever and anon, during the long vacation days, he may be found at the old homestead of the octogenarian, where in communion with each other, many joyful hours are yearly spent beneath the venerable oak that yet stands to shelter the little red sandstone school-house.

CHAPTER XVIII.

NICHOLAS AND HIS ESCORT LOOKING BACKWARD INTO THE PAST.

"IT is with feelings of pleasure mingled with sadness that I ask you, my young friends, to join me in a visit to the scenes of my early childhood," suggested Nicholas, as we sauntered forth from the old homestead on the morning following the Thanksgiving ever to be remembered with pleasure. After a short walk we reached the substantial iron bridge, beneath which flows the same familiar stream as in days gone by, winding its way onward through an undulating surface until lost in the wilds of Shaky Hollow.

"The quaint wooden bridge has long since been swept away," musingly sighs Nicholas; "but the yellow pebbles that glisten in the bright sunlight beneath the bridge are just as of yore, and will remain the same as long as we read years from the dial of time. But the little bubbles, as they skip dancingly along in quick succession beneath our feet as we lean over the iron column and watch their strange antics, glance up as if to say, 'No, we are not the same listless, idle fellows that playfully

meandered along beneath the old wooden bridge
when you, Nicholas, were a lad. Listen to the
sound of turning wheels and revolving spindles
farther down the stream, and you'll soon discover
that we too have a duty to perform. No time to
waste on idle curiosity-seekers; for the wheels of the
new electric station away below are waiting, and
we must be promptly on time.' And a moment
later they seem to say: 'Good-bye, old man;' and
on they rush until lost in the distance, lisping the
words of the poet:

> "'We chatter over stony ways,
> In little sharps and trebles,
> We bubble into eddying bays,
> We babble on the pebbles.
>
> "'We chatter, chatter as we flow
> To join the brimming river,
> For men may come and men may go,
> But we go on forever.'"

A few steps to the right of the bridge stands the
gray moss-covered church and its time-worn tomb-
stones—lone sentinels that yet stand to perpetuate
the deeds of noble men and women, and serve to
awaken within us long-forgotten memories of old
Parson Hoskins, who in years gone by dwelt within
the ivy-covered parsonage; of Oscar Bently, the
portly inn-keeper of the "General Washington,"
and of Squire Benton, who for many years dealt
out justice and mercy in his rough way to the
denizens of Shaky Hollow. We look in vain for

THE SCHOOL-HOUSE UNDER THE OAK.

(220)

the old town pump as it stood in the days of our youth, administering to the wants of the thirsty, and sigh for the low thatched cottage, wherein dwelt a sainted mother with her little flock. Beyond the weather-beaten church, on what was once the village green, we pass an elegant and commodious school building of modern construction; but where is the little old red sandstone school-house to which Nicholas Comenius so often refers? Has it at last fallen a sacrifice to the inroads of civilizing influences? No, there it stands, beneath the spreading branches of the venerable oak, where so often it has greeted the eye of Nicholas, returning from a long day's journey— the last representative of a type of old school-houses, once numerous, but destined soon to live only in tradition, or in the hearts of the few who still linger among men, in ripe old age. Ah, how impressively are we here made to feel and appreciate the lines from Whittier's " In School Days:"

> " Still sits the school-house by the road,
>   A ragged beggar sunning ;
> Around it still the sumacs grow,
>   And blackberry vines are running.

> " Within, the master's desk is seen,
>   Deep scarred by raps official ;
> The warping floors, the battered seats,
>   The jack knife's carved initial."

" In these respective types," remarked Comenius, " we behold on one side the new Emden in

all the power and glory that belongs to a new era;
on the other we see dear old Emden, the dream of
Paradise in our boyhood days, with its rough-
hewn landmarks fast vanishing from the stage of
life, leaving us only a sweet and fragrant memory.
Each in its turn conveys a lesson full of meaning,
both to the young and the old. Around the
modern house the green lawn, the silvery maple
and the linden add their charms; bright-eyed girls
and light-hearted boys come and go with each
recurring morning in the enjoyment of their innocent pastimes; even the teacher, young, active and
full of youthful aspirations, mingles in their out-
door amusements; while within they pursue the
even tenor of their way, unconscious of the old
house and its early associations. If around that
time-worn deserted structure ever lingered any endearing memories, they have either long since
passed away, or dwell only in the fast-failing
memory of—whom, I may well ask," continued
Nicholas with a sigh.

"Yes, within its bleak walls there may have
been as loving hearts and as devoted a master in
the days gone by; but if so, what use has this
modern teacher either for his example or his
methods? The old master and his traditional
environment have no abiding-place in his memory;
the future alone, with its endless variety of new
methods and possibilities, is the absorbing interest
in his life. The old pedagogue may have been

what the teacher of to-day loves to designate as one of a long line of superannuated old-time masters, to whose charge was entrusted not only the moral and intellectual status of the entire school, but of the whole neighborhood as well; or he may have been a second Doctor Arnold or a Christopher Dock—schoolmasters who were not simply masters of the school, but rather of the souls of their pupils, shining examples of that noble army of educators whose memory should be cherished by every teacher in the land.

"Who was the last master that taught this particular school, whence he came and whither he went, is of little moment to his successor. Whatever may have been his intellectual qualifications, his virtue and kindness of heart, his mental and moral attainments are now considered to be symbolized by the rude floor and crude furniture of the old house; while his outward appearance, whatever it once may have been, is assumed to have been a counterpart of the dingy, weather-beaten walls of the old house without. If it were cold and uninviting, he was the same; if its walls within were bleak and cheerless, his nature was equally so. In fact, the average teacher of to-day would seem to prefer not only to ignore the better qualities of the old master, but to hold him up to scorn and ridicule, and by way of extenuation assert that his knowledge never extended beyond the single and double rule of three, the spelling-book and the

birch rod, that universally accepted panacea for all
the ills and shortcomings of a boy's nature. Many
still rejoice in the fact that with the incoming of
the new system his light went out, as suddenly as
though it had never existed.

"Let us, however, my young friends," continued
Nicholas, "call upon memory to conjure up a picture of the ebb and flow of daily life, with all its
shades of stern or pleasant duty, that once went on
within the walls of this old school-house. Let the
picture be bright enough in color and remain long
enough before us to make an impression; then let
us invite the rising generation of young teachers,
whose judgment and conceptions of the old master
and the house in which he kept school some sixty
years ago are so ill-founded and untenable, to step
to our side and study its suggestive features. Let
us reverse the dial of time, and re-enact the conditions as they existed when old Jimmy McCune was
monarch of all he surveyed as master of the village
school. Let us summon before us some disconsolate educator, who is ever longing for the better
days when the teacher's calling shall have become
self-sustaining; and turning his back on the cosy,
well-equipped rural school and its manifold blessings, let him turn old-time schoolmaster for one
short term and mark the result.

"Ah, here you are, my old master" (turning to
one of our number: "a little too flashy in your
get-up to please the constituents, but a few months

of boarding round on your three-penny-a-day collections will adapt you to the changed conditions. Now, hurry along, old man, and lend a helping hand, as we proceed to restore the old house to its former status, in order that we may get you comfortably installed before the bleak storms of winter set in. Come, let us make haste to repair the roof of the old house; reset its three scant window-frames with new four-by-six glass; relay the floor with unhewn slabs, that the air may circulate the more freely among the little urchins of the school; plaster up its crevices; resurrect the ten-plate wood stove, with the cumbrous wood-box, axe, saw and saw-buck. And now, while the old desks and slab benches are being arranged around the wall, your first half-hour's experience will be devoted to wood-chopping over in yonder clearing; for the long winter days will require a goodly supply of hickory to keep the room in proper condition. Hurry along now, my old pedagogue, and get a move on, for the time's drawing near for the exercises to begin.

"Ah, here you are, with a pretty good armful, my busy man!" cries Nicholas, a half hour later, as the master enters the room in a stooping position, with disheveled hair and blistered hands. "The next in order is the steel and flint, and we'll soon have a blazing fire in the old stove, that'll drive away the blues in short order."

"But the room is so dark, the walls so dreary

15

and the windows so small! Oh, I fear I shall
never feel at home under such conditions," comes
the plaint of our disconsolate schoolmaster, as he
casts his eyes upward among the unhewn rafters in
the direction of a ray of light that comes through
an open crevice.

"Ah, my old master, be not dismayed at the
very threshold of your new undertaking," sym-
pathetically suggests Nicholas, laying a large, bony
hand upon his shoulder; "there'll be other blessings coming along in due time that you've never
dreamed of."

"Yes, yes," was the rejoinder, as a ray of hope
dawned upon him; "the room will show off to
much better advantage with a new set of improved
furniture, a furnace in the cellar, and when the
blackboard, outline maps, mottoes and pictures are
arranged along the walls. Then a full set of
Encyclopedia; a Webster's International Dictionary; a set of astronomical charts; a line of geographical and historical works; a new library for
the use of the pupils; the daily newspapers and
the magazines—and possibly an organ to help
teach the young folks music. With these necessary appliances and the regular visitations by the
County Superintendent, I think," he added, with a
half-suppressed smile, "the long winter days may
prove very pleasant and profitable indeed. Of
course, the Board have made provision for an eight
months' term, and draw their check promptly at

the end of each month; allow for a week's attendance at the County Teachers' Institute; provide for uniform free text-books, and arrange for a comfortable boarding-place for the teacher within easy reach of the school?" came the question, as he proceeded to thrust a chunk of hickory into the old stove, rub his eyes, and watch the curling smoke as it circled upward along the pipe, playing hide and seek among the rafters above.

"Ho, ho, my inexperienced friend," retorted Nicholas, as he saw him rush to the window and throw up the sash, that came down with a bang on one of his fingers: "Whence came you and whither are you drifting? Who, among the good people of Emden district, ever heard of a County Superintendent, or an outline map? Stop your dreaming, old man, and prepare to meet the wild lads who are already pushing their way toward the door of the school-house."

A moment later, with a tramp, tramp, comes a troop of youngsters of all ages and sizes, crowding and pushing their way with raw-hide boots and shoes, on and over the tops of desks, in search of a peg whereon to hang their dinner baskets, hats and bonnets. Order being restored, the arrangement of classes begins and an account of stock is taken. But what a conglomeration of text-books! —a dozen Spellers of various names and of as many different editions; an equal number of Arithmetics, from Pike's and Rose's down to Emerson's Part III;

a multiplity of editions of the Bible. A few sheets
of rough paper constitute the only writing material,
with ink of various concoctions in bottles of every
imaginable shape. Up rushes one to have his
quill sharpened or mended, while another steps
forward to recite his lesson alone; a third is using
his jack-knife to advantage on the desk before him,
while a fourth is initiating the new master into the
conditions in vogue by closing up the chimney,
thus filling the room with a cloud of smoke so
dense as to eliminate the few rays of sunlight that
had found their way through the dismal windows.
The master raps and thunders for order: but the
louder he raps the more unruly the school becomes; then he tenderly appeals to their young
manhood, gives them a lesson in moral suasion,
reads them a story in the life of George Washington, prays and beseeches them to preserve order for
the good of the school. In the midst of this confusion in steps the President of the Board, looks
the master over, and says: "It's a pretty good beginning you're making;" but with that the bedlam
of sounds recommences: paper wads and all sorts
of missiles are hurled at his head; a raw-hide boot
is extended here or there over which he lands
sprawling on the floor, at the very feet of the
worthy President. When he rises, he appeals for
support and friendly advice in his dire dilemma,
but is met with the retort: "Flog 'em! flail 'em!
The master who isn't good on his muscle had better

skip this neighborhood. Wade in, old man, and give the ringleaders a good trouncing, and it'll be a feather in your cap with the trustees! No use trying to keep school unless you're good on a tussle." The next instant the entire school's in confusion, and with a hurrah they land the master hatless and coatless in the playground without—

"Wake up, young man, for it's only a trance into which you have fallen! Want to linger longer among the environments of the old house?" added Nicholas. "No? Then follow me!"

CHAPTER XIX.

NICODEMUS THE ACADEMICIAN—THE FREE SCHOOL FIGHT—GIANTS OF THOSE DAYS.

PASSING beyond the confines of the last remnant of bygone days, the old school-house, we were startled by a voice from beyond the majestic oak :

"A bright, crisp November morning, Nicholas, my old friend."

"Why," retorted Nicholas, "how do you do, Nicodemus? Allow me to introduce to you these young professional gentlemen, whom the institute very kindly appointed as my escort of honor." Then turning, he added, "My young friends, this is the venerable Alonzo Nicodemus, the worthy president of the Collegiate Institute of Emden town."

"Glad to meet you ; yes, always glad to welcome a committee of strangers to Emden soil. It speaks well for the town, and is liable at almost any moment to start a financial boom—something most devoutly to be wished for," said Nicodemus, as he grasped each by the hand. Then, with a change of attitude, he continued : "Maybe you're about purchasing a farm, or may be you're after investing

230

your hard cash in a financial enterprise? Plenty
of eligible corner lots still lying around, waiting
for an honest investor, who isn't afraid to risk a
dollar in a growing town."

We assured him, in as few words as possible,
that the object of our visit had no financial significance.

"Ah, ha, I see, I see; a local historian, then,
bent on writing a history of Emden school district.
Well, well, who would have thought it? It's a
mighty fertile field, boys, you've struck; richer
than a gold mine that's never been worked! All
that's necessary is to jot down all the facts old
Nicholas Comenius has stored away in his memory,
and it'll create a sensation, sure as you live; for
there isn't another place in America where the
new school system's had a harder road to travel
than right over among the constituents of Shaky
Hollow. While I'm bearing the new system no ill
will, my young friends, I'm not more than half
reconciled to the havoc it's played with the old
academic institutions all over the country. The
truth is, according to my notions, the new system,
that started out all right in the beginning, hasn't
been making a very creditable showing of late
years. Since the State's been supplying most of
the cash, that's been squeezed out of the taxpayers unbeknown to them, it appears to Nicodemus
that there's too much show and expenditure for
the practical results obtained. Of course the con-

stituents aren't saying very much, but they're doing a mighty sight of thinking in a quiet way.

"What the public want, and what Nicholas Comenius is able to give," continued Nicodemus, as he stroked his long white beard, "is a history that'll give the poor old masters, now dead and gone, their proper place before the young educators of the country. The fact is, the young masters have been having a monopoly of the history business; for there hasn't been a teachers' meeting for the last twenty years from which the young chaps haven't gone away feeling that they knew more than even Pestalozzi or John Amos Comenius did in their day. It don't seem more than half right, my boys, that the old masters, who invented the machine and set it in motion, should be forgotten, while the young professors who are now running it under high pressure should have all the glory. No offense, I hope; only giving you a few thoughts that have been weighing upon my mind for quite a season," concluded Nicodemus, as he turned to depart.

"One of the old-timers," we suggested, as Nicodemus passed through a cluster of maples and entered an antiquated sandstone structure, with four gables and gray limestone trimmings.

"Yes," answered Nicholas, "one of the conservatives, full of reminiscences of bygone days, and a little given to old fogyism. You see," he continued, as his voice grew stronger and his step more elastic, "disappointments, if they come singly and during early life, may in time be forgotten or healed over; but if they come too late or too often, they at last embitter our whole nature. There was a time, my young friends, some sixty years ago, when yonder old Seminary building was among the most pretentious of its class in the Commonwealth. Like hundreds of others, its promoters, at the time the common school system was inaugurated, instead of giving encouragement to the cause of universal education, either stood aloof or joined the army of dissenters. Liberally endowed as many of these worthy institutions were by private bequests, they believed they could afford to bid defiance to a system of schools that were to be the common heritage of all, supported by the strong arm of the State. Experience has shown their mistake.

"It is an historical fact, although not generally remembered, that the four years from 1834 to 1838 were the most eventful in the annals of school legislation in Pennsylvania. It is true the story has been often told in connection with other political events, but it still remains for some modern educator to gather and present the facts from the standpoint of our day, as an inspiration to the rising generation.

"Yes, my young friends," continued Comenius, as we stood facing the old Seminary building, "how many of the rank and file of Pennsylvania's

army of teachers can intelligently portray to those
under their charge the stirring events in the halls
of legislation during those four memorable years
away back in the thirties? They are familiar with
the pages of American history from the landing of
Columbus down to the present day; even the names
of the three little ships of the daring old mariner
of four hundred years ago, when he set sail from
Palos, are daily being impressed upon the youthful
mind. The names of distinguished Pennsylva-
nians, from William Penn down to the men of our
own day, embellish the pages of the school history;
but how many know the names and services of
George Wolf, Joseph Ritner, Thaddeus Stevens and
Thomas H. Burrowes, that quaternion of Pennsylvania's noblest names, which are too often passed
over with only the slightest reference? Which of
our modern school Readers contains an extract
from the great speech of Stevens, delivered in the
House of Representatives in 1835? How many
of our teachers are sufficiently informed on these
points to have imbibed the spirit of these great
educators of the past generation, so that they can
picture to the next the incalculable blessings that
we have reaped through those men's efforts in
behalf of the organization and the preservation of
the common school system? True, the initial step
has lately been taken, as it should be, by the State
Teachers' Association, whose committee, with the
liberal-minded McCaskey at its head, has placed a

life-size picture of Burrowes in nearly every school in the Commonwealth.

"Ah," continued Nicholas—pointing to a slab directly over the doorway on which was engraved, Erected in 1790—"it was in that year that the Constitution of Pennsylvania was adopted. Strange as it may seem, from the time of the first Governor, Thomas Mifflin, down to the year in which the new system was inaugurated, each of the seven Executives in his message to the Legislature made some reference to a system of schools for the education of the masses at the public expense. Men of all shades of political opinion had studied the question in the abstract, with the hope that the time might come sooner or later when the sons and daughters of every Pennsylvanian, whether of high or low degree, might enjoy a perfect equality in educational privileges.

"It was during the campaign of George Wolf, in 1829, if I remember correctly," said Comenius, as we moved away from the old Seminary, "that James Buchanan, in a public speech, uttered these remarkable words: 'If ever the passions of men could be excused in a man ambitious of true glory, he might almost be justified in envying the fame of that favored individual whom Providence intends to make the instrument in establishing common schools throughout the Commonwealth. Ages yet unborn and nations yet behind shall bless his memory.'

Little did Mr Buchanan think that within five short years, plain George Wolf, of Northampton county, would be that favored individual whom Providence had ordained to subscribe his signature to a law that was to be a blessing to generations

GOV. GEORGE WOLF.

yet unborn. But, though the Rubicon was passed, it was merely the first skirmish in the great battle.

"To pass the act creating the new system was a victory over which the friends of education might well rejoice; but to put it into successful operation among a people many of whom believed that education was not only useless but dangerous, was quite another question. Cumbrous and unwieldy, it served but to stir up the deepest feeling of opposition in all parts of the Commonwealth. Though the education of the people was enjoined by the constitution as a solemn duty which could not be neglected without disregard of the moral and political safety of the people, the principle was contrary to the traditions and beliefs of more than one-half the people of the State.

"There was one saving provision of the act, however, that prevented what otherwise might have resulted in anarchy or revolution. The bill provided 'that when any township or district in any school division votes in the negative on the question of accepting this law, said township or district shall not be compelled to accept the same.' This mild provision, which was strictly in conformity with the constitution and the theory of free government, threw the responsibility of accepting or rejecting the system directly upon the people of the various districts, to be decided at a special election, the result of which was that in nearly half the districts the system was rejected by large majorities.

"It was to the incoming Legislature, that of 1835, that the people anxiously looked forward. The system, it was argued, had been tried and found wanting. In the Senate a proposition for repeal was adopted, and the Act of 1809—that for educating the poor gratis—substituted. From the Senate the resolution went to the House, among whose members the sentiment in favor of the repeal of the 'iniquitous' free school system was even

THADDEUS STEVENS.

more pronounced, as many of them, like the Senators, had been elected on a strictly free school issue.

"The battle opened with the forces of the opposition jubilant and expectant. On one side of the House sat young Thaddeus Stevens, surrounded by a few faithful adherents, calm and self-reliant. When the critical moment came, he took his position in the broad middle aisle facing the speaker's desk. Wrought up to a pitch of intense excitement, he there delivered the greatest speech of his life. It was in the closing sentences, so full of inspiration, that he uttered that startling and majestic declaration: 'I shall place myself unhesitatingly in the ranks of him *whose banner streams in light.*'

"At the conclusion, the House broke into the wildest excitement of delight. The magical sentence was caught up and passed from lip to lip. Before the vote was taken it was felt that the Senate bill was beaten, and the system, even in its crude form, respited at least for another year. A moment later the good news had prevaded every department of State, to be transmitted by friend and foe to every portion of the Commonwealth, with congratulation on the one hand and denunciation on the other. When Stevens entered the Executive Chamber, in response to an invitation, Governor Wolf threw his arms around the neck of his old political enemy and with broken voice and tearful eyes thanked him for the great service he had rendered the cause of humanity.

"Thus, my young friends," said Comenius, "ends the first chapter in the history of a struggle for free schools, that should be indelibly engraved upon the minds and hearts of young and old. At the following session of the Legislature, that of 1836, the battle was renewed under somewhat altered conditions. Governor Wolf had been defeated, and Joseph Ritner installed as his successor, with Thomas H. Burrowes as Secretary of State.

GOV. JOSEPH RITNER.

For a time the firmest friends of the cause stood in doubt, hoping that the much-abused system might find in the newly-elected Governor and his official adviser friends instead of foes.

"To the surprise of the most ardent advocates

of the system, as well as to the astonishment and indignation of its enemies, Burrowes had prepared, before the meeting of the Legislature, a new bill, eliminating many of the undesirable features of the Act of 1834, and embodying such important additions as the most careful observation and investigation could suggest. After a contest such as has never been equaled in school legislation, this act passed both houses of the Legislature.

"It was now, as many predicted, to meet its doom at the hands of the new Governor, Joseph Ritner, the descendant of a long line of Dutch ancestors. For Ritner, a native of 'Old Berks,' and a self-made man, rising from obscurity by the force of his own high qualities to the position of Chief Magistrate, to fasten upon his unwilling constituency a measure as iniquitous as the common school system was pictured to be, was counted as scarcely within the range of possibility. But it was not the nature of Ritner to allow a victory achieved under such trying circumstances to be lost to a free Commonwealth. His own early trials and discouragements, his lack of opportunity to press forward in the field of activity as a struggling youth, had implanted within his strong nature a desire to open to others an easier road to that knowledge which came to him only under the most unfavorable circumstances.

"To attest the old Governor's undying love for the free school system, it may be only necessary to

16

add," continued Comenius, "that at the age of eighty-three, Joseph Ritner was appointed, in the year 1861, by his old friend Thomas H. Burrowes, then Superintendent of Schools, as one of the inspectors of the Edinboro Normal School. To be

THOMAS H. BURROWES.

present at its dedication he traveled over five hundred miles by rail and stage. Joseph Ritner deserves that his portrait be displayed with that of Burrowes in every school-house in Pennsylvania.

"But if at that early day the action of Governor

Ritner and his enthusiastic Secretary of State, in the enforcement of the new law, was considered an arbitrary assumption of authority, twenty years later it was looked upon as a righteous act in comparison with the passage and enforcement of the law creating the office of County Superintendent of schools. In the eyes of many this legislative act was equaled only by the Boston Stamp Act of 1765. Protest after protest was hurled at the Department of State, from all parts of the Commonwealth. Many were outspoken in their wrath, claiming that the law had inflicted a fatal stab upon their cherished rights, and that religious liberty was a thing of the past in free America.

"And yet with the passage of this most beneficient law creating county supervision, which superseded the 'squire and committeemen,' came the long line of modern methods, theories and schoolroom appliances. The black-boards, outline maps, works on teaching, made their way into the school on every side. Pike's Arithmetic, Cobb's Spelling-book and the old English Reader fell by the wayside. In this evolution, more radical in its scope than the inauguration of the system itself, the log school house, the slab benches and the rod, as well as the conservative schoolmaster, disappeared, and the school-boy's millennium, like a bright ray of hope, dawned in the midst of the surrounding gloom."

It is through this early period, embraced

between the years '34 and '54, when people began to see the immense power exercised by education over moral, intellectual and physical conditions, and found in it, when properly conducted, the surest guarantee against individual vices and political corruption, that I would ask the reader to follow Nicholas Comenius, the aged historian. It is to this history of the schools of Blackwell county, hitherto largely enveloped in tradition, and transmitted, like many a fairy tale, from ancestor to posterity, that the succeeding pages will be largely devoted. The following picture of the first examination, of which Nicholas Comenius was an interested eye-witness, may be somewhat highly colored, but in the main it reflects the conditions as they existed in many parts of Pennsylvania nearly two generations ago.

CHAPTER XX.

OPPOSITION TO THE SYSTEM—IMPROVED ELECTION
METHOD—THE SQUIRE AND THE OLD MASTERS.

"Has Nicholas Comenius forgotten the first attempt to force the new system upon the people of Emden district? No; but it's a long story, that has never been told, and it's been a long time ago, and did more to disturb the peace of the old town than the running of the first locomotive through Blackwell county. You see, my young friend, while the taxpayers had been hearing of its operations in other sections of the State, many of them had made up their minds, from the first day the law was passed, that the old way of educating their children suited them better than the new. And so when an effort was made to put the new system in operation, they declared at a mass meeting, by a series of resolutions, that they didn't want outsiders to be forcing any of their pernicious doctrines upon the people of Emden district. But it didn't end there; for the masters, who were set in their ways, got to arguing that the adoption of the new system meant the loss of their occupation—and in this they wern't very far out of the way," suggested Nicholas.

245

"But the worst opposition came from Old Parson Hoskins, who kept preaching against the new law, and telling his congregation that as the world was coming to an end before long anyway, they'd better keep their hands off the wicked State system, otherwise they'd be sure to be left behind when Ascension day came around. Yes, it was the spiritual advice of the old minister that settled the system for a time; and if it hadn't been for the cunning and ingenuity of old Squire Benton, poor old Jimmy McCune, the master, wouldn't have died of a broken heart long before his time, and old Jeremiah wouldn't have spent the last years of his life in the workhouse on account of the loss of his calling.

"Now it came about in a rather peculiar way, and while it mayn't be very creditable to the memory of Squire Benton, who has long since passed beyond the river, from whence no old Squire ever returns, still it's part of the record, and it isn't Nicholas Comenius that's going to suppress any of the unwritten facts that belong to the early history of Emden district. While the Squire at first caught the constituents napping, the law-makers, inspired by young Thaddeus Stevens, were too smart for even Squire Benton, as you'll soon discover.

"It was on a rainy day along about Christmas, that the Squire and Ebenezer Lukins, President of the Board, put their heads together in the back office and began to tackle the provisions of the new law. When they had given it a pretty careful examination, the squire went into the next room to meditate, as was his custom, and when he came out he said, 'It's all right, and a tolerably fair state paper for a lot of legislators to pass. So I guess we'll give it a chance, as it don't differ in any particular from the old, except in raising money from the taxes to pay the masters, instead of letting the little ones pay by the day as before— a mighty uncertain way of keeping school at best.' Then holding the bill before him, and pointing with his long finger, he said: 'See; it don't contemplate any new teachers, or new books, or new school-houses, and in no way interferes with the masters' boarding around. Best of all,' said he, with a smile and a sly wink of his left eye, 'it leaves the examining in the hands of the Squire, which is very right and proper, and protects the old masters as before.'

"But the constituents who didn't have any youngsters of their own to educate, shook their heads and declared they wouldn't pay taxes to educate other people's children; and so when election day came round they voted down the system by a large majority. This was more than the Squire had counted on, and so the very next year he started through the district on an electioneering tour; but with all his argument and persuasion the result was the same.

"Now while old Orlando Hoskins was congratulating the members of his flock, and while the constituents were rejoicing over the defeat of the new system, the Squire was planning and studying, so that by the time the next election day came around he had invented a scheme which brought the answer, with a big lot of votes that he didn't have any use for. It was the Squire's own invention, and for years he kept right along selling out his patent to other districts that had the intelligence to understand how to work it.

"You see, the squire handled all the tickets, as was his custom, and the day before the election he wrote the word 'SCHOOL,' with jet black ink on each ticket; then he took a fresh quill, moistened it with saliva and wrote the word 'No' in large letters right before the word School; and when he emptied the sand on it, there was the ticket with No SCHOOL so plain that anybody could read it without spectacles. Next morning bright and early the Squire planted himself right at the place where the voting was going on, and as each constituent came up he got a ticket, and when he looked at it and saw the words No SCHOOL, he smiled, nodded his head, and in it went. When the election was over and the counting began, the Squire carefully rubbed each ticket between his fingers, and then handed it over to the election clerks, who recorded it on the tally sheets, which they signed and turned over to the Squire, who proclaimed the system adopted by nearly every vote.

When the news became known over the district that the majority of the constituents had voted for the new system, there was more commotion than ever was seen at a first-class county fair. Bright and early the morning following election, crowds of angry tax-payers from Shaky Hollow, headed by Parson Hoskins, began to gather around the Squire's office, examining the returns and clamoring to see the tickets; but there they were, with only the world 'SCHOOL,' and no mistaking it. Legal proceedings were at last instituted against the election clerks for tampering with the votes; but they were acquitted of course, because no one could see through the new scheme the Squire had invented for running the school election. To their dying day many believed and said that old Squire Benton knew more about the returns than he was willing to disclose, and that old Satan himself was at the head of the new system. But Squire Benton only smiled, and kept the secret locked up in his bosom.

"Rather a doubtful statement, think you, my young friends?" queried Nicholas, as he noticed a look of surprise on some of our countenances. "True, every word; and while it could not be defended on the principles of honor and justice, it was in those early days considered simply as a means to an end. You see, the system had become part of the law of the Commonwealth, and to enforce its provisions was considered a sacred duty on the part of the progressives, while the conservatives were equally sincere in their opposition, believing it to be their religious duty to oppose it by every means within their power. With them, to spend time over books was worse than so much waste; for they believed that every able-bodied person, old or young, was in duty bound to employ his time in useful manual labor. On the other hand, with Justice Benton it was simply a matter of political expediency, as a better acquaintance with the Squire will ultimately show.

"For a long time the new system kept moving along pretty much in the old way, with little improvement, either in the line of new methods, school appliances or new school buildings," continued Nicholas, as we returned to the old-fashioned sitting-room of his home. "As Squire Benton held the enviable position of examiner under the old system, so he was equally fortunate in holding the same position for nearly a score of years under the new. For over two decades, as shown by the records, no vacancy, through death or resignation, had been known to occur in any of the schools of Emden district. In fact, the eight old masters were as much a part of the system as the Squire himself. With these old-timers, it was not a question of the survival of the fittest, but rather one of physical endurance. In due course of time, however, through a most important legislative enactment, a radical change swept over Blackwell county, not unlike a cyclone over the prairie; and within a few years thereafter the eight old schoolmasters, like hundreds of others, fell by the wayside, one after the other, to be followed in time by the aged Squire.

"It was during the month of May in the year 1854, that the first Directors' convention was held in the old court house. Fortunately or unfortunately, a young New England Normal school graduate, with ideas far in advance of the educational sentiment of the times, was elected County Superintendent of Blackwell county. It was the day after the election took place, if I remember correctly," continued Nicholas, casting his eye in the direction of the old school-house, "that Jimmy, the master of the village school, with the seven other old masters, was summoned to Squire Benton's office to hear the news.

"'For more than thirty years, my worthy co-workers,' exclaimed the Squire, with a doleful shake of the head, 'it has been my pleasure to extend the hand of good-fellowship to one and all of you. At each annual examination held in this office, your character and educational standing have never been questioned. But now your liberties and the rights of the honorable School Board of Emden district are to be trampled in the dust by the iron heel of oppression. Are we, as free-

men, to stand idly by without seeking to be
avenged on this presumptuous tyrant who proposes to usurp the rights of every examining
committee in Blackwell county? The day has
been set apart for you, the conscientious schoolmasters of Emden district, to meet this official and
undergo an examination in all the new-fangled
branches that the new system has invented. Are
you, my old friends, prepared to enter into compe-
tition with perhaps an equal number of dandified
professors, who are ready to flock into the district
from distant Normal schools? Are you prepared
to meet this young professional tyrant? You have
my sympathy, old men, and when the fatal hour
comes round, you shall have Squire Benton's encouragement and support.'

" 'We'll bar the door and smoke him out,' came
the reply from Patrick McDeever, the master of
Shaky Hollow school.

" 'Oh, that will never do,' retorted the Squire.
'A justice of the peace is bound to maintain the
law. It's the Squire that'll be on hand with a
pointer or two, my faithful old friends. Yes, yes,
keep a sharp eye on Squire Benton for a shake of
the head or a sly wink of his left eye. And now,
my old schoolmasters, as there's no time to be lost,
it might be well to be looking up the old text-
books, so that you won't be caught napping.'

" At the conclusion of the Squire's address, the
eight old masters arose from the long bench and

passed, one after another, out into a world that seemed suddenly to have grown colder.

"Now, my young friends," continued Nicholas, "the Squire, it must be remembered, was the most important public functionary in Blackwell county. In law and politics he stood preëminently without a rival, as all were ready to admit who, on more than one momentous occasion, had heard him addressing his constituents on the political issues of the day. But it was before the School Board that the Squire always appeared at his best. His dress on these occasions, which corresponded with that worn by the gentry of pre-Revolutionary times, was out of all comparison with the plain homespun worn by many of the sturdy tillers of the soil. His stylish beaver gave to his stout and stubby form dignity and grace; his breeches were of the finest sheep-skin; his coat, with large cuffs, wide skirt, lined and stiffened with buckram, and wadded almost like a coverlet to keep it smooth, contrasted favorably with his plaited neck-stock, with its large silver buckle. This ornament kept his shoulders in close relation with his cranium, in which was stored all the knowledge and wisdom of Emden district. Yes, yes, the old Squire was generous to a fault, was kind and accommodating, and when election day came round, the boys always got the benefit of his advice, while he gathered in the votes to suit his own convenience—a pretty even exchange," laughed our genial narrator.

"If any dispute arose among the constituents of the district, he settled it to the satisfaction of all. They didn't go lawing as nowadays, but trusted their little differences to Squire Benton, and when he gave his decision, there was no appealing to a higher court. After each important election he'd start for the old court house to meet the Board of Return Judges, with the returns securely stored away in the inside pocket of his great-coat. Whether the Squire was early or late made little difference, as the result could always be estimated within a vote or two. You see, my young friends," said Nicholas, "few of the leading politicians of Blackwell county, in those days, possessed this intuitive knowledge to a greater degree than Thomas Benton. Indeed, it often became necessary on the very eve of an important election for the Squire to reverse himself—in other words, to advocate the very measures he had been opposing just before. You see, the Squire bore the same relation to the political world that Parson Hoskins bore to the spiritual; so that with the Squire on the one hand and the Parson on the other, there was little possibility of any portion of the community going far astray.

"And as the Squire managed the politics of the district, so he managed the schools," continued Nicholas, getting back to the thread of his story. "He always kept a sharp eye on the eight old masters, but made them feel that he was their friend. The day before his annual examination he would summon them all before him. There on his broad-topped desk were arranged dozens of volumes, bearing on almost every conceivable subject. Then, with all the dignity at his command, he proceeded to address them, by way of impressing them with what they might be expected to meet on the day following: 'Another year has gone by, my faithful educators,' he would say, 'and another examination day is near at hand! Hope you've all been improving your time, and that you'll be ready to toe the mark by high noon to-morrow! You see, my old friends, a full line of applications has been pouring in on the Justice from a class of young Normal school graduates from over the State line. They all seem anxious to serve your constituents, and claim to be prepared to stand a most thorough examination in all the latest improved text-books, many samples of which are before me, and to which I have been giving most careful consideration. These are stirring times, Timothy, (whom I see dozing before me,) and it behooves one and all to be on the lookout for new and advanced ideas.'

"A general stiffening up took place all along the line, when, directing special attention to certain letters before him, he'd add: 'Here's an important official communication from the Secretary of State, calling the Squire's attention to one or two new branches that have but recently been added to

the school room curriculum—a newly invented
term, by the way—any one of you able to spell it,
eh?' And so the word goes the round until it
reaches Gad Day, the walking encyclopedia of
Shaky Mountain, who manages to spell it correctly.

"'Now it may be necessary for the examiner to
reach out along new lines of advanced thought.
Here for instance is a new work on United States
History, telling all about the war between this
grand old country and Mexico, a subject that's
been agitating Congress and old Zachary Taylor
for quite a spell : and here's a Geography and Atlas
—two works in one, or rather one for the master
and the other for the youngsters, if my understanding of the two volumes is correct ; but as the time's
not yet ripe for the study of Geography, it had
better be laid aside with the History until you
have a call for it from the constituents.

"'Here is, however, a very important pamphlet,
calling attention to some recent inventions, called
globes, outline maps, black-boards, charts, and a
treatise on a new system for keeping school without the use of the shillalah, entitled Moral Suasion;
and another, on Theory of Teaching. These latter
subjects, men, have been puzzling the brain of the
Squire more than a district election. Seems impossible to get the hang of the new-fangled
schemes ! I've been writing the author of this
treatise, as he calls it, for information, and here's
his reply : " Moral Suasion," he writes, " presup-

poses the governing a school from the higher
standpoint of the moral attributes of the ideality
of the teacher, when brought into the closest rela-
tionship with the inner nature of the child." And
that Theory of Teaching also presupposes the
teacher to be so thoroughly conversant with the
subject-matter to be imparted as to enable him, to
a dead moral certainty, to instil into the minds of
a half hundred youngsters the essentials of a practical business education, while they are skylarking
around through Emden district. But how these
newly-invented subjects relate to keeping school in
the old way, this court is unable to decide. Of
course, men, these are only a few of the recent discoveries that are yearly working their way down
from the Yankee States, through the book ped-
lars, who've been remembering the Squire with
numerous samples of late.'

"Then, pushing the letters aside, with a sudden
change of attitude as well as of voice, he'd turn
first to old Patrick McDeever, the master of Shaky
Hollow school, and with a broad smile upon his
face exclaim: 'How does Squire Benton stand,
anyway, among the constituents of Shaky Hollow?
Any considerable opposition to his re-election as
Justice for his fifth term? As popular as ever,
eh? Well, mighty glad to hear it, Pat, my honest
old schoolmaster. And over along Sassafras Ridge,
Timothy O'Neal? Any falling from grace in that
neck o' woods, my good man? No? Ah! such

17

flattering compliments speak well for honest,
faithful, conscientious service, and reflect the utmost credit on your observing faculties as an educator! But over along the charcoal beds, Dennis?
What are the chances for the Squire among those
dusky charcoal-burners?' 'And by my faith,'
replied Dennis, 'there isn't a dissenting voice,
and neither will there be a dissenting vote, for its
Dennis O'Reilly that's judge of the election board,
begorra! It's Squire Benton first, last and all the
time—'tis for a fact!'

"'Ha, ha, glad to know the sentiment of my
constituency,' laughed the squire, as he grasped
each man by the hand. 'It's public sentiment,
men, that controls public affairs, and it's public
sentiment that governs the schools of Emden district. Now, my faithful old schoolmasters, it isn't
the Squire that's going to depart from the usual
procedure of the examination, with his own election hanging in the balance. It's Squire Benton
who's been watching your operations in the school
room; and it's the Squire that's been observing
the movement of your minds while sitting here.'

"Shifting his position and leaning forward with
hands resting upon a pile of law-books, he hesi-
tated a moment as if in deep meditation over some
intricate problem, looked squarely into the faces
of the disconcerted schoolmasters, and said: 'The
verdict of the court is, men, that the master who
can correctly diagnose the political situation of

Emden district, when Thomas Benton's political standing is at issue, is perfectly qualified to conduct a district school! Call round, my faithful co-workers, by high noon to-morrow, and the certificates will be signed, sealed and ready for delivery.' "

And the Squire was always as good as his word.

CHAPTER XXI.

"FULL well do I recall the first examination held by the County Superintendent in the old house over there, just forty years ago," said Nicholas, after hesitating a moment to make sure of the correct date. "They seem to come along every season as regularly as camp-meeting, and while the crowd that gathers round isn't over religiously inclined, it measures up pretty well in size and standing. Of course, not more than a dozen or so come to answer all the hard questions that it is always claimed the examiner's been gathering out of the latest text-books during the time he hadn't much else to think about."

"And what is the opinion of Nicholas Comenius as to the practical utility of these public examinations?" we made free to ask.

"In my judgment, based on practical experience," he replied, "it isn't using the young folks more than half right to compel them to sit for six long hours in a close, ill-ventilated room before a whole house-full of country folks, many of whom

260

are ill-fitted to pass judgment on the qualification
of the applicant. My opinion is, that the longer
these examinations continue, the more nervous the
candidates become, and the less able they are to do
themselves entire justice.

"Now, there was our old master Jimmy—as
straight as an arrow and as quick-witted as a judge;
learned in half a dozen languages; could make all
the straight lines and pot-hooks as if they'd grown;
could outstand any fellow in the whole school in a
spelling match; could work the double rule of three
backward and forward; knew every chapter in the
Bible even better than Solomon himself—and yet
when the new Superintendent got hold of him, he
trembled like a leaf in a storm. Yes, it was the
first public examination that killed many a poor
old master; for within a year or two they began to
fall off like flies on a frosty morning. Many believed at the time that the law was passed for the
sole purpose of shelving the old masters. It was
charged openly that the professor who invented
the new Arithmetic and the new Etymology had
kept them all in the big schools among the young
professors, so that the poor old masters never got a
look inside of one to their dying day. Then what
seemed to break up old Jimmy and the other old
masters was when they had to stand before the
Superintendent and tell all about how they'd teach
a school this, that and the other thing, when they
didn't have any school before them to practice on.

"Of course many a time I've heard the old Squire give the masters plenty of good wholesome advice; tell them all how he had courted half a dozen girls at the same time at an apple-butter boiling, unbeknown to the others hanging round; show them how he could swing a scythe or a cradle in the harvest field and be back attending to the duties of his office long before the others had gotten more than half through with their day's work. 'It's one thing to catch an eel,' he'd say, 'but the scientific thing to do is to hold him when you've got him.' And so the Squire'd lay awake nights meditating how the masters were going to stand before that Superintendent and explain how they were going to educate and discipline from sixty to seventy youngsters, while they were off playing ball or cutting up all kinds of capers at a barn raising. 'Easy enough,' he'd say, 'if he's smart and got them all inside the school with the door barred. No other way to learn music, except by attending singing school and joining in the exercises. It's practice makes perfect, and there's no doctrine under heaven that beats practice.'

"Yes, yes, it was a trying time for the old masters, as the day approached for the first public examination, under the new examiner; for the Squire and I sat up half the night with old Jimmy and the seven other old gentlemen, trying to stiffen them up for the terrible ordeal that was to come off the next day. It was an awful night—reading and spelling, ciphering and memorizing. There wasn't a sum in the old Arithmetic that Jimmy couldn't work with his eyes shut, nor a page in the old Grammar that he didn't know by rote. But he was pale and nervous, and when the fatal morning came he didn't go into the harvest field as usual, but said he felt something terrible was going to happen the old man. The old masters were taken by surprise and caught napping from the very first, for they didn't have a chance to prowl round as nowadays to find out the lay of the land, or to discover the strong and weak points of the enemy."

Bright and early on the morning of the first examination held in Emden district under the new law, people began to gather round the little red sandstone school-house, and none of them looked very pleasant either; for they didn't like the new system any way, and hated the new Superintendent like poison for robbing the Squire of his vocation. By seven o'clock Jimmy came down the stairs of the old inn, on his way to the Squire's office, dressed in his best suit of linsey-woolsey, with the Speller, Arithmetic and Grammar under his arm; while from different directions came the other seven old masters. Some trudged their way on foot, while others were on horseback, with their shining nankeen breeches drawn upward toward their knees, and their long, lank legs dangling beside saddle bags that were so well filled with books published in Noah Webster's day, that there could be no mistake as to the preconceived arrangement on the part of the Squire and the masters to circumvent the new Superintendent.

A little later, in the office of the venerable Justice stood the eight old schoolmasters on one side of the long desk, looking as solemn as the gravestones over beside the ancient church, while on the other side stood the six trustees. At one end of this little coterie of district magnates stood the learned Squire, in his stylish outfit; and to the extreme right of the column, President Ebenezer Lukens, for so many years the pronounced champion of the people's rights. In person, Ebenezer was a short, thick-set man, who wore his hair long and parted in the middle. His face was round and fat, his manner ardent and impressive, and in point of intelligence and general information, his whole bearing was calculated to impress his colleagues with his superiority.

Beside the window, and with eyes intently fixed upon the old school house—the objective point of so much interest—stood Orlando Hoskins, the aged Parson, and altogether the most disturbing factor in the educational history of Blackwell county. For many long years Parson Hoskins had held the unenviable reputation of being the great expounder of the doctrine of Millerism in its most radical form. His voice, pitched at all times in the minor key, with falling inflection at the end of each sentence, corresponded with his grotesque attitude, as he swung from side to side in the old pulpit, harassing and terrorizing his subservient followers.

"There he goes!" exclaimed the now agitated Parson, "and followed too by a straggling crowd of hangers on!"

"Ho!" came the voice of the Squire, as one and all made a rush for the door to catch a glimpse of the young Superintendent.

"Ah, and a handsome-looking official he is," sneered the Parson.

A few moments later, one excited individual after another rapped at the office door, all eager to bear witness that they had actually seen, with their own eyes, the superhuman being who had been specially ordained to examine every old schoolmaster in Blackwell county. After a few moment's hurried consultation, in which it was arranged that the Squire's tact and ingenuity were to be thrown in the masters' favor at the most critical moment, and after each Director had given the old men a few words of sympathy, encouraging them to uphold and maintain the dignity of their calling, they mournfully wended their way toward the little red sandstone school-house.

Half an hour later the eight old masters stood under the aged oak, comparing notes and asking each other all sorts of hard questions, like this: "If a certain number, and the half of the number, and seven and a half make eleven and a half, what

THE OLD MASTERS UNDER THE OAK.

(266)

is the number?" Under the linden stood an equal
number of dandified professors, making remarks
about Moral Suasion, Mental Arithmetic, Analysis
in Grammar, and Theory of Teaching, and casting
sly glances over at the old masters. But the trying time began when the Superintendent stepped
to the door and said: "All applicants for schools
in this district will please occupy the benches
along the walls, facing the examiner."

Before the old masters could reach the doorway,
the young men had taken their seats one beside
the other, while the old gentlemen ranged themselves on the opposite bench, where they sat with
arms folded like a set of mourners at a funeral.

Closely following the applicants came the six
trustees, headed by Justice Benton, in his gorgeous
outfit, marching in single file to the remotest part
of the room, where they seated themselves in a
little group. But no word or look of recognition
passed from Director to Superintendent, or vice
versa. It was evident to the mind of the new official before he had crossed the threshold of the old
house, that he was to encounter a public sentiment
of the deepest hostility. Nothing daunted, however, he concluded to follow closely the line of his
professional duty, whatever the consequence.

After a few suggestive remarks by the Superintendent, admonishing each applicant to keep his
eye firmly fixed upon his own work; that any sly
glance to the right or the left would be sufficient

THE ORDEAL BEGINS.

(268)

cause for disfavor; that no prompting by outsiders would be tolerated; and that if any member of the class should be found to have Cobb's Speller or Pike's Arithmetic concealed about his person he would be denied a certificate, the examination proceeded. This latter remark, that no prompting by outsiders would be tolerated, naturally threw the Squire completely off his base, as he had placed himself in direct line with the old masters, bent on rendering them any assistance that might come within his range.

At the head of the long bench, and directly opposite the young students, sat Patrick McDeever, the master of Shaky Hollow school, as brawny an old Irish gentleman as ever leaned upon a genuine blackthorn; to his left sat Dennis O'Reilly, Michael O'Farrel, Gabriel Thomas, Jeremiah Todd, Gad Day, Timothy O'Neal, and at the end the master of the village school, Jimmy McCune.

At the close of the Superintendent's rather severe remarks, all eyes were centered in the direction of Squire Benton, who now began squirming in his seat, as though a stray humble-bee had accidentally been awakened from its snug winter quarters on the old bench upon which the Squire had seated himself. That the chilling remarks were in part intended for this officious legal gentleman, admitted of no doubt. For Squire Benton, the mainstay of the old masters, and on whom they had for so many years relied in all things pertaining to their schools, thus to show signs of wavering, even before the Superintendent had commenced operations, was a sad beginning for the old men, I can assure you. A moment later, the Superintendent, foreseeing the demoralizing effect his pointed remarks were likely to produce on the minds of the masters, made this announcement:

"As the law requires an answer to the following questions, each applicant will be prepared to give his full name, age, number of years in the profession, schools previously attended, and number and kind of educational works read from time to time."

This simple request acted on the old masters' spirits like a ray of sunshine on a drooping plant, and had the immediate effect of stimulating their latent energies into renewed activity. Under the delusive hope that age and long service were to be considered factors in the new certificate, a ray of hope now broke in upon them, only to vanish as it came. Even the Squire now began to readjust his plaited neck-stock and to straighten out the skirt of his stylish coat, which in his excitement had become sadly disarranged. Starting with the young students whose whole experience was embraced within a few years of Normal training, the examiner's eyes were soon directed toward the older men.

"Will the first gentleman please rise and "—but before the question had been fully stated old Jimmy stood erect and in a clear ringing voice that almost brought the Squire to his feet, exclaimed:

"My Christian name is James and my surname McCune, but known among the lads of the village school as plain Jimmy. Born in county Donegal, North Ireland, sixty-five years ago, if there be no mistake in the records. Graduated with honor before attaining my manhood. Have kept school in the old house from the day I made the treaty of peace with the wild lads of the school under the old oak over forty years ago, as the exact date marked on the tree will prove to your honor. My reading comprises the whole category of pedagogy, from the time of Pestalozzi down to the beginning of the new system, which hasn't a history worth speaking of, if my judgment serves me right. In the dead languages, I have never had an equal in this neighborhood, as many of the young men whom I've trained will bear me witness."

"A pretty long service and a ripe old age," suggested the examiner, as he cast his eyes around the room to observe the effect produced by the speaker's remarks.

"Yes, it's pretty long and faithful service; but I'm still the equal of any two of the young professors, either at keeping school or at swinging a cradle in the harvest field," was Jimmy's rejoinder, as he took his seat amid the sly nods of approval from the trustees, who were leaning their heads forward, eager to catch every word of his statement.

"I believe I have the pleasure of addressing Timothy Neal," suggested the superintendent.

"Timothy O'Neal, may it please your riverence, and no mistaking the O," said Tim, as he looked the Superintendent squarely in the eye. "Me birth-place is by the Lakes of Killarney, where I first saw the light o' day sevinty-wan years ago. Here's me parchment, if you care to examine it, in altogether as good condition as though your honor had penned it with his own quill. For more than fifty years it has been me passport wheriver me feet have carried me; and should be as good as gold, even under the new system, which is after knocking the props clear from under me. You can please the ould gintleman immensely if you'll but subscribe your own signature right below that of the ould Bishop's, and thus give it a new lease o' loife."

A wave of the hand was sufficient to satisfy Tim that his time had already expired.

"Will Patrick McDeever be kind enough to"—

"And by my faith I shall be only too willing to stand up, ef it's me history ye wants from mimory; but ef it's me diplomy you're afther seeing, you'll never lay your eyes on it, begorra; for if the truth must be told, I've never resaived one from ony college or University. I'm a self-made mon, as you'll diskiver on a more intimate acquaintance, if I shud be fortunate enough to wade clear through the list of new doctrines widout swamping mesilf. It's from the time I landed in Ameriky that I've swung the firule over the back of ivery young rapscallion, to the entire satisfaction of all the intelligent constituents of Shaky Hollow school. That me years hang heavy on me shoulders, some three score and tin, is not for Patrick the schoolmaster to deny; but that I'm young in me ways, even yourself may diskiver if ye give me but a sight of a chance. No, it's nayther a diplomy nor a certificate that's been me stock in trade, but a strong arrum and a good-sized firule that's given ould Patrick his standing among the gintry of Shaky Hollow. If it's the certificate that's to make the skule, I'm afther thinking it'll be a long way off when the ould mon is willing to give up his saplin' for a bit of parchment to hang up in the skule-room to frighten a skule of sixty or seventy wild lads, that know a good shillaly only whin they feel the shtrokes a-fallin' like a flail on the barn flure."

"That will answer for the present," mildly suggested the Superintendent. And so Patrick, yielding to conditions which he could not control, fell back into his seat with quivering lips and trembling frame, clearly indicating the severe mental strain to which he had been subjected, in his determination to uphold the dignity of the profession as handed down by his predecessors.

"Will the next gentleman proceed with the desired information?" said the examining official, as he caught the eye of Gad Day.

18

"It will afford me the greatest pleasure, Mr. Superintendent," came the reply of Gad in one of his well-rounded sentences.

Now Gad, it must be remembered, was a lineal descendant of one of the old time New England schoolmasters, was endowed with more than the average natural ability, tact and cunning, if the judgment of the Squire could be relied on. In fact, he prided himself on being the oldest of four brothers, Ira, Dan, Asa and Gad, the combined letters of whose Christian names did not exceed twelve characters of the alphabet; but at the same time the shortest-set schoolmaster in Blackwell county. Gad, being of a roving propensity as his name might imply, was doomed to ramble idly without any fixed purpose, bobbing up here and there when least expected. He was the champion speller at country spelling-matches, where he was at all times sure to carry off the coveted prize. Armed with the Bible in one pocket and the Speller in the other, and a cotton umbrella under his arm, he was the conquering hero who bade defiance to every old schoolmaster whom he chanced to meet. He was familiarly known, when not in the school-room, as the "walking dictionary" of Sassafras Ridge, and was ever ready to entertain and enlighten the loungers in by-way inns and country stores. He could out-walk any other pedestrian—ped-es-'é-rian, as he was accustomed to pronounce the word —and in the spelling and pronunciation of Biblical

words was considered the champion. To hold the
enviable reputation of always standing at the head
of the class in a spelling-match was considered an
honor second only to that of being the best wrestler
at a fox-chase or at a country fair. With Gad, and
the community at large, all other qualifications
were considered of secondary importance. It was
but natural, then, that Gad should enter somewhat
into a plain presentation of facts, in order that the
Superintendent might proceed accordingly. It
was his determination also to impress upon the examiner, at the very outstart, that what he lacked
in stature was more than made up in literary qualification.

As Gad Day had inwardly resolved before entering the class to take issue with the new Superintendent on every technical point that might arise,
to enter into a personal controversy with the
avowed purpose of placing the examiner in a com-
promising position before the class and the constituents of Emden district, it is not at all surprising
that he should become the target for a fusillade of
direct questions from the very beginning; and the
result was what might have been expected.

"To take issue with the Superintendent on
every disputed point," observed Comenius, recalling incidents of the many examinations he had
personally conducted, "has resulted in settling the
fate of more than one irrepressible schoolmaster,
however well informed he may have been on the

subject-matter under consideration. The folly of such a course is often offset, however, by the disposition of certain examiners, who abuse the authority their office gives them, by holding up to ridicule some unfortunate applicant for the amusement of the assembled audience. There is no other profession in the world wherein a little knowledge, combined with a vast amount of self-assurance, is more dangerous than in the teacher's calling, and especially so in that of a Superintendent. Far better that a young man or woman should never enter upon the work of a teacher, than to imagine that they constitute 'the hub of the universe.' This was perhaps the one besetting sin of the schoolmaster of earlier days. Settling himself in some secluded neighborhood, forever after he was a law unto himself in all things pertaining to the training of the young. As reading, writing and arithmetic were the three essentials, he was prudent enough never to overstep the danger line. If an occasional boy manifested a taste for geography, history or grammar, in opposition to the expressed wishes of teacher and parents, the master would generally sacrifice the former for the latter. To demonstrate his ability to 'keep school,' the solution of one or two intricate mathematical problems at a country store or wayside inn was sufficient to establish his reputation."

These observations of our aged narrator commend themselves to every observing mind; and so it was not to be expected that these eight old masters would submit to conditions against which their very natures rebelled, without asserting their own individuality in a way most pleasing to the Squire and their constituents. But the result could not be other than disastrous to themselves.

CHAPTER XXII.

EXAMINATION IN ARITHMETIC AND GRAMMAR—
MOTHER BENTON—THE SPELLING BOOK—
THE OLD MASTERS DISCARDED.

UP to this point, no exception could be taken to
the examiner's method of procedure, for the widest
latitude had been given the old masters in the preliminary exercises. But when the next series of
questions came—" What works on theory and philosophy of teaching have you read?" " Explain
the difference between the pouring in and the
drawing out process?" " What are the conceptive
and the perceptive faculties?" " Wherein do the
deductive, inductive and objective methods differ
from the old alphabetic method?"—it was evident
that the line of demarkation between the New and
the Old had been reached, and that the masters
were to be relegated to the rear for a newer dispensation.

But the trying ordeal only came when the examiner drew from his grip-sack a small, innocent-
looking volume, bearing on its outer cover in gilt
characters, " Mental Arithmetic." To this novel
piece of ammunition all eyes were turned; for how-

278

ever small in size, there was death to the old masters lurking within its covers. When the eyes of
Jimmy fell upon that destructive weapon, he
turned to Tim and whispered: "I'd sooner run
against a dozen hornet-nests, my old boy, or all the
wild lads of the district, than to tackle that newly-
discovered Arithmetic!" But the way the young
students rolled off the big cup-and-cover questions
was enough to startle even the Squire, who by this
time began to rub his eyes and gather himself together.

That Jimmy, the old master, was considered the
best fisherman in all the country round, had caught
many a slippery old fellow with his own hands
along many a fair stream, was acknowledged on all
sides; but when he took hold of the fish question,
which the Superintendent kindly repeated three or
four times in order that he might get a tight grip
on it, he couldn't manage the one side of it. With
a good grip on the head he'd lose sight of the tail;
and with both head and tail well in hand he
couldn't manage the body; and so, after getting the
slippery creature divided up, he couldn't for his life
put it all together again.

Timothy O'Neal's turn came next, and he had
the same experience with the tree problem. He
could swing an axe, could cut more timber in a
day than the whole row of those young professors
could in a week, and measure it too in the bargain;
and yet he squirmed around, now holding on to the

trunk, then to the top, but he couldn't, to save his
reputation, manage the shadow. "Yes, it was the
shadow," remarked Tim many times thereafter,
"that bothered me more than the surveying of a
ten-acre timber tract."

"Yes, there was freer breathing all along the
line when that little book was laid aside," commented Nicholas at this point. "All right at the
present day, when every school-boy in the land
can go through a Mental Arithmetic as easily
as he'd go through the multiplication table—
and yet fail on the first practical question involving a simple business-like solution. There
wasn't so much show about the old master's mathematical operations; but when the result was
announced it wasn't necessary to be looking up the
answer in the key to make sure of the accuracy
of his solutions."

"Now, please," said the examiner, after directing
a few questions to the young students, "define the
term Moral Suasion, and explain how you would
govern a school without the use of the rod."

"Holy Saint Patrick!" exclaimed Gabriel
Thomas, who had risen to his feet, and who now
recalled the statement of the Squire a year before;
"and would ye take away from the old master his
only means of defense; place him at the mercy of
all the wild lads of the neighborhood by robbing
him of his shillaly? And is it this the system's
coming to, that would strip an old bird of his

wings, and make ould Gabriel Thomas, the respected schoolmaster, strut around in the school
like a young fledgling, with his arms tied behind
his back, unable to defind himself against the
young rapscallions of the district!"

"Next!" quickly interposed the examiner. But
for once Gabriel had gained an apparent victory,
inasmuch as he had received an appreciative nod
from the seven other masters, who were intensely
interested in maintaining their rights, so long
recognized throughout Blackwell county.

"But support of this kind didn't amount to very
much," laughed Nicholas; "while to his right
could be heard the snapping of no less than half a
dozen fingers of as many impatient competitors,
ready to repeat word for word the contents of some
new work detailing how it was being done so suc-
cessfully away over in the Boston schools."

In grammar, however, the masters thought they
were completely fortified, having committed the
contents of the first edition of Kirkham's old
Grammar, in which could always be found authority on every knotty sentence or stanza in English
literature. It was an undisputed fact that, however
widely any half dozen of these old-timers might
differ on any particular point, each disputant could
securely fortify himself behind this most valuable
adjunct of the teacher's stock in trade. So there
was hope pictured on the faces of these trusty old
educators when the subject of grammar was au-

nounced! Indeed, the flush of renewed confidence
illumined the countenances of the six trustees, as
they leaned forward. On the brow of the Squire
also sat hope renewed.

But to the consternation of these old veterans,
the Superintendent drew for a second time from
his grip a small work entitled, "Language Lessons,
or New Education." Holding this little volume
before him, and glancing around to take account
of any weak material, his eye fell on Jeremiah
Todd, who was at that very moment engaged in readjusting his wig, which in the excitement of the
moment had become sadly disarranged; for indeed
there were moments when Jerry was at a loss to
know whether he had not come away bareheaded.

"Will Mr. Todd please state into how many
parts grammar is divided?"

And Jeremiah, bounding to his feet, blurted out:
"Into four, of course—Or-tho-graph'-y, Ety-mo-
lo'-gy, Syntax and Pro-so'-dy."

With this prompt answer, coming within the
scope of the old grammar, Jeremiah was about to
subside full of honors, when he was confronted
with this sentence for analysis: "The days of the
old schoolmasters are fast drawing to a close."

"And what shall I do with it?" said Jerry.

"Separate it into its parts, and give its preposi-
tive, substantive modifiers, and the analytical relation of each component part, in a synthetical sense,
to the subject and predicate."

Now Jeremiah was a genuine type of many an
old Irish master: his face at times may have been
rough, bronzed, and rugged lines may have marked
its contour, but there was neither meanness nor
selfishness in his nature; his massive chin and
straight brows indicated an unyielding will, while
from his big gray eyes shone forth both tenderness
and sympathy for his little flock. And yet, beneath the coarse gray clothes which hung loosely
about his person, there slept a passion that when
kindled into a flame through some intended or
imaginary insult, knew no limit. As Jeremiah
stood up, head and shoulders above every other
member of the class, his face assumed a deep scar-
let red; the little bob of hair protruding through
his wig disentangled itself, and in a moment each
particular hair seemed to stand on end. His whole
being was up in arms, eager for the fray, as he
looked the Superintendent squarely in the eye, and
said:

"And is it Jeremiah Todd that you'd have me
siparate and pull apart? If you'll come out on the
green, it's yourself that I'll siparate, and it's ivery
bone in your body that I'll analyze to find out what
manner of mon ye be, to ask a poor ould schoolmaster sich outlandish conundrums that even a
mon of me years wuddn't be afther asking the
worst boy in the howl schule, for fear me conscience wouldn't rest aizy to me dying day. It's
not the first of your size and intelligence, Mr.

Superintendent, that I've analyzed, but not according to the new system, as you'll soon diskiver.''

For a moment the wildest confusion prevailed. The young students left their seats and gathered round the Superintendent, seemingly for his protection. The eight old masters were gesticulating and pouring out invectives on the head of the interloper, as they termed the examiner. The six trustees gathered into a corner of the room and urged the Squire forthwith to commit the young official for contempt; while the Superintendent stood at his post as little disconcerted as though it were but an every-day occurrence. Orlando Hoskins, on the other hand, betook himself to the outside, where he gave free expression to his pent-up wrath, urging the young folks to storm the old house from without.

In the midst of this confusion, Squire Benton, it must be said, continued to maintain that dignity of composure that had on more than one previous occasion shown the strength of his character and the fertility of his resources in the hour of greatest difficulty. Stung to the quick by the unfair treatment he felt had been meted out to the old masters, his manner was yet in keeping with the important office he had so long held. Stepping forward through the crowd that had filled every portion of the old house, until he stood face to face with the new Superintendent, he spoke for the first time since he had entered the room:

"My name, Mr. Superintendent," said he in a firm voice, "is plain Thomas Benton, for many years a citizen and justice of the peace of Emden district. You will do me a favor by adjourning the examination until after the dinner hour, if I am not trespassing on your time."

A moment later the Superintendent, feeling that he had possibly compromised the dignity of his office in some way not entirely clear to his own mind, made a few conciliatory remarks, which acted like oil on the troubled waters, and then adjourned the examination until afternoon.

" If the crowd that gathered within and around the little red sandstone school-house during the exercises of that historic forenoon had been unusual in number, that which collected in the afternoon far exceeded any similar uprising during the many years of my own experience as County Superintendent of Blackwell county," said Comenius. "As young and old came pouring into the village, their presence could only be accounted for, by those who had not heard the cause, on the supposition that the annual autumnal Fair week had arrived."

" All dissenters or conservatives?" asked one of us.

" No," replied Nicholas, as he drew his easy reclining-chair closer toward the low window; "not by any means! There were brave men in those days—men with hearts full of love and devotion to the cause of popular education. Earnest and en-

thusiastic as they were, there was no shouting, no
frothy demonstrations such as moves the multitude
at teachers' or directors' meetings nowadays. And
if there were brave men, there were even braver
women—women who gave encouragement by word
and action to those who were ready to give their
lives, if necessary, that the principles represented
by the common school system might be established.
For where, in the history of our modern rural
life, stands a name more worthy to be revered and
honored than that of plain Mary Benton? The
conceptions of a broader and more perfect life : the
sunlight of a kindly nature ; unbounded faith in
an over-ruling Providence—these were the cardinal virtues of her life. In the darkest hours, when
superstition and fanaticism had taken possession of
the minds of the multitude, it was Mother Benton
who kept her light burning amid the gloom, ever
hoping for the coming of a better day. Yes, it was
woman's intuition that prompted her to rescue
Robert Rayland from the surroundings of the old
inn, and from the charge of insubordination at another critical moment. It was her intuition that
saved the old Parson from bodily harm, when the
entire populace stood ready to condemn and punish.

"Yes, my young friends," continued the aged
father, as the big tears began to trickle down his
cheeks, "it was a woman's deep convictions that
moved her even to exchange old Jimmy, the master of the village school, who had kindly cared for

her own little ones, for a young and progressive teacher. We all thought at the time that Mary Benton had become infatuated with some peculiar mental hallucination, but time eventually justified her wisdom.

"But these little episodes happened long ago, when the system was not as yet crystallized into that perfect mechanism over which the present generation delights to dwell in its Fourth of July oratory. It was such unselfish interest as the devoted wife of Squire Benton at all times manifested in her daughters, that eventually gave to young women that high position in the schools of the state for which they are by nature and training so well adapted. For it should be remembered by the young teachers of the Commonwealth, that at the time Jimmy McCune conducted the village school, the records failed to show the name of a single young lady teacher employed in any of the public schools of Blackwell county, and comparatively few in the whole State."

But we must not let our aged narrator anticipate the history yet to be related, and will return to the examination. For a time after the noon recess, only the wise counsel of Thomas Benton among the rank and file without, and the judicious deportment of one of the younger students within, prevented what otherwise might have resulted in a riotous demonstration, or possibly the ejection of the new Superintendent. Like the good Samaritan

of old, this young man pressed his way forward,
and taking each of the old men by the hand,
whispered words of good cheer to one and all.
These expressions of sympathy, coming as they
did from one of the youngest professors, had a most
conciliatory effect, which lasted until attention was
diverted by the placing of an outline map of the
United States on the otherwise blank wall. With
this modern school-room appliance placed directly
before the class, the examination was renewed; not
however in the old-fashioned way, for a new craze
had recently entered the educational field—that of
singing the States, capitals, and other important
features to the tune of Yankee Doodle. As the
Superintendent was a newly-converted disciple to
this modern method, the younger members of the
class made the four corners of the room resound
with the echo of their voices: the other members
were the eight old masters, who sat as silent observers of the scene before them.

But when Michael O'Farrel's turn came to explain the roundity of the earth, there was music in
the air; for however well informed Mike may have
been in geography and travels, he had never out-
grown the prevailing superstition of many otherwise well-informed people who honestly believed
that the earth was as flat as the rims of their broad-
brimmed hats. For many years Mike had been a
seafaring man, and the variety of anecdotes which
daily enthused the loungers at the wayside inn

made him an undoubted authority in the line of geographical teaching, and gave him a yearly passport to a school without examination. And yet on that fatal occasion, the sturdy old pedagogue became so confused that he could hardly have described the road to the old grist-mill.

Confronted with the direct question: "What is the shape and size of the earth?" the old schoolmaster straightened himself up, cast an observing eye over at the Squire and replied:

"Some say it is flat, Mr. Superintendent; some say it is square, while others say it is round; but if I succeed in getting a legal paper, I am willing to teach it any way the constituents may desire."

The Squire nodded his head, which was followed by a similar expression of approval from the six duly authorized school trustees of Emden district. Michael was encouraged, and felt himself equal to the occasion; and when the Superintendent turned to a small globe which he held before the class, and asked him where he would come out on the other side, were it possible for him to pass clear through the earth, a bright idea dawned upon Mike:

"And where should I come out on the other side, Mr. Superintendent, but out of the hole at the other end, of course, if I ever lived to get through without swamping myself in the broad ocean."

If this application of the principles of mathematical geography failed to carry conviction to the

19

mind of the examiner, it nevertheless struck a responsive chord in the breasts of the listeners, and found expression in repeated nods of approval from the custodians of the school interests of Emden district.

That Michael O'Farrel could answer a question that to the average mind was only to be grappled with by the Squire's superior wisdom, at once gave him a standing in the community which he had never before attained. For the Superintendent to assume that the earth was round like a ball, was to the minds of many well-meaning people simply preposterous: and yet, accepting the theory as correct, where else but at the other end of the hole was it possible for the old master to appear?

But Michael's ambition, stimulated by the evident impression he had made, tempted him still further, and he added:

"To sustain me position, Mr. Superintendent, I might state that there is a lake over in the ould country with no bottom at all, sorr."

"But how do you know that?" asked the Superintendent, with a smile.

"Well, sorr, I will tell ye. Me own cousin was showing the pond to a gintleman one day, sorr, who looked incredulous like, just as you do yerself, and me cousin couldn't stand it for him to doubt his word, so he said, 'Begorra, I'll prove the truth of me words,' and off with his clothes and in he jumped."

The Superintendent's face wore an amused and quizzical expression.

"Yes, sorr, he dived under, and didn't come up again, at all, at all."

"But," said the Superintendent, "I don't see how your cousin proved his point by recklessly drowning himself."

"Sure, sorr, it wasn't drowned at all he was; for the next month comes a letter from him in Austra-lia, askin' to send on his clothes."

There was triumph in the eye of Michael O'Farrel as he took his seat on the long slab bench, followed by a buzz of admiration from all who had crowded their way into the village school.

After this brilliant display of wisdom, which brought a smile even from the young Superintend-ent, the examination finally closed with that most vexatious of all tests, the spelling exercise: for it has ever been a custom, even down to the present day, either to begin the examination with the spelling-book or to close the day's work with that most difficult branch of the school-room curriculum.

"I've attended nearly every examination since the new system came into use," was the comment of Nicholas; "and it's my opinion that the spelling-book has caused more worry than all the other branches of the school-room combined."

"It was easy enough for Gad Day to stand up in a spelling match and spell all the hard words of the old Speller, as fast as even Noah Webster could

have pronounced them; but when the examiner
pulled out that new Etymology, with a long list
of lately-invented words, with their strange pronunciation, it was evident that the old men were
going to have a trying time of it, unless Jimmy
could persuade the Superintendent to ease up a
little by substituting old Noah's Spelling-book for
that new Etymology. This might easily have
been accomplished had the Squire held the reins;
but old customs, habits and even methods, like the
old masters, were now to be swept away for a
newer dispensation.

It was a caution to see how the masters tried to
"juke" many of the words they had spelled fifty
times over at the spelling-schools; for the new examiner had such a peculiar way of twirling them
round. One of the easiest words in the language
Gad Day missed the moment it reached him. Now
Gad had studied As-tro-no'-my, as he pronounced it,
for years; knew all the signs and stars in the
heavens; could predict the coming of a storm to
the minute; understood the various eclipses and
changes of the moon to a dead certainty; and yet
when the Superintendent gave him the word Jupi-
ter, he was the first to go down by insisting on
calling it Ju-pe'-ter. Then there was Dennis
O'Reilly, who was a great believer in the mythol-
ogy of apparitions; could never pass within a mile
of a graveyard without its recalling a line of myth-
ical narratives, which he took great delight in re-

peating for the benefit of his friend the Squire; but he went down in the first skirmish, because he persisted in pronouncing the word my-tho-lo'-gy. Old Gabriel Thomas, who was noted for his happy faculty of belaboring more discipline into the obstreperous lads of the school than any other master in the district, met the same fate on the words bel-a-bor'ing and ob-stre-pe'rous, as he obstinately insisted on pronouncing them.

As the examination drew to a close, a sense of relief seemed to permeate the whole class. Half an hour later, the Superintendent announced that while he would personally desire to favor the old masters as far as possible, the obligations of his high position demanded the strictest impartiality; and that feeling it to be his duty to sustain the new law by granting certificates to those only who had met its several requirements, he was reluctantly compelled to—

Before the sentence could be completed, Patrick McDeever, the master of Shaky Hollow school, arose, and in a commanding tone said: "Brace up, old men," and out of the little red sandstone schoolhouse the eight old masters trudged their way into the cold world, leaving the eight young professors masters of the situation.

A moment later the Superintendent handed to each of the young men a small four-by-eight paper, bearing the official imprint of the State, upon which was inscribed: "This is to certify that you

have passed the examination, and are entitled to
teach in the schools of the Commonwealth during
the ensuing year."

" As the Superintendent passed out of the door,"
added Nicholas, rising from his easy chair and
standing erect as in his early manhood, " I looked
him squarely in the eye, and could see that away
down in his own heart he felt he had broken the
hearts of the old schoolmasters. He didn't give
them a good-by shake, and I noticed that Jimmy
McCune didn't carry his grip across the lawn by
the old oak, as he had in the morning.

" Looking here and there for a word of encouragement which he failed to receive, the new Superintendent drove away with a heavy weight resting
upon him. It was sad to see the eight old masters
standing round with bended heads. They were
not the victors that day, but they had plenty of
kind words from the Squire and the trustees, and
kindly looks of sympathy from a loving constituency. An hour later, and the news had reached
every portion of the village that the old schoolmasters had been discarded, and their places filled
by an equal number of young professors, representing all the new methods and theories in the educational world."

To cast adrift those eight old masters by one
sweep of the pen was the prerogative of the new
Superintendent; but to eradicate the deep-seated
superstitions, superinduced in part by the mistaken

teachings of Orlando Hoskins, was a psychological problem, the solution of which was, for the time at least, entirely beyond his jurisdiction. Could the advocates and the defenders of the old system, however incurably defective in the eyes of the others, be expected to discard the same at the instigation of this new official, and accept a system diametrically the reverse of that under which they themselves had been nourished, under the fostering care of the old masters, who had ever found a welcome at every fireside?

The six directors, however superficial their own qualifications, and while they stood ready to obey the strict letter of the law, which forbade the employment of others than those holding valid certificates, were at the same time unalterably determined to maintain a close supervision over the schools under their control—to hold each teacher to a strict accountability for a violation of any of the prescribed rules, among the most important of which was that which forbade the introduction of any of the new-fangled methods and theories. For hours after the examiner had departed, here and there around the old oak stood little knots of sympathizers in consultation with the discarded masters, offering words of condolence; while within the old house sat the duly constituted authorities. Finally, after a prolonged discussion, the eight young teachers were duly appointed to the various schools.

CHAPTER XXIII.

THE NEW TEACHER — THE FIRST MORNING —
MODERN METHODS—ORLANDO HOSKINS
INDIGNANT.

IT was on the morning of the beautiful October
day when Robert Rayland, the newly-elected
teacher of the village school of Emden, crossed the
threshold of the little stone house as the successor
of Jimmy McCune, that the climax was reached
and the seed sown which in God's own time was to
take deep root, blossom and bear fruit—the fruit
of the old system regenerated into the new. While
the evolution of the old master into the modern
teacher was to be complete, and at the same time
so radical in its tendency as apparently to sweep
away the educational landmarks and early traditions of more than five generations, it was nevertheless but the beginning of a struggle, with the
masses solidly arrayed on the one side and fearless,
conscientious young teachers on the other. It was
furthermore a contest in which clear grit, conscience, and self-reliant determination to carry the
light of the new educational system even to the
very depths of Shaky Hollow, were eventually to

296

crown our young hero's efforts with victory, and
emancipate the good people of Emden from the
thraldom of superstition, as the sequel will show.

Unlike the old master, the new arrival, modest
and unassuming as he at all times appeared, was
not permitted to make his entry into the village
quietly and unobserved; for on that most eventful
morning the entire place had assumed a holiday
appearance. From sly nooks and remote corners
the unsophisticated country lad was quietly surveying the new-comer with that keen penetration so
common in the denizens of many a backwoods district; while at an open window sat Malinda, the
Parson's oldest daughter, with thoughts but half
concealed, casting sly glances and wondering at
whose fireside the new teacher was to find a welcome during the long winter evenings. That he
was young and handsomely attired in a well-fitting
suit of black, contrasting most favorably with the
plain homespun of the old master, was appre-
ciatively noted by all the marriageable girls of
Emden; but in the eyes of the many good housewives this was viewed in a light entirely opposite.

If the Squire was active in the local and political
affairs of the district, his faithful wife was none the
less active in looking after the proper education of
her little family. In many respects she was his
superior—in birth, as well as in advantages of education, for she had in early years attended a good
school in a distant town. Since she had known

Jimmy for so many years thoroughly and inti-
mately, and had heard so many disparaging remarks concerning the young professor, it was
natural to suppose that her prejudices would be as
deep-seated as those of her husband. And yet,
with an intuition peculiar to her sex, she had resolved from the moment the news first reached her
of the new appointment, to withhold whatever
opinion she might have formed until she could
verify it by meeting the young teacher face to face.

It is true, in many ways she had learned to respect and admire Jimmy McCune; for had he not
always faithfully looked after her family of growing girls over in the old school? And yet, was
there not away down in her very nature a consciousness that after all, her three daughters, fast
blooming into womanhood, needed a different kind
of training, and that perhaps in the new teacher
she might find the fruition of her many longing
desires? And so, while the village gossips who
had called on her for sympathy and consolation
were engaged in making all kinds of invidious
comparisons, she simply replied in her quiet and
unassuming manner:

"Well, we'll give the young man a chance to
show what's in him; may be the gold which glitters in his fine clothes isn't all on the outside, after
all. He looks like a sprightly young chap, that
has good breeding and polished manners, and by
his walk I'd judge he isn't a bit lazy, either. I

don't want to prejudge the young fellow, for the
Scripture says: 'Judge not, that ye may not be
judged.' And so I'll wait until the Squire comes
home, and then we'll argue the question from an
intelligent standpoint.''

From this unexpected and unlooked-for decision
there was no appeal, for surprise kept the usually
nimble tongues silent.

If the atmosphere hung heavy without, an even
denser gloom shrouded Robert Rayland as he
moved in the direction of the little stone house,
filled to its utmost capacity with young and old,
who had assembled to witness the installation or
possible dismissal of the newly imported teacher.
In fact, the latter was what the great majority most
desired. To see Robert Rayland commit some
gross indiscretion or violate one of the prescribed
rules, and be thereupon summarily dismissed and
Jimmy McCune reinstated in his place, was what
every village lad had anxiously looked for.

And yet it was evident, even to the prejudiced
mind of the Squire, who sat at the head of the six
directors on the long slab bench, their backs resting against the damp wall, that Robert Rayland
bore no resemblance whatever to the long line of
itinerant Yankee schoolmasters who had for a generation or more annually made application to his
worship for a certificate. Whatever his ancestors
may have been in their day and generation, it was
evident that he had been educated under a system

so different from the old as to make it absolutely
impossible to follow in the footsteps of Jimmy
McCune, however much, for the sake of peace and
harmony, he might have so desired.

Robert Rayland was at no time dependent upon
the school-room for a living, having come from a
distant school, like hundreds of others before him,
rather to spread the light of the new educational
gospel, which had illumined every New England
village, than to earn a livelihood as the teacher of
a village school. And so when he surveyed the
old school building which loomed up before him
in the distance, he never for a moment doubted
that in the end he would come out victorious.

It is true he had entered into a solemn contract
that under no circumstances were any of the new
doctrines advanced by the new Superintendent to
supersede those which had for so many years prevailed in the schools of Emden district; but he had
always reasoned on the principle that desperate
cases require desperate remedies, and that " sufficient unto the day is the evil thereof." He had
also hoped that he might be permitted to enter the
school without attracting the attention of the outside world, and by proceeding slowly and cautiously, disarm any criticism which might otherwise arise. But scarcely had he turned into the
pathway to the school-house, when he began to
realize that in this he was greatly mistaken, and
that he would have to meet the issue in a straight-

forward way, or end his mission in ignominious failure.

To resurrect one of the old-time masters and induct him into one of the modern schools of to-day, would scarcely provoke more criticism than the induction of a down-east educator of fifty years ago into the school of a backwoods district. And so it is but natural to rely upon the recollection and experience of eye-witnesses yet living for any knowledge of historical value pertaining to that early day. We will let our old friend tell the story of Robert Rayland's first day in Emden school in his own words.

"I've attended many a meeting of the elders over in the chapel," said Nicholas, "when old Parson Hoskins was engaged in reckoning up the exact date for the Ascension, which had 'missed fire' so many times before; and I've seen the Squire standing over a stack of law-books arguing a point of law with a lot of hot-headed clients from away over the hills; but I've never seen a young beginner with no practical experience handle a school in the way that young professor did. He didn't even wait for an introduction by the president of the board to the boys and girls sitting around, but began operations as if he had been in the business longer than old Jimmy himself. Nor did he stop to explain to the school how he'd gotten permission to step into the shoes of the old master; nor ask the Parson, who was waiting for an invitation, to offer the opening prayer, to ease up things a little, as was the custom of old Jimmy McCune; but he walked straight up to the desk beside the old wood-stove, which was warming up the youngsters pretty lively, and setting his foot down firmly and looking straight into the faces of the larger boys, who were turning and twisting, said: 'We'll open school by reading a chapter from the New Testament.' I don't recall the whole text, but remember distinctly the words 'He that receiveth a righteous man in the name of a righteous man shall receive a righteous man's reward.'

"Now for a dozen or more years I'd sat under the preaching of the Parson, and I'd heard him read many a long chapter before he'd begin his discourses on the final ending of the world; but I don't recall any readings to compare with the new teacher's. The words as they fell from his lips, so clear and forcible, so full of divine inspiration, made a deep impression; but why he chose that text I could not at the time understand.

"That there was a deep meaning and purpose on the part of the new teacher, was apparent to all. Even the Squire melted, and the whole school looked solemn; and I made up my mind that the only mistake the teacher made was that he didn't get to preaching instead of teaching, as he wasn't engaged to read the Scriptures himself, but to let the big boys and girls do the reading. It was a big feather in his cap with some, but the members

of the Parson's congregation said it was a reflection
on the minister, and so on this point a dispute
arose the very next Sunday over in the chapel. It
seemed like a bad break for the professor to make
at the very outstart, but it turned out all right in
the end.

"The Parson, as has been mentioned, had for
some years been preaching the 'Millerite' doctrine,
and only two months before had made his fifth prediction that the end of all things terrestrial was to
come to pass the day previous to that of the stated
meeting in the chapel; but as he again failed to hit
the mark, and no ascension took place, there was
the liveliest kind of a disturbance. So the Parson,
to account in some way for the mistake in the date,
charged the failure to the new system, to be forced
on the people by the new teacher and the Superintendent. Before the professor came around there
was no freedom of conscience among the people of
Emden district, except what was allowed by the
Parson, who kept a strict watch over the whole
neighborhood; and Orlando's word was law. Yes,
the Parson did all the thinking necessary to be
done, and it saved the people a power of trouble
and worriment in reconciling all the knotty and
conflicting points in the Scriptures.

"Well, the next thing the teacher did after he
had finished reading the chapter, was to go right
among the children, and in less than no time he
had taken down from fifty to sixty names; and

some of them were mighty tough ones at that, such
as Ebenezer, Ezekiel, Hezekiah, Jeremiah, and the
like: but when he called the roll he didn't miss a
single one. Up to that time no particular fault
could be found with his work, as he was following
in the master's tracks pretty closely; but from that
on he got the Squire and the Board so tangled they
couldn't begin to keep up with the exercises—and
yet they couldn't get over the reading of that chapter in the New Testament, for it kept telling them
inwardly that perhaps after all they'd better ease
up a little on the new teacher, and not try to hold
the reins too tight on him.

"After he had finished calling the roll, and
while all were in doubt as to the next move, he
had the school stand before him in rows—the little
codgers in the front row and the larger ones behind them, like a set of soldiers on dress parade.
Then he unrolled what he termed a newly-invented
chart, used, as he said, throughout all the New
England schools, and about half the size of the
Squire's window shutter, and hung the queer-looking machine on the wall, right over the heads of
the trustees. Looking around, he soon caught on
to a sapling about the size of Farmer Stevens'
wagon-whip. When the eyes of the trustees got a
view of this they were greatly pleased, for they
thought after all he still had a little of the masters'
blood in his veins; but the big boys standing
around began to look pale and nervous, for they

didn't know how soon he was going to begin operations in the old-fashioned way.

"However, when he opened up that chart, it was all covered over with the queerest lot of ciphering, and what he called 'phonics' and 'vowels,' big and little words, long and short sentences, so that it puzzled even the Squire to figure out what it had to do with keeping school in the old way. First he took the little codgers on the short words, then the larger boys and girls on the large words and sentences. When he got through with one side he turned the other over, and still kept pointing and the whole school kept repeating after the teacher for more than an hour.

When he finished the geography lesson—which almost paralyzed the trustees, for they had never before seen a school taught by wholesale—his eyes fell at last upon the brightest girl, the eldest daughter of Squire Benton. Addressing her in his firm but kindly manner he said, "Will Hannah please step forward?" And Hannah, the modest, unassuming village girl of fourteen, stepped to the front, took the pointer from the hand of Robert Rayland, and to the surprise of all pointed out and repeated word for word the entire lesson as thoroughly as though she had studied the various topics for an entire winter. But while this new departure, so radically at variance with the established methods of the old system, met with a hearty response on the part of the boys and girls of Em-

20

den, there were loud mutterings of disapproval
among the local authorities.

"For well-nigh another hour the professor kept
right along teaching the youngsters by wholesale,
and running the school according to scientific principles, pretty much to suit himself. He never
once cast an inquiring look over at the trustees,
nor in the direction of the Parson, who was standing over in the corner taking notes, and preparing
to take a hand in the exercises when the time
came for inviting visitors to say a word or two, as
was the custom under the old master. But as I
was on the lookout for squalls," continued Nicholas, "I kept my eye now on the professor and then
on the trustees and the Squire, who were boiling
all over with rage, waiting their turn to get a
whack at the school. From what I knew of the
fighting qualities of the old men in their younger
days, I felt a little uneasy for the safety of the
young man; and so I stepped over to his side in
the midst of the exercises, and whispered in his ear
that the safest thing for him to do under the trying
circumstances was to slip out as soon as the exercises closed, and strike the shortest trail for Boston."

"Did he skip the town?" we asked.

"Skip? Not if the old man's recollection serves
him right! After reading the thirteen verses of the
thirteenth chapter of Corinthians, and marching
the whole school in single file around the room,
then through the doorway, he turned and planted

himself directly in front of the school authorities.
Looking the old men squarely in the face, he smilingly said :

"'Well, gentlemen, I have now tried to do my
duty to the school to the best of my ability : how
were you pleased with the first morning's exercises?
Any suggestions to offer? If so, I shall be pleased
to hear what you may have to say.'

"Now this flank movement on the part of the
teacher was more than the six district overseers
had counted on. For a moment they all sat eying
each other in a quizzical way, then, amid mutterings of disapproval, one after another attempted to
rise to the floor. But the teacher gracefully waved
them back into their seats, and planting himself
between the Squire and Ebenezer Lukins, the
President of the Board, said: 'One at a time,
gentlemen; we'll hear whatever objections you
may have to make.' It was a mighty well-laid
plan to capture the old men before they could recover themselves; and if it hadn't been for the
shrewdness of the Parson, the young teacher would
have been master of the situation from that
moment, without a struggle.

"But Orlando Hoskins wasn't a believer in the
new educational system, and had made a vow only
a few months before that he'd have the young
stranger out of the school inside of a week ; and it
was the Parson's teachings that were working on
the minds of the trustees more than any particular

ill-will they bore to the new teacher personally. So while the young man was sitting on the long bench explaining points of the new doctrines to the old men, who were bending over to catch every

ORLANDO HOSKINS.

word, the Parson rushed up before them with clenched fist and said: 'As your pastor and spiritual adviser, I command you to bounce this young Bostonian instanter ; otherwise every mother's son will be left behind when Ascension day comes around, and the time fixed for the Upward Journey isn't very far off.'

"At this peremptory summons the whole six district fathers made a plunge for the door, in their haste to unhitch and bridle their horses, which stood without. A few moments later the several officials might have been seen galloping in various directions in eager haste to reach their homes, lest the fatal moment might overtake them on their way. Arm in arm the Squire and the Parson jogged along on foot, leaving the young

teacher standing alone within the doorway of the
now deserted school-room.

"Seeing the young professor standing there
alone," continued the aged father, "I couldn't pass
over to the old homestead with an easy conscience
without giving him a word of comfort. Of course
I hadn't much love for the young fellow that had
robbed old Jimmy of his calling, but as I thought
over the closing chapter which the teacher read—
'Though I speak with the tongues of men and of
angels, and have not charity, I am become as
sounding brass or a tinkling cymbal '—I stepped up
to the door and said: 'Young man, I rather pity
you; you're a stranger in these parts, trying, I
suppose, to perform your duty. You don't seem to
have a friend in the town, unless it be the Squire's
wife, who has befriended more than one stranger
when the whole village was against him. It's a
mighty tough time you'll have at best, in trying to
plant the seed of the new doctrine in this district.
The truth is, it isn't the kind of seed that suits the
soil, nor the kind of soil that suits the seed, and
that's where the trouble comes in with your teaching. There's no use in your trying to convert the
trustees to your new kind of notions until you have
first succeeded in converting the Squire and the
Parson; and that you'll discover to be a mighty
ticklish operation.'

"Finding the young master willing to listen, I
continued: 'While I have no personal feeling

against you, I see your plan of teaching school in
no way agrees with old Jimmy's. His plan may
not have suited the youngsters, but it pleased the
Squire and the Parson immensely, while your plan
suits the little codgers better than it does the
trustees. It's the overseers you must reach, young
man, and to reach them you've got to make terms
with the Squire and Parson. There's the Squire's
been running the politics of the district for more
than forty years, and there has never been a trustee
elected in all that time that was not the first choice
of Squire Benton. There is a way of working the
old man if you can manage to get his daughter
Hannah on your side; but in doing so beware of
the Parson, the Parson's wife and Malinda, who
are mighty jealous of the Squire's wife and his
young daughter Hannah, to whom you were kind
of showing partiality this morning by having
her stand before the whole school pointing to that
machine over on the wall.

"'There's a mighty sight of difference, young
man, in the way of keeping school, as I've observed
in my day. When the trustees don't want any
highfaluting studies, it's best to stick to the old
way of doing things, and give them what they
want. It's only a hint I'm giving you, but take a
stranger's advice and send that patent machine off
to Boston on the first coach. It's plain teaching
the people want, and in the old way. If you get
down to retailing out your knowledge, instead of

wholesaling it; if you'll call the youngsters up one at a time and let them read the Scriptures themselves, and stand your ground for a year or two, maybe you'll come out all right in the end.'

"As I kept looking down at the old step, then up at the young master, I couldn't help feeling kindly toward him, as he stood with a big tear rolling down his cheek; but he never said a word. It was getting well nigh time I should be over at the farm; so I took him by the hand, and said: 'You seem like a young man of good home training, that has come over to these parts to earn an honest living in keeping school. It may be up-hill business to secure respectable quarters for one of your style of living. If you can't get accommodations over at the inn, perhaps I may be able to help you. So good-by.'

"And as I turned to leave him, he placed his hand upon my shoulder, and looking into my eyes, and then at the old stone house, spoke in language so full of hope and tender feeling, that for a moment I scarce knew where I stood. Then, as he drew from within his pocket a small Bible, he concluded, 'Though the way be dark and gloomy, yet within this little book shall I find consolation.'

"It was a sad parting, my friends; and as I passed through the gate to the old homestead, I saw the young master turn the key in the old door, and then pass onward by the old oak toward the village, as I supposed for the last time."

(312) HANNAH DIRECTS ROBERT TO THE INN.

CHAPTER XXIV.

SEEKING QUARTERS—THE GENERAL WASHINGTON
—"INSUBORDINATION"—A FRIEND IN NEED.

WHEN Robert Rayland left the school-house on that lovely autumn noon he met with no words of encouragement save those of Nicholas Comenius, but quietly and alone, in communion with his own inward thoughts, went in search of bed and board. Not knowing which way to go, as the boys and girls had preceded him in their anxiety to carry to their homes their impressions of the new teacher, he halted at the intersection of the only two streets in the village, when Hannah, the fair, bright-eyed girl to whom he had handed the pointer but a short while before, stepped forward and in a clear, gentle voice, said: "Is it the inn you are looking for? Come, and I will direct you." So, walking side by side, they soon reached the only tavern in the town, a dingy two-story structure, built away back in the early part of the seventeenth century. Giving his young guide a pleasant 'Thank you,' he stood for a moment beside the old sign-post, on which was suspended a large-sized image of George Washington and directly beneath, the word "Inn."

313

(314)

ROBERT AT THE GENERAL WASHINGTON.

For a moment he stood, interested in one of those
ponderous Conestoga teams, with white canvas
covers drawn tightly over the bows, laden with
grain, pork and poultry, and drawn by eight strong
horses, equipped with rows of bells, their constant
jingle keeping time with the horses' hoofs on the
solid compact road, as they passed through the village. Echoing through hill and dale he distinctly
heard the sounds of the antiquated stage-horn,
which in days gone by gave promise to mine host
of well-filled coffers. A moment later there came
rushing up to the old inn a stage coach, drawn by
a spanking team of four-in-hand, and bearing on
its sides the legend, "United States Mail." A few
minutes' halt, exchange of mails, and with a flourish on the horn the stage was again on its rapid
way, and Robert, opening the rickety old door,
found himself in the midst of a gaping crowd of
hangers-on. Some lounged on benches, others
leaned against the dingy bar, behind which stood
the form of the portly landlord, dealing out
draughts of that deadly poison, the very fumes of
which nearly took the breath of Robert Rayland,
and almost made him regret he had ever left his
quiet and happy New England home. The innkeeper being thus busily engaged in appeasing the
thirst of the "regulars," Robert was left to bide
his time, and how long he might have waited he
knew not, had not Hannah stepped through the
open door, and in a low sweet voice addressed the

host: "Mr. Bently, this is the new teacher, and mother says you should please give him the best room in the house." With this remark she disappeared as quietly as she had entered.

Adjusting his spectacles beneath his heavy brows, and surveying the new-comer from head to foot, Oscar exclaimed, in the vernacular so common to by-way inns of that day: "And so you are the young professor the new Superintendent sent to take the place of old Jimmy McCune? You look like a slick sort of a chap with no whiskers on your face, but I don't think you'll ever suit the trustees of this district. However, as the Squire's wife has given you a recommend, I guess we'll have to find a room somewhere that isn't occupied by the regulars. How long we'll keep you will depend; that is, the fellow that expects the best room in the house mustn't be too particular what he eats and drinks, and must be liberal down here at the bar; because with the high price of pork and other provisions nowadays, a landlord might as well shut up shop and go to teaching school himself, unless his boarders fall in and give him a lift at the bar. So the price of good living will depend; that is, we'll take you on trial for a week, and maybe the price will go up, and maybe it'll go down; and if the latter, it'll be because the spirits go down accordingly—understand, eh?"

Whether Robert Rayland took in the exact situation he gave no outward indication, either from his expression or his manner; but wheeling on his heel he sought the bright outer world, where he stood for a moment, his eye resting on the sign-board, from which the face of George Washington was reflected in the soft rays of the autumn sunshine. Long and intently he gazed on those noble features, now faded almost beyond recognition by the blasts of many a long winter. His reflections naturally carried him back to his boyhood days at school, and he vividly recalled the first book he had ever read. It was none other than the life and character of this same George Washington; and as he surmised that possibly the old tavern stood not far from a famous Revolutionary battle-field, he concluded that it was altogether possible that in years gone by, he too might have occupied the best room in the old inn. With these thoughts revolving through his mind, a new inspiration seemed to revive within him, and he reasoned within himself that what George Washington had withstood, Robert Rayland might also survive.

A moment later, however, he was awakened from his meditation by the sound of voices that seemed to reach his ear from an open window of a red sandstone dwelling on the opposite side of the road; a structure so antiquated and so unsightly as to bear the unmistakable imprint of the last century, and on the door of which was painted in large letters "Law Office of Squire Benton." It was also evident from the intonations which fell

upon his ear, that among the voices there was at
least one female striving for the ascendency in the
argument, whatever the subject might be.

Before he could realize the cause of this sudden
and unexpected commotion, his attention was attracted in quite an opposite direction. In the
vicinity of the village school a motley crowd had
gathered, for what purpose he could only surmise.

At this moment the portly form of the innkeeper appeared at the door, announcing that the
noon-day meal was now ready. Whatever appetite
Robert may have had when he left the school-
room was banished by the general appearance of
the surroundings; yet he had but one alternative—
either to seek quarters elsewhere, whither he knew
not, or fall into line with the regulars. Following
the proprietor through the bar-room, and thence
along a dingy passage with low ceiling, he reached
the dining-room, if this modern term may be applied to what was nothing more or less than a cold
and cheerless room extending the entire length of
the building. A pale glimmer came through the
four small windows, with their four-by-six lights.
If the blue-marked walls were uninviting, how
much more so was the table, with a gray oil-cloth
covering whose ragged edges indicated its age, and
along both sides of which extended slab benches,
without backs, over one of which it was necessary
for the teacher to step in order to crowd himself
between two of the regulars as best as he could.

For a moment Robert sat in bewilderment, surveying an immense bowl which stood in the centre of the table, and an old-fashioned tin dipper in the hand of the trusty landlord, who was at that moment engaged in dealing out a plentiful supply of what he termed pumpkin-hash, a dainty and familiar dish "not to be sneezed at" by the hangers-on in the only tavern in the town of Emden. A second supply was tendered Robert long before he had exhausted the first, and upon his refusal to hand up his dish a second time, the burly inn-keeper grew impatient, and looking him straight in the face said: "Young man, I see you aren't accustomed to good living. Now pumpkin-hash in September and October is like turkey at Christmas, or pork and beans in January. It's stimulating and good for the blood; in fact it beats snapper soup all hollow, and why shouldn't it? Look at the pumpkins out in the field, growing among the corn and turnips. Of course you're from the city, and aren't used to the flavor; but in time your taste will be cultivated so that you'll want it like the regulars, every day in the week and twice on Sunday. My good woman's been making and I've been serving this dish out to the boys for more than twenty years every September and October, and I tell you it knocks all your high-toned bills-of-fare higher than a kite. In fact I've had old Dr. Henry diagnose the whole pumpkin family, and he has certified in writing that the yellow pumpkin will cure more ailments than half the drugs in the materia medica. It will cure dyspepsia and laziness in any young fellow that hasn't got anything more to do than keep school and mind the children. It beats the bayberry bush at curing the toothache, and discounts Seneca rattlesnake oil at making the whiskers grow. So take my word, young man, and eat a plentiful supply of pumpkin-hash. Have another dish? Well, maybe by supper time you'll enjoy fried turnips and carrots, another dish that'll help digestion even better than the hash, if it hasn't got the flavor."

After Robert had succeeded in getting one foot and then the other over the old bench, had reached the bar-room, and was in the act of selecting his hat, which had become part of a heap of possibly more than a dozen, of every size, shape and color, proposing to seek relief in an adjoining field where the yellow pumpkins lay basking in the bright sunshine in all the glory of an October noon, he was met by the shrill voice of the inn-keeper, who had followed him into the bar-room:

"Want a little spirits to settle your dinner? Have got something nice and mild that's invigorating to the system. A little after dinner always makes the regulars feel cheerful, and whets up their appetites for something stronger later in the day. It's what always stimulated the mental faculties of the old masters, and set their minds to

working like a spinning wheel when in the school-
room. If you aren't prepared to plank down the
cash we'll start where Michael O'Farrel left off,
and you can settle up at the end of the month,
when the trustees pay off in hard cash. Here's
Michael's account-book still open for the last
month, unsettled, and maybe you'll obligate yourself to square up his account when you pay your
own. You see, the example set by the new teacher
at the start has a powerful effect on the whole
district. If he's polite and accommodating, and
stands treat now and then, it kind of keeps up the
reputation of the house ; but if he's stuck-up and
high-minded, and won't take good advice, he'll run
ashore before he's been in the district a month.

"So I tell you it's the General Washington inn
that's done more in shaping public opinion around
this neck of woods than all the school-houses in the
district. There's the Squire across the way, who's
been dealing out law for more than forty years, has
been taking his nips three times a day, unbeknown
to his woman, who's a mighty intelligent sort of a
housewife, but her head's twisted so badly on tem-
perance and manners, education and the like, that
you can hear them arguing for hours at a time.
Yes, the Squire would have been lying in the old
churchyard over there long ago, or gone clear
beside himself from worry, if he hadn't lost the
hearing of his right ear, or couldn't get something
comforting over here at the bar to ease up his mind

21

a little after the old lady's got him all tangled up.
May be you'd better take a seat, for the Squire'll
be along for a nip as soon as the argument ends
which has been going on for over an hour in the
office. Take my word for it, young stranger, and
don't get mixed up with the women-folks of this
town, or you might just as well pack up and take
the next stage for Boston. It's as plain as teaching
school that you can't play in with the Squire and
the old lady at the same time. You might as well
try to mix the water from the old well with the
straight stuff from the old still, and expect to get
it off on the Squire as the genuine article.''

The next moment there was a sudden creaking
of the door leading from the hall-way, and Squire
Benton, pale and nervous, stood at his accustomed
place at the bar. He made no effort to indicate
his mission, for before he had made it known the
keen instinct of Oscar Bently had placed before
him a little brown jug. After satisfying his thirst,
and before he could turn to depart, his eye, keen
and piercing, fell on the form of Robert Rayland.
Drawing a small slip of paper from his pocket he
handed it to Robert, saying, "Read this!" and
without trying to explain its contents withdrew.

For a moment Robert sat spellbound on the long
bench, holding the note unopened in his hand.
Then he rose and left the bar-room, without a
word, and walked away slowly in the direction of
the school-house. A few moments later he might

have been seen standing before the old building,
where he opened the Squire's note and read:

"School closed. Report at the office of Squire Benton at
seven to-morrow evening, to answer the charge of insubordination."

On the panel of the door he also read, "Closed
on account of insubordination of teacher."

Whatever effect the environments of the old inn
and its surroundings may have produced on Robert

Rayland during the one short hour when he took his first meal therein, he was no longer the half-hearted individual he had been the moment before, when almost determined in his own mind to yield to conditions which he was led to believe he could never control. From the very depths of his inner nature a self confidence seemed to arise, and he stood strong in the strength of his own character and manhood. Tearing the note into fragments, and rising equal to the occasion, he exclaimed: "Yes, stranger though I am, yet will I face not only the Squire and his emissaries, but a regiment of school officers, if necessary."

Pursuing his way in the opposite direction, where he might commune alone with nature and his own thoughts, he at last reached a cluster of cedars, beneath which he sat himself down to meditate over the course he was going to pursue in the trying ordeal that awaited him. How many thoughts of home and its associations throbbed through his mind! Was the compensation equal to the sacrifice he had made, in abandoning home and friends to accept a situation in a backwoods district, surrounded by deep-rooted prejudices which it might take years to eradicate? While these meditations were uppermost in his mind, he was startled by the sweet voice of Hannah Benton. He was hardly able to realize his position when a note was handed to him, the bearer hurriedly departing. A glance at the inscription satisfied him

that it was not the Squire's handwriting. It read
as follows:

" Mr. RAYLAND: You are a stranger in our village, but fear
not; you have one friend here who will see that justice is done
you. Stand firm. Your cause is a just one, and justice must
always prevail in the office of Squire Benton.

"MARY BENTON."

Retracing his steps, he was soon within the
shadow of the old inn, around which had congregated a number of idle loungers, intently engaged
in discussing the probable outcome of the trial.
Foremost among the motley gathering was a tall,
handsome-looking man of perhaps forty, of more
than the average intelligence. His remarks were
distinctly audible to Robert as he stood half-
concealed behind the old town pump, which had
done service for many a long year in quenching
the thirst of man and beast.

"I'll tell you now, men," said he, "that young
chap is going to come out of this scrimmage without losing a feather, because the Squire's wife is
on his side and against the old man. I know what
I'm saying, for I heard the fracas along about noon
over at the office, where the Squire was reading up
the law on insubordination. Before he had got
more than half through, the old lady took the big
book and pointed out the law to the Squire and
turned down the corner of the page, and that
set'led it There'll be no conviction in this case
unless Mrs. Benton gets another spell of the

rheumatism before the thing comes to trial; and I
don't think there is any danger in that direction,
for she's been flying around with Hannah and the
other girls all day, in better spirits than I've seen
her in twenty years. If they convict the young
professor they'll have to bounce the whole crowd,
for I heard the Squire say that all the other
teachers had been suspended for teaching the same
kind of pernicious doctrines."

This last expression satisfied Robert that, whatever the outcome might be, he would not stand
alone in the ordeal which awaited him.

CHAPTER XXV.

EMDEN FAIR WEEK—ORLANDO'S UNFULFILLED PROPHECY.

MANY indeed were the strange visions which disturbed the slumbers of Robert Rayland in his dismal attic during the first night's sojourn at the General Washington. However well fortified he may have been against the superstitious influences that surrounded the native inhabitants, the very appearance of the dingy stairway over which he directed his steps by the pale glimmer of a tallow dip, produced within him a feeling of loneliness. As the long hours wore on, the creaking of a door on rusty hinges, the rattling of a window sash, the gnawing of a chipmunk within the cornice of the weather-beaten roof, unconsciously acted upon his imagination. Forebodings of coming trouble with the crusty Oscar, grave apprehensions as to the result of the trial upon which his own position depended, the lurking opposition of Orlando Hoskins—all these combined to render the long night one of intense anxiety.

At the first hour of returning day, however, Robert's attention was directed toward the Market

ROBERT SEES EMDEN FAIR.

Square, which extended directly beyond the gable
of the historic hostelry. What strange combination of circumstances had so suddenly transformed
this staid old thoroughfare, in so short a time, into
a Babel of moving, active life? As far as the eye
could penetrate, every available foot of space
seemed to be occupied by a motley crowd of grunt-
ing, noisy animals, rickety carts, cackling fowls,
and nondescript horses. The Bedlam of sounds
which met his ear was equaled only by the hurry-
to and fro of men, women and children in their
efforts to arrange their products to the best possible
advantage. To his bewildered mind it seemed
that the entire rural community had during the
early morning hours deserted home and fireside,
accompanied by all their earthly possessions.
Even the pigs from the sty, the sheep from the
fold, the lazy curs from the kennel; mothers with
squalling babies in their arms, followed by sprawling youngsters at their heels—all had taken possession of the Square and its surroundings, but for
what purpose Robert was unable to determine.
Prompted by curiosity, and a desire to learn the
cause of this sudden upheaval, Robert dressed himself, and a few moments later stood face to face
with the erratic proprietor of the famous inn.

"Ah, ha, my young friend," said Oscar, greeting Robert with outstretched hand; "a pretty
early riser for a young schoolmaster! Take my
advice and keep retiring early and rising with the

lark, and you'll grow rich by the saving of tallow
dips alone. Up early preparing for the trial, eh?
Awfully sorry you've made such a break in your
first day's teaching, for I've kind of taken a liking
to your ways, even if they don't suit the trustees.
Keep an observing eye on the Squire's office across
the way, for there's something brewing unbeknown
to the Squire, but it's hard to reckon out whether
it's in your favor or against you. I noticed the
best horse in the stable's been missing since long
before daylight, and the best rider in the village is
astraddle of 'Captain Jim,' galloping away to the
Capital with a message from Hannah's mother.
It may be encouraging news to you, and it may be
the reverse; but keep a-hoping, young man. Have
a nip on the sly before the crowd comes pouring in
and the commotion begins?"

"Commotion?" repeated Robert, who was not
without serious misgivings lest the crowd had
already come to witness the trial, which was to
take place during the early evening.

"Why, young man, have you never attended a
country fair? Come now, and don't be pleading
your ignorance. Never hear of Emden Fair week?
Biggest thing on earth when it gets under full
blast, and known all over the land, from Canada to
the Gulf. Take my advice, young man, and get
to practicing on your muscle, for your fine clothes
and occupation will get you into a fracas with the
wild lads of Shaky Hollow before you've seen more

than half the sights. Keep your hand on your
wallet, and don't get to betting on the first horse
in sight. Yes, take an old man's advice and keep
an observing eye on the jugglers and fellows prowling around, the fakirs and light-fingered gentry,
and don't pick 'em up for hayseeds, or you'll be
short in your boarding account before the week's
half round. Fair week! why, bless my stars, it's
worth more to the General Washington than half-
a dozen years of camp-meeting, and discounts
circus and battalion days two to one. It's a great
school for educating the public, and gives the
young men on the farms more practical experience
than the masters could give them out of books in a
life-time. It's a wonderful help to the village, and
starts money flowing around the General Washington freer than air; for it's an old saying, that when
the landlord's prosperous and the potato crop's a
success, there's no danger of a famine.

"If my memory serves me right," continued
Oscar, as he cast an observing eye through the
window at a long line of conveyances passing
toward the Square, "there's been only one Fair
week in the history of the village that didn't
measure up in size and standing, and it came
mighty near bankrupting the whole town. It
wasn't the fault of the weather, nor the hard times
either; for the crops had been bountiful, and the
prices had gone up a peg or two in anticipation of
a skirmish between Mexico and Uncle Sam. No,

it was owing to what some call a Divine visitation, threatened by the Parson, to punish the wicked sinners of the town who had been neglecting their spiritual duties, and giving all their attention to worldly affairs."

"The Parson?" mildly interposed Robert, anxious to learn anything of interest concerning the aged minister, whom he had cause to fear. "Was the Parson running the Fair?"

"No, it wasn't his running it that brought on the trouble, but his bursting up the machine before it had gotten under full head of steam. Understand, it all came about in a miraculous sort of way, and many of the people haven't gotten over the scare, and aren't likely to till their dying day. It occurred in this way," said Oscar, with a motion of his short, stubby arm. "While the Parson was reckoning on a bright, crisp morning for the 'send off,' he accidentally struck the middle of Fair week for the appointed day, and kept the secret tied up in his bosom until he had gotten all the wicked old sinners planted, with all their earthly possessions, right over in front of the parsonage. It's an awful sad story I'm relating, young man, and to think of it starts the cold shivers running down my back faster than the blood passes through my veins; for it was a mighty narrow escape for old Oscar to make, and still be doing business at the old stand.

"You see, while the proprietor of the General

Washington was standing behind the bar, making
the young chaps feel kind o' merry, and while the
whole town was promenading around, taking a
hand in the races and betting their last dollar on
their favorite nag, the Parson stepped over into the
thickest of the crowd and began proclaiming at
the top of his voice: 'Gentlemen, I see you have
all been having a pretty lively time winning and
losing, but it's time you're turning your attention
to spiritual affairs. Better stop to consider what
preparations you've all been making for the Upward Journey; for the time has arrived, and the
hour is set for the Ascension, ten to-night, full
moon.'

"You seem to be smiling and making light of
my story; but if you had been old Oscar instead
of a stripling of a master, you'd have more practical experience and less of what they call theory in
your get-up. It was a sorrowful occasion, and the
announcement came so sudden that even those
who were enjoying the hospitality of the house
rushed out, one after the other, forgetting to square
up for the last round, which is still on the slate,
unsettled. But out on the race-track, among the
'professionals' who came from the city, there was
the liveliest kind of a commotion. In less than
five minutes by the sun-dial, every old sinner who
had been reaping in the cold cash from his next-
door neighbor got to paying it back with interest,
by way of easing up his conscience. Then the

fellows that were swearing the hardest got to praying the loudest.

"My young friend, have you ever seen a campmeeting broken up by a hornet's nest at the very moment the congregation was shouting and rejoicing the loudest? Well, before night came along there wasn't a sign left of the Fair, except a lot of provisions and a stray horse here and there. It was the worst stampede that ever befell the country since George Washington drove the Hessians out of the old fort beyond. It was easy enough getting out of town for some, who took to their heels, and over the fields and fences they went flying, expecting every moment to feel old Satan hanging to their coat-tails. But the worst scared chaps you ever laid your eyes on were the professionals, who came to teach the country boys how to make enough money in a week to keep them in easy circumstances for the balance of the year. Yes, it was the first experience of a religious turn that they'd ever had; and on they came rushing, one after the other, up to the door of the General Washington, looking as pale as death and inquiring for the departure of the first stage, which wasn't booked to arrive until the following morning."

"Converted to the Parson's new doctrine?" asked Robert.

"Well, some were and some weren't; but as the time set for the Upward Journey was approaching,

I felt it was a pretty sad predicament they'd gotten themselves into, away from their families and friends; so I took pity on them and said: 'As you look rather crestfallen and broken up, I shall be only too happy to make your last moments as easy as the circumstances will permit. If you need any spiritual advice, I'll send for the Parson, who's a mighty forgiving kind of a man under such trying circumstances. Or if you want to make your will, I'll send over for the Squire, who's got more than a hundred of those documents stored away in his iron chest for safe-keeping in case a stray relative should turn up here and there after the ceremonies.'

"Then I approached the leader, who was leaning against the bar for support, like this," continued Oscar, imitating the action, "for he looked as if he had been a sinner all his life, and said to him, 'Maybe, old man, your winnings are troubling your conscience more than is good for your health. You see, there's a disadvantage in carrying the precious metal and the cards around in your clothes, as the weight may interfere with the Upward Journey, and prevent your getting a seat in the front row beside the Parson and his family.' But he only shook his head in a sorrowful way. By this time a change seemed to be working in the young professionals, but the hardened old sinners, dressed up in their broadcloth and diamonds, kept swearing one minute and praying the next.

"For a time I couldn't understand what kept

the old wood stove boiling and steaming, for there
hadn't been a stick of hickory thrown in for more
than an hour. But I soon made a discovery. First
one pack of cards went in, and then another; and
after they'd gotten rid of the cards, thimbles and
the like, they all took their seats around the stove
and began confessing their sins one to another, for
parting company with the cards seemed to ease up
their feelings. After more than half an hour of
this confessional, one after another arose, and their
leader said : 'Old man, it's a mighty sad predicament we're in, and no way of getting out of the
town except going out with the old minister in a
way we're not accustomed to traveling; but we're
all reconciled to joining the procession.' It was a
curious sight to look into the faces of those men, I
can assure you.''

"And did the Squire take charge of the cash?''
inquired Robert.

"No, they said they'd take the chance of taking
it with them; and if it hadn't been for Amelia,
who had been keeping an eye on the strangers,
they'd have skipped out without settling up their
account with the General Washington.''

"And so,'' remarked Robert, "the proprietor
of the General Washington had also become reconciled to leaving all his earthly possessions behind?''

"Let me tell you, young man, an old soldier of
the war of 1812 has no fear. It's Oscar Bently
who has kept his eye on the old General out on the

sign-board—General Washington, first in war, first in peace, and first in the hearts of his countrymen."

" But how comes it you are still in evidence, dealing out the straight unadulterated spirits?" suggested Robert.

" Ah, ha, my inquisitive young friend," retorted Oscar, with a slight twitch of his shoulder; " it was all a mistake in the date of the old almanac."

The rumbling of heavy wheels, the tread of horses' hoofs, and a moment later there alighted from the old stage-coach a contingent of professionals who pressed their way into the inn, and whom Robert recognized as members of the class described in Oscar's story. So he left them to the tender mercies of their host.

A few hours later, Robert, in company with one of the other professors who had come to see the Fair, was strolling here and there amid the hurly-burly of excitement which everywhere held sway. In fact, it was his first object lesson in industrial economy, and presented to his young mind a new condition in rural life. And yet, while the external conditions surrounding the population of Emden were vastly different from those under which he had been trained, his education had been such as to adapt him to different phases of life. Physically, he possessed no outward indications of muscular strength ; but his gymnastic training had fitted him for any emergency that might arise, either within or without the school-room. And

22

while Robert was at all times diffident and reserved
in his demeanor, his high moral courage never
failed him, even under the most trying circumstances.

While engaged in pursuing the natural bent of
his mind, Robert was besieged on all sides by a
gaping crowd of rustics, who, having discovered
his identity, kept pressing around him. In the
distance he distinctly saw the tall, slender form of
Jeremiah Todd, a former master, surrounded by a
score or more of the populace, and beyond was the
aged Parson. As the crowd came rushing toward
him a shout rent the air, and for the first time he
realized the peril in which he had placed himself.

It was fighting and racing week for the young
bloods, who had been practising at barn-raisings,
corn-huskings and the like; and as they were in
for a tilt, a stranger always suited their purpose
better than one of their own set. Of course there
wasn't much danger of the young professor being
double-teamed, for it was fair play and honest dealing with a stranger in a scrimmage, as it was in a
trade or in bidding at a sale. If two bidders
claimed the same horse and a dispute arose, a
knock-down argument settled the ownership, while
the other boys formed a ring and kept hands off.
It was the worst of times for a teacher to be walking around "on his dignity," as most of the young
chaps had been schooling under masters who were
growing too old to keep up their end of the line;

and it only needed a word from any one of the old men to start the ball rolling, and that word was soon supplied, for it was noised around the public square that the young professor had said he "could lay out any lad in the town of Emden." There wasn't a word of truth in the report, of course; but it wasn't the truth they were seeking, so much as a chance to punish the new-comer for robbing old Jimmy of his calling.

"We'll send him a challenge in writing," said Paul Sanders, a six-footer, to a dozen others who had gathered around, "and we'll find out what kind of metal he's made of."

"And I'll second the motion," said young Jere Todd.

"I'll write the challenge and deliver it to the young stranger," spoke forth Pat McGinnis, who was known throughout Emden district as Reckless Pat.

Seeing this unruly mob pressing towards him, Robert's first impulse was to make an effort to reach the old inn, and thus extricate himself as best he could from his unpleasant surroundings; but as the words "Fear not, your cause is a just one," flashed through his mind, he turned, faced his pursuers, and with a look of determination in his eye, said: "Gentlemen, what does all this mean?"

"Read this," said Pat, as he thrust a small slip of paper into his hand.

"I see, gentlemen," said Robert, in his calm, dignified manner: "It is a challenge to Robert Rayland, the new teacher, to disgrace the position he holds by entering into a personal contest with the young men of the village without provocation."

"Yes, but it's one at a time and fair play," said Pat, who stood facing the professor.

"Well, gentlemen," retorted Robert, "I hope you'll excuse me, for I've never had a personal controversy with any one in my life; and until now, have never received a challenge of any kind."

"Come now, young man, no apologizing! Form a ring, boys, and we'll see what kind of metal the young schoolmaster's made of," said Paul Sanders.

"One moment, gentlemen," said Robert, as the crowd began to hustle him toward the centre of the ring; "who are the ringleaders in this disgraceful proceeding?"

A moment later there stood facing him Paul Sanders, the champion of Shaky Hollow; Jere Todd, a wayward son of Jeremiah the master, and Reckless Pat, as he was known and feared at every backwoods gathering—a trio of young pugilists, whose frequent encounters had made their names famous among the denizens of Shaky Hollow.

"Now, gentlemen, I regret exceedingly to be placed in this most disgraceful attitude; but as I have never shirked a duty, I shall not hesitate to defend my fair name and manhood. All I ask is fair play and one at a time."

As Robert stepped forward as fearless as though he were entering the old school-house, a shout rent the air, and by his side stood the rugged form of old Patrick McDeever, the discarded master of Shaky Hollow school, with the exclamation:

ROBERT DEFENDS HIMSELF.

"And by my faith, young mon, and it's fair play ye shall have, or Patrick McDeever's body will be lying cold on the ground before ye."

A moment later there came rushing from the

direction of the old hostelry a contingent of regulars, headed by old Oscar, whose purpose was to rescue Robert by main force and convey him out of harm's way.

"No, gentlemen," said Robert, as he motioned his rescuers aside (having divested himself of coat and hat): "We'll start with the ringleader."

The next instant Paul Sanders sprang before him, stripped to the waist, and with a plunge rushed at the young teacher with a well-directed blow, the effect of which the young man warded off with his left arm; and with a counter-stroke of his right fist on the side of Paul's neck, sent him sprawling headlong among the bystanders.

Before he could regain his feet, the young teacher called in a pleasant voice, "Next!" And as Reckless Pat made a bound forward, the young teacher kept warding off the blows one after the other in a playful way, without attempting to deliver a blow in return. This manoeuvering on the part of the young man seemed to exasperate the Irish lad; and as he made a desperate effort to clinch in on the young teacher, he was met by three terrific blows, following each other in quick succession, which landed him squarely on the broad of his back, where he lay until the young men stepped over and raised him to his feet.

Turning and surveying the crowd, Robert called out: "Come gentlemen, it's getting late; who's next?"

With these words a shout rent the air, and Paul Sanders, limping forward, held out his hand and said: "Young man, I want to ask your pardon, and I want to make a confession. I see there is no use in we un's standing up fighting against science. You don't seem to be more than half our weight, but you're a fighter on scientific principles, and there's no use in comparing muscle to science."

Then Robert, shaking the would-be champion by the hand, said: "Are you all satisfied, gentlemen; if so, we'll continue our sight-seeing without further delay."

It took but a little while for the news to spread to every part of the Fair grounds; and as the crowd began congratulating the young master he simply turned and said: "There's no occasion for congratulations, gentlemen. What I've done was simply the demand of stern duty, and reflects little honor upon my character or standing." And off he marched, as unconcernedly as if nothing unusual had occurred.

When the news reached the Parson, he shook his head and murmured to himself: "Yes, yes, this young man must be gotten rid of at the trial this very night, or Orlando Hoskins is a ruined minister of the gospel."

CHAPTER XXVI.

THE TEACHER ON TRIAL.—MOTHER BENTON IN-TERPOSES—INSUBORDINATION IN THE CITY—CHANGE OF QUARTERS—VILLAGE GOSSIP.

As the warm October sun disappeared behind the distant hills and the shades of twilight began to cast their shadows over Emden, here and there might have been noticed a horseman moving in the direction of Squire Benton's law office; and when the hour of seven arrived there sat in the large square room, with its low ceiling and three dismal windows, the six trustees, with the high-topped beavers they always wore on important occasions, the Squire and Robert Rayland; while around the outside, crowding the windows, half the villagers of Emden had gathered. After the Squire had succeeded in arranging side by side a number of legal authorities consisting of some half dozen shelf-worn law books, their appearance indicating that they had done service in Revolutionary times, he read the charges and produced the contract, signed by Robert Rayland some four months before.

Dressed in his stylish outfit and drawing his red

344

bandanna from his hat, he began by saying: "Mr. President and Gentlemen of the School Board of Emden district, for nigh unto forty years I have practiced law in this village, and in all my experience I have never had a case appealed to Court, for when I give my opinion that settles it; but gentlemen of the Board, here is a young man charged with trying to break down the school system, by sowing seeds of a new doctrine. He isn't following in the steps of Jimmy McCune, as he promised to do. Now I have looked up the law and meditated over it, and the verdict of the court is that insubordination means, according to Blackstone, disobedience to lawful authority. The school has been closed, and it is for you, the trustees, to say whether Robert Rayland is to continue the teaching of all kinds of new-fangled ideas, or to pack up his trunk and get out of town on the first stage. Gentlemen of the Board, you have been witnesses over in the old school, and as seeing is believing, it is for you to accept the law; and I now pronounce Robert Rayland guilty in manner and form as he stands indicted. Shall the young professor be dismissed, and the ever-faithful Jimmy McCune be elected to fill his place?"

A vote was taken, and as the Squire was about to declare Jimmy victorious, a woman of perhaps fifty years, neatly attired, stepped from a side door, and handing a heavily-sealed envelope, bearing the coat of arms of the State, to the Squire, said in a

MOTHER BENTON SETS ASIDE THE VERDICT.

(346)

clear voice: "I demand that you withhold action until the contents of this letter shall have been read."

Then the Squire, adjusting his glasses, read as follows:

"STATE OF PENNSYLVANIA, SS:

"Having learned that Robert Rayland and seven other teachers, holding valid certificates, issued in accordance with the school laws of the State by the regularly appointed County Superintendent, and regularly assigned to the schools of Emden district, are about to be dismissed for the conscientious performance of their duties, I hereby direct you, Thomas Benton, Esquire, to withdraw all legal proceedings, of whatever nature, and require the Board of Directors to abstain from all interference with their rights and duties within the school-room proper. Should the Directors persist in ignoring the contents of this, my official letter, the entire Board (along with yourself) will be summoned to the Court of Quarter Sessions to answer the charge of obstructing and violating the school laws of the Commonwealth.

(Signed) "—————— —————— .
"*Secretary of State.*"

If a thunderbolt from a clear sky had fallen in the office of Squire Benton, the consternation could not have been more complete. Big drops of perspiration trickled down his face, and the trustees sat in astounded silence. Before they could recover their equilibrium, the Squire's better half —for such in reality she was—stepped forward and said:

"Now, gentlemen, I hold myself entirely responsible for the message that has just been read.

I never met Robert Rayland face to face until he
appeared in this room, but I had seen him pass and
repass, and I made up my mind that justice should
be done him in Squire Benton's office.   It was I
who dispatched a messenger to the capital, stating
the facts to the head official of the schools of the
State, and you have the result before you.   If you
disobey the contents of that letter, you do so at
your peril.   Although not kin to you by birth, yet
for more than thirty years I have lived among the
people of Emden and its surroundings; and through
this young man the first ray of hope of a brighter
educational future has dawned upon our village.
For years Jimmy McCune and the other masters
have plodded along, like the wheel over at the old
mill, sifting the bran from the meal in the old-
fashioned way; just as for more than twenty years
the Squire here has been dressing up in his velvet
suit, that was doing service in George Washington's time.   Is it not time to be throwing off the
old and putting on the new?   Remember that God
said 'Let there be light,' and there was light; and
so I say to you, the trustees of Emden district, re-
instate Robert Rayland in the little stone house
and you'll live to see the day when the light of the
new system will dispel the clouds of superstition
which now darken your firesides, and when your
boys and girls shall rise up and call you blessed."

While these words, falling on the minds and
hearts of that assembly like the gentle rain of

heaven, were only met with looks of silent contempt, coming as they did from a woman, who had
no voice in the management of the schools, and
while they were mostly like seeds sown upon stony
ground, yet a grain unseen may have taken root
here and there. After a moment's hurried consultation, in which the Squire advised strict obedience
to constitutional authority, it was unanimously
though reluctantly decided that Robert Rayland
and the other teachers should re-enter upon the
discharge of their duties the following morning,
without any further interference.

This determination on the part of the authorities
of Emden district was far from being the result of
conviction. If anything, the feeling of opposition
became more intensified. It would have been as
easy to put new wine into old bottles as to place
new heads on these old shoulders; and as long as
the old heads remained, little fermentation in the
direction of progress could be expected.

Owing to the rapid transition from old conditions and methods to the modern, few teachers of
the present day can fully understand why a teacher
of fifty years ago should have been arraigned before a school board and censured for the introduction of so simple a piece of school-room
apparatus as a school chart. But in fact the chart,
the blackboard, outline maps and globe, met with
the same determined opposition that has at all
times marked the progress of all other mechanical

inventions. "We did not have such apparatus," said an old teacher; "and if we had it would have been of no value, as we would not have known how to use it." Indeed, the weary task of the individual pupil was a daily struggle for weeks and even months through the twenty-six arbitrary characters of the alphabet, with scarcely an effort on the part of the master to use them in their proper relation to words and sentences, until the letters in their regular order had been indelibly impressed upon the memory. From this primitive and arbitrary method there seemed to be no appeal on the part of the learner. Committing the alphabet to memory was one of the first requisites of the old master, and then with rapid strides he never rested until the unfortunate pupil was pushed into the New Testament, where he was allowed to flounder along among the difficult Biblical terms for the remainder of his school days, often in dense ignorance of their true meaning.

Robert Rayland's trial and ultimate acquittal of what was termed "pernicious teaching," not only attracted the attention of leading educators and the outside public, but at the same time gave him a standing in the educational field which he could in no other way have attained in so short a time. So forcibly impressed were the members of the Board of perhaps the largest inland city in the Union at that early day, with the wonderful results attained by Robert Rayland in the little

stone house, that a committee was appointed to
confer with him, and report on the expediency of
introducing his scheme into the primary grades of
that city. An extract from the report of the
committee which here follows is remarkable, inasmuch as it conclusively proves that while the old
masters may have been learned in the higher
branches and conscientious in the discharge of
their duties as they understood them, they were in
many instances wofully lacking in the methods
upon which the early training of the young so
much depended. The report of the committee
reads verbatim as follows:

"Having witnessed the practical operation of
this scheme, we believe it important to introduce
it into those departments of the school concerned
in the instruction of the youngest and least advanced scholars. Cards are suspended, upon which
the alphabet or syllables of two or more letters are
printed in large type, so that the attention of the
whole class may be easily directed to every part of
the card. There is a two-fold advantage in this
method. The principal is greatly relieved, so
much so that one of the teachers who has never
taught before is able with great ease to instruct in
the alphabet and in the spelling of words of one or
two syllables, more than eighty young pupils,
divided into four or five classes. The classes are
severally called up, and the teacher pointing with
a rod to the card, the scholars all pronounce the

letter or spell the syllable or word. The alphabet is commenced at the beginning, and the rod passes from letter to letter to the last; then the course is reversed, after which the teacher points to the letters promiscuously, and the whole class pronounces them. Lastly the rod is placed in the hands of some one or other of the class, who is required to point out such letters as the teacher may name. Mr. Rayland declares that he can teach a dozen or twenty at once by this method sooner and better than by the ordinary plan, and prefers a number of pupils to a single one."

For a time, but from an entirely different cause, the same opposition which had confronted Robert Rayland in the village school of Emden appeared in a more intensified form in the schools of the city in question. Among its excellent corps of teachers were a number of old masters; prominent among them stood Thomas Yarrell, as typical a specimen of "ye olden time" master as it was possible for the old system to produce. Now Thomas was more noted for his obstinacy and his ability to swing the ferule than for his learning and power to develop the mental faculties of his pupils. While he had taught continuously for nearly two generations, he never succeeded in getting beyond the work of the primary grade, although many of his pupils had attained an age which at the present day would have brought them up to the graduating class of the high school. However, Thomas reasoned on the principle that as there was no possible opening for a boy in those days until he had reached his majority, running up and down the alphabet in the primary school at least kept him out of mischief, if nothing more. It was Thomas Yarrell's mission in life to teach the alphabet in the old way; and if by the end of the term he had succeeded in planting the letters from A to Z in a boy's memory, in regular order, he always rested easy in the consciousness that he had performed his duty to the school authorities.

Consequently, when "sets of charts, cards and syllables, and words of spelling," were ordered "for all the primary grades," and when Thomas was directed to reform his methods in accordance with these modern appliances, the seat of war was temporarily transferred from the district of Emden to the city. As the professional dignity of Thomas was in a measure compromised, he rebelled, and politely refused to obey the instructions of the Board, or to depart one iota from the old established method. He was in consequence summoned to appear before the school authorities to answer the charge of insubordination. This he considered an insult to his standing as a teacher, and as a consequence handed in his resignation and abandoned the profession forever.

Here, within a brief period, were two charges of insubordination; one by the trustees of Emden district against Robert Rayland for the introduc-

23

tion of a chart inimical to the best interests of the schools of a backwoods district; the other by a progressive city Board against Thomas Yarrell, for neglecting and refusing to adapt his teaching to this same school-room appliance. But while it is evident to the mind of every modern educator, that Robert Rayland at that early period was imbued with the progressive spirit far in advance of the age in which he labored, and that Thomas Yarrell was among the very last apologists for a system destined to pass into oblivion, it is also evident, in the light of recent events, that the vast multiplicity of charts of every variety and style has in many directions overstepped the line of usefulness. What were in the early days of the system considered essentially necessary as aids to the young and inexperienced educator, have in recent years been thrust by wholesale upon School Boards throughout the length and breadth of the land.

For a time things moved along in the even tenor of their way with Robert Rayland, except in his relations with the grasping innkeeper. He soon discovered, however, that in Robert he had a boarder of more than the average tact and ability, who showed no disposition whatever to affiliate with the regulars. At the close of the first month Robert concluded that some definite arrangement should be determined on with the innkeeper, so, approaching him at the bar, he said: "I have been boarding with you one month, Mr. Bently, and if you will tell me how much I am indebted to you I will settle my account.''

"Well now, young man," replied the innkeeper, "you remember what I said when I gave you the best room in the house—that with the high price of pork and other provisions, the price of board would depend; that is, if the spirits go down freely then the price of board goes down accordingly, but if there is no downward movement in the straight unadulterated stuff, then the price goes up—understand, eh? How much do you get a month for keeping school three or four hours a day? Yes, I understand. Well, we'll split your salary in two, for that's what the landlord always expects from the regulars. Fifty per cent. discount makes easy figuring, and don't require any calculating by that new arithmetic book, which has been the cause of more disturbance around this neck o' woods than was ever seen since the day old Orlando Hoskins started out on his white horse to direct the final ending of the world."

Within a week from the night that Robert Rayland settled that bill with the innkeeper, it was well known that he was quietly dreaming the dreams of the pure in heart on a downy bed in the best room in the house across the way, at the pleasant home of Mrs. Benton. In fact, he had hardly succeeded in arranging his scanty wardrobe before the news had reached every nook and corner of the old town. Every mother with eligible

daughters was on the tip-toe of excitement in her
anxiety to carry the news to her next neighbor.
Of course, "it was all a deep-laid plot on the part
of the Squire's wife to entrap the young teacher
into marrying Hannah;" and the gossips not only
could no longer see anything to admire in his personal appearance, but began to shower gratuitous
pity on the young man.

"I'll tell you," said Mrs. Orlando Hoskins, the
minister's wife, in conversation with a half dozen
members of her own church circle: "There's no
use disguising the plain truth—I'm disappointed.
If Orlando's five children had been boys, they'd
have been following along in the old gentleman's
footsteps, preaching the gospel; but as they happen
to be girls, the responsibility of marrying them off
rests where troubles have always rested since the
beginning of the world, on the shoulders of the
women-folks. Perhaps I've been keeping Malinda
a little too strict, since the young teacher got to
boarding over at the old inn. In my eyes, a
tavern's no place for a young man who's had good
religious training to hang around. Now, while
the girls and I were arguing and trying to persuade
Orlando to forgive the new teacher for meddling
with the Scriptures over in the school, and while
we were all planning how to get him into a respectable minister's family, where he could have married my eldest daughter, Malinda, and assisted the
parson in his parish duties, the Squire's wife got

to coaxing the young professor to leave the landlord and go a-boarding with her. It may be all
right for one of her kind, that's never been converted and that's got no fellow-feeling for even the
landlord's wife, who has been struggling along
trying to make both ends meet by boarding the
new teacher. I'll venture my standing in the old
parish that Hannah will never marry Robert Rayland without the Squire's consent, and he'll never
give in to his daughter's marrying a down-east
New England Yankee school teacher, with no
other recommendation than a certificate from the
new Superintendent. No, Mrs. Orlando Hoskins
hasn't been a pastor's wife these many years, and
she hasn't been a-working among the congregation
and giving good advice to all the young people in
the chapel, to be deceived by a young foreigner
who's got no social standing in this community."

The next moment the door opened, and Malinda,
pale and nervous, stood amid the group of sympathizing friends who had gathered at the parsonage
of Mrs. Hoskins to offer words of sympathy to the
pastor's wife in regard to the action of the misguided young teacher. Before the seemingly
broken-hearted girl could give expression to her
thoughts, her very countenance told the story of
her chagrin and disappointment. From the moment
her eyes had fallen upon the manly form of Robert
Rayland, when he entered the village of Emden
for the first time, there was a preconcerted move-

ment on the part of the whole Hoskins family, ultimately to capture the young and handsome professor. Robert was not unconscious of these manifestations on the part of Malinda, for every time he passed or repassed the Parson's residence, Malinda was either to be seen peeping through the window or gazing from some half-hidden nook.

But Robert, unlike most young men in their first sojourn in a distant village, pressed forward and onward in the line of his professional duties, turning neither to the right nor to the left. If occasionally he happened to meet old Jimmy or any of the other old masters, he never passed them by without a kindly greeting. He would often sit for hours under the old oak with his predecessor Jimmy, whose health seemed to be fast failing, listening to his many anecdotes of strange experiences, and in return would portray to him, in glowing colors, the strides made in educational development in his Bay State home, and at the same time endeavor to picture to him the educational blessings in store for the people of Emden, which in God's own time were sure to come.

While neither the trustees nor the Squire again visited Robert in the little school-house during the term, he would sit for hours in the back office, making deep impressions where the Squire's wife had failed, and slowly but surely weaving a network of influences around the old man, which were destined to bear fruit as time moved on.

CHAPTER XXVII.

NATURE STUDY—NICHOLAS APPOINTED SUPERIN-TENDENT—DEATH OF HIS PREDECESSOR.

As the long months of winter passed slowly by, the school at Emden grew in size and strengthened with each recurring day. While the clouds at times hung heavy without, the genial sunshine reflected from the many young and loving hearts, and mellowed by the tender words of Robert, made the old school at Emden a place of beauty and a joy forever. At the close of the second month, those who had been accustomed to view its bleak and cheerless walls would almost have failed to recognize the complete transformation that had taken place within. A fresh coat of white-wash, a picture here and there, a new broom brought into daily use, a cedar bucket with a bright tin dipper—all these gave the old house an appearance that blended harmoniously with the clean hands and faces, and the neat and tidy appearance of the little workers within. And the faithful Hannah, far above the average in natural endowments, never missed a day. What books of the higher order the Squire refused to purchase,

Robert supplied from his own private funds; for he was not slow in discovering that the intellect and character of the mother were duplicated in the daughter, now only a modest, unassuming school-girl.

And so, while doubt and uncertainty pervaded the atmosphere without, there was one consoling thought that nerved the young teacher to even greater efforts in the school. Were not the boys and girls at the close of each day's session eager to join him in his periodical strolls to the neighboring hills and valleys surrounding beautiful Emden, there to commune with nature in all its varied forms? And how many ever returned empty-handed, or without a store of useful knowledge which the meadows and hills were ever sure to provide? Not a plant escaped the notice of the girls, nor a rare stone or mineral the attention of the boys. Could not any one of a dozen girls give the botanical names to all the plants that grew in the meadow down by the ivy-covered parsonage? And the boys—were they not equally prepared to distinguish the various rock formations and the different varieties of soil, and the effect produced by proper fertilizing?

And there was Jack McCabe's son Richard, a sprightly lad of thirteen, who had never before seen a history in his life—nor his father the old repairman either, for that matter. And didn't Dick keep the whole family sitting around the

table after the evening meal while he kept explaining to his brothers and sisters all about the
battle of the Brandywine, which had taken place
so many years before, on Pennsylvania soil? And
wouldn't he lay out the whole plan of the battle,
using the cups and saucers and the knives and
forks to illustrate the position of the troops, with
the Hessians and red-coats on the one side and
Washington and his famishing army on the other,
and Valley Forge in the centre?

Had not Sim, the old charcoal-burner's son, a
lad of ten, made the startling revelation before
he'd finished his second month, of the number and
cost per thousand of every shingle on the old
wagon-shed? And could he not compute at the
same time the number of cord-feet in every stick
of timber that grew on Farmer Cooper's strip of
woodland?

Ah, but what a commotion over at the corner
grocery, when the miller's son, Ben, got to figuring out the weight and cost per bushel of all the
grain stored in the granary over in the old stone
mill!

Wouldn't it make all the older heads turn to
hear young Ike, the only son of old Oscar, the
proprietor of the General Washington, skirmish
around among the Presidential administrations,
repeating the name of every President in regular
order from Washington down to old Zachary
Taylor?

And so for weeks after the opening of the village school its unrecognized influence was imperceptibly permeating every rural household. Whence came this new inspiration among the boys and girls of the village school?—this sudden quickening of the mind to enter untrodden paths, in search of hidden treasures, never before dreamed of even by those of maturer years? Was it but the reflex of the recent public examination, the first ever held in the village of Emden, that had so imperceptibly stirred the youthful mind from the sluggishness of indifference to an awakening like that produced by the rays of the morning sun? Or was it the influence of the young teacher, unconsciously operating like the gentle dew from heaven upon young and old alike?

With Robert Rayland the absence of a multiplicity of text-books was a blessing in disguise. Thoroughly trained in the art of imparting knowledge, and with a mind ever ready to draw upon nature's vast storehouse, Robert never lost courage or faith in the power of the means at his command eventually to liberate the good people of Emden district from the thraldom of ignorance and superstition.

But after all, was there anything in the school at Emden of such vastly superior merit and importance that its counterpart is not readily to be found in hundreds of district schools at the present day? Does not every locality have as many Robert Ray-

lands and as many intelligent girls in all respects
the equals of Hannah, yet of whom mention is
seldom if ever made? Why then delineate the
character and personal qualities of this or that individual, whose counterpart may be seen in every
village and hamlet in the land?

Is the name of the engineer, we ask, who pulled
the throttle that sent the first locomotive through
the land at the rate of but ten miles an hour, or
that of the electrician who touched the key which
sent the first message on its way from Baltimore to
Washington, some fifty years ago, to sink into
oblivion because modern engineering has since en-
circled the earth with the steel rail and the electric
cable? Are those who stood as beacon lights in
our educational system's darkest night—who stood
face to face against public opinion, oppression and
ignorance, when to battle for the cause of popular
education was considered by many almost a crime
—are those heroes of other days to receive no recognition from the enlightened public of the latter days
of this nineteenth century? Does the cosy little
brick school-house, with its interior adornments,
decorations and hygienic appliances, bear no relation to the dilapidated time-worn structure yet
standing—so near and yet so far? Is the professional teacher of the present generation so completely absorbed in the multiplicity of his labors, or
in the importance of his mission, as to justify him
in ignoring or looking with contempt on a Robert

Rayland, or even a Jimmy McCune? If such there be in the teacher's profession, let them in their quiet moments revert to the past, there to gather new inspiration from that noble army of martyrs who built upon a foundation as enduring as the human race. If the embodiment of their ideal lies far above and beyond the types herein represented, let them dwell for a time amid the environments which cluster around the life of Dr. Arnold or of Pestalozzi.

As the busy bee goes forth in the early morning, only to return when the shades of twilight appear, laden with the very essence of the honeysuckle, so should the young teacher, when he has gleaned from the text-book all that is worth gathering, go forth and mingle with nature and the great masters who have given to the world all that is worth knowing.

At last spring-time, the most delightful season of the year, and especially so to the young and enthusiastic teacher, came in all its glory. The aged oak, the monarch of the forest, once more put forth its clustering foliage; beside the old familiar pathway the wild briar and the coarse weeds began to push their way upward in search of light and heat; and even the old school-house seemed to have thrown off its robes of mourning for old Jimmy and assume a more cheerful aspect, when an event occurred of vast significance to the educational interests of Blackwell county.

There on the long bench were seated a number of strange-looking faces—young and middle-aged, with and without experience, headed by Robert Rayland—for the appointed day for the second examination had arrived. The old slab bench, however, upon which had been seated the eight old masters the year previous, was vacant. Even the Squire and the aged Parson were strangely absent, as well as the six trustees. There were none of Emden's constituency to be seen loitering around the venerable oak without, nor within the old house, on that memorable occasion, to remind one of the excitement that pervaded the very atmosphere of the year previous.

A carriage drove up to the door of the old house, and the young Superintendent alighted and entered the school for the second time. There was no elasticity in his step; his every movement indicated the severe physical and mental strain under which he was laboring.

"Calling me aside at the close of the examination," said Nicholas, whose own words we give now that his own personality enters so largely into the story so graphically related, "he turned and with the deepest feeling of emotion said: 'Nicholas Comenius, allow me, in the name of the Governor of the State, to present you with this certificate of appointment as Superintendent of the schools of Blackwell county for my unexpired term of office. The responsible duties, the tax on physical endurance, the severe mental strain, coupled with declining health, have forced me to resign a position which I have endeavored to fill to the best of my ability for one short year. May you, Nicholas,'

NICHOLAS COMMISSIONED SUPERINTENDENT.

continued he, 'under the guidance of an over-ruling Providence, so direct the educational move-ment that the various discordant elements may be brought into that perfect union which the very

name of Comenius should aid you to harmonize
and adjust.' The announcement of the young
Superintendent's resignation, with that of my appointment, coming so suddenly and unexpectedly,
produced a profound impression upon the members
of the class," added Nicholas, with his eye upon
the ruins of the village school, as his voice fell
almost to a whisper.

"As the young Superintendent passed through
the doorway, now relieved as he was from all official responsibility, his step seemed to quicken;
but I noticed deep and furrowed lines on his
manly face. He uttered not a word until he stood
beneath the shade of the great oak, when he beckoned me to his side and said, in a low tone:

"'I want to talk with you, my friend! Tell
me where to find Jim and Tim, and the other old
masters. I missed them in the class to-day, as I
have missed so many others in my second tour
over Blackwell county. Tell me where they are,
and why they have not been here. After leaving
the examination a year ago, I began to think of
the old men, and I said to myself, No, it wasn't
right to treat them in that way; if I live till
another year I'll give them a chance, for they're
old and cannot live long anyway. These thoughts
have followed me,' said he, with quivering lips,
'through the long days, on many a lonely pilgrim-
age, when bereft of that good-will and support
without which life is a failure. So tell me where

to find the old school-masters, and why they are
absent?'

"'The masters,' said I, 'let me see. Yes, come
with me, and we'll go and see Jim and Tim.'

RETURNED FROM THE CHURCH-YARD.

"So arm in arm we walked over through the
gate by the church, and thence to the graves of
Jim and Tim. As we stood I noticed a big tear
like a rain-drop fall on the grave of Jimmy. Retracing our steps to the oak, he said:

" 'Now where are the other old men, and especially my old friend Patrick, so full of genuine Irish wit and humor?'

"So I gave him their history as well as I could recall—that three of them were in the county work-house, and the others tramping the county round among old friends, kind and true. But I couldn't help saying a kind word for my old friend Jimmy McCune, for I saw it struck a responsive chord in his very inmost nature : and so of Jimmy we talked as we sat till the sun disappeared behind the distant hills. I told him all about Jimmy, for I loved him; he was so generous and forgiving, without an enemy in the world. I told him how he had met the boys some thirty odd years before under this same oak, as he came to take charge of the little village school; how we had all gathered there one beautiful October morning, wondering what kind of a master we should all have to meet, when a tall, handsome young man stepped into our midst, and said, in a mild tone, 'Good morning, boys.' Before we could reply, he added :

" 'Boys, did you ever hear of William Penn, and how he made the famous treaty with the wild men of the forest under an old elm tree—the only treaty never sworn to and never broken? And now,' he continued, 'while I am not William Penn, but plain Jimmy McCune, the master appointed to teach this village school, I want to form a treaty with all the boys and girls under this oak.'

24

"So beneath its sheltering branches, which weren't as old then as now, nor Jimmy McCune nor Nicholas either, we all gathered around the new master, took each other by the hand, and there pledged ourselves, each to the other and all to the master, that as long as the old tree stood we should be friends. Then young Jimmy led the way, and with hats off we followed him over the threshold into the little stone school-house. Once within, silently we stood with eyes intent on the master, when the same soft voice continued :

"'Now, my dear boys and girls, we'll try to find a nice high seat for the large ones, and the little ones will sit beside the master, and help him keep school.'

"First month there wasn't a half-dozen books in the whole school, but the master said he didn't care for books, as long as he could give the boys and girls all he had stored up in his head; that a master, like a doctor, didn't amount to much if he had all the time to be looking into the books to find out what kind of medicine the patient needed. No, there weren't many books that I can recall; we didn't need them, for the master had a mind chock-full of knowledge, and it flowed through the school as the waters of the spring spread over the meadow, giving new life daily to each tender blade.

"There was no forgetting what the master taught, for there was experience back of his teaching, and what Jimmy McCune drove into a boy's head stuck like beeswax. He never hitched them all together in a string as now-a-days, to make the smart young chap pull the whole team along, or to be held back by the weight of the drones; but he called them up one at a time, and in this way measured up each and every boy in the school, and knew where they all stood. And those old copy-books, the head-lines of which the master wrote with his own hand! What golden thoughts and words of wisdom those lines contained! Yes, they've been the old man's guiding star all through life, and will remain with him to the end. Nothing like them to be found in the printed copy-books of these days."

"Was the treaty made under the old oak ever broken?" we asked.

"Broken? No; but once a year, as long as Jimmy stayed, it was renewed. And since Jimmy has passed over the river of Time, the boys and girls, every first of October morning, carry wreaths of autumn leaves and flowers from the garden-plot around the old house, and place them over Jim and Tim's graves. There wasn't one of Jimmy's first boys joined the last procession except myself, for the others had long since passed away. Yes, yes, old friends and associations may pass away, but the recollections of Jimmy McCune, as I knew him when I was a lad, struggling with adversity over in the old homestead, can never be effaced. Well do I remember the old leather-bound

family Bible as it rested on the mantel of the huge
stone fireplace, around which during many a cold
winter evening we huddled ourselves together as a
protection against the bleak winds, waiting in joyous anticipation for the master; for it was a family
custom never to retire until Jimmy McCune had
read a chapter from the old Bible, and pronounced
a 'God bless you' on the heads of old and young.

"It was evident," continued Nicholas, "that
the Superintendent was much affected. The very
mention of the old family Bible had struck a responsive chord. Reaching into a side pocket he
drew forth a small leather-bound volume, and
placing it in my hand said:

"'Here too is a memento of the past, worn and
old, but as dear to my heart as are the recollections of her who gave it to me. It may not
have the wear and tear of time which marked the
one out of which Jimmy McCune read the blessed
words of truth; but it contains those same golden
thoughts and wholesome lessons. This small
volume was given me many years ago.'

"As he passed it into my hands he paused a
moment, and then said, 'Read the inscription,'
and as I looked, I saw the words: 'Holy Bible:
From mother to son.'

"The old Bible, thought I—the little book
which the Superintendent prized so highly was
the same blessed word of truth that old Jimmy so
often read to us when I was a boy!

"'Then I reasoned within myself:—Jimmy Mc-Cune has passed away with the days gone by, but now the essence and strength of his personality are embodied and centered in the new teacher; the one symbolizing the dead past, the other the living present, each the representative type of his respective day and epoch. Evidently, thought I, the world moves, and he who fails to keep in touch with the future must fall by the wayside, broken and disheartened. The old oak, a silent observer of the scene below, has lived for the past; but does it not now also live for the present? Then why should I be of less worth to the world than the aged oak?

"So grasping the Superintendent by the hand, I then and there mentally resolved that as long as God gave me health and strength to battle for the cause of popular education, and against bigotry and fanaticism, there at all times would I stand.

"As he turned to leave me, his very countenance indicated an intense desire to give expression to some thought that for a moment failed to find utterance. 'I noticed in the class to-day,' said he at last, 'that of all of Emden's corps of last year's teachers, only one has had the moral fortitude to hold his ground and to continue the good fight to the end.'

"'True, my friend,' I replied, 'those young men were never cut out for pioneers. It is their province in life, like the rolling stone that gathers

no moss, to shift from one position to another
until they shall have reached the acme of their
ambition, far beyond the profession of teaching.'

"'But what has prevailed upon young Robert
Rayland so nobly to stand his ground?' said he, as
he leaned against the aged oak.

"'Robert Rayland?' I replied. 'We may not,
my friend, live to see the day, but the time will
surely come when this young student will make
his mark in the world; and when that day comes,
the name of Mary Benton will be the one to which
he will love to do honor and reverence. While your
pathway, my worthy friend, has been strewn with
thorns and thistles in your lonely pilgrimages over
Blackwell county, remember that you will ever
have the satisfaction of feeling that in Robert Rayland there lies the inspiration of an unseen power,
which as years roll by will penetrate every school
district of this great county.'

"Alas, my young friends," said Nicholas;
"only a few weeks later, the sad news reached the
village of the passing away of the young Superintendent, in a distant city. Overcome by the
weight of a multiplicity of duties far beyond his
strength, this noble young educator had fallen a
martyr to the cause he so much loved."

And here the narrator paused for a moment to
master the emotion caused by the recollection of
his departed friend.

CHAPTER XXVIII.

ANOTHER DATE FOR ASCENSION—ORLANDO MIS-
TAKEN AGAIN—OSCAR BENTLY IN THE
OLD FORT.

"IT was late that evening when we reached the
old homestead," resumed Nicholas; "I say we, for
I was not alone, but was joined by young Robert
and a number of those who were anxious for appointment. Later on, one after another of Jimmy's
friends began to drop in on us. Even the trustees
and the Squire came around, as they said, to relieve
their minds a little, unconscious of the presence
of young Robert Rayland, and rather to avoid if
possible the fearful consequences which that night
was to bring to their sorely-stricken souls. For a
time, as we sat on the porch, not a word was
spoken, each being intent on watching the full
moon as it came into view from over a neighboring
hill. There was something intensely significant
about the appearance of the heavens on that eventful evening; for in accordance with the prophecy
of Parson Hoskins, proclaimed months before, the
final dissolution of the world was to take place at
that full moon.

THE ASCENSION DOES NOT TAKE PLACE.

"No noisy demonstration occurred on the village streets of Emden—only the loud shrill voice of Orlando Hoskins, as he galloped to and fro through the town, proclaiming his 'midnight cry' and carrying consternation at times to many hearts. From farm-house and cabin came the rushing multitude to the call of his trumpet's piercing sounds; rich and poor, old and young—some rejoicing, others praying for deliverance and bemoaning their sad condition—all impressed with the fearful consequences so soon to overtake them.

"In the pale glimmer of the full moon, in the distance, came the portly form of old Oscar Bently, his eyes now on the Parson and again directed toward an old abandoned fort, which in Revolutionary times had protected the village of Emden and its surroundings from the Hessian soldiers. He chose the latter; and securely entrenched within the portals of this ancient citadel, Oscar bade defiance to old Time with his sharpened scythe, and laid himself down to sleep—'perchance to dream.' On housetops and elsewhere in Shaky Hollow sat many a fair maiden, dressed in white robes, hoping yet fearing the moment when she should bid adieu to earthly scenes and join the celestial throng.

"Anon, while piercing shrieks, mingled with the sweet strains of a hymn, floated on the air from a distant corner of the village, there rested on the little assembly on the porch of the old stone man-

sion no darkling gloom, but the hope of a glorious
future, built upon a foundation against which the
efforts of the Rev. Orlando Hoskins could not prevail. Our guest took occasion to refer to the
superstition so often exploded; and as the words
of wisdom fell from his lips and those of Robert
Rayland, who but a short time before had been
shunned, and persecuted, and unjustly censured, a
new revelation seemed to dawn upon the vision
of the older men beside them. It was not, however, until the old grandfather's clock, which had
stood for more than five generations in a secluded
corner of the old homestead, had struck forth the
hour of midnight, that Robert was called upon to
solemnize the parting moments by reading a chapter from the old family Bible.

"After a night of intense agony and long-suffer-
ing, disappointment and remorse, came the bright
rays of the genial morning sunshine. Over hill
and dale, with here and there a notable exception,
peace and quietude reigned supreme over Emden
and the shades of Shaky Hollow. Along secluded
hedges and lonely by-ways a draggled rescuing-
party might have been seen, in search of those supposed to have strayed along the outlying ridges.
Many a frail form lingered for months thereafter on
a bed of sickness from nervous prostration, in some
lonely out-of-the-way cabin. Even the old Parson,
at times kindly disposed and generous to a fault,
but now broken-hearted and dejected, kept himself

hidden for weeks thereafter within the narrow limits of the ivy-covered parsonage. Malinda and her mother, on the other hand, were not so easily disconcerted. It was their mission to re-establish confidence among the weak, the doubting and hesitating; to hold the old almanac accountable for any and all errors or mistakes in date, and at the same time arrange for another ascension later on.

"When Oscar Bently, the old innkeeper of the General Washington, awoke from his peaceful slumbers at the first dawn of returning day, he called loudly for his dear Amelia. Receiving no reply except the faint echo of his own voice, as it reverberated from the walls of the old fortress, he flew into a violent rage, declaring he was another Robinson Crusoe, bereft of friends and destined to roam amid the wilds of Shaky Hollow a lonely wanderer to the end of his days. With one desperate effort he removed the barricades from the numerous port-holes, into each of which he proceeded to thrust his head and stubby shoulders, to ascertain the lay of the land and compute the value of his landed possessions. With heavy heart he took in the surrounding landscape far and near, but no living form of man or beast met his eye, nor sound his ear. 'Hum!' he unconsciously murmured, in his endeavor to extricate himself from the confines of his narrow enclosure; 'yes, yes, all have been taken except old Oscar himself! Poor Amelia, for more than forty years the old man's stand-by over at the General Washington, gone too, with the Parson and the Squire, the regulars and all the wicked sinners of the village.'

"With big tears trickling down his troubled face, Oscar's eye at last fell upon the form of Robert, who was at that early hour pursuing his usual morning's walk, prior to his departure for his summer's vacation. Rushing to the door he exclaimed, 'Ah, ha, my good young friend, back to stay for good?—or only on furlough? Old Father Time has mowed them all down with one swing of his scythe! Only old Oscar Bently and the young master left, to run the school and the General Washington. What will the honest innkeeper do without Amelia and the regulars, and the master without the little codgers?'

"'Wait a moment, old man,' said Robert; 'what's the matter with you, anyway? Too much schnapps last night? Better hurry home, for the old lady's about sending out a contingent of regulars as a searching party.'

"'What! Amelia alive, and the regulars on duty? How about the Squire and the Parson?'

"'Oh, they're all safe.'

"'The Parson safe, eh? Well, I'd never have believed it! Yes, yes,' muttered Oscar, 'more trouble ahead for the old innkeeper. Now, young man, take a pointer from the old man. Say nothing to Amelia. I'll slip in at the back door and make the old gal believe Oscar's been sound asleep

in the spare room.' With this monologue the
jolly innkeeper went puffing along with all the
speed his short limbs could command, to explain
as best he could his night's absence from the General Washington.

OSCAR RETURNS TO AMELIA.

"When old Oscar reached the famous inn over
which he had for so many years held sway, with
disheveled hair, his trousers tucked into his long
untanned boots, and his old felt hat, which had

done service as a bolster the night before, jammed
down over both ears, he was met by the full complement of regulars and his ever-faithful wife. It
seemed useless to make any attempt at defence.
As he was pressed on all sides for some explanation of his miraculous escape from the old fortress,
he at once proceeded with a satisfactory explanation. As no one in all the country round had ever
had the moral courage to enter this Revolutionary
landmark, owing to certain mysterious powers
supposed to emanate therefrom, he who had the
moral courage to enter this old fort, even in the
light of day, was considered a hero. Trances and
visions had their origin in this old relic of other
days. In fact, all the mysterious local tales and
midnight superstitions started in the old fortress
of Emden.

"'Oh,' said Oscar, 'twas a frightful night for
any other than one with a strong arm and a brave
heart. Yes, it was Oscar Bently that was spirited
away by the old Parson from the bosom of his
family in the wee hours of the night, and forced
into the old dungeon. But what a night of
troubled spirit and vexation of mind! All night
long there was a little army of Hessian soldiers,
with presented arms and fixed bayonets, standing
right before the old man, as he lay on the hard
stone floor. Open my eyes, and away they would
bob behind the barricades; close them, and there
they would stand, with their little gray bobtail

coats, pointed hats, and boots turned up at the toes like sleigh-runners. And the Captain—I mustn't forget him, for he was a dandy sort of a little chap! Well, these little devils kept coming closer and closer, and so at last I got my blood up, raised myself and said: "Don't you know the war's been fought and won many years ago? Who am I? Well, I'm none other than the proprietor of the General Washington." "The General Washington?" replied the Captain! 'Yes, that same old General that met and defeated the whole Hessian army at the battle of Trenton." And with the mention of George Washington they all scampered away as fast as their legs could carry them. Now, when daylight came, there were the door and the port-holes barricaded as tight as they'd been the night before. How did the little imps get in? That's the question that bothers old Oscar.'

"And with this explanation Oscar, Amelia, and the whole contingent of regulars, made their way into the bar-room, thankful for the mysterious escape of the host of the General Washington."

CHAPTER XXIX.

ROBERT RETURNS TO EMDEN—WHY DID HE COME
BACK?—THE PARSON'S WIFE—WELCOMED
BY THE DIRECTORS.

AND so the intervening months of spring and
summer, with meadows teeming with wild flowers
and broad acres with golden grain, passed slowly
by, to be followed by early autumn with orchards
laden with luscious fruit and broad fields bedecked
here and there with shocks of corn, interspersed
with the yellow pumpkin so necessary to the health
of the regulars and the success of the thrifty innkeeper, who stood ever ready with an eye single to
the main chance. Was it anticipation of Robert
Rayland or Jimmy McCune, that caused the faces
of the half hundred boys and girls standing around
the stone school on that lovely October morning to
be wreathed in smiles? Of that throng of happy
hearts, how many were longing for the return of
old Jimmy, the master, to whom but a short year
before they were so devotedly attached? No mathematical demonstration is necessary to solve the
problem of child-nature. To gravitate from the
old to the new—from old associations, habits and

384

customs, to new conditions, as exemplified in the personality and character of Robert Rayland—was as natural to the young mind as are reveries and meditations on the past to the aged grandfather.

The transition from the old master into the young teacher was the result of a condition in which the child was the essential factor; for as the young and tender plant reaches forth in the direction of the sun's rays for light and warmth, so the tender hearts of the young obey the same law of nature and gravitate one toward another. For the old master there may have been a certain reverential respect, as there is and at all times should be for old age; but for Robert Rayland's return there was a longing desire, akin to that filial love which a boy experiences during his first visit from home; and so when the sound of the stage-horn, announcing the arrival of the coach which was to bring the teacher back to the village of Emden, fell upon the ears of both old and young, no cold indifference manifested itself among the throng which had gathered before the old inn.

A glance at the stone mansion of Squire Benton was sufficient to satisfy the most incredulous that a generous hospitality awaited him who had come the year previous as an entire stranger. The happy smile on Hannah's face was a sufficient guarantee that an event of no secondary importance was about to occur, and that Robert had been triumphantly re-elected for another term. But why dwell longer on the personality of the plain, uncultured country school-girl of Emden? the impatient reader will remark, as he pictures her in the light of a fickle-minded girl in love with the new teacher. To accept such a hastily-pronounced verdict would be doing an injustice to her sterling qualities. That Hannah had tasted of the cup whose waters had been drawn from the very fountain-head of intellectual development, that having so imbibed she was prone to discover their hidden source, was not for a moment to be doubted; but to infer that she was moved by an impulse such as the world might impute, would be doing injustice to her ingenuous nature.

With Robert Rayland, however, it may have been in a measure the opposite; but to attribute to him other than the highest motives consistent with an exemplary character, would be doing an equal injustice. His conception of the true intent and meaning of the new law was far in advance of the average educator of his day. He was in no sense of the word, then or in after years, an extremist in the methods to be sought in the development of the young mind, but held to the psychological fact and pedagogical maxim, that the expansion of the mind should go hand in hand with that of the heart and soul. He sought to cultivate the observing faculties rather than to overtax the memory—a monstrous error into which the system has since drifted. To proceed from the known to the unknown, and

never to let the letter stand for the spirit, was also
an axiom, which to his mind needed no demonstration. Practical, and yet with a perfectly clear
comprehension of theory, Robert built upon a
foundation which his keen foresight at all times
assured him was what the common people of every
class so much required in the daily walks of life.
And while he believed implicitly in higher educational facilities, he nevertheless devoted his best
energies to the equipment of the average school, in
which the masses were to be educated. Whether
Robert Rayland misconceived the true intent of the
framers of the law, which was to found a system
on the broad principle that the ninety-five per
cent. of all those attending school should have the
same advantages in the grammar school, the school
of the people, that are now held out exclusively to
the five per cent. attending high school, is a question on which there should be but one opinion.

But why should Robert, with his natural ability
and past experience, again risk his reputation by
taking charge of Emden school for the second
time? Had he not already been vindicated, and
were not other more available and desirable positions awaiting him in other more favorable locali-
ties? His first venture may have been largely an
experiment, in which so many young men love to
risk their chances in life in the hope of gaining
experience as well as notoriety; but why should he
return to a district with but few of the refining in-

fluences under which he had lived from early infancy? Was it the love he bore the old school,
with its bleak and cheerless surroundings, that
induced him to make the sacrifice—for such in
reality it was—or was he moved by some mysterious force over which he had no control? And
yet, aside from these minor considerations, what
object other than Hannah, the one and only one in
the whole school who had befriended him in the
hour of his deepest anguish and humiliation, could
have exerted over him a more lasting and to her a
more unconscious influence in shaping his future
course in life?

Yes, it was the influence of the modest school-
girl that had followed him to his far-off New England home, and had made the elegant and commodious school building of his native town sink into
insignificance in comparison with the little stone
house with Hannah as a pupil. Even the flowers
which grew wild around the old house seemed far
brighter and sweeter than the cultivated geraniums
that grew, under the fostering care of the gardener,
around the new structure. The stately elm, in-
digenous to every New England village and hamlet, and beneath which he had received his first
lesson from the lips of his sainted mother, appeared
to have lost its symmetry and majestic bearing in
comparison with the rugged old oak under which
Jimmy McCune had formed his famous treaty of
peace, some forty-odd years before.

Four long months had now passed since Robert was the guest of Comenius, on that lovely moonlight evening of early spring. The intervening days were in the fullest sense of the word vacation days—a season of recreation unknown to the old masters; for how many weeks or even days had old Jimmy for study or rest? From the schoolroom to the drudgery of the farm, and back again to "teach the young idea how to shoot" was the yearly rotation of the old pedagogue. Yet it was not simply a preference on the part of the master, it was a demand on the part of public opinion; for he who paraded himself as a learned professor, however well he could sustain the character, found little favor among the people. And so may it not be said that vacation days, in so far as they relate to the teacher's calling, are a modern innovation, co-incident with the incoming of the new system?

As young Robert alighted from the coach at the door of Squire Benton's law office, even the now good-natured innkeeper, his helpmate, and a goodly number of the regulars, pressed their way forward to wish him a happy return and a "God bless you." At the other end of the village, however, around the Parson's mansion, there was nothing but cold indifference manifested.

"I never in my life could understand," said the Parson's wife, "why all this fuss should be made over a common school teacher who hasn't been out of town for more than a month or two. It's ten to

one he's been away down East making love to some
Yankee girl. I've been telling Malinda that there's
better fish in the sea than have ever been caught;
but the poor girl keeps fretting over her disappointment more than is good for her health, which
has been failing wofully of late. But there's one
consolation—yes, one consoling thought; and that
is Orlando's prediction, and he has never yet made
a 'predict' that wouldn't have come to pass to the
minute, had the reckoning of the old almanac been
correct. Now Orlando says that before the teacher
can marry Hannah Benton, the world is going to
collapse and knock the wedding ceremonies all
into smithereens. Only last week the Parson sold
the best cow in the stable to provide Malinda with
a suitable outfit for the next Ascension. Guess
when the professor gets a glimpse of her white
robes as she goes soaring upwards among the
planets, he'll be after relenting, and will want to
call her back. See, it's been all arranged to send
her off a day or so before the day fixed for the
final dissolution. Now Malinda has been trying
to persuade Orlando to invite the new teacher
around when the send-off occurs; for we're all
kind o' persuaded to give him one more chance to
marry the poor girl while there's time. But it's
awfully mortifying to think that after all the
preaching on the day of judgment that Orlando
has been doing for more than a score of years, the
new teacher should be stirring up the congrega-

tion and telling them that Orlando's doctrine is all
a humbug. There's the Squire and the trustees,
for example. Who'd ever have thought that their
heads could be twisted around against the Scriptures, and in favor of the new system? But their
wicked souls will have to wallow along on this
unregenerated and sinful planet, while Orlando
and his family are sitting in the front pews of the
New Jerusalem. I tell you, my friend, it's the
Parson's wife that's been walking the straight and
narrow path, and that's bringing her four daughters
up in the way they should go. If Malinda is destined to meet with disappointment down here,
she'll receive her reward in the sweet bye and bye,
where the weary cease from trouble and the wicked
never rest."

At this moment, the Parson's eye was attracted
to the opposite side of the road, and rushing into
the room, he exclaimed: "Malinda, Malinda!"
and the next moment every eye was turned in the
direction of the old stone house.

"How perfectly handsome he is!" ejaculated one.

"How gracefully he walks in his new broadcloth Boston outfit!" exclaimed another.

"Yes, he's Malinda's size exactly, and his dark
hair is just the opposite of hers; and it's two oppo-
sites that always make the best matches," said the
Parson's next-door neighbor's wife.

But while this spirited conversation was going
on in the Parson's house, there was a sudden com-

motion; for Malinda had fallen in a swoon, and had to be carried into an adjoining room.

"I have forgotten," resumed the reminiscent Nicholas, "a good many things that are new and some that are old, but I shall never forget the reception the Squire and the trustees gave the professor when he reached the old house. The very next Sunday after Robert and the Superintendent had exploded the notion that the world was coming to an end, the Squire got religion, but it was a new faith that didn't require any of the Parson's wings. In fact it suited the Squire better than the doctrine preached by the Parson; for he said he wasn't ready to give up his practice at the bar anyway, and wanted a little more time in his old days to help along the modern improvements. For the regenerated Squire became one of the foremost advocates of the new school system, and the personal friend of every young teacher, as he had been of every old master. Some say this change of heart was brought about by the young professor, while others incline to the opinion that it was the work of Hannah and her mother, who've been working wonders for good among the women folks of this town. But whatever the source of the change, it was genuine and permanent. Yes, the Squire's conversion was felt all over the district, and it almost paralyzed the old innkeeper of the General Washington; for he didn't pay him any more visits, but kept at home, reading the Scriptures."

And so when young Robert Rayland, happy in the realization of duty performed and conscious of the reward which must sooner or later crown every noble effort, stepped within the little stone house on the morning of the first day of his second term, there was neither faltering of step nor doubt of mind as to the complete transformation public opinion had undergone during his temporary absence from the Emden district.

Was this sudden revolution effected by the personal work of one individual, and that a teacher of a rural school, of no consequence to the great army of educators which the system has since produced? Is a victory achieved even in a backwoods district, under trials and difficulties almost insurmountable, of less value to the educational world than one gained in any other vocation of life?

Dear teacher, has it ever been your fortune or misfortune to be ushered into a district school, with apparently the highest prospects, only to appreciate the lamentable fact later on, that while you were seemingly the choice of the entire School Board, some less qualified applicant held a petition signed by every patron in the district? In no way personally responsible yourself for the unhappy conflict between directors and patrons, was it your misfortune to fall by the wayside, disheartened and discouraged? Or have you the proud satisfaction of looking back to those early trials and difficulties in which your own force of character and

perseverance carried you safely through to the
end? And do you recall your triumphant return
to the same school the year following, and how
you were met at the very threshold with open
arms by those who had been most active oppon-
ents? These little episodes in the early experience
of the average teacher are often among the most
sacred and cherished of a long and eventful life.
Happy indeed, then, must have been Robert Rayland in the realization of his fondest hopes and ex-
pectations, as he looked upon faces wrinkled with
age, yet mellowed by that mysterious influence
which only one strong individuality can unconsciously produce upon an entire community.

"If memory serves me right again," remarked
Nicholas, "not even General Lafayette, in his triumphal march through the village, met with a
more hearty welcome than that which now awaited
the new teacher; for it had all been arranged to
give him a handsome send-off. There on the long
bench sat five of the six trustees and the Squire in
their Sunday outfits; for I tell you there was no
discounting the old men of that early day when
they got their heads set in a certain direction. Of
course, they couldn't change their natures in a day,
any more than they could their love for old Jimmy;
yet when they got well started under a full head of
steam they gave the new system such a send-off,
and it's been moving along ever since at such a
rapid rate, that the only wonder is, with the load it

has had to carry, that it hasn't jumped the track
long ago. For a long time the system kept moving
along pretty close to the safety line ; but the older
it gets the heavier the load becomes. As soon as
one of those modern educators gets hold of a new
scheme, he manages to get it off on the teachers at
conventions, and they in turn unload it on to the
little codgers much in the same way as they receive
it. It's quantity without regard to quality that's
undermining the mental faculties of the rising
generation. But as it's all in the line of our
modern high-pressure system, that controls every
other department of life, there would seem to be no
other way than for the multitude to move along
with those who've got their hands on the lever,
and take their chance with the young men in
charge of the machine."

CHAPTER XXX.

PRESIDENT LUKINS IN FULL DRESS—HE ALARMS
OSCAR BENTLY—EBENEZER'S SPEECH TO
ROBERT.

It was Ebenezer Lukins, the President of the
Board, who on account of his standing in the community and recent conversion was chosen to make
the presentation speech to the young teacher.
Well, no sooner had he been appointed to officiate
than he began to look wise and hustle around for a
new outfit, suitable to the occasion; for he wasn't
to be outdone, even in his old days, by any of the
young chaps. Of course, as he couldn't borrow a
suit, he decided to fall back on his wedding costume, which, although a little off in color and
style, and never worn since the day he married
Nancy over in the parsonage more than fifty years
before, he considered as in all respects most appropriate for the position he was to occupy. But
Ebenezer never realized until the morning of the
entertainment that while he had nearly doubled in
size and weight, the old swallow-tailed coat and
broadcloth breeches had if anything grown smaller
both in width and length. However, after a hard

396

tussle, Nancy and the girls managed to get the old gentleman well inside the ancient costume, and seating him astride the saddle-bags of old Nan, his favorite mare, started him off, happy in the reflection that Ebenezer Lukins, for so many years President of the Board of Emden school district under the old system, was now also to reap fresh honors under the new. But if Nancy was proud of the honors which awaited her husband, she was at the same time overcome with a feeling of sadness as her eyes followed him through the long lane which led from the farm-house to the main roadway.

"Fifty years is a long time," thought Nancy, as her mind reverted to the old associations of her girlhood days, to the parsonage and the old Parson. Then, quietly and alone she stole over and into a silent room, set apart for the quaint oddities of other days, unlocked and raised the lid of a leather-covered chest, and drew forth her own wedding garments. A moment later the antiquated mirror had reflected back her own image—but oh, how changed! There, true enough, were the gorgeous silks and satins, and the bright-colored bonnet; but all these contrasted so oddly with her present form and appearance, that she muttered, with a shake of the head :

"Yes, yes, they were gay and handsome in their day, as were Nancy and Ebenezer ; but who would ever catch a woman of my years parading through the town all tucked up in such an array of finery, for no other purpose than to please the young master? And what would Orlando Hoskins, the minister, say to see old Nancy Lukins strutting in among the young folks and the new teacher, when she should be at home preparing for the final send-off, and the ending of all earthly pleasures? Verily, the new system has completely turned the head of Ebenezer, and driven him from the straight and narrow path of his spiritual duties, to seek a new salvation, as proclaimed by that apostle of the new educational system.''

And with these inward meditations, Nancy replaced the semi-celestial robes, silks and satins, within the sacred precincts of the old leather-bound chest, to find consolation among her many household duties.

Quietly and alone Ebenezer wended his way toward the little stone house, repeating to himself the little speech which he had committed to memory, unconscious of the sad reflections which had crossed the mind of Nancy in that silent room, since he had bidden her a brief good-bye a few moments before. Nothing of importance occurred to disturb his peaceful reveries until he reached the old hostelry. At this moment his strange attire, rendered doubly impressive by the peculiar style and shape of his high-crowned head-gear, began to attract attention; for by each alternating motion of the old nag, his cranium had been forced upwards into the crown of the old-style beaver.

Whether it was the peculiar effect a stranger always produced on the nerves of the score or more of lazy, half-starved curs that were part and parcel of the dilapidated surroundings, or the unsightly appearance of Ebenezer in particular, now unrecognizable even by his most intimate friends, as he came joggling along on the back of the old nag, has never been definitely ascertained. That the Bedlam of sounds at once awoke old Oscar from his nap, as he sat in the sunlight surrounded by a contingent of regulars, was apparent even to the unsophisticated mind of Ebenezer, who was unable to discover what relation, if any, he bore to the great army of tramps that had infested the country for years.

"What strange specimen of humanity has suddenly found his way into the very heart of Emden?" thought Oscar, as he began to recover consciousness with a start. Was this a second edition of Rip Van Winkle, returning to his long-lost home after an absence of twenty years?

"I declare by the shades of Shaky Hollow," spoke a tall, slender, middle-aged hanger-on, rising from his lounging posture, "that it's none other than one of the advance guard of the old prophet William Miller, or else that long-looked-for personage himself."

The idea that the fatal hour of reckoning had at last come at once took possession of the bewildered mind of the now thoroughly frightened innkeeper, as he beheld the strange and grotesque figure preparing to dismount at his very door. Rushing into the bar-room with all the haste he could command, he summoned his devoted wife to his side and tremblingly exclaimed, with big tears trickling down his cheeks:

"Amelia, my good, faithful Amelia, we're ruined, we're ruined. Send for the Squire, for I must make my will. Square up the accounts with the regulars, and make a liberal discount for cash payment. It's all up at last with the honest old innkeeper of the General Washington, who has never done a mean act in his life, if I do say it myself. Get your Sunday clothes ready, Amelia, for the old prophet has come in person to proclaim the end of terrestrial things. Oh, if the old man could only be spared for a week longer, I'd clear the bar, empty out the wine and spirits, start a prayer-meeting among the regulars, and get myself measured for a new suit, that would give me a respectable standing among the church-going people when we all go soaring off together among the planets! But it's too late—too late for repentance now!"

At this important juncture a bright idea struck Amelia, who replied: "Bring him in, Oscar, and maybe you can buy him off with a little of the best schnapps in the cellar, or get him to postpone the exercises until the old man can get himself worked up to the starting point."

But while the landlord was still trembling in

every nerve, the door suddenly opened, and in stepped Ebenezer, followed by the throng of idlers who had by this time discovered the true character and purpose of the old gentleman's mission. Cringingly the terrified landlord approached the stranger and said :

" In the name of my good wife and family, have mercy on the old man and give him a few days longer to prepare himself; and don't take him off with this old outfit, which, while it may be all right for the General Washington, isn't at all suited for the Upward Journey."

Beckoning the old lady, Ebenezer approached the bar, and after succeeding by a desperate effort in removing his head-gear, said: "A little schnapps, and hurry it along; for Ebenezer Lukins is down for the presentation speech over at the old school, and he must be moving."

Hearing the familiar voice of Ebenezer, Oscar, bounding to his feet, exclaimed : " Amelia, Amelia, run down into the cellar and bring my friend Ebenezer a little of the straight unadulterated spirits, that's never been tapped ; and call in the regulars to join with old Oscar, now himself again." Then, taking Ebenezer aside, he related in most graphic language the trance through which he positively declared he had passed ; the strange hallucinations that had flashed upon his mind while the queer spell was on.

But however inclined the disingenuous proprietor

26

of the General Washington may have been to de-
ceive, as well as conciliate Ebenezer, he was in a
manner irresponsible; for the wily intrigues of the
Hoskins family had completely encompassed him
with a net-work of their own false doctrines.
Even men of stronger mental and physical endowments than Oscar were at times so thoroughly
imbued with the idea that the end of all things
mortal was destined to come in the near future,
that every stranger was looked upon with awe and
suspicion, as a messenger direct from the Prophet
himself. And so for many years, after all these
evil prognostications had failed to materialize,
many of the earlier superstitions were so well
grounded into the very nature of the people of
Emden, that it required all the great force of
character of Robert Rayland to make possible any
new departure in the direction of a healthy moral
and intellectual development among them.

If Ebenezer's mind, up to the time he reached
the old inn, had been peaceful and tranquil, it was
no longer in that condition. Was there anything
in his general appearance so changed or grotesque
as to mislead the old landlord into mistaking his
real identity? or had Oscar's mind suddenly given
way under the fanatical strain which had so often
tested the strength of his own mental faculties?
These reflections seemed to be uppermost in Ebenezer's mind as he jogged along, the observed of
all observers, with here and there a motley crowd

of idlers, who stood content with simply a glance
at his stylish outfit. He had not proceeded far
when he was intercepted by an advance committee,
who assured him that without his august presence
the entertainment was doomed to ignominious
failure. This assurance of renewed confidence on
the part of the committee caused him to redouble
his speed, and a moment later he stood like a
second Daniel Webster beneath the old oak, his
mind concentrated on the momentous topic which
was to engross his attention and that of those who
had been so anxiously awaiting his appearance.
Entering the old house with that firm and elastic
step which is always an indication of self-reliance
and assurance, and surveying the audience with the
dignity which age and gorgeous costume always
add to those who are entrusted with the discharge
of some official duty, Ebenezer allowed himself to
be escorted to the only vacant seat at the head of
the column, thus filling out the complement of
exalted literary personages, comprising the highest
culture, the most comprehensive learning and the
broadest statesmanship of Emden's inhabitants.

Owing to the delay at the General Washington,
the exercises were well under way when the President of the Board arrived, so that in the delivery
of his remarks the charge of plagiarism could at
least not in truth be made against him. At the
opportune moment, Ebenezer was conducted by
that noble personage, the Squire, to the centre of

the platform, where he stood for a moment sorely
perplexed at the formidable array of eyes, which
seemed to take in at one glance the glitter of his
superb adornments, bedecked here and there by
rows of large brass buttons, appropriated for the
occasion from an old Revolutionary uniform and
polished by the strong arm and nimble fingers of
the faithful Nancy.

While all had noticed the change in Ebenezer's
appearance, how many understood the bent of his
mind, or could fathom the depth of his understanding? Were his remarks to be in keeping with his
outward demeanor—a mere rambling harrangue
intended to draw attention to himself? Or was
he, notwithstanding his peculiar and unbecoming
costume, deeply impressed with the solemnity of
the occasion? There could be no mistaking the
responsibility which he felt rested upon him, as he
gave expression to the very first sentence:

"My good friends and neighbors, for more than
sixty years I have lived among the people of Emden; and yet sixty years is but a span with the
great chronicler of time. More than eighteen
hundred years ago there was decreed to the world
by the greatest of all teachers, a new dispensation;
and while the words of that Blessed Man of old
have since fallen upon many cold and unwilling
ears, the light of His countenance has been the
guiding star under whose divine inspiration our
ancestors, driven as they were from their homes

beyond the sea, at last found an asylum in the New World. Here in a dense wilderness they settled more than one hundred and fifty years ago, and built and dedicated to the cause of religious freedom, as they understood it, this old sandstone structure. Within the sacred walls of this temple of learning our forefathers and their children—whose hearts were quickened by a new hope of a more glorious future—received their first lessons from the pages of the old Bible. From its pages our young minds were fed and nourished, and from its teachings we grew from youth into old age; accepting at all times the very letter of the text, rather than its living spirit.

"From the time the Great Teacher first preached the Sermon from the Mount, proclaiming salvation to all mankind, the world has had its false prophets; and with our forefathers, driven as they were from the fatherland, came these same false teachers, who have ever since resided among the plain and simple-hearted people, binding their hearts and consciences with fetters of iron. If in our quiet moments a bright ray of hope sparkled forth from the pages of His holy word and found an abiding place within our hearts, it was as quickly dispelled by those whose mission among us was to expound the faith in accordance with their own narrow and imperfect interpretations. But after more than five generations of bigotry, superstition and false teaching, the dark clouds of religious fanaticism have at last been dispersed, and to-day the bright and glorious sunlight of heaven shines upon this little assembly. The dark and gloomy forebodings which hung over me when I left the old farm no longer enshroud my vision. The little episode which occurred at the General Washington has taught me that the teachings of Orlando Hoskins and his class are a part of this same false doctrine, which has held in subjection the hearts of our people these many years."

Then turning to Robert Rayland, he said: "One short year ago you came among the conservative people of this village an entire stranger. Then the hand of every man was against you. We believed in the old system, in the old minister, and in the master, Jimmy McCune, while you represented a new system and a new faith. While the old men who are here to-day to welcome you back to their homes and firesides can look deeper into a ploughed furrow, you, a much younger man, can look far deeper into the mysteries of the human mind. While the old Parson has held strictly to the letter of the text, and while he has cast a gloom over many a fireside by keeping his little flock in constant dread of a calamity which was sure to befall them sooner or later, you, in your plain interpretation of the Scriptures, have filled the hearts of our boys and girls with a deep love not only for their parents, but for the new teacher as well. There is, however, one other who shall

ever be held in grateful remembrance by the
people of Emden. I refer to Nicholas Comenius;
for it was he who in the darkest hours dispelled the
clouds which hung over our minds, on that beautiful moonlight evening as we sat on the porch over
at yonder farm. The words which fell from the
lips of that great and worthy disciple of the new
system will ever have an abiding place within our
hearts.

"And now, Robert Rayland, allow me, on behalf of the school authorities of Emden district,
and in the name of Nicholas Comenius, who has
been the defender of this old house these many
years, to present to you this old leather-bound
Bible, which for so many years has rested upon the
ancient mantle-piece. May the inspired words it
contains be a blessing to your little flock, and a
comfort and solace even to the end of time."

At the close of Ebenezer's speech, which was in
such marked contrast with his outward appearance,
a death-like silence prevailed throughout the
assembled multitude, to be finally broken by Robert Rayland, who in a few modest, appreciative
remarks, accepted the gift, and thanked the President for the honor conferred. Opening the old
Bible, he read a chapter in his clear, forcible manner, and after a benediction the exercises termi-
nated, with the new system firmly anchored among
the conservative people of Emden district.

CHAPTER XXXI.

PARTING WITH HANNAH—THE HOLIDAY SEASON
—ORLANDO BRINGS MALINDA TO SCHOOL.—
ROBERT DENOUNCES HIS DOCTRINES.

FOR a time, and until the holiday season approached, Robert Rayland was monarch of all he surveyed in the sandstone school at Emden. There came a time however when a parting became necessary; not that Robert had resigned, nor that the school authorities had closed the school "on account of the insubordination of the teacher." On the other hand, Robert was too deeply interested in his little flock to think of leaving them, and the directors were too loyal to the young teacher to question his authority. What event then had cast a shadow over the little school of Emden? Why, at the closing hour preceding the Christmas holiday season, should Robert Rayland look sad, and the boys and girls leave the old school with heavy hearts? It was simply because of the announcement by Hannah that her schooldays in Emden were ended, and that she would depart on the first day of the New Year, to complete her education in a distant Normal school.

168

If the closing hours at the village school were sad, the intervening days, following Christmas and ending with New Year's day, more than compensated for them in social pleasure. The present Christmas-tide was one for which the good people of Emden had abundant cause to be thankful; for a kindlier feeling and a more generous hospitality prevailed among them than ever before. Had there not been a divided public school sentiment only a short year before, and had not the doctrine of Millerism been making deep inroads among the pious people of the village? Now, however, with an exception here and there, peace and perfect good-will prevailed, making this Christmas a holiday season in which young and old joined in hallowed enjoyment of the olden-time simplicity.

But above all, was not this Hannah's last week in Emden? And why should not this in itself have added to the charm encircling each family fireside? Among many doors of hospitable homes that were thrown wide open to welcome the young girl, that of the Parson's mansion was certainly no exception; for however bitter may have been her dislike for Hannah and Robert Rayland, Mrs. Orlando Hoskins was too discreet and judicious in her deportment to fail to manifest at least an outward regard for the civilities which the holiday season demanded. Besides, there was one peculiarity among the rural population in those early days of simple manners, that atoned for a host of imper-

fections and shortcomings: for when the Christmas
season approached, the tongue of gossip was as
silent as the graves over in the old church-yard. ·
Unhappily, many of those old-time customs no
longer prevail among the more educated and prosperous people of Emden at the present day.

At last the first day of the New Year was ushered
in, amid the jingle of sleigh-bells and the creaking
sounds of ponderous wheels of the Conestoga
teams, on hard, frozen snow. All Emden seemed
to be on tiptoe of excitement, as the boys and girls
hastened to join the throng of saddened hearts to
bid their schoolmate farewell, as she was wrapped
in the warm robes of the old sleigh en route for
her distant school.

A few hours later, and the observing visitor at
the old school would scarcely have noticed any
marked change, either in the band of little workers
or in the appearance of Robert Rayland. If away
deep in his manly nature there was a feeling of
sadness, he kept it hidden within his own breast.
With the morning following, however, came new
and unlooked-for responsibilities. Robert had
scarcely finished reading a chapter from the old
leather-covered Bible when the door opened, and
bowingly entered the tall, slender form of Orlando
Hoskins, and by his side Malinda, with a half-
suppressed smile upon her face, that betrayed the
satisfaction she felt in anticipation of occupying
the seat vacated by Hannah.

Before Robert could recover from his surprise, the old Parson began in his most gracious and persuasive manner to explain the object of his visit. Now it was evident to nine-tenths of the people of Emden that Malinda was the very opposite of prepossessing, having inherited many of the physical peculiarities of her father.

"I believe I have the honor of addressing Mr. Rayland," hesitatingly said Orlando, as he extended his hand, with a peculiar bending movement of his body, in the direction of Robert, who stood some distance away, quietly surveying his distinguished visitor. "I regret exceedingly that the Hoskins family has been denied a more intimate acquaintance with the successor of the late Jimmy McCune, that Christian and scholarly old gentleman, and that you have failed to give the minister's wife that attention and due respect which her station in the community would seem to demand from the new teacher. But I am willing to overlook the past, with the assurance that in the future our relations may be more pleasant and profitable. However, as my visit is purely one of business, and exceedingly important at that, I shall hesitate no longer in making it known without further ceremony. Allow me, therefore, Mr. Rayland, to introduce to you my daughter, Malinda or 'Malind,' as she is more familiarly known over at the parsonage. You will readily perceive, after a more intimate acquaintance, that Malinda is a girl of many striking and remarkable traits of character. That nature has endowed her with a vigorous constitution, an open expression, and a tender and harmless disposition, must be admitted by all who have had the pleasure of an acquaintance with one so young in years and yet so matured in all the attributes which constitute the perfect female character. In fact, she graduated under the master, some two years ago, in all the branches except possibly the dead languages; and by a more thorough acquaintance with these most indispensable attainments, in addition to her many personal accomplishments, there is every reason to believe she will stand as the leader of Emden's most intellectual society. Now if you can give her the seat recently vacated by Hannah Benton, the Squire's daughter, who I understand has been spirited away to college, without any special training or social standing back of her, I'm sure she wouldn't mind assisting the larger boys and girls, now and then, in their studies. Yes, 'Malind' has always been an uncommonly bright girl, and before she was eight years old she could skip clear through the whole alphabet from A to Z, and could count from one to one hundred quicker than Orlando Hoskins could rattle off a chapter from the Old Testament."

"To what extent has your daughter pursued her studies in the common branches?" inquired Robert, who up to this time had remained a silent observer.

"Speak out, Malinda, and enlighten the teacher's mind on these trifling subjects. Name the branches in their regular order, daughter," suggested Orlando.

"I've graduated in readin', 'ritin', 'rithmetic and manners," said Malinda, in her supercilious tone of voice.

"Have you ever studied Analysis of Grammar, Rhetoric and Composition, Geography, History, Chemistry, or Botany, or any of the underlying principles which constitute the foundation of a thorough education?" suggested Robert.

"Come, now, Mr. Rayland," said Orlando, growing impatient and gesticulating with both arms, "do not press a young, diffident girl too severely on the new-fangled studies, that have sprung into existence like a bed of mushrooms. Confine your questions to the subjects in which my daughter is proficient, and don't hurt her feelings at the very start, by straying off among the doctrines and theories that the new system has invented."

"So you have graduated in Reading, Writing and Arithmetic? Well, as your father suggests, I will confine myself to those important subjects, and will give you a few questions in arithmetic in order to ascertain your proficiency in that important branch. If the globe upon which we live is twenty-five thousand miles in circumference, what is its diameter?"

"Hold on a moment, young man, and don't be

getting yourself mixed up in the Scriptures, unless you want the old man to take a hand; and when Orlando Hoskins gets started upon that point he'll cut a broad swath clear through the school. Confine yourself to the questions in the old Arithmetic book, and don't be running into Geography and the like. Take my advice and steer clear of the Scriptures, and don't be teaching any of your false doctrines around this neighborhood. It isn't Malinda that's going to admit that the world's round, any more than the old Parson, who for more than twenty years has been knocking all such absurd nonsense clear out of the heads of the parishioners. Malinda,—read the tenth chapter of the book of Genesis for the new teacher, and show him how you can rattle off the big names without skipping one.

"Now, if I'm a judge," continued Orlando, "it's in reading and pronouncing the Scriptural words that you make your record and receive your standing in the school. Malinda, by actual count, has read them through no less than thirteen times, and if it hadn't been for that unlucky number she'd have broken the record. As it is, the poor girl's mind has been giving way of late under the strain of trying to harmonize all the conflicting statements as you find them scattered through the big Book.

"Of course, 'Malind' has had her share of disappointments of late. In the first place, a young

man coming into a strange town don't always
know what's good for him, and is apt to go clear
through the cane-brake and get a crooked stick in
the end—understand? It's been my experience
ever since I was a young man, that the only safe
course for any young fellow to take is to hang
pretty close to the Parson's teachings, and to manage, if possible, to get accommodations in the minister's family. The truth is, and I may as well
confess it, Malinda was a little disappointed that
the new teacher had gone astray and fallen from
grace; but she couldn't help it, as she has all her
life been a most tender-hearted girl."

At this moment the attention of the whole
school was directed toward Malinda, who was apparently engaged in wiping the big tears from her
eyes with a red cotton handkerchief.

"But the saddest blow of all to the dear girl,"
continued Orlando, "was the disappointment she
suffered when the Ascension did not occur. True,
it was a mistake on the part of Orlando, and one
that cost him many a follower; but it was no fault
of his, but of the miscalculation in the almanac,
that the prediction didn't come true to the minute.
Come now, dry your eyes, my daughter, and read
a chapter for the teacher, and show him how you
can rattle off the hard names."

A moment later, and Malinda was floundering
among the long list of difficult Scripture names,
hesitating at this one and almost choking at the

next, until Orlando, who by this time had become almost frantic with rage, attempted to extricate the poor girl from her difficulties. At this most critical juncture, Robert interrupted her by saying, in a kindly and yet determined tone of voice:

"Mr. Hoskins, while I have no doubt that you have a very exalted idea of your daughter's attainments, I am at the same time of the opinion that you have very much over-estimated them. Yet, while my school is somewhat over-crowded, I shall be pleased to give her a seat. It will be necessary for her to submit to the same regulations I require of all my other pupils. And furthermore, for the present at least, all thoughts of what you term the dead languages must be abandoned. Malinda may be well versed in your peculiar construction of the Scriptures, but the common school system recognizes no particular faith or doctrine, and rests upon the New Testament in its broadest and most comprehensive construction.

"Let me here say that I am unalterably opposed to your dogmas and doctrines, and in my individual capacity shall use every fair means in the future, as I have in the past, to liberate the good people of Emden from the meshes into which you have for these many years sought to entrap them. If it should be necessary for me to take the stand publicly to denounce your false doctrines, I stand ready to sacrifice all that I have to accomplish that most desirable end. I therefore now serve warning on you, to prepare to meet that righteous public sentiment which sooner or later will drive you from the village of Emden; and that I cannot be enticed from the straight and narrow path of what I conceive to be my plain duty, either through the soft words of flattery, or through any other means by which you may seek to retard my purpose."

At this unlooked-for rejoinder on the part of Robert, who stood erect in the full strength of his manhood, there was no recourse for Orlando except a hasty retreat; so, taking Malinda by the hand, he said: "Young man, prepare yourself to meet the wrath of Orlando Hoskins;" then, bowing, he withdrew from the school, leaving Robert to pursue the even tenor of his way, at least for a time, unmolested.

When the hour of noon arrived, the news of the encounter between Robert and the Parson spread to every part of the village, and before the day had ended congratulations began to pour in on the young teacher. Even the Squire and the inn-keeper were among the first to congratulate him, and to express their satisfaction that one man at least had been found to measure swords with the old Parson. There was general rejoicing throughout Emden that the Rev. Orlando Hoskins had been overthrown, and that the hour of deliverance was at last come. Freedom of conscience from the thraldom of bigotry and persecution seemed at last to smile upon the good people of Emden. That

Orlando had met his Waterloo at the hands of the young teacher was accepted on all sides as the beginning of the end. And yet, on the other hand, after the excitement of the moment had subsided, Robert was not unmindful of the fact that he might have committed an indiscretion; and that there was after all a question as to the justification of his course in making an open attack upon the old Parson and the cause he represented. That he had assumed a grave responsibility, in striking at the very foundation of a religious creed whose adherents included not only the Parson's family, but hundreds of others of his blinded and devoted followers, became more apparent as he reviewed the situation.

Orlando Hoskins had been humiliated and mortified before the whole school, many of whose boys and girls were the sons and daughters of his present and former parishioners, and he was not the man humbly to submit to such a gross indignity without an effort at least to vindicate his self-respect. Not only was self-preservation, with Orlando, "the first law of nature;" it was a cardinal principle with him never to be attacked without a return in the same shape and measure. "An eye for an eye and a tooth for a tooth" was still part of his creed. He did not believe in returning good for evil. And so he resolved to crush the New England school teacher and the "godless free school system," as he termed it, at one blow, if it took the whole power of the church to accomplish his purpose. If the deadly hatred lurking in the heart of Orlando found expression at all, it was confined to a chosen few of his trusty adherents. The other members of the Hoskins family were even more circumspect and considerate in their outward expressions than they had ever been before; and yet those who were at all familiar with the Parson's family were not slow in reaching the conclusion that beneath this thin disguise there was something deeper than was apparent on the surface.

Even the expression of Malinda, instead of being downcast and dejected, was that of perfect contentment, as if in anticipation of some event that was to startle all Emden from centre to circumference. But the movements of the old Parson were shrouded in mystery, even to the inquisitive minds of the innkeeper of the General Washington and his contingent of regulars, who were ever on the alert to gather and magnify every rumor afloat throughout the surrounding country.

But if amid the quiet that prevailed, such as oftentimes is the precursor of the coming storm, there was a lack of town gossip, the lull was of short duration.

CHAPTER XXXII.

SHAKY HOLLOW — A MYSTERIOUS PROCESSION —
ROBERT DISAPPEARS—ORLANDO TRIED FOR
KIDNAPING—THE LOST IS FOUND.

CERTAIN nocturnal pilgrimages of Parson Hoskins on his dapper little gray mare had caused Oscar Bently profound cogitation as to the probability of some deep-laid plot. It was not however, until exaggerated rumors had reached the village from Shaky Hollow, that the reverend gentleman had been seen in one or more of his midnight strolls in that dark and secluded retreat, that old Oscar began to consider the fearful consequences which might result to the General Washington should that important personage issue another prediction. From certain signs upon which he had always relied, and which heretofore had never failed him, he was satisfied in his own mind that new trouble was awaiting the good people of Emden.

In the general appearance of its surroundings and in the peculiar character of its people, their superstitions and habits, Shaky Hollow might well claim pre-eminence over that other tradi-

420

tionary defile in the Catskills, known to all the
world as Sleepy Hollow. Shaky Hollow, even
during pre-revolutionary times, was known far and
near for its peculiar sect of Christians, commonly
nicknamed Shaking Quakers, from which the spot
received its name. It was among these simple and
misguided people that Orlando Hoskins happened
to settle, before his removal to the village of Emden, where a broader field of usefulness seemed to
await him; and it was there in the broad virgin
forest that he began his missionary work, and laid
the foundation of the doctrine of Millerism so
firmly that none before Robert Rayland had ever
had the courage to question his authority. From
this obscure settlement Squire Benton drew a great
part of his clientage from year to year, and the
regulars their never-failing supply of tales of
mystery.

It was drawing well on towards midnight of the
day following the first definite report of Orlando's
pilgrimages on these lonely by-ways, that a rap
on the door of the old inn startled Oscar from one
of his dreamy meditations. Entering the dusky
bar-room, the traveler, for such he proved to be,
related in graphic language how a very strange
apparition had crossed his pathway that night in
the region of Shaky Hollow. He declared that
while strolling along through a narrow defile he
had suddenly encountered in the darkness a dozen
or more riders, muffled and disguised, guarding a

rickety old dearborn, in front of which rode, on a little, shaggy gray mare, a tall, gaunt-looking individual, so disguised as to preclude the possibility of recognition.

These startling words had scarcely been uttered when the venerable Squire, rushing into the room, made urgent inquiry as to the whereabouts of Robert Rayland.

As had been his usual custom, Robert had gone to the little red sandstone school-house during the early evening to pursue his studies, but thus far he had failed to return. That Robert Rayland had been kidnaped and spirited away to the wilds of Shaky Hollow, amid the howling of the storm without, was at once accepted as the only reasonable explanation of his disappearance. Had the village been enveloped in flames the consternation could scarcely have been greater.

A moment later, and the stubby form of old Oscar might have been seen standing beneath the tower in which had hung for so many years a heavy bell, used in days gone by as a signal announcing the arrival of many an old stage-coach. His short but muscular arms were stretched upward, with hands grasping the greasy old rope, with his body swinging backward and forward, as the sounds of warning rang out over all Emden, awaking both young and old from slumbers such as only a clear conscience and a tired body can give. The contingent of regulars, whose actual

mission in life had never before been fully determined, now seemed for the first time to realize the
object of their creation, that of scouring the wilds
and hidden recesses of Shaky Hollow in search of
the missing Robert Rayland.

Before the bright sun had begun to cast his re-
fulgent beams over the glistening snow and
through the heavy-laden branches of woodland,
teeming with myriads of sparkling diamonds
which the storm had deposited but a few hours before, as if to make the gloom within a perfect contrast with nature without, all Emden was in the
wildest state of confusion. A hasty inspection of
the old house seemed to furnish all the evidence
needed to warrant the conclusion that a dastardly
crime had been committed in the very heart of the
village. Who the instigators of this cowardly out-
rage were, whence they came, and whither they
had conveyed their captive, was a problem the
solution of which needed manly courage and
prompt action. Before the echoes of the old bell
had died away among the distant hills, the regulars, headed by Oscar Bently, were on their way to
Shaky Hollow, with a determination to liberate
the victim and capture the perpetrators, if strong
arms and brave hearts could accomplish the purpose.

That suspicion from the very first rested upon
Orlando Hoskins, was admitted on all sides, notwithstanding the fact that he was among the most

active in rendering every assistance possible, and that Malinda and her mother were loud in their outward expressions of grief and sorrow. But notwithstanding the circumstances connecting the minister with the kidnaping of the young teacher, there was one, and only one, who amid the clamor for speedy measures to convict and punish, stood like a guardian angel in the full strength of her womanly nature, urging deliberate counsel and moderation.

At the end of the second day the most indisputable evidence came with the return of the searchers. A shoe from the Parson's mare had been accidentally found close to the spot where the stranger had seen the singular conveyance; also a spur which fitted the heel of the Parson's right boot; besides numerous other proofs which in themselves were sufficient to surround that unfortunate personage with a network of evidence from which it seemed there was no escape. The fact that, though a minister of the gospel, he was a personal enemy of the young teacher, and had harbored against him the deepest resentment; even the notion that he was possessed of certain supernatural powers, combined to convict him before the bar of public opinion.

Another day passed with no word of the missing Robert, and as night again approached the excitement became more and more intensified, in anticipation of the return of the regulars; and when late in the evening the familiar voice of Oscar was heard, announcing another failure and disappointment, the feeling increased to such an alarming extent that an additional guard became necessary for the better protection of the Parson's family. Even the Squire's wife came in for a share of abuse, for attempting to defend or shield the sinful old false prophet. But to all such remarks she would simply reply in her own quiet way:

"Yes, yes, he may be a wolf in sheep's clothing, and he may have spirited away our beloved teacher; but only last night I had a deep and startling presentiment. In the vision which passed before me, I beheld Robert lying helpless among strangers, whither he had wandered alone in the darkness of night. And yet this strange apparition may have been caused by his sad and careworn expression as he started in the direction of the old school-house. Orlando may be guilty, and if so he deserves the full penalty the law may inflict; but until you have proof positive and direct, judge not too harshly."

While these words of wisdom fell from the lips of Mother Benton, addressed to the group of angry and excited men who had met to consult with the Squire in reference to the advisability of organizing a vigilance committee, for the ostensible purpose of stringing up the Parson to the nearest limb of the old oak as a warning to all future evil-doers, the motley crowd which had gathered around the General Washington, in anticipation of some posi-

TRIAL OF ORLANDO HOSKINS.

(426)

tive information concerning the whereabouts of
Robert, had become by this time a savage mob,
waiting only for some courageous spirit ready to
lead the way. At last, as a compromise, charges
were preferred against Orlando for kidnaping, and
against Malinda and her mother for complicity in
the crime; and the trial of the defendants was demanded without further delay.

If the crowd of faces without bore evidence of the
deepest anxiety, those within the Squire's office
were affected to even a greater degree. On one
side sat the Board of School Directors of Emden,
headed by Ebenezer, the President, and several
prominent citizens who had been summoned to
attend as witnesses; while on the opposite side
were Orlando, Malinda and her heart-stricken
mother. In the centre of the group stood the
dignified Squire, whose countenance indicated conflicting shades of feeling, alternating from the
most poignant grief and despair to doubt of his
own ability to administer justice in so important
a matter, in accordance with the law and the
evidence.

Having heard the testimony for the complain-
ants, which seemed to point unmistakably to the
guilt of the defendants on the charge of kidnaping
and spiriting away into the wilds of Shaky Hollow
the missing teacher, the Squire adjusted his spectacles, and after a protracted research through a
half-dozen authorities, announced that he had de-

cided to commit Orlando Hoskins for trial at court, and would proceed to prepare the necessary papers.

While all eyes were riveted upon the defendants, who sat with bended heads and shattered hopes, the proceedings were temporarily interrupted by the sound of carriage wheels, halting at the door of the Squire's office. A moment later, and the severe expression on the faces of the assembled crowd changed to one of speechless astonishment, when a tap at the door ushered into their midst the living form and presence of Robert Rayland. If an apparition from another world had risen from the floor beneath their feet, it could not have produced a more startling effect. It was only when the familiar tones of Robert fell upon their bewildered ears, that they fully realized that it was not a supernatural but a natural phenomenon, whose meaning was about to be explained by the central figure of the strange drama.

After expressing a deep regret that he had figured in a role which had disturbed the peace and quietude of the people among whom he labored, and whom he had learned to hold in profound esteem, Robert began his story, assuring them that he alone must be held responsible for his strange disappearance; that he only must be blamed for any errors made, or suspicions created, in the excitement which his singular absence would naturally produce in the community.

"I am extremely anxious," he continued, "in as

few words, and as far as possible, to explain my
movements for the past few days. For some time
before I made my last visit to the old school-house,
I was suffering from an acute attack of insomnia,
superinduced by the pressure of worry and over-
work. My nerves were wrought up to the highest
tension; at times an excruciating pain would seize
my head that would make it throb like a trip-
hammer, and for the moment arrest and suspend
the current of my thoughts. I stood up bravely
against this insidious foe, and, with the aid of
reason and common sense, expected in time to
allay the excitement and recover my usual health.
But the rush of work, combined with worry
brought on in great measure by the fatal and far-
reaching influence upon young and old of the
fanatical teachings of a doctrine which in its very
essence is at variance with the ordinary facts of life,
were too much for my enfeebled strength. I
needed rest and change of scene to rally my
strength, but foolishly turned a deaf ear to the demands of an abused and protesting system.

" On the evening I last went to the school-house,
I was suffering from severe and protracted neural-
gia. When I reached the school-room the pain
became so violent, the very atmosphere grew so
hot and oppressive that it seemed like a flame of
fire. In an agony of pain I rushed out of the room
to drink in the cool air, like a man famishing for a
drink of water. The delirious craving for fresh

air carried me farther and farther away from the
old house ; finally I lost consciousness of my personal identity, yet kept on rushing over fields and
woods. My strange conduct at last attracted the
attention of a good man who kindly took me into
his house, and under the sedative influence of rest
and gentle nursing I regained my powers of mind
and soon established a chain of connection between
my situation at the home of my friend and my
former self. To-day I felt strong enough to make
the ten-mile drive—the distance I had wandered
from Emden—and with the exception of fatigue
and a general weakness incident to my strange experience, I feel that the crisis of my peculiar condition has been passed."

Pen fails to picture the scene which followed the
words that fell from the lips of Robert Rayland,
but it will ever be held in remembrance by those
who witnessed it, and transmitted from father to
son until it is finally stored in the archives, along
with the many other traditions which have cast a
halo around the simplicity of rural life in the olden
time.

CHAPTER XXXIII.

ROBERT VINDICATES ORLANDO—THE PARSON'S RE-
CANTATION—THE FADED FLOWER OF SHAKY
HOLLOW—PEACE AND GOOD-WILL.

HESITATING for a moment, as if under some severe mental restraint, Robert suddenly turned, and
grasping the aged Parson firmly by the hand, said
in a clear, unfaltering tone of voice: "However I
may have been impressed at the time by the unhappy occurrences which took place in the old
stone school-house, prior to my singular and mysterious disappearance, justice demands that I
should declare you, before all present, innocent of
the crime with which you stand charged."

Then Orlando, raising his bended form, and fully
realizing the unfortunate position in which he had
been placed, replied: "With heart overflowing
with the deepest anguish and humiliation, consequent upon the unfortunate position in which I am
here placed to answer the charge of one of the
highest and most ignominious crimes known to
the law, it is not my purpose to offer any evidence
in my own behalf. The living presence and the
clear and forcible statement of the one alleged to

431

have been spirited away to the wilds of Shaky Hollow, are before you as my vindication. That the circumstantial evidence, confirmed apparently by my seemingly strange conduct and repeated absences from Emden, prior and subsequent to the sudden disappearance of Robert Rayland, pointed unmistakably to my guilt, would hardly seem to admit of a doubt. And yet, notwithstanding the intense feeling manifested on all sides, I have never doubted for a moment that the time would come, sooner or later, when my innocence would be fully established. But the many severe trials through which I and my grief-stricken family have so recently passed, have opened to our hitherto benighted vision a new hope and the realization of a brighter future.

"I started in life fully conscious of the innumerable blessings in store for a mind ever on the alert to grasp every moral and religious opportunity in the great struggle. For years I kept in the straight and narrow path of a pure and simple faith, turning neither to the right nor to the left; but as time rolled on I ceased to be a meek and lowly laborer in the vineyard of the Blessed Saviour, and relying upon my own strength, set myself up as the expounder of a doctrine in direct conflict with the inspired words of that Blessed Book, which in my early years I learned to love and venerate at the footstool of a sainted mother. These sad words, falling as they do from the lips of an old man tried in the balance and found wanting, are but introductory to a confession I am about to make to you, and to the hundreds of misguided victims who for so many years have been my devoted followers; many of whom would neither sow nor reap, nor allow others to cultivate the soil, resting content to await the disappointment which followed my unfulfilled predictions."

Deeply moved by his own strange deliverance, Orlando continued: "Many years ago, when filling a lucrative position, and in the enjoyment of the confidence of a thrifty congregation in a well settled community, it was my good fortune to spend my summer vacations among the cascades of the Highlands. It was while returning from one of these delightful annual pilgrimages that I unfortunately fell in with the founder and expounder of the doctrine of Millerism, William Miller, 'the prophet.' After conversing for a time, and listening in breathless astonishment to his most extraordinary exposition of the fulfilment of the prophecy of Daniel, he handed to each of his hearers a small pamphlet, entitled 'The Midnight Cry.' After carefully reading its contents and pondering the same alone in my quiet moments, something seemed to whisper to my inward soul: 'Go, tell it to all the world.'

"From that moment I was no longer satisfied with my pure and simple faith. I returned to my flock and cheerfully resigned my position as their

28

pastor, and became a wanderer on the face of the earth. I believed and faithfully proclaimed on highway and byway that Jesus would appear a second time in the year 1843 in the clouds of Heaven; that he would raise the righteous dead, and judge them together with the righteous living, who would be caught up to meet Him in the air; that he would purify the air with fire, causing the wicked and all their works to be consumed in the general conflagration, and would shut up their souls in the place prepared for the devil and his angels: that the saints would live and reign with Christ on the new earth a thousand years; that then Satan and his wicked spirits would be let loose and the wicked dead be raised—this being the second resurrection—and being judged, should make war upon the saints, be defeated and cast down into hell forever.

"If, for many years, during the lifetime of Miller himself, I was doomed to adversities and disappointments, after his death I continued the work, making numerous predictions which likewise one after the other failed to come to pass. It was among the innocent and unsuspecting residents of Shaky Hollow that I at last found an abiding-place; removing in due course of time to this village of Emden, where for years I have industriously striven to implant in the hearts of its people the doctrine of 'The Midnight Cry.' At times my own disappointment was so great as to almost shake my faith in the ultimate fulfillment of its prophecies; but with an obstinacy born of fanaticism, I continued to battle against my better judgment.

"It was during the several nights preceding and succeeding the stormy night in which Robert Rayland so mysteriously disappeared from the old stone school-house that the saddest event of my life occurred, in a low thatched cottage among the pines and cedars of Shaky Hollow. The world may never care to know, and from the lips of Orlando Hoskins shall never learn the true story which has led to my return to the pure and simple faith of my early days. But as calamities are oftentimes blessings in disguise, conveying to the very depths of the soul the lesson that 'as ye sow so shall ye reap,' this double affliction may yet prove to be the frail bark destined to convey Orlando Hoskins and his sorely-stricken family through the rolling billows, over which these many years he has been sailing devoid of either rudder or compass, and in the end to bring them safely to the Rock of Ages, beyond the reach of the waves.

"And now, standing as I do before this assembly of my former friends and neighbors, I hereby renounce every letter and syllable of a doctrine conceived in iniquity and in league with the devil and his angels. Let judge and jury bear witness to this confession; and may these solemn words be conveyed to high and low, rich and poor, and even to the remotest corner of Shaky Hollow, where yet dwells many a deluded follower of Orlando Hoskins."

At this trying moment, when all eyes were riveted upon the penitent old minister, the trampling of feet without, followed by the creaking of the old door on its rusty hinges, attracted the attention of those who sat within the old mansion. Another moment, and the portly form of Oscar Bently pressed its way into the centre of the group. A momentary glance at his outward appearance was sufficient to indicate the severe strain through which he had passed in his forty hours' search in the wilds of Shaky Hollow. That he had made important discoveries was noticeable at a g'ance, but whether in the minister's favor or against him could only be determined by hearing his story.

Oscar's statement was substantially as follows: Having lost his way the evening previous, he was compelled to put up for the night at a cabin at a cross-road leading to one of the many caverns which during the seven years' struggle for Independence had sheltered hundreds of deserters from the Hessian army. Entering this lonely habitation, and making inquiry as to the missing Robert Rayland, Oscar was impressed with the melancholy appearance of the inmates— one of whom he recognized as none else than old Patrick McDeever, the master, the other his grief-stricken and brokenhearted helpmate. After partaking of a scanty meal, a seat was offered him in one corner of the stone fire-place, where for some time he sat, vainly endeavoring to enlist his unhappy host and hostess in conversation, hoping thereby to elicit something definite with reference to his important mission. For a time the only words uttered were those of gentle reproof to three ill-dressed and half-fed urchins that lay half-concealed from view on the floor in an opposite corner of the old cabin, unconscious of the mutterings of the storm without, or the guests within.

But as the long moments rolled by in silence Oscar's anxiety and suspense increased, until, pressing the old schoolmaster for some explanation of the deep gloom which seemed to rest upon their hearts, he learned the melancholy story from the lips of old Patrick, which has since become a household legend among the simple-minded people of Shaky Hollow, to be repeated and enlarged upon as it passes in tradition from generation to generation. After replenishing the fire, and drawing himself into closer proximity to his welcome guest, Patrick related in simple, yet forcible language, this story of a broken heart:

"It is not," said he, "of old Patrick himself, and the trials through which he has passed as the discarded master of Shaky Hollow school, that I would speak; but of the loss of Myra, our only daughter, the Flower of Shaky Hollow.

"From her childhood Myra, a lovely maiden

of unusual intelligence, and the hope and mainstay
of her devoted mother, had become infatuated with
the prophetical teachings of the Rev. Orlando
Hoskins, who many years ago settled among our
people.   Within the little church whose gray outlines may be seen from the window of the old
cabin, when the November blasts have driven the
dead leaves from the forest trees, Myra, when but a
mere child, was deluded by the old Parson's persuasive appeals. As time wore on, and as Orlando's predictions failed to come to pass, the disappointment of her ardent hopes and longing desires
began to prey upon both mind and body, and it became evident that her end was not far distant.
Her dying request was once more to meet the old
Parson face to face, having in her last peaceful
hours awakened to the happy realization of a new
and undying hope of a blessed hereafter, whose
foundation rested not upon the teachings of a pernicious theory, but upon the blessed Saviour and
Him crucified.

"Night after night Orlando stood by the bedside
of the dying girl, over in yon corner where the lads
lie huddled together, returning to his home in
Emden before sunrise. Though the Parson was
gentle and kind, and resorted to every means
within the power of his faith to rally the faded
flower of the mountain defile to health and
strength all his promises of speedy recovery were
powerless to revive her energies.

"During his last visit, it was evident that upon his own conscience were resting grave responsibilities. That he had lost confidence in his own ability to restore the poor girl to life through any one of his many miraculous faith-cures, was apparent to those who sat by her side; while the faith of Myra in a higher Power shone forth resplendent as her young life fast ebbed away. At last, rising to a half-sitting posture, and taking the hand of the Parson in her own, and looking straight into his eyes, she said in a sweet calm voice:

"'Orlando Hoskins, as the expounder of a religious faith these many years I have known thee, worshiping with bended knee at thy ministrations, but henceforth I know thee not. The salvation that has come to Myra is not of thy faith, nor of thy teachings; it rests with me at this moment, like the sweet perfume of heaven, falling upon the just and the unjust—upon your heart, as well as upon my own. Before I close my eyes in peace, and pass to my Maker and Redeemer, I ask you, as my last dying request, to accept this blessed faith. I beseech you to abandon your false doctrines, and accept salvation from the lips of one who for so many years accepted without a murmur your false teachings under the guise of religion. Promise me to fulfil my last parting request. Will you?'

"And as the last words of the dying girl fell to a whisper Orlando replied, 'With God's help, I will.'

THE BURIAL OF MYRA.

"As Myra's wish was that she should be laid to rest the day following, on the highest point of the mountain pass, a plain coffin was hastily constructed, and at the hour of noon the earthly remains of the Flower of Shaky Hollow were conveyed in the old dearborn to their resting place. It was a sad picture. On each side of the hearse rode a body-guard of my nearest neighbors and friends, while in front, leading the way, sat Orlando on his gray mare. Hour after hour we mournfully wended our way, passing but a single lonely traveler. The shades of night were falling when we discovered to our surprise that we had lost our way, and were compelled to retrace our steps. And so we laid Myra to rest on the craggy heights of the mountain summit as the full moon came into view.

"This is the story of Myra, the bright-eyed, light-hearted girl, the flower of our flock," sighed old Patrick as he raked together the half-dead coals: "Go, my friend, and tell it to all the world, that Myra, my only daughter, died a Christian, and that Orlando Hoskins has been re-converted to the same pure and simple faith."

At the conclusion of Oscar's plain, straight-forward statement, Orlando Hoskins simply bowed in humble acquiescence; the Squire of course declared the aged minister innocent, and dismissed the complaint. In the general reconciliation which followed, and which ultimately extended to the remotest depths of Shaky Hollow, deeply impressed

with the solemnity of the occasion, Mary Benton
stepped to the center of the room, and with one
hand upon the head of Robert and the other on
that of Orlando, said: "May the blessing of God

" BLESSED ARE THE PEACEMAKERS."

rest upon you both, and may the angel of peace
forever hover over Emden and its people."

And at parting all joined in the pledge that
thenceforth peace should reign in Emden.

CHAPTER XXXIV.

THE OLD SCHOOL-HOUSE DESERTED—ROBERT IS WANTED ELSEWHERE—HANNAH AS TEACHER— MAY-DAY FESTIVAL—THEIR WEDDING.

THREE long winters had come and gone since the reconciliation between teacher and Parson so happily consummated in the office of Theophilus Benton; and Time, the relentless destroyer of wind-flower and violet, wild rose and golden rod, had been reaping rich harvests among young and old.

On a bleak November day, amid naked woods and meadows brown and sere, old Patrick, the last of the discarded masters, was laid to rest beside his Myra, the child of the forest, at the top of the mountain pass; and close by the moss-covered church, in the old grave-yard beside Jim and Tim, peacefully rest the last earthly remains of Ebenezer Lukins, the venerable President of Emden school board. While here and there other notable changes affecting the material prosperity of Emden district were noticeable, the red sand-stone school-house now stood as forsaken as the deserted fortress beyond. No sweet, soft voice of

443

gladness came from within; no gay peals of
laughter nor tread of merry feet broke in upon
the breathless silence. Though the genial sunlight of Heaven still found its way through the
small windows, it fell upon empty benches, cheerless walls and high-topped desk, beneath the raised
lid of which the old master was wont betimes to
bury his head as if in deep meditation over the
solution of some vexed and intricate problem,
which the key to old Emerson (always securely
hidden within) was sure to supply, to the entire
satisfaction of the unconscious youth who stood in
waiting by his side, amazed at the power of his
intellect and the fertility of his resources; but the
little brood of happy workers had flown. Last
first of December morning one and all had bidden
the old house a last farewell, and following Robert
Rayland, entered for the first time the cozy, well-
equipped modern structure, bearing the superscrip-
tion, "Emden School."

In these words engraved on the stone lintel,
there may be nothing suggestive to the professional
teacher of to-day, whose eyes are often dazzled by
the beauty and the stateliness of architectural design displayed wherever the blessings of the free
school system have been most largely felt and the
broadest school sentiment prevails. But for months
thereafter, the results of the efforts of Robert,
though devoid of ostentatious display, were felt
and appreciated even beyond Emden district.

With gentle rains and early spring flowers came the end of the long winter term of the village school of Emden. Every preparation had been made by willing hands and anxious hearts to render the parting of the teacher from his pupils and patrons one long to be remembered. To close the school with appropriate exercises, in which the boys and girls should participate, had never before been the practice in Emden. And what a beautiful conception these closing exercises are! How they have grown with each succeeding year and strengthened with the growth of the system itself, leaving the imprint of the teacher indelibly impressed upon the tender hearts of the young! Years may come and years may go, but these little episodes at the end of the school term will ever remain among the brightest and most touching of early childhood. While at the opening of the school there may be a certain satisfaction, mingled with anxiety in anticipation of meeting the new teacher and playmates, the hour of parting has a peculiar significance of its own.

It is at the moment when the sad word "Farewell," falls from the lips of the teacher, that the lad forgetting his real or imaginary resentments, steps forward, and placing his hand in that of the teacher, hesitates a moment, and then in an apologetic tone says: "I know I haven't been doing what was right, and I haven't obeyed more than half the rules of the school; but I'm awfully sorry,

teacher, and I hope you'll forgive me. I had such
a heavy feeling against you when I came to school
this morning that I never thought I could even say
good-bye; but it's all gone, and if you'll promise
to return next winter, I'll promise you right before
the whole school, that I'll never break another
rule as long as I live."

Forgive him? Of course you forgive him; and
in after years, when you see him manfully holding
up his end of the world's work, memory will carry
you back to the closing exercises of that little
school, where the lad, now a man, so frankly con-
fessed: "Teacher, I know I haven't been doing
what was right."

And so one after the other, from the rosy-faced,
bright-eyed girl of eight to the bashful lad of fifteen,
looks up in his face, bids him a fervent good-bye,
and then passes homeward.

In his address upon the ending of his fifth term
as teacher of the village school, Robert paid a
glowing tribute to the memory of Old Jimmy, for
so many years his predecessor in the old stone
house; recounted the hardships through which, in
their latter days, the other old masters had passed;
reviewed the past, with its sunshine and clouds of
adversity; paid a tribute to the memory of Ebenezer Lukins, the School Board's venerable President; and at the same time admonished them to
remember that from Him above all good things
come.

As he ceased speaking, a sealed envelope was placed in his hand. Breaking the seal and glancing over its contents, he stood for a moment half bewildered. There was a flutter in the little assembly, the knowing older heads began nodding backward and forward in a quizzical manner, and a sly wink of the Squire's eye indicated that he had guessed the contents of the epistle.

"You see," continued Nicholas, as he drew toward the end of his story, "it was by putting this and that together that the Squire was able to understand the workings of old Jimmy's mind when things weren't running along very smoothly over in the old stone house; and he wasn't to be caught napping."

And so, while the teacher was looking around over the school, with big tears in his eyes, the Squire said in a confidential manner to the school trustees who sat beside him:

"I'll bet the best copy of Blackstone ever printed that the Professor's fortune is sticking right inside of that epistle; and so he may just as well relieve his conscience and make a clean breast of the whole business, for it will come out sooner or later, anyway. You see," he continued, with one eye on the teacher, while the point of his finger was directed from one to the other of the trustees, "it's by cultivating the observing faculties that you get inside of whatever's going on, and can discount the newspapers two to one; for if you keep your mouth shut, and your eyes and ears open, you can always manage to catch on to the best things, which for some reason or other never get into print. It's all right to cultivate the memory, but take my advice and stick to the observing faculties; they'll carry you through life with less worry of mind and body than all the figures ever taught in Emden school since arithmetic was invented. You see when the shingles of Solomon's Sloan's barn began to flare up like the bark of the old shell-bark tree, I just kept on observing and smiling; but when the posts of his rail fence went down as if they'd been buried in a snow-drift, I'd point to the 'Long Lost Friend' and say: 'The fellow that never observes, but persists in following the perversity of his own crooked nature, deserves no better luck.'

"And now I tell you, gentlemen of the School Board of Emden district, you may just as well put your heads together and begin to look for another teacher for Emden school; for either there's a fortune lurking within that message for the young master, or else there's a wasting away of Theophilus Benton's observing faculties, which up to this time haven't shown any disposition to part company with the old man."

Robert also felt that, however inclined to reticence, it would be useless longer to withhold from his friends what they had already grasped by intuition. "It becomes my duty," said he, "to make

known to you all the contents of the message
which was unexpectedly handed me but a moment
ago. To one whose mission in life has been to
labor within the narrow limits of the school among
the vine-clad hills and valleys of beautiful Emden,
the unexpected announcement that duty has called
him to a broader field of usefulness has a deep significance. I should no longer withhold from
friends true and dear the announcement that I,
who here stand before you for possibly the last
time, have been chosen to fill a responsible position
in a distant state."

If, in after years, the stern realities of life, with
their responsibilities and the rewards of higher intellectual development, tended to chill and harden
Robert Rayland's emotional nature, his thoughts
would wander back to the scenes of his early
labors, where he was sure to find consolation,
recreation and inspiration under the branches of
the majestic oak, beneath which long years before
sat the eight old masters, as the words: "All applicants for schools in Emden district will please
occupy the benches along the wall, facing the examiner," fell chillingly upon their ears. And how
those other words, uttered by a simple school-girl,
"Teacher, are you looking for the inn? Come,
and I will direct you," would throb through his
soul, as his mind's eye took in the broad expanse
of country and the moss-covered church in whose
old graveyard Jim and Tim are peacefully resting.

29

A week after the closing exercises of the village school, Robert was energetically engaged in the duties of the new position in his far-distant home. While his scholarship and the purity of his character had never been questioned, there were those who now began to look into the early history of young Robert Rayland. It soon became known that while he had received his education in New England, his birth-place was a small hamlet along the base of the South Mountain, a village of some importance as a manufacturing centre of army supplies during the Revolutionary times. We mention Robert's birth-place as an historical incident, rather than from any desire to reflect upon that large class of professional instructors from New England soil, who, immediately after the adoption of the new system, had found a fruitful field for their labors in many other States, and to whom, unlike their predecessor, the Yankee schoolmaster of thirty years before, the appellation of "Schoolmaster Abroad" could not with propriety be applied. Most of those young educators were cast in a mould entirely different from that of the wandering itinerants of the preceding generation, whose mission it was

> "To stroll and teach from town to town."

These young men were trained especially for the life of the educational pioneer, in its most comprehensive sense. Wherever they went their influence strengthened the system, so that at last, when steps were taken to organize Normal schools, hundreds to the manner born flocked thereto from all directions. Country lads, under the influence of trained instructors, began to realize their own ability, when better equipped by Normal training, to fill positions of importance, and soon supplied the demand for professional instructors largely from the immediate vicinity. In fact, the numbers who have attended the various Normal schools within the past forty years are perhaps the best evidence as well as one of the most important factors in the success of our system of education. Every profession and business has among its numbers those whose early years were spent within the walls of a Normal school. They may have long since deserted the teacher's calling to engage in other more profitable avocations of life, and in so doing may have lowered the standard of the teaching profession; but their influence and inspiration, in addition to their force of character, have been an element of strength to the system wherever support was needed.

If the withdrawal of Robert temporarily cast a gloom over the village of Emden, it was of short duration; for with rapid strides, the village school took a high place among its sisterhood of schools. Over them the sweet influence of womanhood began to assume dominion; and among them she will ever continue to wield the sceptre of love and affection. Five years, to older people, were as a fleeting shadow; but to the young hearts who on that New Year's morn had bidden farewell to Hannah, as she was wrapped in the robes of the old sleigh-coach which was to convey her far from friends and old associations, these years had an inexpressible meaning. How many of her young friends, now grown into womanhood and manhood, could then have foreseen the return of Hannah, years later, as the successor of Robert Rayland in the village school of Emden?—not arrayed, however, as their young minds had so often pictured her, in silks and satins, but adorned with the graces of true womanly character.

If the transition from master to teacher, as exemplified in the reform which had substituted for a Jimmy McCune a Robert Rayland, was as complete as it was sudden, the induction of Hannah into the village school at this critical period was the final step in advance, which was to assure the perpetuity of the system itself. And so when Hannah carried with her into the school of Emden the results of a thorough Normal training, it sent a thrill of renewed hope through the hearts of the supporters of the new system—a hope that the hour of emancipation had at last come, in which the true worth of young womanhood was to be felt and recognized in every school district of the state. It was not that any immediate advantages were to accrue to the village school in the high standard it

had already attained under Robert Rayland, but
rather in the establishment of a principle—the
recognition of woman as a factor in the teaching
force of the State at large. Hannah Benton at that
early day was but the representative of a type of
young women claiming recognition all over the
Commonwealth. Their numerical strength, which
at the adoption of the system was but an insignifi-
cant factor of the whole, has since assumed the
proportion of nearly three to one.

It is not to be presumed that Hannah, accomplished as she was, would be permitted to enter the
duties of her calling without opposition. Although
following methods wherein perfect discipline lay at
the very foundation of success, there were those
who were ever ready to predict her failure. If
Robert spared the rod, it was not that he did not
possess the physical ability to apply it, should it
become necessary to do so. Hannah, on the other
hand, still a mere girl in the eyes of many, was
possessed of no such reserve of physical force ; and
even yet it was considered almost suicidal to entrust the unruly elements of the neighborhood to
those who could not swing the birch rod with the
strong arm of a backwoodsman. In fact, at the
present day, in districts remote from the centres of
population, the rights of woman are discriminated
against for the avowed reason that the strong arm
of a male teacher is considered absolutely necessary
to the success of the school.

Another sort of opposition came from a class of school-ma'ams whose methods were still like those of the pedantic old-time masters who yet held sway in adjoining districts, and who were ever on the alert to join hands with their gentler, if not younger co-workers, in holding up the village girl to scorn and ridicule. The confidence and sympathy existing between these schoolmistresses and schoolmasters were at times something peculiarly touching to behold. Whenever occasion offered, these old-timers, "birds of a feather," would flock together to defend and uphold the system of the old masters, with a tenacity of purpose which compelled the wonder, if not the admiration, of the advocates of progress.

"But when, with the advent of Normal training, the various synonyms, master, pedagogue, tutor, instructor, professor, were united under the comprehensive term of Teacher, which includes them all," here commented Nicholas, "it was no longer a question of age, long service or former conditions. It was the survival of the fittest in the teacher's calling, as it has ever been in all other departments of life, and as it will continue to be to the end of time; and so the old master and mistress of by-gone days fell by the wayside, and, like Jim and Tim, were laid to rest with the happy consciousness of duty well performed. Of many of them it might truthfully be said: 'Well done, good and faithful servant.'"

Five more years had made further changes in the life of Hannah Benton, the unpolished diamond of a few years before. Then her daily life lay within the limits of the village school and her own pleasant homestead; since, she had risen to the head of one of the leading seminaries in a distant city. Following in her footsteps, a number of her former schoolmates had taken a course in Normal training, and were later engaged as teachers in the schools of the district.

As a result of the deep impression made upon his mind and heart, the Rev. Orlando Hoskins had become an ardent advocate of popular education, and as if to atone for his previous shortcomings, had entrusted Malinda to the care of a matronly lady in charge of a young ladies' college, from which she had graduated and subsequently opened in the village a select school for young girls.

Squire Benton, or "The Squire" as he was still familiarly known, then and for many years thereafter led the life of a retired gentleman. His opinions on all knotty and conflicting law points were never grudgingly withheld from his successor, who had read law under his personal supervision, and who has since been reaping a name and fame in another commonwealth. While Mrs. Benton, during these years, had of course grown older, she was still the same dignified woman. Her features seemed to grow more beautiful as the wrinkles of time impressed themselves upon her forehead.

And now, dear reader, our story draws near its end. At Emden, on a beautiful May morning, the sun seems to shine as it never shone before on the hearts of young and old, without a cloud to dim the azure of the heavens above, or cast a shadow over the dreams of those below. But why this grand ovation, this meeting and greeting, this clamor, this hurly-burly, as rider after rider, with fair maiden perched behind, hurriedly presses his way toward the village green? Why all these venders of cakes, bonbons and small beer, lining both sides of the roadway? And the aged Parson! What impels him to hurry to and fro through the village on his little gray mare, marshaling into line, here and there, a stray horseman? Why is everybody dressed in the brightest of colors, with nosegay on coat or bosom? What has come over the dreams of Oscar Bently and the regulars of the General Washington?

Why should the moss-covered church and the ancient parsonage, and even the old school-house, be decorated with evergreens and wild honey-suckles? Ah, it is the revival of an old and cher-ished custom—the May-day festival—the last sur-vival of the holiday festivities held in out-of-the-way towns and villages, years ago, when every house put on a holiday garb—when the farmer laid aside his plow, the schoolboy his books, and when business of every kind gave way to merry-making and enjoyment. But how many yet living can recall this, the last of Emden's time-honored customs, or the merry scenes of that lovely May morning, when fresh from the craggy heights of Shaky Hollow came the May-pole, loaded upon the strongest wagon in all the country round?

"Ah, my young friends," said Nicholas, "how it thrills the old man's heart when he recalls to mind that picture never to be forgotten? There, along through the village, came the wagon, with its thirty oxen, each with a nosegay tied to its horns, and the wagon and pole decorated with ribbons and flowers; and upon it sat Hannah Benton and Robert Rayland, the former to be honored and crowned by the multitude as May Queen, and afterward both to be made one in the holy bonds of matrimony by the Rev. Orlando Hoskins."

Dear reader, is your sensitive nature shocked, and have the two objects of your admiration fallen in your estimation? Can you imagine "the proprieties" which would justify two cultured people entering into the sacred bonds of matrimony amid such scenes of confusion in an out-door promiscuous gathering at the present day? Be not too hasty, my over-fastidious friend. The impropriety, if such it be, lies not in the customs which prevailed in the good old days of simplicity of rural home life, but rather in the degeneration of modern-day habits and morals. Robert Rayland was neither over-fastidious nor over-elated with the

WEDDING UNDER THE MAY-POLE.

(458)

honors that had been thrust upon him.   His early
training had placed no barrier between himself and
the common people.   If anything, it had broadened his nature and taught him what many young
students since have failed to comprehend, that fine
clothes and a few years of higher educational facilities make neither a Lincoln, a Clay nor a Webster.
He may, it is true, have failed in the modern
theory of earning his bread by the sweat of his
father's or his grandfather's brow.

But while the reader may be indulgently inclined
to overlook the indiscretion of Robert, upon what
principle of modern-day etiquette, they will exclaim, can the gentler sex justify Hannah Benton,
an accomplished teacher, even at that early day,
being perched upon an improvised country conveyance, bedecked with wild flowers and evergreens,
first to be crowned the May Queen, and then to
become the wife of Robert Rayland?

"Yes, dear reader," concluded the aged Comenius; "out on the village green, under the May-
pole and close by the moss-covered church, where
now rest in grateful remembrance Ebenezer Lukins,
the Squire, Jim and Tim, and almost beneath the
branches of the old oak, occurred that event, which
Nicholas Comenius will never tire of rehearsing
while he lingers among the living.   Here, amid
the peals of the old church bell, on that lovely
morning, surrounded by young and old, Robert
and Hannah gave their hands and hearts each to

the other, as the aged Parson repeated the beautiful
and solemn words, 'Robert Rayland, wilt thou
have this woman, Hannah Benton, to be thy
wedded wife? Wilt thou love and honor her so
long as ye both shall live?' Repeating the like
questions to Hannah, he pronounced them man
and wife; following with the words: 'The Lord
bless and keep you, Amen.'

"A moment later the solemn service was followed by a burst of joyful merry-making, though
a tear trickled down the faces of some older people
who looked upon the face of Orlando Hoskins as
he kissed the bride and shook the hand of Robert
Rayland. Impressive as the scene had been, it
was rendered doubly so when Malinda and her
mother made their way through the crowd and
congratulated the young couple, wishing them
many years of happiness and prosperity.

"It was only, however, when Mother Benton, in
her quiet, unassuming manner, stepped forward
into the centre of the little circle, that those present began to feel and realize the unseen power
through which the bright sunlight of education
had dispelled the dark clouds of ignorance and
superstition which for two generations had held
the minds and consciences of the good people of
Emden in subjection. 'All honor to Mary Benton,
and may her spirit of love and good-will continue
to permeate every domestic fireside,' came the
voices of one and all, as they scattered to join in

the festivities which only a May-day celebration
could produce.

"As the last faint glimmer of the descending
sun began to disappear through the shades of
Shaky Hollow, one after the other bade adieu to
the last scene of Emden's May-day festivities, to
seek their own firesides, leaving Robert and
Hannah to spend the days of their honeymoon
among kind friends and old associations."

CHAPTER XXXV.

IT was well toward noon on the day following
that Thanksgiving ever to be remembered with
gratitude, that we took our last stroll through Emden town, preparatory to our return to witness the
closing exercises of possibly the most successful institute ever held in the metropolis of Blackwell
county. Every effort had been made that time
and money could command, to give the closing exercises such standing and dignity as, in the estimation of the young Superintendent, were best
calculated to ensure hearty co-operation and harmony among the great body of teachers and the
public at large. The lecturer for this, the final
session, had been secured at great expense; and
being an ex-United States Senator from one of the
great belt of States lying beyond the Mississippi,
it was but natural to suppose that his presence
would attract more than the average attention.

"It is hardly to be supposed," said Nicholas, as
we stood face to face with one of the many old

462

landmarks yet prominent among the new conditions, "that very striking changes would be noticeable in Emden town, since forty years ago, when
Robert Rayland taught the village school, except
possibly in that steady growth of intellectual development that had its origin under the inspiration
of the young teacher. Yes, forty years have rolled
by since Robert bade farewell to one and all."

"And never once returned to the old town, with
its early associations?" we asked.

"Yes, once, but 'twas many years ago, while
Mother Benton still lived. Then it was my pleasure to take Hannah and the young master by the
hand for the last time, as they stepped into the old
stage-coach for their distant home. But I have
never lost hope during all the years since, that the
love he bore the old town would one day reassert
itself, and that Robert would once more long for
the hillsides and valleys of beautiful Emden.
Singular as it may seem," continued Comenius,
"the programme for this very evening's entertainment bears the name of a Senator Rayland, and
only a week ago the Postmaster received a letter
post-marked Washington, D. C., asking whether
the little red sandstone school-house was still standing beneath the venerable oak as it stood forty
years ago. Of course there may be nothing in
these coincidences," added Nicholas, as though trying to formulate some rational connection between
these facts.

"True enough, my venerable friend, but the name of the lecturer for the evening happens to be Ryland instead of Rayland—only a slight dissimilarity in the spelling," we suggested.

"Yes, yes, but the change of a letter or two has often changed the ownership of a landed estate, as I have discovered," came the retort as Nicholas stepped into the post-office, leaving us for the time to pursue our sight-seeing alone.

As we reached the old town pump our attention was attracted by the presence of Nicodemus, who was earnestly engaged in a spirited conversation with several elderly gentlemen and a matronly lady of perhaps sixty, who had alighted from a handsome coach in front of the old inn only a moment before.

"Ah, ha," exclaimed Nicodemus, as he grasped the hand first of one and then of the other, with the freedom that only the presidency of a collegiate institute could inspire; "glad to welcome to Emden soil strangers with daughters to educate! Not another institution in the land that affords better facilities for the proper care and training of young ladies than Emden Seminary. Step right across the way, Madam, and I'll introduce you to Malinda, the matron, the only daughter of the Rev. Orlando Hoskins, who many years ago held forth in the ivy-covered parsonage down by the old church."

"Malinda, did you say?" suggested the gentleman, with a slight tremor in his voice.

"Yes; the poor girl had her own trials and misfortunes in her younger days, but they've all been a blessing in disguise. Disappointed, you see, in her early love affairs ; but experience has proven that these disappointments, especially if they come during early years, always insure discipline and stability of character in one's after life.

"I am sorry to be compelled to confess to the president of a young ladies' seminary that my own family consists of four grown boys, instead of an equal number of girls," said the lady, with a smile and a blush, as preparations were being made to re-enter their comfortable carriage.

"Sorry to hear it, madam, but maybe it's all for the best. Won't be any danger of their running away with a young schoolmaster, as was the case with Hannah, the eldest of Squire Benton's four daughters."

"Squire Benton !—and is the Squire still a resident of the town ?"

"Why, bless you, no! After Hannah left the village, the Squire died of a broken heart, and Mother Benton followed soon after. In fact, strangers, there aren't any of the old residenters living except old Nicholas Comenius, long ago Superintendent of Blackwell county; and the only companion that's left him is the little red sandstone school-house down near by the village green, under the great oak. Seems that the old house, with the thoughts of the old master Jimmy, and

30

his worthy successor young Robert Rayland, who many years ago married Hannah Benton, the Squire's daughter, have been keeping the old man as fresh and green as the old oak tree itself."

"Can you, my friend, direct us to the old school-house?" said the elderly gentleman.

"Come this way, only a short distance to the old structure," said Nicodemus, as he led the way, only too willing to lend his aid to those who he had reason to feel might in the end say a good word for the most worthy institution which he had the honor to represent as its president. And so through the streets of Emden Nicodemus conducted the visitors to the little red sandstone school-house, followed at a safe distance by Stephen Smithers and Teddy.

A moment later Nicholas rejoined us, unconscious of the episode that had occurred almost within his hearing. What a strange combination of circumstances! Who could the strangers be? Could that elderly gentleman be Robert, or Senator Rayland, the lecturer of the evening? Could there have been simply an error in the spelling of the name! Could the matronly-looking lady be Hannah Benton, whose young image the aged father had so indelibly impressed upon our minds? Had Nicodemus, in his enthusiasm, lost the shrewdness for which he had been noted from the day he first entered the village? What apology or amends could the old man make for the apparent insult to Robert and Hannah, if such they should ultimately prove to be? But aside from the peculiar position in which Nicodemus had placed himself, how should we break the startling discovery, if such it were, to Nicholas Comenius? Or had we only imagined we had seen Robert and Hannah?

To dismiss the little drama from our mind was perhaps after all the very best to be done under the circumstances. And so from one point of interest to another we proceeded to wend our way, until the hour of noon once more found us under the roof of the hospitable Comenius, arranging for an early afternoon departure for the county town. We had almost forgotten the occurrence, when a rap at the door of the old homestead startled Nicholas from the reverie into which he had fallen; and a moment later in stepped Nicodemus, as pale as a sheet and trembling from head to foot.

"Nicholas! Nicholas!" cried Nicodemus, "the lost are found! yea, verily, the dead have been restored to life!"

"Nicodemus, are you bewitched? Speak out and explain yourself! Has another of those periodical spells overtaken you, Nicodemus, or has Old Nick at last taken possession of the old sinner, as a punishment for the abuse often heaped upon those who now rest in peace over in the churchyard beside Jim and Tim? Begone, you old"—

But before another word could be uttered, there, resting on each arm of the easy reclining-chair, sat

Hannah and Robert, with arm encircling the
aged patriarch's neck, while little Teddy and
Stephen Smithers stood smiling within the open
doorway.

FRIENDS REUNITED.

Yes, there in the old homestead, near by the
majestic oak, beneath which still stood the remnant of the little red sandstone school-house, sat
Robert and Hannah—Robert, now a Senator of
world-wide reputation, and Hannah—the mother
of four stalwart lads—verily a second Mother
Benton.

For what passed between the aged father and the young schoolmaster of forty years ago we have no words. We have fulfilled our mission. We have given you, largely from his own lips, the story of Nicholas Comenius, the big-hearted, broad-minded pioneer of the early days of the common school system. A few years more, and he too will peacefully rest over near the gray old church, beside his old friend Jimmy, the former master of the village school. If any there be among my readers who wish for the sequel, they must follow Robert and Hannah to their far-distant home, beyond the broad Mississippi, "the father of waters," and there gather from them the inspiration that may thrill the hearts of the rising generation with the realization of a brighter and a more perfect future.